I0557462

BACK TO THE GARDEN
Arnold W. Porter

© 2016 Arnold W. Porter
All rights reserved
ISBN-978-0-9937472-2-9 (Back to the Garden)

For the old ones

Back to the Garden is a fictoir, a work of fiction woven around the memories of a specific time and place. Though at times the author has created stories around locations, events and persons that may be recognizable, the stories themselves are fictional and the product of the author's imagination. They should in no way should be taken as an accurate history of the events portrayed.

We are stardust
We are golden
And we've got to get ourselves
Back to the garden
  Joni Mitchell

Memory fails and the sea of oblivion rises around him, leaving only disconnected peaks, islands of memory, standing above its water. He will have to paddle out to that other island, the one that's over there, to see if he can remember exactly what happened. Or maybe he will have to make it up, create something that feels right, something that would fit, like a palaeontologist putting a face and a personality on a skull... Ah yes, the skulls that once sang and danced, told stories, stored memories and did a thousand foolish and wonderful things before they became artifacts, empty seashells that fell to the bottom of the sea.

Sometimes, on an island of memory, he finds an old house. There is a picture of a person in it, left tacked on a wall or buried in a pile of leaves and old boards. Who were they? He remembers a few things. He rummages through his memory as though it were one of the jumbled boxes in the Vasquez Island Free Store. Sometimes he finds a shirt that he remembers someone having worn. He holds it up in the darkness of the store and says out loud, "if you see yourself in this book, fear not, it is not really you, it's just one of my characters dressed up in some of the old clothes you threw away."

--From *In A Time of Magic* by Arnold Porter

PROLOGUE

Up on the mountain tonight the storm is closing fast, a giant white eraser washing away the stars, washing away the moon, washing away the luhm of the coastal cities. All up and down the Gulf of Georgia the rain turns to snow.

Tomorrow, the mountains will rise like teeth above the dark forest, and the forest will be dusted white with snow. In Vancouver, the air will reek with the fumes of oil furnaces. Little black balls of soot will fall from the sky. At first the world will be pristine white; all the junk, all the candy wrappers, all the wine bottles, covered by this virginal bridal veil. Too soon it will be churned into grey slush. In Vancouver, in winter, all colours seek grey.

The storm picks up in ferocity, obliterating everything that was visible only yesterday.

1
The Commune

Ryan entered their land, stopping to re-hook the gate that had been left undone. The yard was crowded with lilac trees, with old roses, with sweet rocket, lupine, calendula, and foxgloves. Honeysuckle climbed the roof of the ancient house. The robins had stopped carolling and there was silence in the air.

The moss covered peaks of the roof rose above the tops of old fruit trees. Unripe fruit hung like ornaments among their leaves. Ryan thought that the whole thing looked like a Persian miniature, each leaf precisely delineated in the hazy sunlight. He easily imagined a peacock or two strutting through the glade.

He stopped to listen for a moment before going to the door, listened for the children playing, the clank of dishes being washed, the hammering, sawing and cursing of Wylie building something in the yard. There was only silence. He walked around to the back door, which was the only one anyone ever used. The front door was ceremonial in nature and only the Law or a visiting Jehovah's Witness would have thought to knock on it. As Ryan walked around the house, he looked for smoke or a face in the window. No one seemed to be home. Before climbing the sagging wooden steps to the back porch, he looked at Joshua Island, its ancient wind-swept firs and rocky shores barely visible through the great white trunks of the alder trees that hid the house from the sea. Ryan wondered, once again, why everything around Vasquez had a biblical name.

After lunch a bad feeling had come over Ryan, and it was not just from the slabs of coarsely ground bread that he had eaten. The commune truck had come down his road and then returned loaded with people and things. It bothered Ryan that they might have taken people away.

He imagined that they must have gone down to Duke's to buy some of his junk. Duke was an old timer with a halo of long hair, a long prophet's beard and a twinkle in his eye. He identified himself with the prophet Immanuel. After a vision of the end of the world, he had gathered everything that he would need to survive and begin anew. He had put it all on rafts and towed them north but had only gotten as far as Vasquez, and for some reason had stopped there. Everything sat peacefully rising and falling on tides in the sheltered lagoon. His rafts, connected by plank catwalks, comprised a great floating junkyard; a massive collection of machines and equipment, huge fuel tanks, an ancient tractor, a derelict fish boat: bits and pieces of ancient industrial everything.

Ryan had left his house and walked down toward Duke's, feeling the coolness of the road's smooth clay beneath his bare fee. The sky still promised a rain that never came, day after day of the same hazy overcast, not quite sunny not quite cloudy.

At the fork where he had had his fateful meeting with Ariel, he decided to stop and tell her and Wylic that the commune truck had come down their road. Since the debacle in Vancouver, Ryan had been trying to make a new kind of friendship with Ariel, something more practical and earthly than his previous yearning, one that would include her husband and children. Ryan had noticed that Ariel, while polite when he visited, often left to do something in the kitchen or out in the garden, leaving him to talk to Wylie or to play with the girls.

Standing at the open back door, Ryan called into the house and heard only its emptiness. A few morning sunbeams filtered down through the kitchen window panes. The breakfast dishes were still on the table, smeared with yellow egg yolk. There were unfinished remnants of toast left on the sides of the plates, glasses half filled with milk, cups with coffee grounds in the bottom. Ryan called again. There was a thick silence all around. He could hear the chickens clucking out in the yard and the buzz of a passing bee. Ariel was an immaculate house keeper, and he wondered for a moment if they had just decided to leave the dishes and head down to the beach for an after breakfast walk.

When is a door not a door? He walked into the kitchen, into the cool dark room, and into a disorder that went far beyond the plates on the table:

2

things had been spilled out onto the fir floor: a calendar, a trail of lentils, empty paper bags, a jumble of utensils. The kitchen had been ransacked. Its cupboards and drawers had been flung open and everything pulled from the shelves. The sink was piled with dirty dishes; a cereal box was spilled-out on the counter.

Ryan called out again, all their names, as though trying to invoke them: Wylie, tall and dark, shifting between scowl and laugh, lean and a bit stooped from the work of keeping it all together; Jessie and Alia, their blond hair collecting sunbeams, their laughter, tantrums and endless questions about life; Ariel, her beauty and laughter sustaining all of them. Things did not feel right. These images of them flitted like ghosts through his mind in the emptiness of the pillaged house.

He walked through the house from room to room, through the sunbeams and silence and looked at their family's scattered and broken things lying on the floor. A few plastic toys had been squashed under foot. In the living room, the cover cloths had been pulled from the couch and chairs, showing how old and threadbare they really were. Art objects were tumbled on the floor. The drawers of the desk were open and papers, bank statements, bills were scattered around the room.

In panic Ryan climbed the narrow turning staircase up to where the bedrooms were tucked away under the eaves of the house. Everything in Ariel and Wylie's bedroom had been ransacked as well. The drawers had been pulled out. On the floor, the family album was skewed open, bent and trod upon. Its pictures were scattered. Wylie's or Ariel's great grandparents looked up at him from old daguerreotypes, their eyes staring into a future that had suddenly been severed. There were pictures of Ariel and Wylie at their marriage, pictures of their parents in front of old cars, pictures of the girls as babies. Ancestors stared out from their white rimmed borders.

Ryan whirled like a dervish, looking around the room. Clothes had been hastily pulled from drawers that were open and spilling. The bed had been stripped of its mattress and linen. Across the hall, the children's room was in the same condition. The toys, the dolls, the furnishings of their miniature world were tumbled and abandoned on the floor. The little red hotels and green houses of a monopoly game were scattered around the room. Ryan saw the little silver shoe and the silver touring car. The house

3

looked like it had been ransacked by thieves trying to discover something precious and hidden.

Then he knew what had happened. An arrangement had been made. The Commune truck had come this morning. In haste Ariel and Wylie had pulled their clothes out of the drawers and stuffed them into boxes.

All those things that a life secretes around itself to protect its soft meat from the buffets of life, the knickknacks, the beach stones, the children's drawings, the paintings and framed cards, the painted masks from holiday trips, the children's school pictures, the special festive clothes, the favourite books, the crystals in the window, had all been left tumbled onto the floor, or left in their place on shelves or window sills. More important and practical things—mattresses, bedclothes, food—had been taken out to the truck.

There was the mark of so much haste. It looked like the house of refugees who only had time to grab a few things as the sound of the canons got closer. Suddenly he knew that they had fled from the confusion around and inside them; from the endless sequence of altered realities, each as real as the one before or after it; from the inability to distinguish between them; from the inability to make plans and carry them out amidst the shifting kaleidoscope of drug induced worlds. And beyond that he also knew that they had fled from his attempt—he saw it in this broken and fateful moment—to grasp Ariel's endlessly sustaining joy and good nature for himself. To capture her, like a firefly in a bottle, to light his dark realm. Now her light was gone, taken away to the city of plastic huts that huddled below the great stone house.

Did they choose what they took, Ryan wondered, or did someone stand over them and say "take that," and, "you won't be needing this?" He imagined them in the truck, hunkered down, not waving, not wanting to be seen, already learning how to be silent and compliant. They had taken only their clothes, a few boxes, some pieces of furniture, their mattresses and bedding into their new life.

Ryan's eyes filled with tears and he ran out onto the porch, into the sunlight of the bird-filled morning. Responsibility burned in his chest and came out in a wail. He knew that he was partly to blame for having tipped their life over the edge to where it no longer worked; to where it was filled with too much uncertainty and confusion; to where the signposts, the thoushalts and the thou-shalt-nots, were uprooted and scattered like their belongings.

To his mind they had given up trying to lead their own life, trying to make sense of the burdens and gifts given them. They had surrendered to another's vision. They had given over their children and themselves. In that moment he remembered a tale about a Greek village under siege by the Turks. Unable to hold out any longer, the whole village gathered for one last dance in the Khora, every man, woman and child. They danced their sacred dance, the dance of life and freedom, and then, children in arms, jumped to their deaths rather than leave their children to be raised as slaves. A story from another island.

Ryan walked away from the house, out of its darkness, down the trail toward the sea. He sought the openness and emptiness of water. On his way to the beach he came upon a small clearing where there had been a tea party. It looked like a place where elves might have gathered. Magical chairs had been carved out of alder rounds with a chainsaw. They were placed around a table carved from one huge fir round. Its underside had been hollowed away leaving it standing on four stubby legs. On it sat a vase of wilted flowers, left over from spring's ecstasy of lilacs and tulips. The chairs had high backs, the tops of which had been carved into simple heraldic designs. Four in number, they differed in size, like the chairs in the three bear's house: a papa chair, a momma chair and two baby chairs. At the top of the largest chair was carved a large crown, spikes pointing heavenward. On either side of the table were two smaller chairs with little crowns above them for the two princesses; across from the King's chair was a chair with a heart carved at the top, a chair where the Queen of Hearts had sat surrounded by her loving subjects.

The tea party was so full of love and inspired artistry, like a sonnet, that Ryan cracked in grief. It would be left to the weather. It would sit undisturbed for months and years on its promontory over the sea. Leaves would gather on the table. Blackcap vines would twine over the chairs. It would endure the change of seasons and stand as the memory of a moment that was and of other moments that could have been. It would bear witness, as the clouds passed over, to days that had become unspooled and sucked into the void. The chairs would become chairs for ghosts, empty seats for the people he had loved (as much as he was able to love) in a life already filled with endings and leavings.

He walked back to the house. The castle had been sacked; the moat breached; the kingdom broken. They had left in rout, in full flight. He knew beyond all doubt that they had gone to the Commune in search of some routine, some purpose or vision that would keep them together; that the Commune had welcomed them, had come with its truck and taken them away from all this terrible individuality; that the pictures, the toys, meant nothing anymore; that it was like dying; it was letting go and moving on. He knew that the next time he saw Ariel, if he saw her at all, her hair would be short and she would be wearing drab; that she would simply look at him for a moment and then continue with her new life.

Leaving the house frozen in its moment of disaster, Ryan started back up the drive toward the gate. He knew what would happen next. He had seen it before, even with Sheila's things when she had left them at the Pond House. People would come and take a few things that were useful to them, an egg-turner, a bottle brush, a shirt that fit. Things would be scattered and pawed through. Animals would enter. Feral cats would spray. Someone would leave the gate open and cows and sheep would eat the gardens. Grass and brambles would grow. If it stayed empty long enough, boys would come and throw rocks through the windows before running off into the forest. People would take away doors, tables, sinks. His own home had some boards from a beautiful barn that used to stand at the end of Center Road. It was the unwritten Law of Architectural Entropy: in the country, empty houses disappear, board by board, and become pieces of other houses.

He turned around and returned to the house one more time to take the ancestral photographs from the bedroom floor. If their family ever returned, he thought that they might want them. He closed the wire gate behind him, thinking that at least there was hope.

2
The Commune

The day had started out as just any other day in early summer, the sky promising a rain that never came, the garden dried out, the well low and froggy. There was not even enough water to fill the barrel at the back of the house.

Ryan was dribbling water on the garden plants that needed it the most, using a plastic bucket he had scrounged from the bakery in the town across the water. He was dressed in his Mexican chamorra with his hair done up in a braid. His car sat broken at the side of the field. A broken down car. A dirt road. A small shake house that reminded him of the straw roofed houses he had seen in Chiapas. Mexico in Canada.

As he looked around, images crowded his memory. He remembered the tall straw roofs, their scimitar shaped roof caps sticking up out of the jungle. He remembered a woman weaving on a back loom in front of her house. He remembered the hand-woven black cloth she had worn, and how a harness from one end of the loom was passed behind her back, while the other end was tied to the trunk of a flowering tropical tree. After each pass of the flat hand-carved shuttle she leaned back to tighten the warp, all the while singing to a baby on her back. Her voice blended with the song of birds. Her clothes, her food, her house were all taken directly from the earth. Everything was reduced to elemental self-sufficiency; there was no connection whatsoever to the industrial monster of the north, Moloch, devouring the planet and the souls of its children in exchange for possessions and wealth.

The Mayans were used to disaster. The Conquest. And even before the coming of the Spaniards, their great cities had fallen into ruin and lay covered by the jungle. In their mythology the world had ended many times. Each time, a few people crawled through a small hole to start the next world. There was a sparseness and portability to their culture: its basic DNA of loom, axe and seeds that could be passed forward to another time. At eighteen Ryan had been touched by the still living descendents of the people who had built the great limestone ceremonial centres of Palenque, Uxmal, Tikal, Coban, Chichen Itza, Ek-Balam. As he looked at his simple shake house, the names of these ruined cities passed through his mind like the beads on a rosary.

Later Ryan found that the Mayans did use a few things from the industrial north: matches (sparingly), steel machetes, the treads of worn out tires for the soles of sandals, a small radio and batteries for music. These they had adopted, but cautiously, seeming to know that there was a price to pay. For the most part they lived in the ancient way, and could continue their lives if these things suddenly, due to some disaster—something unthinkable happening under inclement stars—became unavailable.

Ryan had become fascinated by cultural collapse; by the descendants of the people who had walked away from the giant ceremonial centres to start new lives in the simple shacks of the Yucatan. He could imagine a time, a future, in which the high-rise buildings of Vancouver would rise out of the encroaching rain forest, hollow-eyed monoliths lived in by tribes who used them as pueblos, each defending their own building.

He was twenty-four now. He had been on Vasquez, an island that was only marginally regulated, an outlaw zone, for two years. He had replaced flashlights and batteries with candle lamps. He had learned to keep goats, chickens, geese; to grow his own root crops, to store apples and pears, to cut firewood from the wild trees, to make tofu from soybeans, to make bread from wheat kernels; to make hinges out of old tires; to make fence posts from the buried cedar logs that the loggers had left behind. Still, his shelves were littered with items from the very civilisation that he was trying to escape, things that he could not do without or make for himself, such as matches, oil, kerosene, gasoline, the chain saw. The whole situation was epitomised in a joke that a friend had told him: "It's a lot of hard work to make your own steel, but it's worth it just to be able to tell U.S. Steel to shove it."

But even if there were enough oolichan left from which to press oil for light, it would have taken many generations of moving backwards to achieve the same self sufficiency that the First People once had, and the eyes of the children were already turned toward the lighted phantasmagoria of the other side, toward Barbie Dolls and Hot Wheel cars.

Ryan had traded away his gas generator, preferring to live in the silence of kerosene lamps, a silence that on windless nights was so deep that each pop of the fire resounded into the cabin and even the hiss of the lamp wick could be heard. In the dim light everything became magic. It was the light of imperial palaces and peasant huts, a pre-scientific light that did not wash out the dim outlines of spirits as they passed through the walls on their errands of the night. This way he could see the ghosts from the past that he was moving into.

He remembered the ghost dance, in which the remnants of the American Indians danced to bring back the dead, and, on the prairies, the buffalo. He remembered that, in the sixties, thousands of protesters made a circle around the Pentagon in Washington in an attempt to neutralize its dark power. The Pentagon remained. The buffalo were gone.

Ryan wondered, as he lay the bucket on its side in the bottom of the nearly empty well, if magic was just the vain delusion of people left behind by the technological rush, people believing that some kind of psychic power, God, prayer, synchronicity, would save them, believing this as they rushed into oblivion, as their images were caught fleetingly in the light of history like the shadows burned onto the walls of Hiroshima.

As he carried his half-filled bucket of water to the shrivelled carrots and withered lettuce, half in this world, half in memory, a truck rattled down past his house, and its sound pulled him from his musings. The truck was green and moved quickly. It looked like a cartoon truck with elliptical wheels that had puffs of dust behind them. To his surprise it was the Commune truck. He had never seen it come down his road before.

Normally he would have waved to a passing truck, but he didn't wave to this one. Experience had taught him that Commune members didn't wave back. It was not that some of them didn't wave back, but that they *all* didn't wave back. It must have been a policy. On the ferry they sat facing backwards, staring at the back wall of the cabin. Today he could make out several of them up in the cab and several more in back. They were wearing their uniform of muted work clothes and rolled toques.

After the truck passed he went back to his watering, but the truck had thrown a cloud over his day. The Commune was ominous. Its tall fences

9

wound further into the forest every day. The silent crew split high pickets and nailed them into place. There was no laughter, no cursing—the time honoured refuge of frustrated carpenters—only silence. It felt like something was hiding there.

Ryan returned to the garden several more times and poured the last of the water around his plants. There were little wet spots around each plant now. When the well was empty and slowly refilling, he closed the picket gate to the garden and placed the bucket beside it. Tomorrow he would do the same thing all over again. He stopped and looked at the sky for the rain that never came.

As he walked through the tall grass and buttercups back to the house, he heard the truck come back up the road. As it went by he glimpsed furniture, boxes, and bags piled precariously to above the railings. People were riding the running boards and hanging off the back. The cab was crammed with people. He watched as the truck disappeared behind the trees and geared down to make the corner. He heard it shift into higher gears and speed up as it turned the corner onto Main Road, heading back to its fenced domain, its gloomy stone house, its shanty town of plastic shacks, its fifty or sixty people who silently cleared the land, planted orchards, and baked bread.

Ryan went inside and made some coffee. He cut a slab of bread from a loaf whose wheat he had ground by hand, passing it three times, in ever tighter settings, through the hand grinder. The daily grind. He spread the bread with peanut butter and jam from Famous Foods, eating to console himself.

As he chewed, he thought about the Commune: rumor had it that they had completed a great stone house on top of the hill; that the leader and his inner circle lived in the mansion while the followers lived in the city of plastic huts at the foot of the hill; that everyone was welcome, rich or poor; that they all contributed what they had, signed over their assets, be it the shirt on their back or their house in Toronto; that a number of wealthy people had joined, giving all their money, and that now they too lived in plastic houses with everyone else; that they all drank a drink called Torah, made from apple cider vinegar and honey, to keep everyone healthy and avoid the colds and flues that could so easily sweep through their population; that they had used the winter to clear some of the surrounding land, had milled the trees into lumber and were building a variety of outbuildings; that they had pulled the stumps and fenced the land where the forest once stood and planted fruit trees to make a huge orchard; that people had visions or heard voices up on the bluffs above the mansion.

Ryan and his friends used to make jokes about the Commune. Having seen the Wizard of Oz, they attributed the voices to concealed loudspeakers or other such trickery. But now that it had taken two of their friends, Julie and Elroy, they didn't laugh so loud. Everybody missed the guitar that Elroy had brought everywhere and the songs that he used to sing.

Ryan had known loneliness, fear, pain disappointment, failure, addiction, all in his twenty four years, but he still wondered what would make people give up their life for such a depersonalised existence. The Commune had him thinking.

3
The Commune

After closing their gate, Ryan walked back up the road to his house and went in just long enough to leave the photos on the kitchen table. Then he left, walking past the garden he had watered in the morning; past the mailboxes at the corner. He turned down Main Road, the way the truck had gone, and walked the half mile down to Sammie and Alexis' trail. He walked through the ferns and stumps down to their little cabin.

Alexis was in the front yard hacking away at the turf and clay to open up a new garden bed. His long curly hair was tied back and dusty.

"Hey man," he said, "What's happ'nin'?" He looked at Ryan with his customary probing sensitivity, indicating that what he had really said was "Hey man, what's happened?" His eyebrows arched above the black frames of his glasses. His face was always mobile, ready to go either way into laughter or into sympathy, like there was a big joke going on but one that it was better not to laugh out loud at.

Sammie was hanging out clothes on a line under the roof of the porch. Ryan thought she gave him a look that said "It takes so much work just to get on out here, that the last thing we need are crazy stoned-out visitors discussing their infinitude of angels endlessly pirouetting on the polished points of pins." Her children were near her, looking out through the railings of the porch to see who had come down the trail.

"Ariel and Wylie and their kids have all gone to the Commune."

"No man, you're kidding." Alexis took his hoe out of the air and leaned on it, like this one was going to take some time.

Alexis and Ryan had talked endlessly about strange science fiction books like David Lindsay's Voyage to Arcturus, Alexis' favourite. It was as though they had read too much of it and now the science fiction world had landed on them in the form of this strange Commune that seemed to eat, among other things, the souls of their friends. Above them Sammy continued to shake out shirts, making small sonic booms before hanging them on the line.

"No, man, I've just been down there. Their house is ransacked, ripped apart, they are gone. I saw the truck go down the road and come back full of people and stuff."

"Yea, when I was out at the road I saw the truck come by here too, but I couldn't see who was in it. Wow, that's heavy, man, heavy. Come on in for a minute." He wiped sweat and dust from his forehead with his sleeve, dropped the hoe and they walked past Sammie into the house. Ryan said "Hi Sammie," but she didn't answer, appearing to be intent on her chores.

Inside Alexis heated up the morning's coffee on a small kerosene burner. They drank it full of canned milk and brown sugar. Alexis rolled a slim joint and they smoked it making all the usual sucking and gulping noises. Drugs were their first line attempt to handle any crisis. The premise was that if you could get a little higher you would be able to look down from above and see the situation more clearly. As Sammie, hanging laundry outside and occasionally glaring in through the windows, knew, in reality that didn't happen. Things only got more muddled. They had been captured by a metaphor.

While holding in a lungful of smoke, Ryan looked up and saw the small TV that he had given Alexis sitting on a shelf above the kitchen counter. It was covered with a cloth to protect it from dust. "How's the TV holding out," Ryan said, coughing out the exhale. "Great man," said Alexis, looking a bit sheepish, "great."

Ryan took another toke and, as he held it, remembered the day that his mother had sent him the miniature battery operated TV. It had come in a huge crushed box that looked like it had been beaten and battered by the best efforts of both countries' postal systems. Surprisingly it had survived, intact in its meninges of Styrofoam packing.

She had also sent another box that contained the battery to which the TV could be hooked. Ryan knew that she saw him as being too insular, out of touch with the world and drifting further away with every passing month. He wondered what she expected from someone who lived on a

13

small island off a bigger island. He knew she hoped that this little TV would begin to bring him back.

As he unpacked it, after he got over his anger at her presumption, he was a little excited at its miniature perfectness, excited to hook it to the battery to see what was on. He knew from his friend Hank who had one just like it, that you could get two channels out on the island. Hank had strapped a TV antennae to the top of a fir tree, much to the consternation of the local ravens. He would sit in his tiny clearing surrounded by dark forest and chuckle at late night comedies.

After the dishes were put away, Ryan had put the TV on the table and hooked it up to the battery. It sprang into life in his quiet lamp-lit house. He fiddled with the rabbit ears, and out of the snowy black and white screen images began to emerge. He moved the set around to various places in the house to clarify the image. Soon he had images of black men in bib overalls talking to a reporter out in the cotton fields of the Deep South, portly farmers with black Southern accents. He fiddled some more and their images became clearer. He could see their faces. He tried to get the other channel, but decided that you must need the tree top arrangement, so he turned back to the black farmers and tilted himself back in the chair to watch the show.

Little by little he pieced it together. It was a documentary about some black farmers who had been experimented on without their consent. Over the years, a number of them had come to a clinic to be treated for syphilis. The doctor, as part of documenting the effects of tertiary syphilis, had given them placebos instead of the drugs they needed. Now, after many years, the truth had come out. They had infected their wives and through them their children. The doctor, it turned out, had been some kind of fundamentalist nutcase who believed that people must experience the wages of their sin. It reminded Ryan of his family dentist who hadn't used Novocain because he believed that children needed to feel the pain so that they wouldn't eat candy. In the dentist's mind he was saving Ryan's teeth by showing him the wages of sin. In Ryan's mind the dentist was a torturer.

Ryan was horrified. He raged around the cabin too fascinated to turn off the phosphorescent eye. He was furious at his mother for having brought this sorrow into his home. There was already enough sorrow in his

14

daily life without having to cope with the suffering of distant farmers in Alabama. Suddenly he couldn't stand the TV and remembered why he didn't have one: it took his time, inserted images into his mind, and created cravings for things that he didn't have. An ad came on showing a swift sports car cruising around the beautiful curves of the Big Sur coast. The people in it were stunningly beautiful and looked truly, perfectly, happy. They were fully in the moment as they drove their marvellous car. He thought of his car, the Red Ant, parked outside, not running since last autumn; the twisted wires that served as an ignition hanging beneath the dashboard; its exhaust system supported by bailing wire and full of holes; its doors not fully closing anymore.

Ryan was angry at the TV. In a whirl of his own energy, he decided that he must give it away; that he didn't need it in his life; didn't need it telling him about syphilitic farmers in Alabama. He picked it up with one hand and its battery with the other. He opened the door and went down the road using the TV as a phosphorescent flashlight. There was no moon and the TV's flickering light played eerily in the fir trees on either side of the road. He had not completely turned off the sound and, along with the crunching of his feet on the gravel, he could still hear the soft voices of Alabama farmers talking into an otherwise quiet northern night. There were no cars on the road and he had kept on going until he had come to Sammie and Alexis' trail. He had walked along the narrow path, throwing pulsing light into the giant sword ferns and shadows all around him.

There were no lights on in Sammie's and Alexis' tiny shake house. They had gone to bed exhausted after putting their two children to sleep in the loft. He knocked twice on their door and then simply walked into their unlocked, darkened home.

Ryan knew that Alexis loved film, loved old movies. He and his film buff friends spent hours talking about films, replaying favourite scenes in their imagination. They didn't even need the film any more. They could just say "Do you remember where Brando walked in the door and saw her sitting on the couch?" They could all see the whole scene. The movie had become so much a part of them they could run it in their heads. Alexis would sit up at night making films with friends. "So then we could have a long shot of the False Bay wharf. The camera closes in on The Captain's face, and then to the wild waves that he's looking at. It cuts back to The

Captain and we don't see fear in his eyes, but a wild pleasure about going out in those waves. We realise that he likes risking his life, likes giving death a chance to end his suffering. It doesn't matter if a whole community goes down with him. It's like Egypt: he'd be The Captain forever, sailing across watery eternity with his captive passengers."

"Yea, and then the boat leaves the dock. It is shot from the lower apron. Ariel stands on the dock watching it leave. Her family is aboard. The boat begins plunging through those cresting waves. We'd have a close-up of the passenger room, people starting to get sick and going into that catatonic trance we go into on a crossing like that; throwing up into barf bags. We'd cut to the sheets of water pouring down the windows. The island looks wrinkled and strange behind them. Then we'd cut back to Ariel—yea, Ariel could do the part, she'd be perfect for it, spunky, a bit crazy, but also grounded and sensible—she is walking up the gang plank and she looks exasperated and pissed off. The wind is whipping her hair around the edges of her hood."

Ryan knew that, unlike him, Alexis would love the TV; that it would be a treasure to him. He would stay up all night and watch the old movies that they play in the wee hours. He would sit alone in his dark house in the dark forest, his family asleep around him, with his eyes glued to the miniature glowing screen. It didn't occur to him that this might have a disastrous effect on his household; that he would be too tired the next day to build chicken coops and cut firewood. That Sammie would have to work even harder. She had once told Sheila—before Sheila had left, "Never learn to use the chain saw or you'll wind up cutting all the firewood too."

Alexis had not known what was happening to him: he was awakened out of deep sleep by a thunderous knock on the door and felt his fragile house shake under Ryan's heavy step. He had just drifted off minutes before and was still partly in the world of dreams. Suddenly, his home was filled with phosphorescent blue light. In his sleep befuddled state, he wondered about invading aliens.

Sometimes they would stay up and freak each other out with tales of alien abductions and the possibility of aliens living in their midst. They speculated about whether the members of the Commune at the south end had been taken over by aliens. These were wild stories that they really didn't believe but they were scary anyway. It was easy for things to become scary in this far-away place. Alexis heard the children stir in their bunks and was worried for them. The light grew brighter and was clearly coming through the open door into their bedroom.

Alexis and Sammie sat up in bed, Sammie clutching the sheet to her. Her eyes were wide in alarm and cast about for the rifle that they used to shoot the mink and racoons that raided the chickens. She looked fierce, like she wasn't going to let them get her that easy. If there was going to be a fight she was up for it. Luckily for Ryan, the rifle was hanging on the wall in the other room.

Alexis twisted half way out of bed to see what was coming at him. Ryan had to hold the TV behind him to get through the narrow passage, and Alexis saw a bright square light bobbing alternately on one side and then the other of a dark humanoid form. It was coming right at him. He heard Ryan's voice mechanically shouting, "Hello? Hello," like a broken mechanism, and also heard the voices of the southern black farmers. It seemed that whatever this thing was, it had sucked all these beings into it and that they were clamouring for release.

Ryan saw the wildness leave Alexis' eyes as he began to come out of the dream world and searched for a more rational explanation. He plunked the TV and battery down on the dresser. "I brought this for you," he said. "My mother sent it to me and I don't want it. It is a gift to you. I thought you might like it."

Then he just stood and looked at them. The cathode ray was illuminating them like bugs being filmed by a night time film crew. They were sickly blue-green under its light and clearly didn't know what to say. They were staring into the screen with wide wild eyes, trying to make sense of a commercial that was selling menstrual products by showing doves ascending into heaven. The song sang about "freedom every day" as the picture cut to a box of tampons. Ryan turned to leave, mission accomplished.

Alexis, always a gentleman, managed to shout after him. "You can have it back anytime you want."

To which Ryan yelled, "I don't want it back."

Suddenly Alexis was pissed off, by the home invasion, by what he perceived as Ryan flamboyantly flaunting his generosity. To Alexis this small TV was a priceless treasure, and he could not believe that anyone would willingly relinquish it. "You'll be back for it," he shouted at Ryan's departing back.

"Hell if I will," said Ryan, going back into darkness and shutting their door behind him.

Ryan had forgotten that there was no moon and stood on their doorstep for awhile to let his eyes get used to the darkness. He picked his way slowly back along the trail by feeling it, step by step, with his feet. Each step was precarious and the sword ferns loomed big around him like many armed creatures of the night. When he reached Main Road, he looked back, and saw faint rays of blue light streaming from the windows of Alexis' house. It looked like one of the uncannily lit windmills from the hell panel of Bosh's Garden of Earthly Delights, throwing a light that was not at all healthy into the surrounding forest, a light that was like radiation, like megatons, a light that was a parody of the light of Heaven. No, he wouldn't be back for it.

Ryan walked back through the darkness, feeling much calmer than when he had come. When he reached his house, it seemed quiet and safe again; out of the reach of harm. He picked up the boxes and Styrofoam packing that the TV and its battery had come in. He had some misgivings about having given the demon to his friend, and wondered if he should have just destroyed it, put it on the chopping block and taken the axe to it, but being wasteful was not in his nature: too many centuries of Genovese frugality had been woven into his genes.

Now, sitting with Alexis after telling him that Ariel and her family had gone to the commune, Ryan exhaled smoke from the joint and realized that he had tripped out on a long memory. His reflection was broken by Sammie coming into the house, shooing the children in front of her. Tiny Sylvia wore a little dress and Lazarus, arisen from the dead of a previous generation, looked like a young prince Valiant with his bangs and shoulder length hair. Alexis looked at Sammie and said, expelling the remains of his lung-full of smoke. "Wylie and Ariel have gone up to the Commune."

"Oh shit," she said, "what about the children?"

"Gone with them."

Sammie sat and took Sylvia onto her lap. She hugged her and nuzzled her neck with her chin while Sylvia's long legs dangled down. She reached out and pulled Lazarus to her as well, so he was leaning against her. She looked at Alexis and Ryan with a look that was remote and far away, tipping between anger and sadness. Then she put the children down and went into the kitchen and began scrubbing the bread pans that she had left in the sink to soak.

4
Ryan and Sheila

Sheila and Ryan had first met Ariel in summer when she and her girls had straggled up through the forest to get their mail. The mail came twice a week to a green metal box at the corner, a box whose compartments were held shut by a collection of rusted locks dangling from bent latches. Only Sheila and Ryan's lock was shiny and new.

First they had heard the children's noisy laughter and unsubdued voices. They went to the door and watched them emerge from the forest, running into the light of the clearing. It was the first time they knew they shared their road with anyone other than Mike, the spooky character who lived on his decaying farm, and Duke, who lived on a raft in his floating pre-apocalyptic junkyard. The children were dressed in the worn end of things, polished up by brightly knit caps and new rubber boots. Their mother, graceful even in her country clothes, came out moments later. She called to the speeding children, "Watch out for cars up on Main Road."

Sheila picked up Lara and they all walked out the short driveway to the road. The children were full of questions: "Who are you? Do you live here? Did you buy this house? How much did you pay for it?" They leaped about in their excitement at seeing new people, and were asking more and more questions when Ariel walked up and shushed them, gathering them to her. "Hello, I'm Ariel, wow it's so great to have you guys living on our road. We have to rush up to meet the mail truck. We've got letters to go out, but we'll visit on our way back."

As it turned out, they all walked up to the corner together and stood talking until distant rattles and clunks announced the arrival of the bent-up red Datsun pickup that served as a mail truck. It emerged from the forest like a terrestrial comet trailing a long plume of dust. When it stopped, the dust caught up with it and settled on all of them while the postman handed out the mail and sorted it into compartments.

On the way back to the house they opened letters and talked about them. The children asked questions about an aunt who was coming to visit. Back at the house Ryan and Sheila invited everybody in and Sheila made toast and jam for the kids and tea—Earl Grey—for the grownups.

The kids poked around and found some jumping jack figures of circus folk, a gift for the nursery from Lara's grandma. They brought them over to show their mother. "Look at these, mom." They pulled the strings and laughed as the circus people's legs and arms flew wildly about. Ariel laughed and tossed her brown hair off her face as she lit the cigarette she had just rolled. Her green eyes sparkled with mirth. "They look like Heads," she said. And so they did, the strong man with his moustache and long hair, a high-wire dancer in her exotic Persian costume, a lion tamer in his cardshark's suit. Somehow their eyes all had that slightly glazed and contented look of the righteously stoned. All they needed was some Canadian work clothes to be right at home here in the bush.

Heads and Freaks were what members of this sub-culture called themselves. Heads was short for pot-heads. Freaks? For freaks in the circus, deformed people who made their living by exhibiting themselves to the normal population? For Freaks of nature, people born different from those around them? It was clear from Ariel's laughter, full of amusement and acceptance, from her comfortable sensuality and ease with her body, that she was a Head, a Freak. It was as though she had entered a doorway to another world, but was still close enough to its threshold to enjoy the pleasure of conversation with Ryan and Sheila. Having cast off some of society's corsets, she found their formality amusing in a gentle sort of way.

Ryan could feel Sheila go on guard. Although she was as polite and personable as ever, he could feel her begin to hold Ariel at arm's length. Even later, when they met Wylie, and began to socialise as couples, Ryan could feel Sheila hold herself back. Their mutual interest in writing and art, their love of the same writers, their talk of Malcolm Lowry's enormous binges, of clarion hangovers and the special insight that came with their pain, their talk about the difficulty of trying to express something honestly, and the fact that they were the only two families living on the same road, was not enough to bridge a certain difference: Ariel and Wylie led a life in disregard of the academy and its values, in disregard of rigor and discipline, in disregard of any assumption about the right way to conduct one's life. Their life had become bigger than the academic preoccupation with specific fields. They had dropped out, while Sheila and Ryan's shelves were still littered with text books from their four years in school.

Ariel had left her life as a group home manager who supervised adolescents into becoming good citizens. She and Wylie had brought with them, or he had followed them, one of her former students, 18 year old Ron. He had escaped from his group home to build his own cabin, a 12' X 12' cedar shake floathouse that rose and fell on the tides of the lagoon below their house. In reality, while sleeping in his float house, Ron spent a lot of time as part of Ariel's family.

Ariel and Wylie were squatters. The old house in which they lived for free was down through the forest, along the fork of the road that did not go to Mike's and Duke's. It had a peaked roof that was covered with large clumps of green moss. Its walls were covered with shingle faded by time to a light green. It stood in a grove of ancient scraggly fruit trees. The grass around them was clipped by the feral sheep. It had something of the Russian fairy tale about it, like a place governed by elementals, with flocks of sheep to mow the grass and bright eyed crows to guard its treasures.

The house sat in its clearing on a cliff high above the water. It was hidden from curious boaters by the white trunks of old alders which grew up from the gulch that fell to the sea behind it. The living room looked out through old-paned windows, through the alders, to Joshua Island, a long rugged rock, crowned by windswept masts of ancient firs. It looked like a windjammer turned to stone and forest.

Behind the house Ariel and Wylie grew a huge garden. Wylie pulled fish from the sea in an old boat that was always breaking down. Sometimes, out on the choppy waters, drifting ever closer to the rocks, he performed intricate repairs with little more than vice-grips and a screwdriver. Sometimes, from the beach where they played with Lara, Sheila and Ryan could hear him cursing the motor and hitting it with wrenches. At times Wylie went away to work and brought back money. He knew about some inlet up the coast, a place where the land fell steeply into the sea, where they paid fifty dollars a day for logging. At the time it was good money.

Ariel and Wylie had nothing to fall back on, no tidy sum of money to subsidise them. There was a fierce survival reality to their life that was lacking in Sheila's and Ryan's, who had seventeen acres and a small cushion of savings.

Wylie was tall and lean with long dark hair and a trimmed beard. There was something angular about him. He flashed between a dancing, animated laughter and slumped, dark brooding. Ariel was all grace and openness. She was more the front-person of the relationship, the one who met the world, while Wylie stayed home and created the kingdom in which they lived.

Though Ryan knew that he and Sheila—as a couple—would not become good friends with Ariel and Wylie, he was fascinated by Ariel, by her charm, her ready laughter, her honesty. He was also attracted in a more physical way to her grace, to her body so bare beneath the summer cotton of her dress. He harboured a hidden urge to kiss the small hairs on her arm.

Ever since his earliest days in high school, people close to Ryan had been dropping out. Whether inspired or just misguided, they would leave the life they were sharing with Ryan and enter some other world. As they left, there was always the tacit invitation: "Wanna come with me?" No matter how far Ryan had dropped out, to the world of Quaker intentional communities, to the world of squatters cabins, to the world of remote islands, there was always someone, in each of these places, who had dropped out further. There seemed to be no bottom to this well of dropping out. Ryan felt that he still carried some code of conduct with him into all these places. He wondered where it would take him, he who had always been fascinated by derelicts and outlaws, if he kept stepping downward.

Compared to Ariel and Wylie, Ryan felt that he and Sheila were like outposts of intellectual empire that had washed up on a primitive shore, stranded but still trying to fly the flag, still trying to keep up appearances. Everything around them was already turning to mildew, and, unless the ship arrived soon, they would be reduced to wearing loincloths and eating with the natives.

Once, on his first trip out to the island with Dave and Celia, Ryan had had a dream about joining, and then escaping from, a tribe out on an island. In the dream, when he had merged with the tribe, Sheila was nowhere in sight. She had escaped long before then.

After tea, Ariel gathered up her mail and her children and started down the road to her home. Ryan and Sheila stood on the porch and watched them go. The children started laughing and talking loudly at the place where the road entered the forest. Ryan felt that it must have been to dispel the imaginary creatures that they felt to be lurking in the trees and ferns around them.

5
Ryan And Sheila

Ryan and Sheila had come tumbling onto the island from Vancouver, with all of their possessions, including their English piano. No-one had warned them about English pianos.

Sheila had brought the piano for Lara, to give her daughter the chance to play music that only a piano can provide for a small child. She had also brought a tape recorder with lots of batteries so that Lara could listen to music. She had salvaged these two precious things, one big and one small, from husband's flight from civilisation.

On the day of their moving, the old red '59 Volvo PV 444 station wagon in which they had come to Canada, lovingly nicknamed the Red Ant, and Sheila's new sky blue Datsun pickup were piled high with all their belongings. Caravaning across Georgia Strait, Ryan and Sheila again found themselves in the belly of a B.C. ferry, waiting to be spit out on Vancouver Island, which lies like a three hundred mile long whale off the coast of British Columbia.

Once debouched, they had driven north on the Island Highway which was still a two lane road. The Red Ant led the way, packed to the roof with the things they would need first. It would roll straight onto a barge to bravely cross the seventeen kilometres of Georgia Strait to Vasquez Island. Once there, it would be hoisted by winch onto the government wharf. It would then carry Ryan, Sheila and Lara with all their immediate necessities to their new cabin. Later it would be used to get around the island, to carry wood, and to carry water in the dryness of summer.

Still later it would be used to careen around the island on moonlit nights. It would be filled with revellers with mason jars full of home brew strained through socks to make it drinkable. That part would happen after Sheila left.

It would drive to a series of beaches, where parties—both holy and debauched—were held around fires. It would age quickly and become haywired on the island's thirty-odd K of dirt road. It would be unlicensed. (Not having to wear license plates had always been one of its secret fantasies). When the RCMP came to look for illegal vehicles, it would be driven into the forest and parked under dark leafy trees. It would hide in the woods. It would secretly burn the cheap purple gas that was legal only for boats.

It would basically lead a life of crime and adventure in its declining years, until finally it was no longer able to run. Then it would sit for many years at the side of a field watching the seasons come and go; having poems written on it; watching children grow up; having its glass knocked out by the self same children throwing rocks. Finally, in tow, it would make its way to a dump high on the shoulder of the local mountain, and there it would sit, surrounded by dark forest and the calls of ravens, presiding, like a senile emperor, over a kingdom of junk and garbage. It would stare helplessly through its socketed headlamps as occasionally, many seasons apart, someone would come to take one of its few remaining parts. There would be nothing it could do.

High on that mountainside it would experience cycles of snow and baking heat. Its red paint would flake off and it would finally become the rich colour of rust. In a distant time there would be almost nothing left. Only an engine block, a transmission, a driveshaft, a differential, a rear axle would still be strung together like the bones of a dinosaur looking as though they wanted to go somewhere. Its skeleton would sit in a pile of red flakes that looked like the ochre spread on the bodies of the Palaeolithic dead.

But for now, as it laboured up the planks onto the barge, the Red Ant did not know—if it knew anything at all—a question better left to the epistomologists—that that was its future. Neither did its owners, its humans, know what lay ahead for them. Thrown up on this shore by this ferry, for reasons that they would only find out, or at least be able to guess at later; spinning and smarting from the turns their lives had taken; they would think they could see the workings of fate, but even then they would wonder if it was fate or just the choices they had made; choices followed by other choices, followed by yet other choices, some good and some bad, that led them to who they became.

Ryan would wonder if what appeared as fate, when looking backward, was only an inner chooser, a composite of training, biological inclination, woundedness and expediency. He would wonder, while looking forward into the blank of the future, if the chooser spins the web. He would wonder if, hoping for pleasure or maybe only trying to avoid pain, the chooser ultimately becomes entangled, wrapped in the intersecting matrix of consequences known as Karma or, alternatively, as The Bed One Must Toss In.

The first few months were exciting. Spring was dawning more every day. It was like having a summer cabin. They made frequent trips to Vancouver to buy necessities, like squares of grass matting with which to cover the massive concrete slab that Bill, the man who had built the house, a poet turned building inspector, said would last a thousand years.

And indeed, after having been on the island for awhile and seen its old homesteads, Ryan could imagine a distant future where someone would wander through a moss covered alder forest, just beginning to give way to firs, and notice a flat spot on the forest floor. They would kick at the leaves and branches and find that the flat spot was an old slab, a foundation. They would wonder about its story.

With the grass mat in place and their old carpets atop it, the house began to take on a homey feeling. On trips to Vancouver they stayed with friends and immersed themselves in the pleasures of city life: movies, Chinese dinners, galleries. Then they returned, car full of provisions, to their little cabin. It was all a bit like a pastoral, like playing at being humble shepherds and hoping that they would find happiness (or it would find them) in the simple, natural life. Their days were companionable if lacking in passion: they worked in the garden; they carried Lara, baby carrier on Ryan's back, down through the forest to lonely beaches; they made their own bread and experimented with cooking oysters and clams.

When night came they lit the lamps. When Lara was asleep, they played cards and read by the popping fire. When Ryan stepped out to pee at night, he was amazed at the darkness of the sky and the multitude of stars. He began to see them in perspective, the layers and layers of them:

they were no longer perforations in a dome over his head, but distant burning fires, fading all the way back to infinity. All this was experienced with cock in hand, his water streaming onto the wet grass like falling rain. Though far inland, Ryan could feel that he was on an island: he could hear the great winds that moved up and down Georgia Strait in the tree tops over his head; in a northeaster he could hear waves breaking on the shores of the Sabine Channel, down through the dark forest below him.

The full moon threw enough light to read by. Sheila and Ryan were amazed and delighted at the night world of silvers, greys and blacks that existed alongside the familiar world of day. Sometimes when Lara was asleep, they explored the land around their cabin, walking in the night as if they were cats awakening from a day's slumber. They never went far or for long. From the hill above their house they looked down to where their daughter slept, all flames extinguished, protected from this sparkling infinity by the house's friendly walls.

It was lonely at sunset. They were the only ones in this little valley. At the edge of the forest was a small tumbledown cottage, empty and looking like it was built in the 20's. As the night came down and blue darkness leaked into everything, the cottage faded into invisibility. Except for the stars, there were no lights that they could see from their cabin, not even on the ridge of the neighbouring island that rose like a whale's back (another whale) above the treeline. Their kerosene lamps, the fire in the hissing, popping wood stove, were all they had. Eventually made drowsy by the dim light and fumes of the lamps, they were ready to sleep. Pausing to hold a lamp above Lara's crib, they savoured her as she slept: her tiny form, her breath, the smell of her head. After a few last kisses to Lara, they crawled into bed and blew out the light. They slept clinging softly to each other in the absolute silence of the dark night.

But there was no escape from the absence of pleasure between them. One day, Ryan climbed into the attic to repair the water line that flowed from the barrel behind the house. The barrel was filled daily, pumped up from the well in three minutes flat by the fiery little Briggs and Stratton pump that waited all day for its special moment. (That is if Briggs and Stratton pumps can experience waiting—another question for the epistomologists). When the barrel overflowed, water cascaded down the back of the house and it was time to shut the noisy motor off.

The well had been the source of water for all the inhabitants of this homestead for several generations. It had quenched their thirst, bathed the dirt from them and watered their gardens. It was a spring that flowed into a three foot deep catch basin dug to hold its water. The hole was covered by planks with boards placed over the cracks to keep out the fir needles and leaves. At this time of year it refilled itself quickly and was soon brimming again, its clear cold water flowing out from under the planks and into the ferns and boggy grass.

Up in the attic, wrenches in hand, Ryan found a mouldering stack of old Playboys, pictures of voluptuous women pulling up tee-shirts to let willing breasts fall in free invitation. He was overcome by these images and masturbated to them, feeling the despair of what had ceased to exist between his wife and himself.

When it all became too much for Ryan and Sheila, being alone in this great spangling void without the well of pleasure to sustain them, they rushed off to Vancouver again. Sometimes it happened toward the end of the day when they felt night coming. A panic would rise as they realised that in twenty minutes the ferry would be gone and there would be no retreat from this sadhana of darkness and stars: if they didn't act quickly the wind and the night birds would have them one more time.

Usually one of them would say something like "Boy I could sure go for some Chinese food tonight" and then, madcap, they would grab clothes, baby, diapers, wallets, car keys and race down the dirt road to the ferry. From its back deck they watched the island disappear behind them and felt audacious in their willingness to make the long journey, audacious in the heady freedom they still possessed to go where they wanted and do what they pleased. They would buy papers and magazines on the brightly lighted B.C. Ferry. Tonight they would eat tofu and chicken lychee in Chinatown and drink wine with friends.

But the jaws of the trap were slowly closing. Each time it got a little harder to make this frantic dash for safety. Little by little their money was running out and the city began to seem raucous, hard-edged, noisy and exasperating, compared to the silence in which they lived. Later, when

Ryan lived alone, he would be reluctant to go even as far as Nanaimo to buy the hardware that he needed, even though he could be back on the same day. He would limit himself to what he could get in the town across the water so that he could get back on the noon ferry. And later, he would begin to put trips off, doing without things rather than having to spend even several hours on "the other side."

He was amazed by what he could improvise from what was lying around; he threw together meals from the sea and garden; he improvised hinges out of scraps of abandoned tire rather than have to deal with the world at large, with stores and cars. In Argenta some of the old timers had talked about people getting "bushed," women staying in their cabin and seeing no-one, becoming fleeting pale faces at the window. It sounded weird to him, this malady known as "bushed," and he would not know that it was happening to him, that it happened in stages, and that marijuana would make it happen more. Later, he would read a warning in the Upanishads that marijuana caused one to "merge with the forces of nature." But by the time he read it, it would be too late. It would have already happened.

For now, Sheila and he felt the danger. They ran as fast as they could toward the hissing highways and glittering lights.

6
Ryan And Sheila

Between trips to the city, Ryan and Sheila began to settle into their new home. Sometimes, during the day, he explored the valley around their house, a chain of grazed down clearings—remnants of old homesteads—strung along a small almost-creek that only ran in winter. Some of the houses were still standing. To the west, across Main Road and up the hill was Smedleys, kept locked by the young university professors who owned it and came out for only a few weeks in summer. Further, down a long series of little clearings and swampy alder woods was the Valley House, still in good condition but empty. Later, Ryan would discover that it was the home of ghosts. Even then he had a tendency to hurry past it.

As autumn blew itself into winter, Ryan and Sheila's relationship closed in around them. It was harder to keep things going with whirlwind trips to Vancouver and visits to friends. Some days the ferry didn't even run because the weather gods were replicating Hokusai's Great Wave out on Georgia Strait. Babe in arms, they would stand on the dock, beaten by the wind, and look wistfully out at the early evening lights on Vancouver Island.

Without the long sunny days, without eating clams in garlic butter under the noonday shade of their cherry tree, without picking green salads from the orderly rows of their garden, without their walks down to Red Sand Beach where they played with Lara, the summer-camp ambience of Ryan and Sheila's life ended. It was replaced by endless wind and grey; by living on top of each other in a small cabin filled with the smoke from hissing alder logs, by the relentless rhythm of rain on the roof; by the moisture from drying diapers fogging up the windows so they couldn't even see out anymore. Under these circumstances, the emptiness of their relationship grew to oppressive proportions.

There was also the emptiness of their artistic aspirations in this lonely place. Vasquez was different than Argenta. There was not yet the community of radicals and rebels there, the flow of the disaffected into the countryside. The ordinariness of life, of getting fish from the sea, of doing the laundry, of buying groceries on the other side, of working in the garden, of building fences, of cutting firewood simply did not support their vainglorious aspirations to contribute to the human medicine chest. In fact, they were frantically rifling through it, looking for an aspirin, or even a Valium.

The Canadian countryside was just too big. The job of making a life took on greater importance than artistic ambition. Keeping the clearing open, cutting back the alders, cutting back the thistles, was all they could do. In the bush, the homesteads themselves, out of necessity, became the works of art.

Ryan and Sheila learned to see in the island's abandoned homesteads the sensibilities of their vanished owners. Their houses stood on knolls that caught every bit of the sun. Their orchards dreamed on windy shelves above the water. Their fruit trees were placed with artistic splendour against a mountain or the sea. Even the chicken coop was placed where the woman who shut in the chickens—every twilight of her life—got one last glimpse of the mountain to lift her spirits in the falling night.

The need to work was serious. Ryan and Sheila learned that whole villages at the north end of Vancouver Island had been swallowed by the returning forest; that the hard working, industrious Finns at Cape Scott had finally abandoned their settlement because even they could not stay ahead of the incoming tide of forest. Ryan and Sheila had fled the city with its urban lifestyle and cash economy, not knowing that these were the very things that allowed them their aspirations. They did not realise—or perhaps Sheila did—that they had put themselves in a position where they would have to become other than who they were. They were sawing off the branch they were sitting on.

They disagreed. They fought more. The old dissatisfaction settled in on Sheila again. She began to wonder if she really wanted to spend the rest of her life in this desolate clearing surrounded by a few old time families and some recently arrived pot-heads. Ryan simply survived day to day— his favourite strategy—growing vegetables and keeping the stove burning.

For firewood, he cut up scraps from the collapsed house behind them, burning a little more of the past each day.

He began to look forward to the days when Ariel came up to get her mail, and to their occasional meetings on the ferry. When he heard Ariel and her family coming up the road, he would go out to say hello. He worked to make friends with them, inviting them in for tea. It was really to Ariel that his affections had shifted, though he did not know it yet, to her easy laughter, her beauty, her fast wit, her stories of the old days back in the city, stories that she told as though the city was from some ancient historical epoch—a vanished Sodom or Gomorra—rather than a simultaneously existing place just half a day away.

Even though he didn't know that his affections had shifted, Sheila did. She stood aside with a weary, resigned detachment, watching him, with whom she had shared so much, become an affectionate puppy dog with the beautiful, and to her sensibilities, shallow woman down the road. Maybe she did not try to intervene because in her mind she was already leaving, moving on, not together this time, not to another city or to another farm; not to another life-style, not to another try. Somewhere inside she finally knew, as painful and scary as it seemed to her, that their life together was doomed, that they had come, for some reason that eluded her, to spend their last days together on this scarcely populated island.

Ariel began to be a guide for Ryan. She told him about the island and its people, the rumours about each of them, the story of their lives, what each had done before they came to Vasquez. In short she told him the oral history that springs up in a rural communities. No detail was too trivial to be recounted. She told him where each family stood in the social hierarchy. It was like an initiation. She was also the first to tell him the rumours about the spooky Commune that lived reclusively down at the south end behind the tall fences that they had built, about their big stone house. Ryan and Ariel talked easily as she told him about life on the island.

More people began to arrive on Vasquez, as presumably they were arriving on other islands, arriving at the empty and broken down farms that dotted the long east coast of Vancouver Island, arriving at the abandoned homesteads along the river valleys and mountain shelves of the interior.

Driving the blue Datsun on the other side, Ryan picked up hitch-hikers who wore the bedraggled uniform of old work clothes, hand knitted caps, and gum-boots. He usually wound up driving them up some dirt road to discover yet another farm that was being reoccupied; houses where plastic windows were held in place by cedar battens, and pieces of salvaged plywood patched holes in the roof. He inevitably helped them carry in their bundles and sat and talked while they got the kitchen fire going to make a pot of tea. Sometimes they drank out of little Japanese tea cups, sometimes out of chipped porcelain mugs that looked like they'd been dug out of the garden. Then they shared the inevitable jay, the doobie, the sacrament that kept this dream of creating a new world going.

For awhile the influx of settlers on Vasquez breathed new possibility into Ryan and Sheila's marriage. They heard with delight the stories of the past, of the great ceremonial centres of the civilisation that lay below them, of Vancouver, of LA, of New York City, of Portland. They heard about the course of events that had turned each person's life sorrowful and had caused them to hit the road in their VW van, their bedraggled car, or with just the pack on their back.

The first group to arrive was a group of young Canadians who bought the old bootleggers house and fixed it up. They lived communally, each couple having their own room. They were younger than Ryan and Sheila, though, and there was not an easy generational comfort. Ryan and Sheila knew all their names to say hello on the road, or to have conversations at the store or on the ferry, but they did not have enough in common to go and visit often. The sheer number of people in the house was also intimidating. They knew how to visit a friend, a couple, roommates, but how did you visit a commune?

Then, one day, Isaac and Miriam walked down the road. He was a disaffected New York painter, stocky, long haired and bearded, with a love of booze. His blue eyes twinkled with laughter and mischief; he was full to overflowing with delicious Jewish humour. She was a Jewish Princess in search of something more real than the luxury of her parent's home. She had a thick mane of blond hair, large breasts and a litheness that spoke of dance classes in far away New York. She had travelled half-way around the world with this man, braving the discomforts of life with him to see what it would bring. She started almost every sentence with a question:

"Do you think that…," or, "Don't you think that…." Ryan and Sheila took them into their home and welcomed them as if they were a long lost brother and sister. They cooked together, shared stories of the now distant art-world, told jokes. Through all this their dog Spot, a Brittany spaniel, slept a well-behaved sleep on the grass mat near the door.

During the day, they drove Isaac and Miriam around to look at old homesteads that were still empty. It was important to find a place for kindred souls if there was any chance they were going to make this remote world work. Isaac and Miriam finally settled on a place far away, at the South End. The South End was more open and windswept than the heavily forested north: the southeast winds had never allowed the forest to get a start there. Open fields and bare rock bluffs looked out over a curved expanse of sea.

The farm which Isaac and Miriam chose felt even more deserted than the little valley in which Ryan and Sheila lived. Of all the farms they had looked at, it had the most beautiful house; the windows were still intact, their panes of glass beautifully rippled by the flow of time. There was a front porch to sit on and even some broken down furniture: a kitchen table and chairs, a rocking chair, an old couch with its stuffing coming out.

The house sat on open fields. The fences had long ago broken down and the land was grazed clean by free range sheep and cows. Behind it tall bluffs, bare outcroppings of rock, were surmounted by the windswept trees of which bonsai are in imitation. Isaac and Miriam salvaged pots and pans from the dump behind the house: a cast iron skillet, an enamelled kettle with some chips out of it, cups without handles, antique plates with chips in them. It all still served. Miriam, used to wealth and pampering, had been cut off by her family in an attempt to bring her to her senses. Isaac, a struggling painter, spent whatever money he could get on paint and intoxicants to raise his spirits. He had never had any money. What they couldn't find they bought with their meagre savings at the SOS thrift store in the town across the water. And so, having arrived with only the packs on their backs, they put together a household. Not being able to afford a pole, Isaac learned to fish from shore with a hand line. He learned to gather oysters from the fertile bays that were only a short walk from his farm.

Old-timers came to visit, at first just to see who had settled at the abandoned farm down the road. They grew to like Isaac and Miriam, and often brought them a chunk of sheep or deer meat. While Isaac didn't hunt himself, he gratefully accepted their gift. Isaac and Miriam roasted it, stewed it, grilled it over a fire pit in front the house, or made it into tsimmis with dried prunes from the orchard. The rest of their food came from occasional trips to Vancouver. While there, Isaac put out his cap and did street painting with coloured chalk, making as much as $20 a day from the passing crowds. They filled their empty packs with a gallon of oil, a bag each of sugar, brown rice, whole wheat and unbleached flours. Isaac brought home loops of discount polish sausage from Save-On Meats. With the flour, Miriam baked beautifully braided and glazed breads. She served them with butter—a luxury from the local store—and jams she learned to make from the local berries.

Later, in the season of mists and mellow fruitfulness, Isaac learned to make wine from the battered but abundant fruit trees that surrounded the house. He borrowed a neighbour's press and filled an old crock with pulpy apple juice. He covered the foaming must with a tightly tied down sheet of plastic and later siphoned and filtered it into gallon jugs. He capped these with balloons to let out the gasses without letting in the fruit flies. The white balloons stood up like ghostly little erections during the weeks of fermentation. He used champagne yeast, which the old timers had told him made a stronger brew.

Eleven miles over dirt roads was a long way, even for Sheila and Ryan who used to think nothing about driving from Marin County to San Francisco for a meal out or a night at the theatre. A new form of visiting evolved where instead of dropping in for tea or dinner, they came to stay the night at each other's houses. They sat around drinking coffee for awhile, but when the visit would have normally ended—when everything had been said—they simply moved into life, helping to pare root maggots out of carrots in preparation for storage, helping to weed the garden, helping to can fruit or stack firewood. Sometimes more things to say came out; sometimes they just worked silently with the occasional comment. They cooked dinner together and then slept in the same house. In the morning, they got up, had breakfast, and worked together some more. Ryan remembered hearing how the California Indians had always worked as they sat and talked, twisting fibres against their thighs to make the chord for nets, or mashing acorns for food. It became like that, a sense of tribe, that one person's work was everyone's work and why not do it while enjoying each other's company.

7
Ryan And Sheila

One winter afternoon, it was 5:30 but already dark. Sheila sat by the wood-heater in her rocking chair, lamp perched behind her shoulder. She read in deep concentration while Lara played on the floor with small plastic animals. Ryan was cooking at the ancient wood stove, when he heard a car stop on Main Road, its doors slam and voices shouting over wind and rain.

He wiped a circle of condensation off the window to see what was happening. Up at the corner, flashlight beams were swinging wildly about, lighting the trees and the rain-filled sky. Outside, winter was gusting. Rain ran off the roof in runnels. The lamps flickered with buffets of wind that came through the weavings of board and shake. The wood heater cast flickering firelight on the cabin's walls. Sheila and Ryan were burning the wood that they had stacked in the woodshed, high under the eaves, and into every available dry space.

Ryan liked going out into the woods with his chainsaw, axe, sledge and wedges; liked bringing back a wheelbarrow full of fragrant newly split alder, liked seeing the butt ends turn orange as they began to dry in the woodshed. The necessity of this simple work kept his head from spinning. The meaning of life became clear: get enough wood to stay warm all winter. Everything depended on the red wheelbarrow.

Ryan heard Ariel and her children come down the road. He opened the front door, letting lamp light flood out and illuminate the puddles and blowing rain. As he stood there, Ariel and her children emerged out of the darkness. The gate slammed behind them. They were in slickers, carrying boxes that were falling apart from the rain. Each was carrying what they could. The girls were stoic and had water running down their faces. Ariel, usually so presentable, looked like a drowned rat. "Can we leave our boxes until Wylie gets back and gets the car running?"

Ryan just held the door open and gestured for them to come inside. As they stood dripping, he shut the door and invited them to take off their rain gear and warm up for awhile. They put their boxes down by the door. "Would you like to stay for dinner?" He added more water and flour to a pizza dough that was already bubbling in their old fashioned bread bowl. Covering the dough with a cloth, he put it back in the warming oven of the stove. Ariel rummaged through one of her soaked boxes and brought out a jug of wine: Calona Medium red. Sheila joined in, opening cans of tomato sauce and grating mozzarella for the pizza. It would be an oyster pizza, a local speciality.

The evening was chaotic. Jessie and Alia played on the floor with Lara's toys. They included Lara even though she was disruptive, sometimes swatting down the model farm they were assembling. While the children played, Sheila, Ariel and Ryan talked excitedly about many things as the wine awakened their brains from winter torpor. Dinner was thrown together, one plate at a time, and served first to the children and then to themselves. Ryan started the Honda generator out in the wood shed and they ate to the Beatles, Bob Dylan, and the Doors. The music was loud enough to drown out the rain, to drown out the tiny Honda generator that whirred in the woodshed, to drown out the desolation of Ryan and Sheila's relationship.

All night long light flashed between Ariel and Ryan: laughter, jokes and double entendres. At one point, how it happened Ryan didn't know, they wound up sitting next to each other on one of the madras covered mattresses that served as couches. He had an arm around her. Perhaps it was the wine that had destroyed their judgement.

He was delighting in her proximity, in the closeness of her body, when suddenly Sheila was standing over them, looking at him with the smile of disgust that she reserved for truly pathetic sights. He sprang to his feet and went over to hold her but she pushed him away.

"That is where you belong," she said, "don't hold on to me, hold on to her."

Suddenly they were all on their feet tidying up. Ariel bundled her children back into their slickers, now warm and dry, and, ever gracious, thanked Ryan and Sheila for dinner. She departed with her children into the rain and wind.

In the woodshed the generator ran out of gas and died. The music distorted and then dropped into silence. Rain drummed on the roof. In silence they put Lara to bed, picked up the toys, and washed the dishes in the pans they had heated on the stove. The silence between them was elemental and unbreakable. Ryan didn't know what to say to bridge the valley. They slept on separate sides of the bed that night and he felt the cold enter into him as the fires died down in the wee hours of the night.

Unfortunately, Ryan didn't really understand yet why you can't love more than one person at a time, or different people for different things; after all, bees didn't gather nectar and pollen from just one flower. The bee did not have to choose between the white apple, the scarlet fireweed, or the yellow dandelion.

He wondered, during the long night, why having children so often condemned a couple to such a boring and grim relationship, full of fighting and despair, like the ones that so many of their parents had had. It was a time of experimentation after all: there were the group marriages in the Slocan; polygyny and polyandry were even out on the air waves. How flexible was human nature? Could they just decide how they wanted things to be and make it so? Unfortunately, much of this utopian vision that floated around in the zeitgeist was fuelled by marijuana. Floating on a cloud of dope anything seemed possible.

At any rate, as spring arrived, Sheila left. She went to live for a short while at the Pond House. Her piano, her mushroom charts, her batiks, Lara's toys, Lara, all gone. The Pond House was a pretty little white house, misplaced from some Canadian rural suburbia. It looked like it had been picked up by a tornado and dropped by the side of a pond that meandered along cat-tail lined waterways. Years later, in winter, at those rare times when his children were with him, Ryan would skate with them there, sliding up and down the wandering channels; stopping to drink hot chocolate from thermoses.

At Sheila's departure he became more of who he really wanted to be. He started smoking pot again and careening around the island from party to party. His response to the salvo that Sheila had fired was to mostly avoid her. His mind was a blur. He did his best to avoid the reality that his wife and child were living down the road now; that his roof no longer sheltered a family. If he moved fast enough, kept driving around the island, perhaps he wouldn't have to feel the emptiness at home.

Why did Sheila continue to live on Vasquez? Perhaps it was out of some hope that they could co-parent and not break the string between them completely. Perhaps it was just a hope that she would not have to go back out into the scary world from which, step by step, they had been withdrawing. She shared the Pond House with a Japanese-Canadian woman, Julie, whose presence was quiet and meditative. They lived mostly in silence, Lara's chirpings and wailings constituting most of the sounds in the house. Sheila spent her time with the L.A. refugees, wild partyers, Jewish jokesters, acid-head philosophers, who had recently settled in the Valley House where they lived among the ghosts with a plenteous supply of home brew and marijuana.

Andy was a law student from UCLA who felt he could do the law program and drop out at the same time, making mad all-night drives down the coast to write his finals. He mailed assignments to friends who handed them in for him. He was short, sturdily built and had large, liquid, slow moving eyes that looked out with innocence from under his curly hair. He had a peculiar S shaped posture: pelvis forward, chest back, head forward. He lived with Dorrie who everybody said was a saint.

Dorrie was a willowy blond, very beautiful; a shiksa princess from Wisconsin, still full of Protestant industry and faith. Her quiet energy held the household together. She served beautifully prepared vegetarian meals to the barbarians with whom she lived; the house was always full of the smell of the bread she baked. She was deeply concerned about spirituality and god, and truly loved the life on Vasquez, while for the rest of her group, it was just a novelty, another thing to do, a place to be wild and out of control, to loose the high-achieving bonds which had restrained them for so long.

After they passed out at night, she put blankets over each of them, and pillows under their heads. She lit a votive candle on the window sill to protect them from the ghosts. During the day she read a book on country house-keeping by Alicia Bay Laurel called *Living on the Land*. It was published to look like a handwritten note book, full of simple little drawings of things. It told her how to make curtains; how to make simple medicines from herbs; how to cook vegetarian meals that had enough protein in them; how to pick flowers for keeping in the house; how to improvise vases out of canning jars and ketchup bottles.

During the day Dorrie had the house to herself for much of the time. Sometimes the ghost of a young mother with a cough would sit in the rocking chair and sooth her sick baby. Dorrie had gotten used to this. She walked around doing her chores and talked to the ghost. "Have you tried drinking a little lemon juice mixed with honey?" "Have you tried feeding the baby fenugreek tea in a bottle?" She wondered if ghosts could get lemons and fenugreek, or if they even ate. She told her: "It would be better to get up and walk the baby. Try bouncing her around a little." She was sure the baby was a girl. The ghost didn't respond to this good advice, however. She just came from time to time to her chair, sat, rocked, coughed, and tried to quiet the baby.

When they were not reading books from the Whole Earth Catalogue that told, step by step, how to homestead, Dorrie's "family" spent much of its time riding around the island in its battered truck. They sampled people's home brew and shared their drugs with everyone. They took it upon themselves to get everyone stoned, just like the song said. This was their contribution to the island's developing society. As Americans, they liked to take private things and turn them into mass movements. They felt easier when a lot of people were doing whatever they were doing. The Valley House people could not be faulted for their generosity. They popped up everywhere, joint in hand, like lawn dwarves, in the unlikeliest places, seemingly materializing even from under the leaves of ferns.

Also with them was Thorn, short for Thornton, a law school drop-out, reeking of east-coast patrician good manners. His long hair and beard could not hide the grace and self assurance in his crinkly blue eyes. Everything about him spoke of the ease and elegance that came from being born to wealth. His contribution was a gift for stealing things. He simply went over to the other side and took what they needed. When they needed a boat, he backed their old truck up to a wall in the garden section of Simpson-Sears where the aluminum boats were on display. He smiled at everyone, put a boat into the back of the truck and simply drove off with it. They soon discovered that the boat was of little use without a motor, so the next week he went back and simply picked up a display model Evinrude, along with its gas tank. He walked out of the busy store, nodding affably to everyone he met. Audacity went a long way back then.

Twenty years later Ryan met him again. In the intervening time, Thorn had become a big time stock broker. They talked about the past and then Thorn laughed, "We thought those were big-time rip offs then." He showed Ryan a brief case full of corporate seals from the dummy companies that he floated on the Vancouver stock exchange. Audacity still went a long way.

Life at the Valley House was a continuous party that rotated around the gracious meals that Dorrie managed to put on the table. All of its residents seemed to have blown their minds on too much acid; all their craziness hung out. The more conservative Canadian drop outs (there were levels and levels to dropping out) referred to them collectively as the LA Crazies. It was as though in front they were human beings that said and did most of the things that humans did, but the back of their heads had been blown out and their human personalities extended far into the universe where no man had gone before. The occasional impulse from Arcturus found its way onto the back roads of B.C.

Sheila found friendship with Andy. Perhaps it was their Jewishness, an inborn understanding of suffering and oppression, that brought them together, or perhaps it was the quality of their intellects. Perhaps it was just refreshing to talk to someone who didn't say "far-out" all the time. At any rate, the drugged outlaw law student and the disaffected mother/artist/moralist spent a lot of time talking together. Since Sheila didn't do drugs, they drank together. They found things in common, a willingness to talk about change, self acceptance, starting over. Andy was very honest. One day when they were talking over homebrew he reflected to her how stuck he saw her: stuck by the need to look right. He told her that he believed the only way she would get unstuck was by accepting how she really was; letting it all hang out and be unsightly; that only if she was willing to do this, would things change for her. He talked to her about how it was only (only) her fears about striking out alone that were keeping her stuck in a life that wasn't working; that life was too fucking precious to piss it away on one empty day followed by the next.

In early autumn, she offered to drive Andy down to L.A for one of his exams. In her heart she knew that it would be her last exit from Vasquez, not just another trip home to where her parent's house boat sat stably on the rising and falling tides of San Francisco Bay. On the last night, she went down to the cabin with Lara to gather some of their things. Most of her things were at the Pond House, but a few had been left behind, like a foot in the door in hope of return. That night Sheila, Lara and Ryan, slept together under the same roof for the last time. Though her conversation was loving and cheerful, tears streamed from Sheila's eyes. Ryan and Sheila slept together in the loft bed and held each other during the long night.

The next morning Ryan's wife and baby daughter left. They all got up early and stood together, for the last time as a family, up on Main Road. Sheila held Lara. Their bags were on the gravel beside them. Ryan stood silently with them, speechless. His car was broken so they waited for a ride, and as they waited, he put an arm around each of them. The day was still and cloaked with mist; the big maples over the old pasture had begun to blaze yellow. They stood, listening to the sounds of the morning and then to the distant rattle and roar of approaching cars. A truck stopped, and Sheila put Lara in back and climbed in after her. She sat with Lara on her lap against the back of the cab. Ryan ran beside the truck for a few feet, holding Lara's tiny hand. Then the accelerating speed of the vehicle forced him to let go and he released her out into a world with which he could no longer cope.

8
Alone

After the truck carrying Sheila and Lara disappeared around the bend, Ryan started walking back to his cabin. He turned his face to hide his tears from the passing cars which raced by for the ferry as he turned down his road. There had been no fire that morning and his house was cold. He threw himself down on the bed and cried.

Now it all came out, loneliness, failure, hurt, anger. When he could cry no more, he sat up and looked around. It was just him and this cabin now. He began cleaning up, putting Sheila's and Lara's things in the storage room so that he would not be reminded of his loss. Weeks later he would still find fallen toys, a small plastic horse behind the leg of a bed, a baby doll hiding in the grass outside the woodshed.

At least, he thought, there had been some warning. Since Argenta it had been like living in a doomed city, like living in Khartoum, knowing that it was just a matter of days before the Mahdi's army would come swarming over the walls. He wondered if he had taken no action because at some level he knew it had to end; if they both had known, and that this had been the only way they could do it.

Sheila was right, he thought, to get out before winter, right to have taken the sky blue Datsun truck that they kept on the other side and headed south. He knew that she would need it on the other side, as he now thought of the rest of the world. He still had the Red Ant which had already become an island car, a sort of power wheelbarrow that, when running, carried loads of wood from the forest and briny kelp from the beach. All summer it had also carried him and his new friends around the island to a movable feast of seemingly endless parties. Sheila's departure left him with no car to negotiate the other side. The parameters of his life constricted further. Soon he would be confined to the island.

In the afternoon of his first day alone, Ron came up the road on his way to the ferry.

"Hey man, is there anything you want from the other side?"

Ryan gave him some money. "Yeah, bring me three gallons of wine." He was thinking of the wonderful dollar-forty-nine per gallon jugs of Red Mountain Burgundy that he used to drink in California. Ron, barely nineteen and not versed in wine drinking, returned on the evening ferry with three gallon jugs of Calona Sweet Sherry. In the weeks to come Ryan realised this was a blessing in disguise: that having the sickening sherry had tempered his drinking and helped him through this time of despondency sooner.

Night came, and Ryan was alone, not exactly at last, with his depression, his sexuality, his hopes, his fears, his history, his inadequacies, his coping strategies, and three gallons of sickeningly sweet sherry. The bottom line was that he would have to keep himself warm, which meant splitting wood everyday and cutting more so that there would be enough to get through the winter.

And that, he thought, was not so bad: At least he had a chain saw and The Red Ant. He was not like Jeff down the road who kept his family warm with a Swede-saw and wheel barrow. Every day it was the same for Jeff: He went out and cut a barrow full of wood by hand, and then came back in and threw it in the voracious furnace of his poorly insulated house. He sat for a few minutes then, and read or had a cup of tea and then had to go out again—into the rain or wind or cold clear sky—to cut another load. He never got ahead. His partner, his "old lady," fed him in the morning, at lunch, and at dinner. At the end of the day he dropped exhausted into bed with nothing left. He felt he was living a myth but was too tired to think about which one it was. It was just a myth, but he still had a family. He started again the next day.

Ryan did not know the word transformation. If he had, he would probably have thought of the stone Chak Mool's he'd seen on top of pyramids, holding out their bowls to receive the still beating hearts of persons given to the gods; or of great limestone cenotes in the Yucatan, where the floor of the jungle had fallen out to form a perfectly round pond, several hundred feet deep and ringed by limestone cliffs. At the bottom of the cenote's dark lake were the bones and gold jewellery of anointed sacrifices. Ryan would not have thought of it as anything so squalid as being left alone to live out the winter in a cabin with not much to do and only sweet sherry for comfort.

That night he went to sleep, a little drunk, lulled by the heat of the cabin and the dying crackles of the fire. He had provided his own warmth. He dreamt of an entry way to another world, another level, a world below this world, a world entered through a lake and full of dark catacombs. It was lit by rippling light from the surface and full of souls who had been thrown in, sacrifices who walked these internalised labyrinthine passages, far from the memories of family, friends and children; far from the ordinary world made up of the little tasks of the living—buying groceries or changing the oil in the car; far from immersion in daily routine; far from known ground, solid ground, any ground; trying, trying to find their way back to the surface, up into the sunny air again; into the light to breathe again, to be warm again; trying to find their way out.

The next day he awakened from these labyrinthine dreams. Later it became a catch phrase: "Today is the first day of the rest of your life." And so it was. Which is not to say that he arose like Lazarus, a new man, released of his losses, his memory wiped clean by the waters of an underground river whose name he could not remember. Who was he? No longer a husband and father, not on a day to day basis, anyway. The gods had smitten him. Would he have a chance to reinvent himself? Would he simply recreate the life he had had before? Would he lose it again in a succession of the same life lived over and over again? Was there some basic humanness, or some basic Ryaness that would seek to manifest itself again and again? A fatal flaw? Was a Ryan a Ryan a Ryan? Once poured would the wax seek to find its original shape again and again? What fires could re-melt it? What hand could re-forge it? Such were his thoughts as he lay in the bed he had made.

The first thing was just to get up, to get out of bed, build a fire and warm the house. The second was to boil water, to make some coffee to lift his spirits, to rise out of this horror of dark emotion, this pudding of fear and loss. Failure, hopelessness and emptiness threatened to drown him and put out his eyes, leaving him unable to go on.

And what was this particular kind of bad feeling, he wondered as he sipped his coffee thick with canned milk. What was so hard about being alone? He realised that until recently he had never been alone for more than a few wonderful hours of hiking. As a child there were his parents, his sisters, their dog Duppy—always ready and willing to be companions. There were a few heady days in Mexico before he had sought out his friends Bob and Ed. Then they had travelled together into the tribes and villages where everybody was so connected to each other. Since then, there had been friends, girlfriends, roommates, fellow students and co-workers. Even when Sheila and Lara lived down the road there had still been at least a sense of family and an endless succession of traveling strangers.

Now he was alone. What was left for him was the island community of his fellow homesteaders, refugees from the outside world. Most of them were living the most subsistence of lives. Stoned, strange, broken, they had left their shattered dreams on the other side. They were all just trying to put some kind of life together: trying to keep food on the table, a roof over their head; trying to stay warm, stay dry, and, maybe, if they were lucky, have someone with whom to share their bed. Was he like them? Sheila and he once would have analysed them, discussed the failure of each to grasp their rich and fast moving lives. Now he didn't talk so loud.

He could not go back, he knew this, into that wider world, to the university, to a job. He had given up on that, something in him had changed. Wanting and yet afraid, he had put down roots in spite of himself. He was a part of this community, of this small piece of land and the erratic and drugged-out crazies around him. He was one of them. And yet, in another way, he was not like any of them. Even here he carried the scar of feeling different from these people who were now his family. His basic needs were like theirs and he could do a convincing job of fitting in, of behaving almost correctly at the rituals—the community picnics, the Legion dances, the school Christmas concert—but in some way he felt that his consciousness had been formed differently; that in the oven of his family another kind of baking had taken place. He feared that he had no place where he really belonged.

No. He would not go to Seattle to be near his wife and child, to be a weekend parent like she wanted him to be. The thought of the thundering planes descending from the sky freaked him out. He also could not be sure that it would end there. They had moved nine times in the course of their time together. Each place had its charms, its dreams, but it hadn't taken long before the ill omened birds of dissatisfaction found them again and it was time to pull up stakes. He knew he could not simply keep following Sheila as she pitched and packed her tent.

He hated the thought of Lara living there under the planes. He dreamed that she and he were on a long journey together. They were trying to get to a primitive ferry which was pulled across a long flat river by cables. They were being bombed and strafed every step of the way. Just before the ferry, they ducked under a concrete picnic table to avoid the spew from strafing jets. Lara had crawled out to retrieve a fallen toy, unaware of the bullets streaming from the diving planes. He crawled out to catch her and pull her back to safety, but she was too fast for him. He couldn't stop her.

He would make a household by himself. He would, he decided, hold out for Lara coming up in summer to share with him, at least for part of the time, the safety of this tiny island, a place without large carnivores, a place where seemingly death didn't stalk. He thought that even if worse came to worse that they might survive on the island. They could hide in the cave at North Bay. When they came out, they could grow their own food. They could learn to make bows and arrows and hunt the deer and sheep. The women could learn how to weave cedar bark and wool, and how to make clothes from animal skins. The men could learn how to make fire. Crosby Stills and Nash sang "Helpless, Helpless, Helpless."

Living on the land seemed like such a brave new world to Ryan. Under the magic of drugs anything seemed possible. Why not weave a world of peace and justice around themselves and throw out the old garbage? Why not live in small communities like ancient Essenes, out from under the throne of Egypt, of Rome, of Usa. They saw themselves as the seeds of a new world. They took from the old what they needed, a few treasures. They sifted and discarded. They wished to start again, to say goodbye to their mothers and fathers, to go into the wilderness, but they knew not how much of the past they carried within themselves.

So, on this day, alone, he forced himself through the motions. He cooked a breakfast and read for awhile by the waning embers of the wood stove. He went out into the driveway and attacked the pile of alder rounds, splitting the quarter rounds into the smaller pieces which he stacked in the woodshed. If he must sleep in the bed he had made, he might as well make it warm and comfortable, he thought. He pulled some things out of the garden for later, savouring the handiwork of summer. The wind had shifted northwest and the day had turned autumn clear. He put on his wool chammorrah, the long tasselled cloak of woven wool, a reminder of his other time alone, and walked through the forest down to the beach. He looked north up the Sabine Channel to where the distant snow caps rose like teeth out of the cerulean waters.

This was too lonely and he soon returned home. In the late afternoon he went down the road to his neighbours where two families lived communally. He arrived as the light was fading and was invited to stay for dinner. He ate their home-made pizza, smoked their dope, drank a bit of their wine and broke the news that he was alone now, that Sheila had left. There was a feeling of shame for him in having to say this, like now he was less than all these family people. To his relief, nobody seemed very surprised.

He walked back up the road, through the starlit night to his home, pleasantly fed, stoned and nurtured by the company of friends—normal people putting their children to bed. He built a small fire in the cook stove, lit a kerosene lamp and sat in the gentle flickering light for awhile before going to bed, soothed by the little popping sounds of the fire in its iron box. He sat in his cabin, swept over by the wind in an enormously empty and lonely landscape, acutely conscious that his fire and dim kerosene lamp were the only spots of warmth in an immense night. Around him was the clearing; beyond the clearing was the forest, and beyond the forest the rolling sea. Above the tree tops at the end of the clearing, the silhouette of another island was just visible against a sky full of twinkling northern stars. There was loneliness, but there was also a sense of peace that his and Sheila's troubles were finally finished, and excitement at what his life alone might bring.

Eventually spring did come, with its activities of turning the soil and bringing in the last bit of wood that his winter supply had fallen short of. Their immediacy delivered him from the suffering of his own thoughts. And then it was summer.

When the sun finally came, he spent time, between minimal survival chores, lying naked on the little knoll behind his house, a place shielded from the road by the house itself. The sunlight was warm, but not overly hot. The wind blew through the guardian firs and an occasional truck rattled by just out of sight on Main Road. It was a very new experience, being naked outdoors, exposed but hidden. For the longest time there was some anxiety, some urge that kept him from relaxing completely, until one day he realised that he was waiting for the phone to ring, to jump to the bidding of its tyrannous bell. Simultaneously he realised that there was no phone—nothing to call him away from himself.

He took to walking naked through the woods along the almost deserted roads of his neighborhood. There were only a few cars and, automotive maintenance being what it was, they could be heard a long way off, roaring, rattling, coughing, backfiring. When he heard a car coming, he simply stepped quietly into the bush and peered out of the salmon berries, a pair of brown eyes, as the truck and its occupants jounced by. Sometimes he carried a staff, like a spear, and experienced what countless people in leafed jungles had experienced as the minions of civilisation, intent on cutting the forest or digging up minerals, buzzed past in their insect-like motor vehicles.

The forest was full of eyes. He thought of the people of Vietnam watching silently from behind dripping philodendrons as squadrons of marines trooped past them. There was kinship with them in this, and kinship with the community of animals, the deer who silently moved along the forest floor and the birds who carolled in its canopy. "I am no longer the hunter, but the hunted," he said out loud, stripped of his armour in the silence of the forest.

9
The Commune

Ariel and her family were the first "new-timers" to settle on Vasquez. Her social graces made her a mainstay of the community, a link between old-timers and the new settlers. Now she was gone.

Those remaining outside the Commune went into shock and grief. If Ariel and Wylie could be taken, it now seemed inevitable that, one by one, all of them would be pulled away from their confused little lives, their subsistence farms, from their plastic-windowed cabins, their Whole-Earth-Catalogue-back-to-the-land philosophy. All of them would be subsumed into the great effort of building communal houses and orchards. In its time the truck would come for each of them and they too would sing in the choir. They would work silently and stare into the forest waiting to see the truth. Their houses would be empty again, shells waiting for new occupants who would also, ultimately, be sucked into the collectivity, one by one, to turn soil and fell trees, while Bob, the ever-gracious father, rode the ferry and read the Globe and Mail.

He would be their intercessor to the confusing outside world, taking from it that which they needed; sparing them its corruption; allowing them to drop the chattering western mind and live forever in agricultural bliss. It was as though a new species was being born, and that there was no resisting the pull of this evolutionary leap, away from being poor, sad, confused individuals, into the realm of Homo Collectivus, blandly acting for the greater good. It seemed to Ryan and Alexis that they and all their friends were being irresistibly drawn by a Darwinian imperative.

The only one who seemed not to be upset by all this was Miriam. She was not as shocked and angry as the rest of them. She did not look upon Ariel, Wylie and their children as having been brain washed, or as having sold out. She did not even seem to consider them as "lost."

"Why are you all so upset," she said. "They have the right to try a different way of life. My parents are upset that I am here. They are upset that I am with Isaac. They see him as controlling me. They think he's got some sort of hold on me. You are acting just like them, like there is only one way to live. Ariel and Wylie are smart people. Who knows, maybe there is something to learn up there."

No one had much time to lick their wounds or puzzle about Ariel and her family's defection. In the middle of the next week, the news came that Miriam had also gone up to the Commune. Of course she was the next to go.

McElwaith and Sherry brought Ryan the news. McElwaith's antique sky-blue pickup rattled up outside Ryan's gate and out they climbed. McElwaith was one of the few people on the island who knew how to keep a car running. It allowed him to get around and find out things. McElwaith and Sherry carried a half empty (or half full, depending on your point of view) bottle of Old Bushmills with them. Ryan invited them into the house and they offered him a drink.

"Miriam—is—gone." McElwaith said it pregnantly, with no explanation, leaving a big space between each of the words. He just let each word drop separately into the silence of the room.

"To—the—Commune." Ryan said." It was not a question but a sombre statement. His eyes meeting with McElwaith's.

"To. The. Commune." McElwaith and Sherry said this in unison, slowly, their voices slightly slurred, like a Greek chorus that had been drinking. Sherry shook her tangled mop of blond hair and laughed at the humour of their presentation. "Yeah, we went down to the farm to bring them some venison," McElwaith said. He was also one of the few new-timers who knew how to hunt, skin, dress and butcher the island's feral sheep and wild deer.

Sherry added: "Isaac told us. He said she just went up for a couple weeks to check it out, but we'll see. Ya da da da, Ya da da da," she hummed the spooky little tune from The Twilight Zone.

They sat around Ryan's table in a depressed, why-is-this-all-happening kind of mood, though even in the midst of it, McElwaith couldn't resist black humour, "Maybe they're all out behind the wood shed, toking up," he offered. His shifty blue eyes lighted up with laughter at the incongruity of the image. It was hard to imagine their friends as zombies, their fire put out, silently working in the collective bakery, silently building the fence, silently working on the firewood detail, silently pulling fir poles through the forest for further additions to the mansion. It was difficult to imagine Ariel not making contact and chatting volubly with the people around her. It was hard to see her moving silently through the world, standing quietly on the high bluffs waiting for a vision, waiting for God to speak. It was difficult to imagine Elroy without his guitar, to see him sitting in his plastic shack, silently staring through the six mil plastic at the blurry world outside. Ryan sat uneasily, not really laughing at McElwaith's jokes, feeling that, in part, his friends were in the Commune because of the night in Vancouver, because of him.

Suddenly there was the sound of a thousand thunders as air force jets from CFB Comox passed low overhead. Several times a month their island world, the canyon of water in which they all lived, was filled with the fighter planes' reverberations. They all looked up. The dark boards of the ceiling, the whisky in their glasses, the hills, the forest, even their bodies seemed to shimmer like tapestries shaken by a gust of wind. To Ryan's drugged-out mind, the jets' roar revealed the enormous emptiness behind the thin tissue of materiality on which their lives were painted. The Curfew Gull had roared, and for a moment Death swirled all around them.

It seemed to Ryan, that the fragile molecular bonds that held this shimmering tapestry together were the very same bonds that held lovers, families, friends, parents, children, communities together; that their love for each other was the same as the force that bound the atom.

But they had tampered with it; had experimented with fast flying relationships and scattered children. They talked about tribe, but really didn't know how to be one: the taboos and prohibitions, the intricate weavings of marrying outside your own clan, the prohibited couplings; the strictures, the very rituals that could have kept it all together, been had rejected as too ancient and quaint.

As they unraveled the restrictions of the million little castles of pain in which they had been raised, the very creation seemed to thin and shimmer. Their little farms and little lives, their gossip, their slights and triumphs, were all built on nothing. Their broken down cars ran on country roads that were a fragile film of dirt laid out over emptiness. Stoned too much, they lived their lives between ecstasy and terror, between matter and energy, looking almost ordinary.

The jets passed. They looked back down from the ceiling. Ryan was feeling that he had crossed some line on that night in the city. For him, it had been an evening of extravagant courtship gone wrong. For Ariel, Julie and Elroy it had been something else, and in the ensuing confusion they had found their lives unworkable and had fled into the Commune's promise of a simpler life, a life with rules and regulations, with a guarantee of materiality despite promises to the contrary.

As McElwaith and Sherry were leaving, Ryan decided to go with them to share solace with his friend Isaac. He got a ride part way and walked the rest. As he crested the final hill, the dry bluffs, grassy fields and big sky of the South End opened before him. He walked along the broken fence that bound Isaac's farm and then turned up the driveway. There were clusters of plum trees all along the fence. In front of the house was an orchard of old apple trees planted around a shallow pond. The house itself was a classical country house. It had shingle, brown boards darkened by the sun, a peaked roof, a porch that provided delicious shade on sunny days. Across the road from the farm were the remains of an airstrip now beginning to grow back in young alders. Ryan paused in the turnaround between the house and barn and listened for awhile to the crickets in the summer fields. Then he turned and walked toward the house.

The farm belonged to a millionaire from Seattle named Bechtol—no one knew his first name. Once in a while, Bechtol came up and tied his yacht to the wharf at Squitty Bay. He walked up the road with a Filipino manservant named Louie—no one knew his last name—to check out the farm he owned. Isaac took him around and showed him what he had done. He played the genial host, offering them home-made cider and some of Miriam's delicious bread, all in his thick New York accent. During these rounds, Bechtol smoked incessantly. As he finished each cigarette he tossed it on the ground. "Could you step on that for me Louie?" he said, and the manservant obligingly crushed out the cigarette with one of his fine Italian shoes.

The first time Bechtol arrived, Isaac was afraid that he would want the farm for a summer house and throw him out. He did not realise that such a house, no matter how nicely Isaac had fixed it up with the furniture he had found in the barn, would be of no interest to a man like Bechtol. If he were to come here, it would be to do something magnificent, something architected in shining glass and west coast timbers. Something on the water.

Several summers after Isaac started caretaking, Bechtol decided to put in the airstrip so he could pop in from time to time. He hired one of the locals to clatter and clank down Main Road in a huge cat left over from the logging days. The cat began to scrape off the little alders that had started growing on the field across from the house. It was much like shaving but on a bigger scale. The cat shoved the broken trees into a huge pile, and a great flat scar of brown dirt was opened to the sky. The plane came in then, just once, and Isaac dropped his brushes to run out and meet it.

Bechtol and Louie climbed down out of the cabin. "How's it going Izzy?" Bechtol said. Behind him Louie carried a bottle of good scotch and a cooler full of ice. Bechtol and Isaac sat out on the front porch while Louie served them scotch on the rocks in the chipped glasses that Isaac had salvaged from around the farm. Isaac made a point of giving Bechtol their one good glass, a flaring crystal one that he had found in the barn, with a stem and flowers etched in smoky glass around its edge. Once the honours were done, Louie poured himself a drink and sat down with them. They sat with their legs stretched out in front of them, looking past the fruit trees, past Miriam hanging out clothing, past the plane sitting in the field across from them, out to the ridge with its conifers reaching up to the sky. Bechtol was content for awhile.

Long before Isaac, Bechtol and Louie had finished the bottle, Miriam pointedly left. She walked up the road and disappeared around the bend into the forest. Isaac knew she was going to visit her friend Clara who lived just around the corner. When the bottle was nearly empty, Bechtol and Louie left. Isaac walked them to the plane. Bechtol climbed into the pilot's seat. He took a final drag off his smoke and tossed it on the ground in front of Isaac, onto the dirt of the air strip. "Mind stepping on that for me, Izzy?" he asked.

Louie smiled down at Isaac from inside the plane, his stainless steel teeth flashing in his dark face, his eyes masked by his aviator's glasses. Isaac crushed out the cigarette with his dilapidated running shoe. He knew that he was part of the organisation now, an official caretaker; that he had passed the test, paid his tribute for the year. Such a small thing. Bechtol closed the door and the plane roared as it bounced along the runway and rose into the late afternoon sky. Heading south over Georgia Straight, Louie and Bechtol watched the island drop into insignificance below them. Over the short distance to Seattle there were many such islands. They all looked as if, aeons ago, some god had splattered pancake batter on a sea-blue griddle. To their right, the sun tilted low and sunk over the mountains of Vancouver Island.

Isaac watched as the plane dwindled to a dot in the sky. As its sound receded, he could hear the crickets and the wind in the trees again. The sun dropped behind the ridge and the shadows of the treetops began to spread across the field. Isaac's grandparents were Russian peasants, Jews who lived in a little village that had stood on the edge of annihilation. His serfdom was light by comparison. Miriam would bitch at him tonight about why he had kowtowed to them, dropped everything to spend the day drinking. That was all right too. It was a small price to pay for this place away from the madness in the U.S.

He walked back to the house where his easel was set up. The painting he had been working on before the plane came in was of a mushroom, Agaricus Campestris, with buff kidskin top and delicate pink gills. It was a small painting, showing the mushroom on the table, the dark grain of the table, a luminous glass of water in front of a window, the trees outside. The window and trees were also refracted in the glass of water. The real mushroom sat on the table near his easel, already withering. Its gills had turned from the delicate pink in the painting to a dark chocolate brown. Louie had left the bottle and there was an inch of scotch in the bottom. Isaac took his chipped shot glass and filled it with amber liquid. Amber. He stood back and looked at the mushroom, then at the painting of the mushroom. The mushroom was dying. The painting would live longer, but even its surface had changed, from the redolent glistening of fresh oil paint to the slightly duller skin that was already forming. In the painting it was still sunny outside. He looked out the window, glass in hand, and saw that the fields and trees were already pregnant with darkness.

As Ryan approached Isaac's house he gave a shout, "Hey Isaac!" Isaac walked out of the house to greet him, smelling of linseed oil turpentine and alcohol. He had been drinking and painting. What else was new? His face looked sad and serious.

"Miriam is gone..." he said, "up to the Commune."

"Yea, I know, McElwaith told me."

"Three days ago she told me that she was walking up to the Commune to see Ariel. I said I'd go with her but she didn't want me to. We hadn't been getting along so good. She just never came back.

"So after two nights I hiked up, bringing a bottle of wine to fortify myself. I asked at the gate to see her and waited around while they went to get her. After awhile she opened the gate and came out. She stood in front of me, wearing a T-shirt and hugging herself to keep warm. 'What's happening?' I asked.

"'I've just decided to stay for awhile,' she said, 'Ariel and Wylie are fine. They like it here. I want to give it a try. I'm sorry I didn't come back to tell you. I was planning to. I just needed to stay here awhile, though. I'll come out though, either to get my stuff or to.... I'm leaving my stuff at the farm if that's alright. I have to go now. I hope you won't drink too much while I'm gone. Your drinking is one of the reasons things are so hard between us. I have to go.'

"She kissed me and we held each other for awhile. Then she went back inside the gate."

Ryan put his arm around his friend's shoulder and gave him a squeeze. They walked arm in arm into the cool transcendental darkness of the house, into its old walls, its creakings, its silence. Isaac's small paintings and drawings were taped and tacked to the walls. There were paintings of many small things, of gates, of apples, of the field with thistles ablaze in light, of the cat in glowing electric black sleep, of rocking chairs and house furniture, of old broken farm implements. They looked like a hundred eyes staring out from the walls of the sequestered room.

Isaac and Ryan sat on the antique couch that had survived years of mice, parties, and being compressed by people's bums. An old sleeping bag covered its protruding springs. From a pitcher Isaac poured out some of last year's apple wine. They sat and talked about New York, about art, about women they had known, about the cult, about western culture, about what all this represented, about evolution, about pain, about their peasant ancestors, about life in the city and life on the island. Then they walked to the beach to gather oysters and made a dinner of oysters from the sea and fresh green Lamb's Quarters from the garden. When darkness came, Isaac lit the lamps. He doodled while Ryan read something by Dostoevsky, a disintegrating paperback held together with a rubber band. Later, Isaac brought him a couple of blankets and a pillow and went up to his bedroom that overlooked the fields and orchard, leaving Ryan to the couch, where he slept embraced by the old house, comforted by the sound of crickets, and secure in one friend's willingness to stay the course.

10
The Commune

Elroy had been the second person to go to the Commune, after Julie, and before Ariel and her family. He was a young cowboy from Texas who was "crashing around," staying a few nights here and a few nights there, singing for his supper. He knew all the rock and roll songs ever written and played them on his guitar. After Sheila had left the island, he often stayed at Ryan's for a few days, sleeping on one of the little beds that served as couches. He always helped out, splitting wood, borrowing Ryan's canvas kayak to catch a fish, making brown rice to eat it with. In autumn, he went with Ryan into the forest and helped him gather gunny sacks of fallen maple leaves to spread on the rich black garden soil to protect it from the rain.

Elroy was lost. He was tall and thin with a muscular pale body and reddish long straight hair. He had great blue eyes that could fill with amusement. He was charming with the ladies, in a tip your Stetson, down-home sort of way, but also lonely as he was just too young for most of them. He wanted to be a singer, but why then was he hanging around Vasquez long after everyone had left with the summer? But, then again, why was anybody?

Ryan liked Elroy because he helped out and didn't make a lot of conversational demands. At night they shared a toke of Ryan's dope and dropped into their own solitudes, Elroy softly playing his songs while Ryan read. For Ryan, this quiet companionship was a relief from the lonely wilds of the cabin. After a few days, Elroy, careful not to wear out his welcome, went on down the road. Ryan knew he would reappear some weeks later and looked forward to his visit.

At first everybody just noticed that Elroy was not around and asked after him. "Maybe he's staying down at Isaac and Miriam's," someone said, but, at one of the Legion bashes, Isaac and Miriam said they hadn't seen him.

It was Miriam who planted the seed. "He was wondering what was going on up at the Commune. He was thinking that he might go up and check it out. But he must be planning to come back: his guitar is still at our house."

"Oh no, he wouldn't do that, would he?" Alexis did a zombie imitation, putting his hands out in front of him and walking around stiff legged with a blank expression on his face, his eyebrows arching above his glasses frames. His eyes looked dead and glazed. Everybody laughed except Miriam. She was offended. "Well why not, we're all curious about the Commune. Instead of sitting around and making up stories about it like all the rest of you, he has the guts to go and find out what they're doing. I don't know why you're putting him down." Her voice had an edge to it.

The Legion. The Legion was a decayed yellow building above False Bay. It was rotting away from too many years of being closed without a fire to dry it out. It was single-storied, surrounded by trees and its roof was covered with thick clumps of green moss. The floor was covered with an ancient floral patterned linoleum from another time. There were still the requisite five members on the island to keep it open, so in recent years once a month they had a night of bingo, alcohol and dancing to scratchy ballroom dance records. These shindigs were attended by the ten or twenty old timers on the island.

Lately, since it was the only game in town, the Legion's members had graciously invited everybody to the party. At first the new settlers came tentatively, politely, to play bingo with the old timers. For Ryan it was very much like hanging out with the old timers in Argenta had been, a bit tedious, a bit polite, a bit formal. For others it was a bit of a giggle to do these outmoded things like playing bingo and trying to dance to ballroom music.

On Legion nights one of the old-timers, usually Thom, who ran the road grader, came in early and fired up the generator in the shed outside. The electric lights blinked into action. There was a pulse from the generator that made everything flicker like a scene from a silent movie. He started a fire in the wood heater and as the building heated up the musty smell began to dissipate. Someone else lugged in cases of beer and cider from their truck and put the bottles in a big wash tub filled with crushed ice. The bar was a little window at the back of the hall, where people could buy coloured theatre tickets to exchange for drinks or whatever baked goods someone had brought from home.

In truth, everyone was a little bored with bingo, but they kept playing it for old Rosa who was in her eighties, overweight and had trouble walking. Unable to dance, she was happy to watch and have shouted conversations over the music in her heavy German accent. But she loved to play bingo, so the whole community generously gathered to play for a while before dancing under the pulsing lights to the scratchy records that they had all heard so many times before. Outside this ancient assembly of light and sound, the stars shone down and clouds floated by in the night. A few of the island's teenagers, unfortunate enough to have been stranded here for the weekend, sat on stumps, clandestinely drinking liquor that they had managed to get from somewhere.

Rosa may have lived on the island longer than anyone. She and her husband came from Germany and had sunk their life's savings into a farm that they had seen advertised in a German paper. He was an artist who saw farming as a way of leaving behind the twisted evils of Europe. He dreamed of painting the pristine and savage Canadian landscape. They got off the train at some small place in Saskatchewan and were taken by the realtor out to the farm they had bought. It was late autumn. Rains had already freshened the air. The sky was blue. The day was pleasantly warm and they drove through golden fields of stubble. He took them to an old house that had recently had new windows put in. It didn't look like it had been lived in for a long time.

The land, unplanted, had a pleasant roll to it; it was a little elevated so they could see the horizon. The silence was immense and they could feel God all around them. Karl saw himself doing great paintings, gold below, blue above, a great flat line under the sky.

They knew nothing about farming. Later, on Vasquez Island, Rosa told Ryan that they had seen fruit hanging from the trees and thought the farm was fertile and prosperous. After they signed the papers, the realtor gave them a ride back to town. They purchased a wagon and horse, bought supplies, and took them back to their new home. Rosa went to pick an apple and found that the fruit had been wired to the tree. They were left alone at the clapboard house to set up their life.

In spring, when the terrors of the Canadian winter had passed, they ploughed and planted. The land around them turned green with the sprouts of wheat. As spring wore on, the well went slowly down until it was dry and empty. Nothing came out of the single faucet in the kitchen. They had been sold a dry farm. The wheat shrivelled and wilted in the grip of summer. Nothing could be done. They sold their last things and headed on a train out west. Rosa had learned to read English and had found an ad for a caretaker on an island off the coast of British Columbia. It was their only option. On the train Karl got up every few hours and walked to the washroom where he washed his hands and returned to his seat. Except for that, everything seemed normal between them. It was a habit that would stay with him the rest of his life.

They were met by Kensington, the wealthy Englishman who owned the north end of Vasquez Island. He took them across the Gulf of Georgia in his speed boat, a dangerous contraption that he loved to drive fast, slamming it through the waves. They were given a house on the north end of the island. It was where they would spend almost the rest of their lives. Rosa planted her crops by watching the snow recede on Mt. Arrowsmith. The beans went in when it reached such and such a rock, the tomatoes when it reached a particular gully. The mountain became the calendar by which she planted and harvested. Karl never painted again. He worked the farm that they didn't really own but of which they seemed to have eternal possession. His only eccentricity, his scar, was that he had a different coloured washcloth and towel for each day of the week. He hung them by the sink, all in a row, and washed and dried with the correct washcloth and towel on the correct day. It was his calendar by which he had created some kind of order in his blown-away life.

He was well enough liked until the war began, when the rumour started that he was really a German spy. This was at the time when the Japanese were being hauled away to relocation camps and their farms and boats sold for a pittance to envious whites. It was a serious accusation.

One night at a dinner party where Karl and Rosa were present, someone got a little too drunk and made reference to Karl as a Nazi. It was a laughing, half belligerent, half outrageous kind of logger humour. "Hey you Nazi, pass the gravy, Ha, Ha, Ha." Rosa looked worriedly at Karl and then stared straight into her plate. Karl, whose friends had told him about the rumours, stood up solemnly at his place and clanged his spoon against a glass for attention. The logger who made the joke said "Hey, just kidding." He laughed his wide laugh and looked from side to side at his friends, like a kid who had just bounced an eraser off the blackboard. Karl clanged away and soon there was a truculent, uneasy, defensive silence. To their surprise Karl, in a greatly exaggerated German accent said, "Ja it ist true." He had their attention now.

The room fell into shocked silence. Rosa looked stricken, alarmed. She looked beseechingly at her husband and reached her arm out toward him. He looked gravely down at her where she sat in her one good party dress, patted her on the arm, and continued his speech.

"Ja, it ist true. Vonce a month, yust at sunset, I row out past da Finertys und vait dere. Up come da German U Boat. Da hatch open und da commander stick out his head. Ve salute. Den he say 'Vat ist da news, Karl?'"

The assembled guests listened in stony silence. So it was true after all.

"Und I tell him: 'McClary's cow fall in da well last week. Da Norman kids haben da chicken pox. Hanson drive his truck into ein tree after da party down at Thomas' und to da hospital gehe im boat to Nanaimo. Simpson's wife run off und live mit Thomson. Simpson mad as hell now und say he going to kill dat Thompson sonofabitch next time he see him."

They listened as Karl, floating in his little rowboat next to the ominous black fish of the German U-boat, told the captain the tales of their little lives, the gossip they all lived on, their little form of literature. Simultaneously they all realised the absurdity of Karl being a spy, the absurdity of thinking that there was anything that he, or anyone else who lived on Vasquez, could possibly know that would be useful to the German High Command. They looked at each other. Cybele, Marsden's wife, started laughing first. She clapped and then they all clapped for Karl. It was his moment. He took the briefest and most formal of bows before sitting down. The conversation moved on. Tomorrow it would be talked about all over the island. Rosa and Karl looked at each other and laughed

64

together. Her laugh was big and hearty, her body shaking in deep gusts. The danger had passed.

In their old age Rosa and Karl saved enough money to buy two and a half acres on Main Road. Karl, with German precision, built them a small house, every joint cut exactly, with all the cupboards and storage rooms that a proper German house should have. It was in a small clearing in the forest and was surrounded by mounds of raspberries and fruit trees. There were borders of St John's Wort and Periwinkle growing along the gravel drive. It was like a tiny piece of the Black Forest that had been magically transposed into the Canadian wilderness. They finally, after fifty years in Canada, owned their own home. Then he died and left her there, along with a ten year supply of firewood that he had stacked in circular piles roofed with bark.

On either side of her hippies moved in, Sheila and Ryan on one side, the Donegals, building a small hippy shack, on the other. On mail days, walking along with her cane, she often invited them in. She always had tea and some kind of delicious German pastry that she had baked for them. They drank tea and smoked cigarettes with her. She was the first among the oldtimers to enjoy the newcomers. She saw that despite the men's long hair, outlandish clothes, and strange behaviour, they were not so different from the people of her own time. In some ways they were freer, not so bent up by social convention, by rules, by etiquette, by propriety.

She was an old woman. She herself had been an outcast, living alone out at the end of the island with her strange husband. She remembered all the snubbing, all the gossip, all the exclusion over petty things and was glad of these accepting new people. She accepted them back.

Now, long after Karl's death, she sat at the Legion in her old black dress, her stockings rolled to just above her knees, attending to the three bingo cards spread out in front of her. Her white hair was tied back; her hand-rolled cigarette dangled at the corner of her mouth. Her old farmer's hands, that had fed so many, dextrously flicked the wooden markers over the numbers.

"B-19."

At the early Legions just a few hippies politely joined the old timers to play bingo and fake waltzes to the old music. But then the island population began to grow. It seemed that every month the ferry brought a few more people with all their belongings. The more affluent ones barged over a truck or van. Some found an abandoned house, swept the floor clear of leaves, stapled up plastic windows and moved right in. There were fewer empty houses now, and the remaining ones were often not accessible by road. They required everything to be hauled in by pack or wheelbarrow. Ryan found these remote cabins to be the most special of all. He loved the long walk through the woods, the grass covered trails—once logging roads—that ran through avenues of slanting alder. He loved coming to the small clearing that magically opened in the middle of the forest; to the ancient battered cabin with its curl of smoke coming out the chimney. Sometimes there was the sound of a guitar, or a harpsichord, being quietly played in the woods.

Before going to the Legion, the hippies usually toked up, took mushrooms or even dropped hits of acid. They wore their work clothes, their hand-knit sweaters, their flowing garments, their Mexican whites, their patched jeans. Sven, Pearl, Blanche, Deana, Thom, Rose, The Captain welcomed the newcomers in an amused sort of way. All of these fine souls amped themselves down for these events, had a few beers so that they were laid back enough to get along with each other. For them it was good to have more life at the party. It was also a chance to get to know these new settlers about whom they were all so curious. Gradually there was a shift in the evening's protocol. It still started with bingo but not everyone played. After bingo, the hippies tried to make music for awhile and, after that, the old-timers closed the evening with their ballroom records.

On the night when they learned that Elroy had defected to the Commune, the hippies took over the dance floor after bingo. Wilf was a powerful young man, born and raised on the island. Versed in machinery, logging, farming, horses and carpentry, he had recently extended his learning into the realms of hippiedom. He climbed boldly on stage with his battered black conga drum. The sheer force of his personality and muscled body, his great arms and bull neck, polarised the other musicians around him. A rising and falling jungle beat began to fill the room and echo out into the rainy forest. On the dance floor, people twisted, contorted, rocked, and wailed to the home-made music. The drums beat wildly. Someone danced around the edges of the hall and unscrewed most of the light bulbs. Bobbing heads flew past the remaining bulbs and their swirling shadows gave a fire-lit, foresty feel to the room. Ryan howled out deep tones that seemed to emanate from the centre of his chest. Others joined in, singing improvised question and answer chants. Their collective voices raised the roof, growling, howling, shouting individual words into the crowd. Freeeedom, Freeedom, Freedom raised itself as a rhythmic chant.

The dance was something out of the tribal past, an archetypal purging of the energies that stood in the way of community. Also demanding release were the frustrations of island life, of bingo, of eating oysters for seven days straight, of trying to burn wet wood, of trying to fix broken cars, of cows breaking down fences and eating gardens, and, most of all, of Elroy, one of their own, disappearing into the Commune. As the jungle drums beat wildly, a swirl of moving bodies, gesticulating hands, and howling mouths danced in the half light. Under the amplification of whatever hallucinatory drugs they had taken, the dancers felt like divine channels through which God's music was flowing.

The old timers stood at the sides of the hall in a mixture of laughter, anger, and disbelief. They seemed to understand, however, that once this sort of thing got started it needed some time to play itself out. They good-naturedly retreated back into the kitchen to talk and drink beer. Some took a turn out under the trees.

Joe was a smart Jewish kid from New York, a fast-talking apprentice stock broker with a fierce competitive streak. He was visiting Miriam, his older sister, and very out of his element among these drugged-out goyim back-to-the-landers, but, nonetheless, was not to be out-hippied. High on a mixture of all the drugs he had been handed, he pulled off his clothes and started dancing naked in the wild crowd. This was too much for The Captain, the very last straw. He went around the room screwing the light bulbs back in and then had a shouting match with the chief drummer, the tough local boy. There was some shoving but eventually the music stopped. It took a while longer for the singing and dancing to stop, but under the Captain's baleful gaze and the bright flickering lights it finally did. Suddenly the room was full of silence and glare. The only sound was the susurration of the generator. Where Joe had flung his clothes, he did not know. The dance floor cleared and he was left standing naked searching the sides of the room for his shirt and pants. His clothes were nowhere to be found. It was like a game of musical chairs where when the music stopped one person was singled out to pay the price for everyone's transgressions.

Joe backed into the crowd and sat against the wall on the ancient linoleum floor. He curled his legs up, crossed his arms around himself, and covered his nakedness. Shame had returned under the bright tungsten glare. Others found his clothes—pants here, gaunch there, shirt under the table—and brought them back to him, one by one, like pieces of Osirus. He re-assembled himself and walked out the door into the night.

The Captain walked across the silent dance floor to the old wooden phonograph. He was a forceful, muscular man, but with a complex delicacy he bent over the phonograph and placed the needle flawlessly on the record he had selected. A waltz sprung to life and he walked across the room, arm extended, and with a small bow, asked Deana, who drove the cab, who milked the cow, who was raising 12 children on her own, to dance. They swirled easily across the floor, in a formal upright posture. They had done this dance a hundred times before. Their weavings and formal steps brought order back into the universe. It was now the old-timers' turn and most of the back-to-the-landers stood around the sides of the room sipping beer to come down from the drugs they had taken. Two or three of them stumbled out onto the floor and cling-danced, or tried to do rock and roll movements to the Tennessee Waltz.

One by one and two by two, in the backs of trucks or on foot, people began to return home through the night. For some it was a long walk. When everyone had gone, Sven, who ran the government dump truck, shut the place down. He made sure the wood heater was damped down, turned off the generator and locked the door. With his wife Pearl, he drove down the island on the gravel road that he kept from being reclaimed by the forest. More than a little drunk, they drove past sleeping farms, recapping the evening, laughing about the wildness these new young people had brought into their lives again. "It's almost as good as the old logging days," he said, thinking back on his own youth, not really so long ago.

11
Ryan And Sheila

Spring in Vancouver. At 5 a.m the robins carolled riotously, awakening Ryan from his fitful sleep. Annoyed at being up so early, he sat drinking instant coffee, and watched the sky change from black to grey over the roof tops.

Unemployed, watching their savings diminish by the day, he felt displaced. From his window he saw the coifed and showered residents of Kitsilano leave their homes for work. For him, there was no creative juice, no story to tell, no picture to paint, no photograph to take. His still unfinished self-portrait was leaned up against a wall behind him. It showed a young academic in steel-rimmed, old-fashioned glasses, standing in a green room with a yellow floor. The door of the room was unpainted, a blank white rectangle. When he and Sheila moved to the island, he would leave the painting in the lane behind the house with other discarded items. Not until all their boxes were unpacked would Sheila realise that he had left it behind. She would grieve for it. He hadn't finished it because he could not see the door by which to leave the room.

After showering, getting dressed, getting Lara up, changing her, dressing her, feeding her, having breakfast, doing dishes, making the bed together, Sheila and Ryan were ready to walk in Kitsilano. Waiting for Sheila to get her coat, Ryan tossed Lara into the air, catching her as she fell back to earth. They both laughed hilariously, again and again, at the catch, at her sudden safety in his arms.

Ryan loved Sheila's chic apartment, the artwork on the walls, the English piano. It had a small balcony off the living room from where they could watch the Greek men come and go on the tree-lined street. The men carried their bodies erectly, greeting each other with with open-armed gestures and a particular dancing grace. Sometimes the smell of grilled lamb kabobs drifted down from the Greek restaurants on Broadway.

Ryan's shortish hair had now grown slightly longer than the norm and Sheila's Greek landlord called him a "Heapy." The word "Heapy" was often shouted at him from porches as he walked down the leafy streets. Greek immigrants who barely spoke English, who could not quite pronounce the word, had already found somebody to despise. Sheila and Ryan had a little joke that a Heapy was someone who left heaps of things about, or promised to be a heap of trouble. It made sense to them that Heapies were despised: these immigrants had suffered centuries of poverty, invasion and civil war and had come to the stability and affluence of Canada, had worked hard to buy their homes on these treed streets, only to find that a whole class of pampered youth was rejecting everything they had struggled to attain; were rejecting the American Dream, which it appeared Canadians had been dreaming for quite a while as well.

Ryan wondered how the American Dream traveled across the border. Did dreams travel singly or in herds? Were they like ectoplasmic paisleys that oozed out of a sleeping person's head at night, floating through the ceilings of their houses into the dark sky above, travelling on prevailing winds over Blaine, across White Rock, through Steveston, over Richmond, and then entering into the heads of sleepers in Vancouver? Did they breed in sleeper's heads? One goes in, two come out? We assume, Ryan thought, that dreams are our own, but are they? Were they parasitic? Did dreams feed us with images to distract us while they munched on the rich and forbidden histories in our heads?

Since Argenta, Ryan had taken to wearing what had become the rural hippie uniform: garishly plaid—blue, red, purple—Chinese work-shirts made of a heavy flannel and very, very cheap. The proportions were a little strange: the arms always seemed too short for the size and volume of the shirt. It made Ryan wonder if Chinese people were proportioned slightly differently than North Americans. The shirts were illegal in The States, as was anything from communist China, so Ryan delighted in smuggling them back for his friends when he crossed the border. He also wore ragged jeans and Pierre Paris logging boots. These were very heavy work boots with Vibram soles. They were called cookie cutters because of the shapes the soles left in the snow—diamonds and clubs as from a deck of cards. They had a jaunty fringe of leather curling up from under the base of their tongue, and steel toes to keep the chain saw from cutting off your own toes or the skidder from crushing them. They were also quintessentially Canadian, made in Vancouver, worn by the fallers, swampers, and chokermen as a mark of pride in their rough and demanding work.

Rural Hippies had begun to wear work clothes, and forest workers, already dressed for the part, had begun to smoke dope and let their hair grow long. At first glance, it was hard to tell whether you were looking at a hippy gone rural or a redneck gone hippy.

For Ryan these boots had a grounding effect, much like the weighted boots of a deep-sea diver. They kept him stuck to the ground, kept him from getting lost in thoughts of paisley dreams as he walked along Kitsilano's shady streets to the occasional shout of "Heapy." They kept him grounded by the sheer effort it took to put one heavy foot in front of the other. In these boots he was a skinny guy with huge feet, like one of those inflatable Bozo's that keep coming back up, again and again.

The hip of Vancouver followed a more celebratory, less burdened, fashion protocol. They wore tie-died shirts, beads, embroidered jackets, jackets with leather fringes, brightly patched pants, retro evening wear, ragged dress clothes gleaned from every epoch of society, all from the profusion of Vancouver's thrift stores. They wore mad hatter hats and brightly coloured caps. To the rural hippies this sort of thing was ostentatious. They only wore this kind of get-up to celebrations such as community picnics or love-ins. They prided themselves in their skill with a chainsaw, their ability to plant a garden, to trim goat's hooves, to grow pot. When they came to town, the Big Smoke they called it, they proudly sported their work clothes, still smelling of wood smoke, to show who they were and who they were becoming.

Heapies. They all had long hair and wore cheap, ragged clothes.

After breakfast, Ryan and Sheila put Lara into her backpack with its blue canvas seat slung on an aluminum frame. They stowed an extra diaper under the seat and set out on their walk up 4th Avenue. Sometimes they stopped for a cup of coffee along the way.

Lara sat erectly in her back pack, looking to the left and right, taking everything in. Sometimes she held up a hand in general greeting to the world, or to some of its many denizens, human and otherwise, who wandered Vancouver's charter'd streets.

Life had settled into a routine again, the routine of being conscientious parents, the routine of spending time with their child in the park. If only they could have settled into this beingness, settled into enjoying the sky, the blossoms falling in drifts like pink snow along 4th Avenue, the green grass, the spring emerging out of the winter wetness. But they were both driven by incompleteness, the need to do something significant. The War, the furore in The States, seemed very far away. They drifted in the circle of their days. Sheila felt a lack of any means of expression; Ryan felt his blockedness, idleness, and lack of motivation. He thought back to Argenta and his time building stone walls, turning the soil, cutting and stacking wood, and missed these simple and satisfying occupations.

On their walks they looked in all the shop windows. Kitsilano was still mostly run down and seedy. Tools stared mutely out at them from the hardware store, spatulas and casseroles from the kitchen shop, left-behind shoes—for sale cheap—at the shoe repair. At Octopus Books they often stopped and looked at the offerings in the window. There they discovered, along with *The Birds of B.C., The Flowers of B.C., The Marine Mammals of B.C., The Mushrooms of B.C.,* a copy of *October Ferry to Gabriola and Other Stories* by Malcolm Lowry. It is as though Malcolm Lowry was an elemental and belonged right in there with the birds, flowers, mushrooms and marine mammals.

They bought the book and found a story in it called *The Forest Path to the Spring.* In his introduction, Lowry stated that the greatest literary effort was usually spent on tragedy. He wondered, "what if the same effort—the same artifice—were to be put into ennobling the fleeting moments of sweetness in life." *The Forest Path to the Spring* was his answer to this question. In it he tells a story about two people living in a squatter's cabin built on stilts over a wild North-Shore beach. They live in harmony with bear and cougar, and, even more dangerously, with each other.

In the story they are making a journey by rowboat to fill their water bottles from the spring, which Sheila and Ryan understood to be a metaphor for the source from which life is sustained and renewed. As they row home, it becomes a story about a love and acceptance between man and woman that transcends their limitations, his alcoholism, and the broken condition that is the human lot.

In another story, they read about how he was driven out of this paradise by the city fathers, who bulldozed and burnt the cabins to make way for a park.

Motivated by the book, Ryan drove the Red Ant over to the North-Shore one day to find where Lowry had lived. There was only an empty beach now, with a few charred stumps of pilings still sticking out of the pebbles. The beach still looked out at the smoking towers and minarets of the oil refineries across Burrard Inlet. The great sign that spelled SHELL, made of separate letters like the ones that spell HOLLYWOOD, was still there. In one of his stories, Lowry had written about how one winter a storm had blown the S down, leaving the smoking oil refinery appropriately labelled HELL.

After having bulldozed and burnt Lowry's cabin, the city fathers had named the asphalt path that they built the Malcolm Lowry Walk. To Ryan, it provided some insight as to the exact manner in which nature follows art. They had paved the Forest Path to the Spring. Ryan also wondered, despite his heavy boots, why Canadians pronounced asphalt "ashfalt." Was it its grey colour? Or was it a Victorian nicety to avoid saying the syllable "ass?"

Years later, on Vasquez, Ryan met a young blond man named Kelly. They talked about transplanting arbutus trees; of the need to orient them to the direction in which they were originally growing in order for them to survive. Finding out that Kelly had grown up on the North-Shore, Ryan asked him if he knew about Malcolm Lowry, the writer. Kelly had never heard of him, so Ryan told him a little about Lowry's life, about how he lived on the North-Shore in a squatter's cabin. Kelly's eyes went wide with recognition as Ryan spoke; he said, "Oh, you mean the old drunk who lived down on the beach." Kelly told Ryan that as a boy he and his friends used to sneak down through the forest and had thrown rocks on the roofs of the squatter's cabins. Out of one, a man would come running, shouting, shaking his fist and swearing at them. He scared the shit out of them. They would scamper back up through the woods to the safety of the highway. They had no idea it was Malcolm Lowry, the writer. They just called him "the old drunk," and thought it was funny to torment him. Kelly was a nice enough young man, "sterling" to use a word from the time. So was Ryan.

From *The Forest Path to the Spring,* Ryan and Sheila took the vision that would motivate the next part of their life: the idea was to live close but separately. Did not Frieda Kahlo and Diego Rivera have separate houses joined by a rope bridge that hung between their third story bedrooms? Maybe, they thought, they could do it that way. Ryan went on a search for squatter's cabins by driving to the South Fork of the Fraser River where he heard that some still existed. There he found long rows of handmade cabins, cheek on jowl, running for miles along the banks of the Fraser. The cabins were built out over the river on pilings and were pieced together from whatever salvaged lumber, mill ends, mill slabs, driftwood, had been available at the time of their construction. Their building materials had floated up and down the river on the tide had been hooked with pikes and pulled into rowboats. Nobody in his right mind would have ever thought of paying for lumber. Fishermen tied their boats to makeshift wharves that they had pieced together from planks and logs that had floated down the river.

Ryan parked and walked along the dyke that protected Queensborough from the fearful floods of the filthy, freaky, frothy, Fraser. Here he met Evie and Cliff, who invited him into their cabin for a drink. Cliff was an old veteran with a plastic leg. He drank straight whisky which he poured over sugar cubes in the bottom of small shot glasses. The cubes stuck to the bottom and became eroded by the whisky, making what appeared to be small abstract ice sculptures in the bottom of each glass. The glasses were never washed. Ryan sat at their table and was offered one of these glasses with the sugar artifact in the bottom. Several other old guys sat around the table in various stages of good natured drunkenness. Just as Cliff was about to pour, he looked into the bottom of the glass and saw the eroded sugar cubes. He apologised and was about to heave himself up and limp to the sink on his bad leg to wash the glass, but Ryan, ever the good sport, said "what the hell, the whisky will kill anything that's in there." He held the glass out for Cliff to fill and tossed it down to laughter and approbation.

Cliff and Evie's squatter's cabin was the kind of bitty space with small windows that fishermen built to hole up in for the winter. Instead of a toilet, each cabin had an outhouse appended to its back. There was a door between this little chamber and the rest of the cabin, both for privacy and to shut out the cold Fraser winds that blew up through the hole in the seat. The occupants of the cabins shat directly into the river. At low tide their shit sat directly on the mud surrounded by a mandala of coloured toilet paper. After many drinks, Ryan went to use Cliff and Evie's outhouse. He looked down through the hole as he peed, and saw what looked like an abstract collage made with clay and colourful tissue paper. Shit on River Bottom, mixed media. Create the natural way. Plop.

Ryan found a six hundred dollar squatter's cabin for sale on the north bank of the south fork of the Fraser. It would be his cabin. Sheila would keep the apartment. The cabin looked across at Annacis Island which at that time still lay mysteriously hidden behind the flowing willows that lined its banks. Many years later Ryan flew over it and, looking down, saw that the island had become a Nissan receiving yard: scraped bare, paved, and turned into a parking lot for five thousand Easter egg coloured Nissans.

The original part of the cabin became the bedroom, dark and tiny. The previous owner had framed in a large space that doubled the size of the cabin before he had died, but this was still in two by fours. Ryan bought battens of insulation and a sling of random length mill end cedar tongue and groove for $30 dollars from a local mill. The Fraser was still lined with sawmills. Cones for burning scraps, piles of logs and stacks of lumber dotted the waterfront up and down the river. Sheila helped him and they laboriously paneled the walls, cutting the boards to fit between the two by four studs. They tore off the back of the house, the side facing the river, and framed in a wall of large windows that they had scrounged here and there for a dollar or two each. They used a hand saw, a hammer and a large steel frame to do the work. The river now flowed visibly by in its murky, degraded majesty.

They tore out the old linoleum and put down fibre board and fed it gallons and gallons of polyurethane varnish until it was hard and glossy. There was no garden space and they made plans to tie a raft to the back of the house and grow things in boxes of dirt. They also ordered mill ends for firewood and bought a seventeen dollar skill saw from Eaton's to cut them to size.

When it was finished, they bought a little enamel #3 to put on the door. The orange three stood out against the pea-green enamel of the plate. #3 South Dyke Road, Queensborough.

The one thing neither of them liked was shiting in the river. It was not nice, not clean. They talked about digging an outhouse into their tiny front yard, into the side of the dyke, but they worried that by doing so they would adversely affect the integrity of the dyke: QUEENSBOROUGH FLOODED, RIVER BREACHES THROUGH OUTHOUSE.

Ryan set up his dark room in the bedroom and printed his first photos: Sheila walking in Kitsilano with Lara on her back, Lara sitting on the grass in a park with that exquisitely upright and present posture that sitting babies have. Photo's of family. Years later, the test strips from these photos remained, fragments from a life that almost came together or maybe never came together at all, despite the effort they had put into it: their attempt at family, their attempt at being ma and pa, which they had somehow miraculously kept together for so many troubled years.

Many mornings Ryan would ride his bike to visit Sheila and Lara. He rode along Kingsway, the Kings Highway, a long strip of fast-food joints and industrial parts warehouses. Biking was ecologically correct, non-polluting. It was healthy and provided exercise. Kingsway was the shortest way to go, the hypotenuse that cut across the grid of the city, the shortest distance between the two points of his life. Unfortunately it was so polluted that he often had an asthma attack upon arrival.

He was lonely in his little cabin, listening to the river flow under him, watching its tides rise and fall. He wrote poems to the Filthy, Freaky, Frothy, Flowing, Fraser. He painted watercolours of the Cascades, which he saw from his windows, across the river, rising above the willows on Annacis Island. In the evening he walked out into the twilight and onto the bridge to Annacis Island. From mid-span he stared down the river, over the flat farmland to the rivers mouth. There were kaleidoscopic bands of grey and darkness out beyond where the Fraser met Georgia Straight. The islands were dark humps rising into the sky beyond.

He would return home and read in bed until, at the same time every night the great oscillating head light of the train came, searching among the willows with its cyclopean eye, as though for babies in reed baskets. As it crossed the tarred plank and piling bridge to the island, it shook the jelly-like mud on which his cabin was built. This shaking marked for him the end of another day as he turned off his lamp and slept through the early winter darkness.

And then—once again at Octopus Books—Ryan and Sheila were caught by the wave of synchronicity that would carry them to a far-away place, pull them apart, and put them out of their deeply bonded relationship misery. It was as though Octopus Books had reached out a tentacle and grabbed them by the ankles.

It was on one of their walks after Ryan had spent the night. They were looking at books when Ryan saw their reflections—through a glass darkly—in the window: he saw himself with his now longish beard and curls; Sheila, her hair parted in the middle and tied behind her neck; Lara in her baby carrier, craning over his shoulder to see what they were looking at and raising her hand in salute to the printed word. Even in the window he could see the soulful cast to Sheila's eyes and mouth.

And then, behind them in the reflection, he saw another couple stop to look in the window. They were holding hands and began to comment on some of the titles. He glanced sideways. They were of similar age to Sheila and himself. The man had long, curly, Furry Freak Brothers type hair. He had twinkly blue eyes framed by steel rimmed glasses and wore a very Vancouver woollen Mackinaw with large red and black checks. She was similarly dressed: jeans, hiking boots, flannel shirt. Her long dark hair was straight and parted in the middle; it flowed over her shoulders and down her back. They could have been hippies, academics, mountain climbers or all of the above. Their fingers came out of their embrace to point at a map of Georgia Strait that was tacked on the screen that separated the display window from the rest of the shop.

It was a Canadian Government (Ryan wondered why Canadians always said "Government of Canada") hydrographic chart of the northern Gulf of Georgia. All the land was yellow and all the water blue. The islands appeared on the map as irregular yellow shapes spattered on the blue water. Details—roads, buildings, topographical lines—were shown only near the coast to help boaters locate their position. A short distance inland, about an inch as it appeared on the map, the detail faded into blank yellow. To Ryan this was exciting. It was like people: you could see their outside, their charted coast, but who the hell knew what lay in their personal outback, "the interior" as it was called in B.C.

On a table in front of the map was a display of books on the Gulf Islands. In addition to all the usual books about native plants, mushrooms, mammals, marine life, and Malcolm Lowry, there were obscure memoirs by original settlers; there was a book on log cabin construction, left open to photos of immaculately crafted dove-tail joints. There was the Whole Earth Catalogue, a great floppy magazine with a photo of mother earth floating in space on its cover. It was full of information on where to buy tools and where to buy books that told you how to grow your own food, grow your own dope, grow your own children, grow your own life. There were country cookbooks. There was Rodale's gardening book and Ruth Stout's book on mulching with hay. There was a book on goat husbandry and a book on how to deliver your own baby without hospitals or doctors. There was a book about how the captains George Vancouver and Juan Francisco de la Bodega y Quadra sailed into the Gulf of Georgia in the same year and played hide and seek among the forested islands, each naming them in their native tongues after crew members.

There were also a few antique tools on the table: a carpenter's plane made from a block of wood with a wooden wedge to hold its steel blade in place, a rusted Aladdin kerosene lamp, a spud for peeling logs, a scythe whose sinuous wooden handle was so weathered and flimsy that it could only have been used for harvesting vaporous souls.

"Look how close Vasquez is to the mainland," said the young woman, "and how far away from Vancouver Island."

"Yea, that was one hell of a ferry trip," said her partner.

Sheila and Ryan looked at the map. Vasquez Island lay far out across the water from where the ferry left. There was a wavy line on the chart that showed the ferry route. Its looked like the coiled line that connects the ear piece of a telephone to its stand. There was another long island with a Spanish name, no doubt named by Juan Francisco de la Bodega y Quadra, which separated Vasquez from the mainland and the rest of Canada. This island created a long and difficult barrier, like the Wall of China, around which boats from the mainland had to travel.

What's in a name? Ryan wondered. Were the Spanish-named islands more passionate, more split into dark and light, more forested, more given to Catholicism, paganism, the occult, and subsistence homesteads than the English-named islands? More donkeys and goats? More rum running and shady occupations?

He imagined that the English-named islands were more open and filled with pastures of grazing sheep. He imagined that the people on them were more rational, given to Protestantism, Zen, vegetarianism, legitimate respectable businesses, political influence, cheery summer cabins, raising horses and keeping up appearances. He made a note to himself to check into this, little knowing how deeply he would become immersed in the little research project he had envisioned. Once again life began to follow art, he, the would-be artist, condemning himself to lead the life he imagined.

He was interested in Vasquez. He had read some interesting newspaper snippets about it. "You've been there?" He ventured, looking over his shoulder. His phrase had that exact Canadian balance between a question and a statement. He'd gotten good at it.

"Oh yea, we went over at the end of last summer, on our bikes. It was amazing. There was almost no one there, just old abandoned homesteads. We met some girls living in a cabin at the foot of the mountain." His hand gestured briefly at the map. "One had blond hair and the other red. They were making pies from the apples and blackberries that were growing around their cabin. They shared a blackberry pie with us. We sat down on the grass in their clearing and ate it in the sunlight. Blackberries grew all over the place. They were living with almost no money, gathering oysters and clams; growing vegetables behind the house; picking fruit from the abandoned orchards. We left them some of our food, good stuff that they couldn't gather: cashews, raisins, coffee, some soup packets."

Ryan and Sheila asked many questions about the island. They asked from where the ferry departed, when it left, when it returned and how much it cost. They learned that it was not a car ferry: that you had to bring your bikes or walk when you got to the other side.

Returning to their apartment with Lara slumped over and asleep in her baby carrier, they decided they would visit Vasquez, this almost ghost town in the middle of the water. In September, Ryan saw a small ad for a house on Vasquez Island at an affordable price. He called about it and the realtor said he would take them over to see it. They decided to go with the realtor. It was easier. There were no bikes to organise, not as many parcels of food and baby things to carry, no figuring out how to get around. With Lara in mind, they had also decided against pioneering. If they moved, they would get a house that was ready to move into and had at least some amenities.

The real question was why Sheila was even open to yet another madcap adventure. Why did she go along with this exploration, just when she had finally settled into a life that answered some of her needs? For Ryan it was about missing the daily tasks of the homesteader that had given structure and meaning to his life in Argenta. Perhaps for Sheila it was just her old restlessness, her need for adventure. Perhaps it was her hope that Ryan might be happier if he was more occupied. Or perhaps it was just her sense of destiny, that this was written and there was no way out.

12
Ryan And Sheila

When the day came, Sheila, Lara and Ryan embarked on their trip to meet the realtor. They drove across Burrard Inlet on the Lions Gate Bridge, through the shopping malls of North Vancouver, then through West Van just to see its old homes. On the Upper Levels Highway, old shingled houses gave way to glass palaces. Their red Volvo station wagon seemed tiny and insubstantial against the mass of the forested mountains. The day was beautiful. The landscape was dark green, punctuated by the sparkling yellow flags of fall maples. They drove onto the ferry.

From Nanaimo they drove north along the Island Highway, past fast-food joints, car dealerships, companies that sold logging machinery, industrial repair yards. The old town centre of Nanaimo had winding streets that reminded them of Guanajuato, another mining town where they had once lived. The rest was strip malls. They sang and joked, full of hope and excitement at going somewhere new. At French Bay they pulled out onto the Government wharf and looked for a sign.

The only sign they were looking for was the one that would tell them when the ferry arrived and departed. It was not yet that time of history when minds loosened by drugs scried the ground, scried the sky, scried people's faces for signs and omens of what was meant to be. A sign was still just a sign, and they were still a family, firmly in control of their own destiny, or so they believed. They had not yet handed their lives over to some force that brought them into contact with mysterious strangers who had messages and instructions to pass on. They had not yet read Jung and did not know about synchronicity, nor had they seen or remarked on anything that might be called that by another name.

So far, chance had not played a large part in their lives, unless one meant the blind chance of Darwin's random mutation. They were materialists, believing themselves to be descended through a very long lineage from something like the amoeba; creatures whose duty it was to evolve beyond the instincts that had carried them so far; to evolve and live by a code of ethics that humans—unique among the animals—had the ability to create. They saw little Lara, who waved from her back pack at the dancing waves, as being born to continue this work, carry it on beyond their failures in the same way that they had tried, somewhat unsuccessfully, to carry it on beyond the failures of their own parents. Lara tentatively tried out her new words: "Bo" for boat; "Way" for Waves. She was as yet mercifully unaware of the heavy burden that she had inherited. There was no ferry, no sign of a ferry, no sign about a ferry.

They walked down the gangway with its red iron rails. The long planks that ran its length were divided into two halves: on one side wooden cross pieces had been nailed to provide footing during the steepness of low tide; on the other side the planks had been worn slick by the innumerable boxes that had been slid down to a catcher below.

Down on the float, a fisherman was loading a huge pile of boxes—food and hardware—into the hold of his troller. They asked him when the ferry was coming and he raised his hand to his eyes and squinted out through the mouth of the riprap to the open water. His long grey hair hung out in strands from under his toque. He pointed a thick crooked finger at the water, toward the island: "There she is," he said. They followed his gaze to a tiny white dot out among the whitecaps. Lara said "Deh shis," and pointed along with the fisherman. Occasionally, like a blowing whale, the boat sent up a plume of spray as it ploughed through a cresting wave. They became aware of the wind that played around them, that blew through the boat basin, tinkling the boat's rigging like wind chimes.

The realtor and house owner joined them as they waited on the slip for the boat. The realtor, Hal, was fifty-ish with wavy white hair combed to one side. He had clear blue eyes. Bill, the owner, was taller, slightly stooped and wore a good natured, humorous expression on his face. He had short dark hair and liked to joke. They were both dressed in wool mackinaws and clean, new jeans and boots, like they were going hunting. Hal explained that Bill wanted to come over with them to do a few repairs.

The boat came wallowing into the basin. Diesel fumes belched from its stack as it reversed and revved its engine to keep from hitting the dock. The "ferry" turned out to be an old logging crummy with thick coats of gummy green paint hiding rust blisters, some of which had broken loose and ran down the hull in orange streaks. It was woebegone, rust streaked and to Ryan, looked like something from a Joseph Conrad novel.

As the deckhand jumped off the boat and tied it to the dock, the skipper, bald with protruding eyes, glared at them from the twin windows of the wheel house. The deckhand, dressed in a military camouflage jacket and hat, didn't meet their eyes. This was not the sort of immaculately maintained B.C. Ferry to which they had become accustomed: no catchy logo emblazoned on its side, no smartly uniformed "personnel" to usher them aboard.

Onboard, the first thing they saw was a hand scrawled sign taped to a steel door that announced that the toilet was "Hors de Combat." Someone had also written on it in an illiterate scrawl, presumably for the sake of those whose French was not so good, "little girls that run around after soldiers." The second thing they saw, as they stepped down into the passenger area, was that instead of the bright rows of plastic seats usually found on ferries, there were six ratty couches, three on each side, covered by equally ratty blankets. Some of the blankets had fallen off and were just bunched up on the seat, revealing the tattered upholstery underneath. The room smelled of diesel and barf.

Ryan was both appalled and exhilarated. The ferry seemed so neglected that it could easily become an unintentional Viking burial ship. On the other hand, it had all the earmarks of a gateway to an outlaw zone, a place off the beaten path, away from the prying eyes of the plastic civilisation that he was trying to escape. Straightening out the tattered blanket on one of the couches, they sat in the belly of this rusted boat, Ryan holding Lara who had been lulled to sleep by the vibrations of the engine. Away from the pale sunlight that had redeemed the day outside, they shivered a bit and waited to cross the great waters.

When the boat left, Bill and Hal took them up the three wooden steps to the poop deck at the stern. It was much nicer than in the dank cabin. Bundled up against the wind, they leaned against the rusted rail. Lara still slept in Ryan's arms, wrapped in the batik quilt that Sheila's mother had given them. The boat turned to the sea and, with much snorting of the diesel engine, left the stone riprap. It was immediately caught by the southeast swell and began to roll and yaw. The spray blown up by the bow did not quite reach them. Bill stood next to Ryan and Sheila and started a shouted conversation over the roar of the exhaust.

He told them that ten years ago there had been four of them who had moved out to the island. Bill to write, another of his friends to paint. Bill said that the painter used to stand on the back of the ferry for hours, watching the motion of the waves, the better to paint them. He told them—with an appraising glance—that Vasquez was an interesting place if you were interested in psychology, particularly the abnormal kind. "Islands are small worlds," said Bill, "They attract people who like to be large frogs in small ponds." Bill had given up writing and worked as a building inspector for the town across the water.

On the tossing boat, they rocked and rolled across the 17k of Georgia Strait to the island. They told Bill about their artistic aspirations. He looked at them thoughtfully and said "Yes, you might do all right over there." When they recapped the conversation that evening, they wondered whether he meant because of their artistic aspirations or because they reminded him of characters from an abnormal psych text.

From a distance the island looked smooth, low and green. As the ferry approached, they saw that in reality it was full of folds, valleys, knobs, knolls, and mountains. It had cliffs that fell dramatically into the sea. Wind-swept trees topped the cliffs. There was no sign of habitation; no summer homes dotted its coast, no vainglorious glass mansions perched on its weathered points. It was dark, wild, and seemingly untouched.

As they rounded the last point, they were sheltered from the wind and swell and no longer had to hold the railing. They saw what the chart in the bookstore had called False Bay: a government wharf with its bright red railings and spindly black pilings; a mottle of pastel houses, yellow, white, pink, and green in various stages of disrepair; a huge Arbutus clustered with red autumn berries like an early Christmas offering; mounds of blackberry plants twining through broken-down fences; a dirt road disappearing into the forest. Invisible from the other side, hidden by the fir clad point that they had just rounded, False Bay looked like a trading post from a turn of the century lithograph, a place where indigenous people might have come in their canoes to trade for guns and blankets. Yet it was only an hour away from the booming subdivisions of Vancouver Island. "Tobacco Row" said Bill with a contemptuous snort.

With much roaring and reversing of engines the ferry manoeuvred into its place at the slip. The deckhand leapt off and slapped the fat hawser over a cleat. The engine shut down. They all climbed off the boat into an immaculate silence that was unmarred by the buzz of air conditioners, the hum of transformers, the rumble of machinery, or chatter of radios. For a moment no-one talked. The pilings creaked and groaned and water lapped beneath the slip.

Up the hill from the wharf, two young children picked blackberries and ate them with red stained hands and mouths. Their voices and laughter seemed loud in the overwhelming silence. The Captain in his grease stained overalls and the deckhand in his camouflage suit stalked up the gangplank like military personnel on parade, looking neither left nor right. They climbed into a rusted red Datsun pickup and gunned it up the hill in a mufflerless roar, spraying gravel all the way. They lurched and careened past the café, past the falling down houses, past the children, and disappeared into the forest. Ryan listened as the truck's sound faded along the twists and turns of the road. Bill looked wistfully around, scenting the air, the smell of the sea and the tar from the pilings. A crow repeatedly dropped a clam shell, trying to break it open on an exposed rock. With each try, it flew a little higher before dropping it again; every time it hit, it made a "Clack," a single repetitive punctuation mark in long sentences of silence.

The five of them walked up the gang plank. Lara struggled along with one hand in her mother's and the other on the red iron railing. Up on the wharf they stood next to the corrugated freight shed and waited for the taxi that would take them to the house.

"Taxi" brings to mind a yellow car with a plastic light on top with the word "taxi" inscribed on it. Ryan wondered, "what if everything was labelled? What if trees had 'Tree' written on them; spoons, 'spoon'; houses, 'house'? What if people had 'philanderer,' 'poet,' 'psychopath,' 'plumber,' written on their foreheads in a plain sort of way? What was it about taxis?

In this case, the taxi bore little resemblance to its platonic ideal. It was a dust covered red VW van that came creeping down the hill in low gear, revving excessively, leaving a rich blue plume of oil laden exhaust behind it. Ryan saw that in False Bay words didn't necessarily mean the same thing that they meant on the other side. "Ferry" was a rusted old boat. "Taxi" was a Volkswagen van with bad rings. He was delighted to find a place this much out of step with the strip mall consciousness that he and Sheila had all too thoroughly explored. He did not know, as he looked around, that he was seeking with some urgency, like a caterpillar, the particular stalk of milkweed on which to weave his cocoon.

Out of the taxi, through the blue cloud of smoke and the haze of dust, climbed a wiry, energetic woman with short blond curls. In a bustle of activity, she greeted them while trying to do six things at once. She was shaking hands, dropping off parcels in the freight shed, picking up other parcels and putting them in the van, running back to the VW to goose the throttle to keep it from dying, yelling at the dog to get back in the van. She was of middle years and her name was Deana. Once everything was packed she shooed the dog into the far back and asked them into the van. Sheila (with Lara in her arms), Ryan, and the realtor, climbed through the VW's side doors into the back seat. Bill sat in front with Deana. They continued to exchange a few pleasantries, asking about people they both knew.

Inside the van, the windows were still coated with summer dust. Condensation had eroded the dust into runnels that looked like the barancas of the Southwest desert as seen from the air. Ryan scraped a hole in the dust with his finger and looked through it as the old van kicked gravel all the way to the top of the hill. With a cloud of dust behind them, they passed a long inlet whose mudflats slept peacefully under the September sun. It was low tide, and even from the van, Ryan could see the sprinkle of white oysters out at the mouth of the bay.

They passed an abandoned three story log house where flat log rounds had been fixed with mortar between hand hewn posts and beams. The rounds had been split into hexagons and fit together like the cells of an enormous beehive. The house looked silent and empty eyed. The brick of one crumbling chimney had been laid in the shape of a teapot, the other looked like a coffee pot. Bill stooped low and pointed under the brows of the VW. "Tea Pot House," he said, "used to be a bootlegger."

Ryan was amazed at how rural Canadian speech was often so terse and confined to necessities. Often, when he went into a fit of verbal diarrhea, he was only acknowledged with a slightly interrogative "Oh yeah?" The ball was not tossed back, leaving him to fall into the silence of the landscape. He was insecure enough then to feel that his words were unimportant, like some kind of intrusion on a silent Knowingness—so much hot air. He felt these rural Canadians to be both wise and judgmental. He began toning down his speech, seeing it, through their imagined eyes, as frivolous university stuff. Gradually he would stop telling his stories, his jokes, his astounding facts. He would lapse into witnessing silence. As an old man, sitting at his writing desk, he would wonder if this silence—taken for wisdom—was really just not knowing how to respond. He would wonder if they felt as awed and uncomfortable around him as he did around them.

They passed a lake that had been flooded. Dead trees that had been left standing stood in its shallows like tall grey ghosts. Bill turned back to them and said. "Reservoir for False Bay. Dammed it to raise the waters. Pipeline. Four inch plastic." Sheila and Ryan nodded mutely.

They climbed a steep hill and traveled through a mixed forest—alder, fir, hemlock, and cedar. The gravel road gace way to smooth damp clay and was full of little rises and falls. Suddenly they dropped downhill past a collapsed corral and fence, past some old fruit trees, into a small open valley that was grazed clean by sheep. The road came to an intersection and they took a left down into the valley. At the intersection they passed a green rural mail box leaning at an angle. Most of its compartments gaped open, but a couple of rusty padlocks still hung off it like medals on the chest of a silent Canadian veteran.

Just past the intersection was the house that they had come to see. As they pulled into its short gravel driveway, Hal said, in his cheery realtor's voice, "This is it." It was a small house surrounded by trees and bushes, presided over by two huge fir trees with drooping branches.

They got out, released by their amiably frantic driver who promised to come back in time for them in to catch the afternoon ferry. As the van fluttered away into the forest, its sound fading through the trees, they sensed the immensity of nature all around them. Even Bill and the realtor seemed stunned. The clearing was loud with the song of birds, an opus magnum of carolling robins. The wind could not be felt in this sheltered spot, but they could hear it soughing through the tree tops on the ridge above. Sunlight filtered through the dust that the van had left behind.

Bill was the first to get his voice. He told them that in addition to driving the taxi, Deana was raising twelve children, kept a cow and delivered milk; that her husband had experienced some sort of religious conversion and was now living on a raft in the lagoon at the foot of the road. From the driveway they looked across the field and down the road. There was another house just before the road went into the forest. It was painted a faded pastel blue and surrounded by shrubs and a broken down fence. Across the road from it was a derelict shed with old plum trees clustered behind it. At the end of the clearing was a row of leafy alders with tall dark firs behind them. Always the forest. Above the tree tops, in the distance, a dramatic mountain rose like the humped back of a whale. Following Ryan's gaze, Bill pointed and said, "Texada. Next island over. Thirty-five miles long."

Ryan would have called the house a cabin or a shack. He had not yet learned the ways of realtors. It was one story, long and low, completely clothed with cedar shakes—roof and sides—the way a hen is clothed in feathers. It had only two small windows high up under the eaves and a wooden front door. Bill undid the small, weathered brass padlock that held the front door shut. The door was a massive thing, made from two layers of locally milled planks held together with bent over nails. It looked more like the door to a mead hall than to a small cabin. Inside, the house was dark and low. The wall and ceilings were panelled with rough sawn planks of local fir that had been darkened by years of wood smoke.

The redeeming feature of the cabin, invisible from the road, was a row of plate glass windows—set between cedar posts—that looked out on a little bluff that had been preserved in its natural state. The effect was of walking into a building that had nature itself as its inner courtyard. Ryan stepped to the windows and saw the trunks of the two huge firs that towered over the house like cloaked guardians. Late morning sun filtered in shafts of light through their branches. Closer to the house, at the foot of the little bluff, was a juniper tree—small for a tree, large for a juniper. It had been pruned into the shape of a menorah, a living Jewish candlestick with all its branches curving in one plane up to the sun. Bill pointed it out with pride, "Took me some years to get it that way."

Bill pointed to the blank wall behind them, with its one little window high up under the eaves. "In the country, when a car goes by, everyone

89

runs to the window to see who it is. We deliberately did not put any windows on this side of the house, to have our privacy."

It was a house with its back turned obstinately to the road; a house that was introverted, that had turned away from the rural pleasures of gossip; of knowing of who was driving down the road; of speculating about what they might be up to.

There was a propane stove, a refrigerator, a tiny dark bathroom with another high-up window, a sink, tub and toilet, all of which drained into a home-made planked septic tank that Bill called "Mohamet's coffin." Next to the bathroom was a cavernous back bedroom. The whole thing sat on a massive solid slab built from piled stone and concrete. Bill stamped his foot and said "This'll be here for a thousand years." It seemed to be a selling point for the poet turned building inspector.

They left the house and walked down the long slope of the field, scattering a flock of feral sheep that were keeping the field mowed. The sheep had long shaggy coats from which hung clay balls—dingle berries— that clacked like dead bells as they ran. Only three or so of the lands 17 acres were cleared. The rest went back into a mixed forest of fir and alder with a few old maples thrown in. They walked into the woods along a small trail through salmon berry bushes that rose to twice a person's height. The property went back a long way. Bill took them to see the corner post, but a huge fir snag had fallen on it, smashing the white survey post.

Coming back, Bill showed them the corner next to the road. The land included the scraggly stand of plum trees but not the shed, which belonged to the house across the road. There was also a six foot square well covered with planks. They pulled off a few of the thick planks and gazed down into its deep watery hole.

Somewhere, on their walk back through the woods, or waiting for Deana's van to come while Bill and Hal did repairs, Ryan and Sheila decided to put in an offer on the house. They wanted to talk about it with Bill when they got back to the other side. Hal advised against it: he said, "It's never good for the seller and buyer to negotiate face to face." They insisted and so they met over tea at Bill's house. His friend's paintings of islands and waves still hung on the wall. They made an offer and tried to bargain but it was of no avail. Bill seemed firm on his price and in no hurry to sell his land.

They went back to Vancouver but the land and the dream of having a homestead stayed with them. For Sheila it was not like Argenta, seven hundred and fifty kilometers from Vancouver. It was closer to civilisation. It seemed to her that maybe they could have the best of both worlds. The thought of moving again, of escaping their troubles, began to inspire and fill them both with excitement. As autumn turned into winter, there were several months of phone negotiations. Finally, in this age before fax machines, papers were mailed back and forth and they were the owners of seventeen acres and a cabin on Vasquez Island.

13
Ryan And Sheila

It was satisfying to own a cabin out on the island. Ryan wasn't bothered by the smoke, by the angry Greeks, by the vacuum of his and Sheila's relationship anymore. Instead, he made the rounds of the used tool shops that were always down by the waterfront in the seedy part of town. Thriftily he bought the shovels, saws, hand-tools he would need out beyond where the electricity flowed. The endless rains of winter poured down around him as he shopped. Rainwater flowed in the city's streets, through its gutters and back to the sea. Vancouver reminded Ryan of a surfacing submarine with runnels of water streaming off it, or Atlantis sinking in torrential rain amidst rising seas. He could never decide which.

Ever since a cataclysmic vision in San Francisco, Ryan had distrusted the civilisation that kept him afloat. It seemed like a thing of the moment, a mayfly. He wanted to get back to basics, something he could trust. Just the thought of their new cabin sitting quietly in its clearing brought him peace of mind as he searched for tools. Some of the tools were new, like the blue Homelite chain saw, the steel wedges, the sledge hammer, and the red wheel barrow upon which so much would depend; some were used, like the antique doublebit axe-head into which he fit a new handle. He had learned how to do that in Argenta. The challenge did not daunt him. He assembled his stash.

Their new place on Vasquez seemed a compromise between the remoteness of Argenta and the readymade world of Vancouver; between doing everything from the ground up themselves, and the ease of driving to the door, flipping on the lights and kicking back to watch TV.

The rusty, plunging ferry was the gatekeeper: few people were willing to go where they couldn't take their car. Of those who came from the other side, only a few stayed for more than an afternoon. They walked up the road and looked at Mud Bay. At low tide it was lavishly sprawled out, exposed like a fertile goddess with her legs open. It smelled of seaweed and iodine. Its shores were lined with oysters. Sometimes they walked a little further to see the chimneys of the deserted Bootlegger's House. They went inside and stared out its glassless windows at its sheep-grazed fields.

In the end, they looked at their watches and walked back to The Sea View Room to have a beer and hamburger before the ferry came. They talked softly, looking out its melancholy windows toward the tiny juniper covered islands at the mouth of the bay. They watched the locals strut in and listened to them talk about the weather, about fishing, about the engine parts they were trying to find at the dump, about how maybe there was a good transmission in that wreck up at the end of Centre Road.

It was a relief when they saw the green hull and white cabin of the ferry round the point. They paid their bill, left a tip, and walked down the planked wharf to meet it. They watched as one or two locals unloaded their boxes of groceries and bags of hardware. The natives were not friendly or informative, just busy, in a hurry to carry their things up to their rusty trucks.

On the boat, if the weather was good, the visitors stood on the back deck to escape the perennial smell of barf in the passenger cabin. Before they returned to their own world of heated houses, plumbing, TV, every sort of diversion, they wanted to get one last view of this island that was so wild and unpeopled, so hidden away in its folds of forest and rocky bluffs. They shivered and buttoned their coats as the island disappeared behind them. Couples sometimes held each other. From the shore they became dots in the distance, vanishing points in the widening V of the boat's wake.

Ryan's first trip out to the new cabin was with their old friends Celia and Dave. They came to Vancouver at the end of winter bringing their baby boy, Thompson. In the little northern California town from wence they had all come, they had been such good friends They had lived near each other and had often eaten at each other's houses.When Sheila and Ryan walked in the hills, they could sometimes hear Dave and Celia's little band practising. Celia's bass carried the most, reverberating the whole house like a giant loud speaker. Celia and Dave were younger than Sheila and Ryan, yet, Sheila and Celia—the young and the much younger woman—had shared their angst about their lives, about their sense of impending doom, about the dissatisfaction with the motions they were going through.

Together again in Vancouver, they shared a blissful reunion from that earlier time. Dave and Celia brought California with them. At night they drank red wine together. Dave brought tapes of the latest rock music and pointed out intricate themes in the music, rewinding certain sections again and again so they could hear what he was talking about. Celia was intensely searching for meaning beyond her daily activities. At eighteen she was full of laughter and full of grief. She was fine boned with a speedy nervous energy that could put a whole house back together in minutes after the children had torn it apart. She and Sheila stayed home with the children and talked intensely while Dave and Ryan went in search of more tools. After dinner the four of them shared relationship tips about how to get through fights, deadlocks, and the ups and downs of marriage. They all smoked cigarettes. At the end of the night Celia and Dave spread out their sleeping bags on the floor of Sheila's elegant apartment

Dave was more easygoing than the rest of them. It was hard for him to be cooped up listening to gloomy conversations. He liked to do things. Even sitting in a chair, his thin body vibrated with the energy of movement. He had straight brown hair, a broad forehead above eyes that laughed but also slid away when the conversation got too intense. For Ryan, Dave's simple stance toward life was a refreshing antidote to the angstful convolutions in which he, Sheila, and Celia all seemed to flounder. He was glad of Dave's presence.

Dave and Celia were eager to go to the island and see the new house; Ryan was excited to show them—and eager to see it again himself. They decided that for this journey just Dave, Celia and Ryan would go: Sheila said that she would rather stay home with Thompson and Lara than try to organise everything that would be needed for a journey with them. Dave, Celia and Ryan organised the bicycles, the sleeping bags, the food and clothing that they would need for a weekend. They packed candles, a kerosene camp stove, canned food, sandwich makings, warm sweaters, and rain gear. Ryan improvised rain gear for Dave and Celia from sheets of plastic. As Californians, this kind of clothing was unfamiliar to them. It would be Ryan's first time back to the island since they'd been shown the cabin—this time without a taxi ride, without a guide.

The first day the three of them quickly rode their bikes the three and a half kilometers from the ferry to the cabin. After a look around and a lunch of bread, cheese and salami, they left their packs and pedaled off to explore the dirt road that went past Ryan's house down into the forest.

They rode past giant-old firs, past ancient split rail fences. They threw stones on beaches so lonely and isolated that the only thing they could see were the snowclad tops of distant mountains rising above the cerulean horizon. Ravens fluttered above them and commented on their coming and going.

On their way to one such beach, guided by the topographical map that they folded and unfolded at every intersection, they met Mike, an old man standing on the road in front of his tumble-down homestead. Thistles and alders were growing up in the tall dead grass of his fields. Beneath last summer's dead vegetation, spring's young green grass was already beginning to push itself up. Mike wore clothes with rips in them and smelled of mildew. His dark Semitic eyes were framed by owlish horn rimmed glasses. He had a trim grey beard and a fringe of grey hair around his bald head. Except for the rotting clothes he could have been some vacationing business man up at his country place, someone used to making decisions and pushing people around. In reality he had spent most of his adult life on the island. Forty years.

He gave them a little tour, seemingly wanting to talk to someone. Whenever they started to ease away from him, to make the body language that signals the end of a conversation, he put his hand on Ryan's arm to hold him a moment more. He grabbed their attention like the ancient mariner, taking them into the fossilised store on his property. As he unlatched its locks and lit a lamp, he told them that it hadn't been open for business for thirty years. They ventured into the dark building where all the windows were boarded up to prevent thieves from entering. Mike held up the lamp for them so they could see the neatly stacked cans that lined the shelves. Ryan noticed that there were brown rust spots spreading on the Gerber baby's cheeks. There were also ancient jars of canned vegetables, faded to yellow over the years, made by Mike's wife, "before she died," he said. After the store tour, Mike took them down the steep driveway to his beach house, through more giant fir trees that he had preserved from logging.

The house was an unpainted log structure that stood guard over a long curve of beach. Mike said he had been blighted, stopped in his tracks, by his wife's death, by her being carried off in a pine box. He didn't sleep here anymore, he said, the waves were too loud for him at night, so with his lantern he went back up through the giant trees and slept in the house that was attached to the store. He gave them the grand tour of the beach house. He showed them the upstairs, the bedroom where he and his wife had once slept. As he swung the door open, Ryan stepped in behind him and caught a glimpse of a figure swathed in cloth and plastic lying on the bed. He turned to look back at Celia, who was standing behind him in the hallway. Later she told him that his eyes had gone round with horror.

They extricated themselves and got back up to Ryan's new house just before dark. In the dimming light they gathered enough bits and pieces of wood to get a fire going in the ornate cast iron heater. The fire flickered eerily through the heater's many cracks. The candles they brought smoked feebly while the Primus hissed as it heated their canned chili con carne. On the way back, he had told Celia and Dave what he had seen in the bedroom and they were all really scared. They had developed a theory that Mike had really killed his wife and secretly lay beside her mummified form at night; that, dressed in his ragged torn clothes, almost dead himself, surrounded by rotting cans of baby food and ancient jars of green beans that his wife had preserved, he had developed the urge to confess, to reveal his secret, and that he had picked them, strangers, with whom to share the awful truth.

Now, they imagined that he was regretting his indiscretion; that he was coming up through the dark woods with a smoky lamp, maybe even standing outside the door listening to them talk about him. In their imaginations he had a rifle in his hand, or a butcher knife, or an axe. The wind soughed outside, the fire popped and hissed, there was no phone, no car to climb into, no neighbour next door to whom they could go. There was only this clearing that stood alone in the moonlight and wind. There was no real lock on the only door, only a flimsy little latch. None of them slept that night. Ryan heard the slightest creak, the slightest stirring. He listened for the door to open and the killer to enter.

The next morning, bleary-eyed, the three of them sat around the table and drank coffee full of grounds which they had brewed in their only pot. They were alive! The terrors of the night before had vanished with the first light.

In the years that followed, after getting to know Mike, Ryan took a friend down to visit Mike's beach. Mike took them on the same tour. He told them the same stories he had told Ryan years before. Once again the bedroom door swung open and this time Ryan looked carefully, heart on fire but eyes as cold as ashes. He saw that in reality there was only a rolled up mattress on the bed, protected from dust or the leaky roof by a sheet of plastic. He laughed to himself about how in the loneliness of the island, in the strangeness of their first meeting with Mike, the bundle on the bed became a symbol of death, decay and murder; a story about clinging to what was no longer alive. It occurred to him that everybody slept with their corpses to varying extents; entered the land of the dead little by little, with a regret here, a memory there, a little memento from a vanished friend, until they found themselves next to the dead body of a beloved. Failing to let go, failing to move on, they wrote stories about the past.

But now, drinking their coffee and poring over the topographical map, they planned their day. Dave pointed out a road that ran sideways across the middle of the island. It wound past some lakes and ended at the foot of the island's only mountain. There were other high bluffs shown on the map, but this was the only one that was actually called a mountain. Ryan remembered the story that the people outside Octopus Books had told him about the hermit girls who lived at the foot of the mountain. He was sure this was the road. The distance seemed doable and they decided to go. They threw their lunch—Italian salami, French bread, Monterey jack cheese, a can of sardines, a few apples—so California Italian—into a bag and headed off, rattling down the gravel road on their borrowed bicycles.

The main road down the island was a mixture of ups and downs. "Like life," Dave laughed. They enjoyed the not too hard peddles up and short giddy coasts down. Today, as they bicycled along in the late winter sun, the fear of the previous night had evaporated like morning mist. They felt more than a little foolish about having been so scared by a little old man. "Maybe it was just rolled up bedding," Ryan said.

To Celia this freedom from her child was rare and wonderful. She pedaled along slightly behind Dave and Ryan's shouted conversation, apparently enjoying the solitude of her distance from them. She enjoyed looking into the dark green forest that was so full of ferns and old stumps. She had been with Thompson constantly for the last three years. Dave left their home to work, to make money, but she stayed and cared for their baby.

Celia and Dave had become lovers while they were both still in high school. After Celia's father died, she was left at home with Guilana, her lonely and depressed mother. It had been through their Italian mothers that Celia and Ryan had known each other for most of their lives. Dave worked part time for Guilana in the deli that she owned. That is how he met Celia and started dating her. Guilana, in her loneliness, enjoyed having Dave's charming, manly energy around the house. As things developed, Guilana let Celia and Dave sleep together in Celia's little bedroom at the end of the hall. He was the first man that Celia had been in relationship with. She was only fifteen.

The sexual revolution had extended itself even to repressed, guilt ridden, Italian mothers. It was as much about the zeitgeist as about her own repressed needs that Guilana allowed her daughter to sleep with Dave under her own roof. "Kids will mess around," she said. She thought of her own sexual experiences high in the mountains above her village, where the children took the sheep to pasture every day; where the older boys took advantage of the younger girls. She remembered the rape she underwent, and the small coin they gave her to keep her mouth shut. She remembered the guilt with which she carried it for fear her father would find it and ask her where she got it. She remembered the mossy stone under which she finally hid it, the stone under which it probably still lies, a tiny horrible secret in the mountains of Liguria.

When Guilana was twelve, her parents moved from the mountains to the city of Lavagna to open a store. Guilana was tortured by guilt and by the visions of hell that gleamed from the flaming murals in Liguria's ancient marble churches. One day, as she walked with her family, she saw the devil looking down at her from a slate roof. He was black, scorched and scaly. The coils of his reptilian tail anchored him to a chimney. He pointed down at her and in a soft hissing voice said, "I will get you." Her parents were aware of nothing. They were just ahead of her, talking about how much squash to buy for the store, and how much they should pay for it.

That was all behind Guilana. Now she lived with her daughters alone in the house that her dead husband had built for her. It was on top of a hill around which suburbs had been stamped down like identical circuit boards. She and her children were lonely misfits in a land of identical houses and identical people. Her son, Josh, had gone to college, of which she was glad, but she thought he was using drugs there. She did not like the people he was hanging around with. He said they were OK, but she knew a thing or two.

Was it not better, she reasoned, if her daughter was going to have sex, as young people will, to have it under her own roof rather than in the backseat of a car? Wasn't this better than what she went through, up in the hills above her village, while tending *lei pecori*, with no adults around, no one even to call out to when things went bad?

Guilana was no longer a Catholic, at least in her own mind. She had left the church long ago when a priest slammed the confessional door in her face. She had been reading Plato at City College in San Francisco then. At confession she told the priest about doubts that she was having after reading him. She was struggling for some way to reconcile the world view of the Greek philosophers with what she had learned in the marble churches. The priest, the confessor, was furious. He yelled through the screen of the confessional "How dare you read this without the the church's permission?" She left. She decided that she would not make her future husband convert, that she would not raise her children Catholic. For the rest of her life she wandered through Protestant churches looking for the connection with God that she had once had amidst incense, stained glass, and Latin chanting. She did not find it. She drank grape juice instead of wine.

She knew that she must get Celia some birth-control. Together they went to a doctor at the bottom of the hill, mother and daughter sitting in a waiting room full of people with colds and flues. She was deeply ashamed, conflicted, at allowing her daughter this freedom. She did not go to their family doctor, an affable alcoholic who had freely dispensed whatever drugs her dying husband had craved; who would have given them whatever they wanted. She did not want him to know. They picked someone from the phone book and descended into the suburbs. Unfortunately, the doctor turned out to be a rabid Catholic. He read Guilana and Celia the riot act: he impugned Guilana's morality for allowing her daughter to have sex under her own roof. "What kind of mother are you?" he asked, "Turning your daughter into a whore, how dare you."

"How dare you," cropped up again. They fled together, not quite covering their faces. Celia did become pregnant. She toughed out a half year of being the pregnant girl at school, and then dropped out. She and Dave married and rented a tiny house in Fairfax where they became neighbours and best friends with Sheila and Ryan. She was fifteen and three quarters.

Today, only two trucks passed the other way as they bicycled along to see the mountain at the end of Centre Road. Their drivers waved to them in a friendly way. They had learned, in their one and a half days on the island, that it seemed to be a rural custom to wave at everyone you passed on the road, a kind of no-risk act of community.

Yesterday they had asked the store keeper how to get to the mountain. He had told them to turn up the road whose sign said Drummond Road but that everybody called Centre Road. This seemed to be yet another oddity of rural communities, that the names on the road signs were not the names that people actually called the roads. What if everybody wore a sign on their forehead but it wasn't what they actually were? What if the sign on Ryan's forehead said George, he wondered; what if the poet had "psychopath" written on his, and the psychopath "poet?" How would that affect everyone's life?

After half an hour of peddling they came to the road. It was part of a four way intersection with Main Road. One of the intersecting branches headed down to the water, which they could just see glimmering through the red haze of budding alder branches. The sea sparkled through the bare tree tops like a lake in a Group of Seven painting. The other crossroad went steeply uphill, through an arch of tall bare maples, into a dark forest. Unlike neatly gravelled Main Road, it was narrow with a surface of native rock and clay.

It looked as though the two man road crew could only keep Main Road smooth and gravelled, and that maintenance on the side roads was minimal. Dave, Celia and Ryan stood on their bikes and unfolded the map on their handlebars. The day had turned beautifully clear with a cold gentle wind blowing steadily from the north-east. They had left their plastic rain sheets back at the house.

According to the map what everyone called the 'south end' was really the east end. The island really lay east and west in the Gulf, but, because of its long and narrow shape and the longitudinal nature of Main Road, everyone seemed to refer to the west end as the north end and the east end as the south end. It was like the convention of maps where the north end is always up. This was yet another disorienting oddity. Being on the island was a bit like going through the looking glass into a place where nothing was quite what it seemed. It was fun, a world that had its own laws—even its own compass points—separated from the rest of the world by water. What else would they find, Ryan wondered, in this strange and wonderful place where they had decided to live?

They dismounted and pushed their old three speeds up the steep hill. The island was still alive with water; somewhere down among the ferns the sound of a creek, along with the hundred rivulets that fed it, rang in their ears. Around them were giant-old alders with great clumps of moss wrapping their white trunks. The moss clumps protruded from the trees and looked like the faces on totem poles. They could see Raven, Bear, Beaver and the faces of protohumans looking wide eyed down at them from the wet forest. It was as though there were spirits in the moss faces on the sides of the trees. Everything was covered with dew and raindrops.

They reached the top of the hill, mounted their bikes and coasted down to another creek. On either side of it they could see abandoned fields and broken down houses through the bare trees. They pushed their bikes up another hill and walked silently under gigantic virgin fir trees. At the side of the road there was a cedar snake fence that seemed to be the boundary to a well preserved homestead. Through the old-growth trees they could just see a small jewel-like lake that was framed by the cliffs of the mountain. The map said the mountain was only 1130 feet tall, but it rose majestically above the twisted limbs of the ancient firs. Old maples dotted the hilly fields around the lake. An immaculately maintained farmhouse sat on a little hill above the lake. It was painted a deep red that stood out against the green fields.

Someone had clearly preserved this homestead, the ancient maples around it, the old firs that ran up the side of the mountain. Dave, Celia and Ryan leaned on their bikes and gazed at a beauty that was not a completely wild beauty, but the beauty of humans and nature living in harmony, mutually embacing each other. It was rare in North America. They were aware that they were gazing back into another time when everything had been different.

They continued on the road as it snaked and turned. It came out of the forest, ran past a modern pan-abode house, ran past the wreck of a derelict backhoe that stood with its jaws open like a tyrannosaurus that had been frozen by freezing clouds of descending volcanic gas. The mountain now towered over them; eagles soared in the sky above it and ravens passed their messages back and forth in the old growth trees that lined its flanks. Birds of light and dark. From a rise where they paused to rest, Dave, Celia and Ryan could see Vancouver Island across the waters of Georgia Strait. Little plumes of smoke were rising from its pulp mills.

As they coasted down the rocky curved road past tranquil meadows full of grazing sheep, past roads that went off into nowhere, the mountain loomed ever higher above them. Suddenly, as they neared the mountain's base, the road ended revealing a cabin in a clearing. Ryan knew at once that it was the cabin that the people at Octopus Books had told him about, the cabin where the hermit girls had served them berry pie. The cabin had taken on mythical proportions in Ryan's mind.

It was surrounded by old apple trees whose bare winter branches looked like arms raised in supplication for the return of the sun. A slight curl of smoke came from the rusty stove pipe that stuck out of the cabin's roof. Plastic had been stapled over its windows. Everything around had been cleaned up. Ryan expected someone to come out at any moment, to say hello, but no one came. They shouted hellos in their most friendly and musical voices, but it was clear that the cabin was empty, with just the remains of the morning's fire smouldering in the stove.

Behind the cabin, out from the shade of the apple trees, someone had fenced a garden with fishnet and recycled page wire. Among last year's ragged cornstalks, they had begun to turn the soil. It looked fierce, black, and sublime in its potency; open to the sky to receive the vivification of sun and rain.

Ryan got off his bike, letting it fall to the ground, and walked to the garden. Two rows of peas were already sprouting in the dance of spring. Walking over to the cabin, he peered through the blurry plastic windows, holding his hands around his eyes to diminish the reflections. Inside was an immaculate little world: an old table, cups on shelves, two beds neatly covered with bright cloths, an ornate antique cook stove, two guitars hanging on the wall, a broom leaning in the corner. A print of a Flemish Christ, head emanating light, hands out in blessing to his supplicants, also hung on the wall. Ryan turned from the house and looked out at the equally immaculate clearing, at Dave and Celia, at the mountain. The mountain towered over them, aloof, impartial, majestic.

"It looks like nobody's home," he said, and looked back into the house. It was like looking into the three bear's cabin, like spying on a secret world. Just then, the sun went behind the mountain and a wave of cold and shadow spread across the clearing. Tiny wisps of smoke still curled from the chimney. Ryan rummaged through his pack to find a gift he could leave and found the can of sardines, all he had to offer. He left it on the weathered doorstep.

They rode away through the lengthening shade, past the homesteads and lakes, through the forest of moss faces, along Main Road toward their own little house. They looked forward to starting the evening fire.

The magical beings with the gold and copper hair had not deigned to appear, but he had seen their home. They did exist. Perhaps they were on the other side, disguised as ordinary women buying things they needed, or down at the beach digging clams or gathering oysters; or perhaps they had changed into birds and had been watching from the trees, giggling softly to themselves. He did not know. The mechanical wheels of their bicycles crunched through the gravel of Main Road. They were headed home.

Tonight they slept easier. Last night the fear of devils had kept them awake. Tonight they slept to visions of angels. Ryan had told Dave and Celia what the people at Octopus Books had told him about the magical beings—the hermit girls—who lived at the foot of the mountain. Tomorrow, Dave, Celia, and himself would shoulder their packs and leave Ryan's little house. Celia and Dave would go back to California; Ryan would continue his preparations to move here—to become a magical being himself, living in a cabin on one of the lonelier Gulf Islands.

The next day they simply rose and packed. They locked the door behind them with the old brass padlock and began the pedal to False Bay. After some mild uphill through the forest, it was a long downhill coast to the bay. A few trucks raced by them at the last minute.

They loaded their bikes and argued with The Captain who wanted to charge them two dollars for each bike. "You didn't charge for them on the way over, why should we have to pay for them on the way back?"

"I don't give a good god dam," he said, "Leave the fucking bikes if you want to, it's the finest-kind with me." They paid the six dollars rather than continue to argue with this obviously hung over being who stared at them with the protuberant eyes of an underworld god.

On the back of the boat they watched the island disappear behind them. Celia and Dave were excited for Ryan. What an adventure he and Sheila were on. Maybe in summer, they would come up and stay with them; maybe look into living here themselves. They were excited about the possibility of living near each other again.

It would not happen. Unbeknownst to Celia and Dave, life would tear them apart and take them in other directions. It would be many years before Dave found his way back to the island and Celia would never come again. But now they laughed together, bundled in their wool clothes against the cool sea winds. The boat rocked like a cradle and they laughed about crazy Mike and how scared they had all been. It now seemed stupid. "We've watched too much Alfred Hitchcock," said Celia.

They were quiet for awhile and Ryan wondered about what the island had presented to him, about Mike, about the girls at the foot of the mountain, about The Captain. They were all a part of his interior landscape now, one of the stories of the world that he filed away in a little chest that he carried around in his head. Now he folded these latest stories and put them back in their drawer again. He would take them out and look at them many times in the course of his life.

Then his thoughts began to move forward again, prompting him to talk about filling up the car, about the ferry schedule to Vancouver, about how Sheila might be doing with the kids. They were all looking forward to having a big breakfast of eggs and hash-browns, complete with bacon or sausage, when they got to the other side.

Ryan opened the chest in his head and looked in a little drawer called "maps and schedules." He visualised the road from French Bay to Departure Bay where the big ferry left on every odd hour. He checked his watch. "We'll have about forty-five minutes for breakfast."

"That should be plenty," said Dave.

Celia snuggled up to Dave and said "I'm hungry."

14
Alone

Early one summer Sarah and Nicole came to camp and explore. With packs on their backs they walked Vasquez's gravel roads, unfolding their map and turning left or right as impulse guided them.

In late afternoon they walked up a road that took them through a virgin forest whose fissured fir trunks rose like columns into a lofty canopy. They were stunned by the immensity of the trees, had never seen anything like them before. Through them, they saw a small lake surrounded by fields. In the middle of the fields slept a small red farm house that looked unoccupied. Above it rose a dramatic mountain, sheer, basaltic, and covered to its shoulder with trees. Mountain, fields, forest, homestead and sky were all mirrored in the lake. It was like a crystal ball, holding within it a pristine world, invitational and serene.

At the very end of the road, past the lake, past the homestead, past the virgin forest, under the mountain, they found an abandoned cabin with empty glassless windows. Around the cabin was an orchard of verdant old apple trees. The grass around the cabin and under the trees had been neatly clipped by the grazing feral sheep. The cabin's door was flung open and odds and ends of pots and pans were strewn about. The sheep scattered as Sarah and Nicole entered the clearing.

They leaned their packs up against the cabin and decided to camp here, at the foot of the mountain. By some impulse, they began to clean the place up, gathering some of the wild scotch broom, originally planted by early settlers to feed their chickens, to fashion a broom and sweep the cabin. They picked up the clearing, piling all the junk in one place; placing useable pans and jars on the battered wooden counter inside the cabin. They built a small fire and cooked their dinner. It felt more like home than anywhere else they'd been.

They stayed in the open house all summer, going to the "other side"—the town across the water—from time to time to fill their packs with food. When summer ended they made another trip and came back with tools and building supplies. Once again they rode the rusty ferry that took no cars. The Captain carried himself with the extreme dignity of someone who had been drinking when no one must know. The silent deckhand wore camouflage gear, his collar pulled up to his ears, the bill of his camouflage cap down over his eyes.

The day had been calm. There weren't many people aboard, so Sarah and Nicole each lay on one of the blanket covered couches and let themselves be lulled to sleep by the thrumming of the engine and the rise and fall of the waves.

The boat basin from which this ghost ship came and went was called French Bay. Why? Probably because, long ago, a French man—probably meaning Quebecois—had lived beside the bay. He had not been known by his name, but simply by Frenchy, a generic name given to all Frenchmen in B.C. In recent times, when the Canadian flag was redesigned, a joke in B.C. was that it should have been 9 beavers pissing on a frog. Then, in apparent innocence, British Columbians expressed righteous indignation as to why Quebec kept trying to secede.

French Bay in the early seventies was a large gravel parking lot full of puddles in winter and dust in summer. Two or three government wharves descended to floats that were protected from the fierce winds of Georgia Strait by a large stone riprap. Mostly fish boats were tied to the floats, with only a few exiled pleasure craft mixed in. It was a hard working sort of place. Not a "marina."

Tourists—always interested in out of the way places—but not too out of the way—arrived on the dock in their campers and Winnebagoes, in their California Cadillac's with *How To Get Rich On Real Estate In B.C.* lying on the back window shelf. Subdivisions were going in apace and the road up island was festooned with signs that said "Lots for Sale." There certainly was.

The owners of these vehicles would stand wistfully on the dock and look out to what locals called "The Dark Island," so called because of its lack of electricity and lack of lights at night. There it lay across the water, like an inaccessible sleeping virgin clothed in forest. They watched the boat come in, tossing and bucking over the water, and were horrified to find out from the three or four people getting off—all of whom were deathly shades of white and green—that it *was* the ferry.

"Pardon me, can you tell me when the ferry is going to come?"

"This is the ferry."

The Captain simply glared at people who asked him questions. The deckhand didn't seem to hear them. Like old hillbillies, they didn't want people poking around. The island was their private realm, where, for whatever reason, they had wound up, far from the bright society of cars and shopping malls. They led their lives on an island off an island. Twice removed, you might say.

The tourists might as well have asked Charon a lot of curious questions about the underworld, when the next boat left, whether there was a laundromat and a place to spend the night, or at what time the boat came back. When they found that there was no way to bring their car over and no place to stay, they returned to their vehicles, wistfully, and drove back onto the restless highway. The boat pulled out without them. In the rise and fall of a Southeast gale, it rolled like a wounded whale; the blanket covered couches slid back and forth; waves broke over its decks; spray obliterated the wheelhouse. It made its way across the slate-grey, foam-crested, wine-dark sea, a few souls tossing in its belly, to the Dark Island that lay 17 k out across the water.

First time across. It was on this boat, in the flat calm of summer, that Sarah and Nicole had first come to the island. They had sat on the roof of the cabin in their flowing hippy dresses and stretched out to receive the sun, putting their packs like pillows beneath their heads.

Now, at the end of summer, they returned with boxes of building materials, bundles of blankets, packs of clothes, rolls of plastic, bags of tools. They were prepared to stay. They also brought with them a spirit of laughter and optimism that this far-away place had not known for a long time.

After the empty ferry was tied to the float, they carried their boxes up to the top of the wharf, leaving them in a pile while they waited for a ride at the small café/store/gas-pumps. Inside, a few locals drank beer and nibbled at the cheese plates—a few pieces of cheese, some potato chips, a slice of bread and three slices of butter pickle—that were served to comply with the law that booze could only be served with food. The locals talked about fishing, or how to repair the generator at the mouldering Legion. The Captain and the deck hand had already driven up the road in a truck that looked like an automotive extra from The Night of the Living Dead. It was not just out of churlishness that they didn't offer the girls a ride, but because they were going the other way. Everyone on the island knew that the girls had set up camp in the abandoned cabin at the end of Centre Road.

As the last of the men got up, he turned to them and, with the exaggerated courtliness of another time, doffed his railroad cap and asked "Would you young ladies like a ride?" Too polite to presume to appear to know where they were going, he asked, as he helped them load their belongings and opened the passenger door of his truck for them. The seat was ripped, there were hydraulic fluid cans on the floor and the cab was pervaded by the smell of diesel. Even though he was only going as far as Centre Road, he decided to take them all the way to the homestead. On the way, they asked him about some of the clearings and abandoned homesteads they passed. They began to hear some of the history of their new home. The creation myth: The first homesteaders... In the beginning…

His name was Ben and he was born on the island, second generation. He owned a mill and a way on which to launch the fish boats he built at the north end of the island. He was a success in the eyes of the world, owned a fleet of seiners, captained by his sons. Not bad for an island boy. All this they found out later, from other people, not from him.

As the truck jounced into the clearing, the sheep scattered into the surrounding woods. For Sarah and Nicole it was nice to see that their little house was still standing in its apple orchard. They had been worried about it while they were gone. Though they had only been away for a week, they were glad to come home to the peace and silence of their clearing. Their summer on Vasquez had changed them: they had looked forward to visiting the city, to eating ice cream, to drinking in a pub with friends, to having some good meals out, but after only a few days it had begun to seem frenetic and overwhelming to them. As Ben helped them to unload their bundles they thanked him profusely. His smile was expansive, his manner somewhere between parental and flirtatious. "Well ladies, give us a call if there is anything you need." He tipped his cap back on his head and, with a broad grin and final wave out the window, bounced back down the road.

Sarah and Nicole stood among their bundles. The silence was stunning. One thing they noticed about the city was that there was noise everywhere, the buzzing of transformers, the hum of refrigerators, the roar of traffic, radios, sirens and honking horns. Even in the middle of the night there was no silence. Here they lived in a great silence ornamented by birdsong and the sound of wind in the trees. Their own thoughts stood out like simple decorative curlicues. Their minds tended to fall into the silence, and in it they perceived things that they had never seen before. Their restlessness, their endless search for something to do stopped, and they just were who they were. I am that I am. They watched the slow procession of the sun across the clearing and the shift of the shadows that marked it. When they were hungry they ate. When they were sleepy they slept, when their garden needed weeding they weeded. It was all very simple and satisfying. As the last sound of Ben's truck vanished down the road, the jangled sense of the city began to drain out of them.

The late summer leaves on the old apple trees stood out in glistening precision. Without talking they picked up their bundles and moved them into the house. The sheep leaked back into the clearing and resumed their grazing. On the third trip back to the pile, Sarah picked up the roll of plastic and leaned it against the cabin, next to the pile of thin cedar battens that they had already split. She wiped a bit of sweat and dust from her forehead. The afternoon was warm.

Nicole bent over a yellow plastic bag that had "Revelstoke" printed in red on its side. She searched through it and pulled out a paper bag full of small nails. This was the moment they had been waiting for; this is what the whole trip was really about, getting plastic to put over the windows, nails to nail on the battens, and a hammer to drive the nails with so they could stay the winter. The summer had already turned crickety-clear, and there had been some light rains, precursors to fall, that had already brought up meadow mushrooms—Agaricus Campestris. Sarah bent over the bag and found the hammer. She couldn't wait to get started.

15
Alone

It was spring, or at least late February—winter's last gasp—when Ryan boarded the Vasuez ferry with a shovel, shiny and new, a Swede saw, an axe, a pack full of clothes, a box of food to last a week. He had not been back since his trip with Dave and Celia, and now he went to prepare things for when he, Sheila and Lara would move to their cabin on 17 acres. Pioneering, he left his family home at the Kitsilano apartment. February was when the only real winter might come, with snow and frozen lakes.

Ryan had sold his squatter's cabin to a Dutch woman, an artist. She would stay for several years and then, later, would follow Ryan to Vasquez, building a cabin at the north end of the island. Later, inexplicably, she would leave the island and join the Hari Krishnas—this intellectual, this artist—and dance in scarves in front of the Vancouver City Hall, the same city hall in front of which Ryan had seen the racoons screwing, a favourite place for public demonstrations of all sorts.

She would become a leitmotif in Ryan's life. They would occasionally meet on B.C. Ferries and he would always ask her if she was still wasting her time in the Hari Krishnas. Being a strong woman and not one to side-step an argument, even in her new-found spirituality, she would ask him if he was still wasting his as a "karmi" out in the world. These meetings took place over many years and it did occur to him that possibly he was wasting his life, but at least his life changed. At their various meetings he was a massage therapist, a Sufi, a Tai Chi student, a worker in a socialist food co-op, a teacher. She was always just a Hari Krishna. Sometimes he would not see her for years and years, and would think of her while riding the ferries, and wish that he would run in to her again. He missed these arguments.

The final time he saw her, she had given her bright young son, Wallace, over to the Hari Krishnas. She showed Ryan photographs of

Wallace wearing his hair in a top knot, Wallace wearing a dhoti, Wallace in white robes with a smear of sacred ash on his forehead, Wallace jumping joyfully into a river with other young devotees, Wallace chanting the Vedic scriptures that he was using his brightness to memorise and become an expert on.

Later, a friend whose brother had dropped out from on high in the Hari Krishna told Ryan that child abuse was endemic in these schools. After the swami died there had been a war between seven powerful personalities for leadership of the cult. There were law suits and even some shootings. Where was the Dutch woman now? Where was her son? Ryan would wonder.

Ryan was able to get a ride to his new house with all his bundles. With his still shortish hair, his academic beard, his good manners, he didn't look too much like a hippy yet. He had always been good at being polite and asking for things. Besides, the locals knew that he had actually bought the house which put him in a different class from a squatter. They also knew he had been a teacher, a highly respected occupation to island folk. They knew everything about everyone on the island and soon Ryan would too.

February had almost turned the corner into March, but there was still a hard frost each morning that took a long time to melt. The sun rose late over the fir trees around Ryan's cabin, cutting a low arc over the clearing. Ryan was surprised at how short each day was: just when the frost had finally melted away, the sun dropped below the treeline on the other side of the clearing and things began to freeze again. Each afternoon he left his shovel like a book mark in the dark black sod he was turning. He was "double digging" the plot where their garden would be, burying the turf two shovel lengths down so that it was too deep to push its way to the surface and take over again. The old-timers in Argenta had taught him that this was better than just throwing it out: as the turf broke down it retained water and provided nourishment for the garden's roots, keeping the soil deep and black.

Just before dark he got out his axe and Swede saw. In the chilled fading light, he approached the fallen-down house in the gulch behind the cabin, cutting enough of the old lumber to build a fire to warm his house.

Night came quickly in February. It was far darker and quieter than anything he remembered since childhood; it closed around him in star-twinkling, no-moon blackness. The silence was so deep that he could hear the kerosene wick hissing inside the lamp. The walls outside the lamp's circle were in a darkness illuminated only by flickers of light thrown through the seams in the firebox of the old wood heater.

From childhood he remembered such silence, remembered sleeping on an old couch on the porch of his Uncle Willy's cabin, Seldom Inn, high in California's Trinity Alps. Seldom Inn was far above the river on rutted roads that ran through dusty cattle country, through great open meadows and sparse forests of ponderosa pine—well beyond the lume of city lights. While his parents, his uncle, his sisters slept inside, he watched the night sky. To him, the night was most holy. In awe he awakened many times to watch the stars beyond the overhang of the porch. On his final wakening, when he saw the fading of the sky that portended dawn, he was disappointed that another night was coming to an end.

He remembered these feelings now as he listened to the deep silent night on an island far out in the middle of the sea, far removed from the lights of civilisation.

Alone. This was his first experience of *Alone* in a long time. He had been married too long. On long bus trips he would sometimes sit out a stopover by finding a bench somewhere downtown. He would savour being *Alone*, savour, in his imagination, what it would be like to live there, to start over somewhere where he didn't know anyone. There was something very savage and alive about it. Yet he knew that he also had another side that craved companionship, warmth, a wife to talk too, lovemaking. He knew that this side was stronger, and, wherever he went, he would find friends and a wife again, would settle into the warm mire of human relationship.

And yet at these times when he could savour, if only for a moment, *Alone*, he felt that there was an immense potential in it, a potential different from having babies and families. He had only spent brief moments in this state, like a climber who stands on a peak for a few moments before his oxygen begins to run low and he needs to start back down. Here on the island he was *Alone*.

113

Day after day, of his seven days away, he worked at the garden. The line of black soil grew broader each day. It felt good to be using his muscles again. Between diggings, he did small things around the house to ready it for their arrival. He swept the floors and cleaned the windows, piled the broken boards and things like kettles with holes shot through them into neat piles to be burned or disposed of.

He took short breaks and went on circling walks into the surrounding forest. During the days, when it got a little warm, there were bursts of frog music that came through the woods, choruses of frogs, such as he had never heard before, limbering up their voices for spring. In search of these voices, he traveled trails past shut up or abandoned houses. He walked through fields growing back in young alder to find swamps lined with cattails, whose soggy edges had been churned to mud by the wandering free range cattle. From deep in the swamp's heart, protected by this ring of mud, came the frog song.

There were only three or so cars going by on Main Road each day, mostly at ferry times. Wednesday and Thursday were particularly lonely as there was no ferry, no chance of retreat back to the warmth of his family, his wife, his baby daughter. There was no phone to connect with them. *Alone.*

There was just enough to do so that he didn't need to worry about his unfulfilled creativity that lay like a dormant seed within him. At twenty-three, he traveled under the curse of feeling misunderstood, of seeing his poems, his short life's work, sent back to him, tender shoots stepped on; he hid his treasured ego dreams inside himself, letting them occasionally peep out only to find that they were not greeted or acknowledged. Now, in the time to which he had arrived, the ego itself was highly suspect.

He did not know, as he prepared this little nest, that he was preparing it for himself *Alone:* That his family would come and shortly leave again; that without the movies, the Chinese dinners, the strolls through the galleries, the emptiness and lack of sustaining pleasure in his and Sheila's relationship would become all too oppressive. He did not know, as he cleaned and tidied, that he had come to a place where even his dreams, those treasured inner parts of himself, would die, here in this place of trees and ravens and abandoned homesteads.

So, *Alone*, he tidied his home, making the bed he would sleep in, unknowingly preparing for events that would rock him and shake the foundation of his life. It was spring, not mud luscious, but the ferocious spring of endings and new beginnings, of the last frosts that kill the last hopes. It was spring when the new shoots had not yet emerged from the fertile black soil. On this island February was the cruellest month. He sat *Alone*.

16
Ryan And Sheila

Before Vasquez. Before Vancouver.

The Red Ant, Ryan and Sheila's '59 Volvo PV 444 Station wagon, was heading down the west shore of Kootenay Lake, away from Argenta. It passed through Nelson and then up the long grade outside of Castlegar, threading through massive green mountains splashed with yellow by the early turning tamaracks. From the summit it coasted down the other side to Christina Lake.

In Argenta Ryan and Sheila had stopped using birth control. They had succumbed to the endless questions from Ryan's Italian relatives, "Well, when are you two going to have children?" Marriage seemed like a progression of things that you were supposed to do; that once having made the initial decision you were locked into a course of events: "first comes love, then comes marriage, then comes Sheila…" Ryan drove while Sheila held Lara on her lap. Mostly they thought their own thoughts as they drove along. Occasionally they talked or sang together.

On the grade outside Grand Forks, they looked down on the haunted ruins of Doukabor collectives. Their huge brick houses looked out glassless windows onto un-pruned orchards. Bears had broken down many branches, climbing to get apples that humans no longer deigned to pick. At one such collective they saw an old babushka, frail and grey, walking among trees that had been planted in her childhood. Tarps had been nailed over the roof of one of the houses, and she must have lived in the one or two rooms that still didn't leak. Pail in hand, her body full of history, she reached up for early Transparent Apples.

They continued to drive, past the slag heaps and Victorian buildings of Greenwood, past its single brick chimney that stood like a ghost of former times. They drove along the Kettle River, through grassland and ponderosa pine, past the lumberyard at Midway, which to Ryan's twisted

116

mind looked like a tree Bergen-Belsin where corpses from the surrounding forest were efficiently stacked.

They climbed the long S curves that rose from Rock Creek to the plateau above. The needle on the temperature gauge was in the red and steam was blowing out from under the hood. The heater was on to get that little bit of extra cooling for the engine. Ryan and Sheila had opened all the windows to survive in the double blast furnace that came from both inside and outside the car. It was one of the last really hot days of summer.

The old Volvo made it to the top with only one stop to let it cool down, and then, blissfully, they rolled through more ponderosa pine hills, past Bridesville, and then, coolingly, down another series of S curves into Osoyoos.

Just after Osoyoos, they passed an intriguing exit marked Nighthawk, a border crossing to the good 'ol USA, just a few miles away. To Ryan the name evoked the Vietnam War. Hawks and Doves were the names used to describe the opposing political factions of the war. In Ryan's mind this was a nighthawk, a hawk poised above the border crossing, ready to swoop down and devour unwary draft dodgers who were trying, under the cover of darkness, to break on through to the other side.

It was a time when many people just walked through the bush into Canada. They came with packs on their backs and followed some north-south river valley up into a country that they saw as a respite of freedom and sanity. They found their way to a highway and appeared as just one more hitchhiker on BC's tortuous web of roads. Then they disappeared. They found their way to Vancouver. They learned to end their sentences with "eh" and say "aboot" instead of "about." They learned to say "in hospital" instead of "in the hospital" and to say "on holidays" instead of "on vacation." They faded into their community and were sheltered by it. Some of them—the deserters—were connected to an underground railway that took them, through a series of small towns, to the east coast where they were spirited off to Sweden, a country which had no extradition treaty with the US. It was a lonely boat ride. They were spirited off to escape the Nighthawk that circled endlessly in the darkness above them.

There were whole river valleys that had been dammed and flooded, the result of the Columbia River Treaty, a onetime cash infusion from the U.S., in return for which B.C., the electric cash-cow, gave cheap electricity in perpetuity. American megalopoli sparkled brightly while whole towns, places like Deer Park and Needles, with their old homesteads and peaceful sculpted fields, sank into darkness beneath the rising waters. O, Moloch, Moloch, Moloch.

Refugees like Sheila and Ryan were finding log houses that families had simply abandoned, leaving the door open, leaving the furniture, leaving the wood stove. The houses were made from exquisitely dovetailed tree trunks squared with a broad axe. The strokes of the axe blade were still visible, marking the spot where, on some day long ago, in a sweaty clearing, the hand and eye of the builder had come together. The horizontal surfaces of the logs were flattened so they fit together closely. The spaces between were caulked with moss or rags or oakum so the winds wouldn't blow through. The roof beams were made out of peeled small trees, the roofs were of cedar shakes, covered with moss and lichen, but still, after all these years, repelling the rain and snow. The roads on which the wagons and jalopies had come and gone were now just trails in the forest with young trees coming up through their mossy surface.

The houses were like the ones in fairy tales, lost in the great silence of the forest. They came alive again with sheets of modern plastic stapled like cataracts over their empty windows. New lives sprang up inside them like thoughts inside an empty skull. Group marriages—the Slocan was famous for its group marriages—lived within houses that had been built by righteous, hard-working Christians. A thousand joyful and anguished experiments in love grew like ground cover in the old orchards. These new people fed themselves on apples planted by their forebears. They planted new gardens in clearings that had been hacked from the forest with hand tools; whose stumps had been pulled by horses.

The old homesteads were strikingly beautiful. They usually commanded a view of a lake, a valley, a mountain. The houses were exquisitely carved from the raw trees. Their occupants, seduced by the trade beads of Moloch, had walked away, gone off to some city where they could earn enough money to have a small part in the American Dream. Sometimes even the kettle had been left on the wood stove, considered unworthy by the vandals who had smashed the windows. Burner plates were scattered around the kitchen, waiting to be put back in their holes. Axe heads, handles rotted away like the ones in Chinese fairy tales, lay out

118

in the yard under the leaves of twenty winters. The fro lay buried in the leaf mould of the barn, waiting to be rediscovered. A new handle was fit, and it was put to work splitting shakes again.

There were even a few old-timers left, living hermit-like lives. Their children had left for the cities and by themselves they could not manage the land. Their homes had begun to fall apart; their barns and fences to sink slowly back into the earth. Still, they lived off the land and watched bemusedly as a generation of long haired, beaded, bearded, bra-less freaks moved into houses long abandoned; watched as they hacked gardens out of land that had grown only weeds for fifty years. The homesteads were so forgotten, so unvalued, that no one even came to kick the newcomers out.

The mountains were nurseries: the great rivers narrowed into spidery little creeks that charged down the mountain sides under summer moons. The salmon traveled far from the sea; laid their eggs in hidden creeks, where their fry sheltered, grew and hardened up before their journey back to the sea.

Likewise, the great highways branched into winding secondary roads. Sleek cars were replaced by logging trucks and pickups with gunracks in their back window. The roads wound up into Gilpin, Kaslo, New Denver, Salmon Arm, Farquar, Argenta, Johnson's Landing. From there they branched into dirt roads that ran up to the canyons and high shelves where more abandoned homesteads and cheap stony farmland awaited. The homesteads were like empty sea shells waiting to be re-inhabited by this new life-form that had travelled to them in second-hand vans with beads hanging from the rear view mirror, with their side windows covered by Indian bedspreads, with strange art painted on their sides. Their owners had come to live in a different way.

Ultimately the old timers swallowed their rancour, their closed mindedness, their worry about some of the weirdness that went on. In a generous overflowing of pioneer spirit, they began to help these newcomers. Perhaps they were simply happy to have someone to whom they could pass on their lifetime of learning; someone who was interested in their tale of self sufficiency.

And so it was that they showed them how to put new handles on old tools; how to build fences, with no money, to keep the deer and free range cattle from devouring their gardens; how to find the fallen cedars, left by

119

the loggers; how to dig them out from decades of leaves; how to split them into fence posts; how to use steel wedges to crack them open; how to make three foot wedges from thorn-apple trees to break open the crack. They showed them how to double-dig a garden, how to prune a tree, how to use the tools they found in the barn, how to trim a goats hoof, how to store the carrots, how to make compost, how to clean the chimneys, how to find the well. They told them the stories of the people who had made and lived on the homesteads before them.

The old timers learned to love these strange ones, passing on to them what they could before they themselves returned to the very soil which they had loved. It was as though their children had finally returned home, back from the belly of Moloch, vomited out, damaged, but willing to learn, willing to try again.

Sheila and Ryan had not completely burned their bridges to the establishment, but lived cautiously somewhere between it and the counterculture. In Argenta they had been given the old Coleman Cabin as their place to live. It lay down a long driveway below below the hairpin turn where the road swings back to the upper part of Argenta. At first they couldn't believe their good fortune. It was a classic Kootenay's house sitting on a sloping field just above the lake. The lake glimmered and winked at them through the fringe of birches just above its shore. The house itself had a peaked roof, complete with resident pack rat, and exterior walls of brown shingle. From the screened porch, a door entered directly into the kitchen, with its table, its windows, the welcoming glow of its wood stove.

They were given a chain saw to use, an old yellow Pioneer. They were loaned gardening tools and paid a salary of $75 a month for food and their other needs. Somewhere Sheila and Ryan had read that Quakers—they had researched it—used to believe that too much money corrupted people and distracted them from their intrinsic spirituality. Unfortunately, this belief had been used as a rationale for underpaying their workers. But it fit right into the spirit of the Kootenays, where Doukobors were regularly burning down the barns and houses of brethren who had become overly distracted by their material success.

For Sheila and Ryan, the small salary seemed like a good beginning step in the direction of spiritual simplicity. They spent their own savings for snow tires and long winter underwear. They bought themselves toques which were a novelty for California kids. They bought a tin heater to warm the house. It was exciting to be preparing for winter in this foreign country; to be living in a log house; to be heating it with wood they had cut, split and stacked themselves. It was exciting to be picking and storing the apples from trees that had been planted in the last century; to be hiding away from Amerika at the end of a valley in the Purcell Mountains.

Driving home from a late night poetry course in San Francisco, Ryan had had a vision of the twinkling San Francisco skyline being evaporated in the blinding blast of a hydrogen bomb, of all his little plans vanishing in the glare of the world's end. It was during the latter days of the Vietnam War.

The seeds of this vision had been planted during the Cuban Missile Crisis when he had sat up all night in Marin County, writing a paper in the mad inspiration of exhaustion, sitting at a desk facing east. Often he looked up at the darkened window panes, waiting for morning to show its colors, wondering if all of them would get through the night, wondering if a blinding flash would come from across the bay. Many people wondered that night.

Several years later, at a gallery and boarding house that Sheila and he had managed on the north coast of California, a rare and beautiful coastal lightning storm descended on them. It was two a.m. and the night filled with flashes and explosions like those in Dylan's *Chimes of Freedom*. Sheila and Ryan went down into the darkened kitchen and pulled back the curtains to better see the great flashes of light arcing over the ocean.

After awhile their guests came down, young women, teenagers really, who were enrolled at the local Art Centre, spending their summer learning how to make raku pots, mix glazes, and build a kiln. They were wrapped in their bathrobes, trembling in terror. Their boyfriends, who had snuck in during the night, came down too, equally shaken. They thought that the end had come.

Ryan and Sheila turned on the lights and made camomile tea with cinnamon toast, a sure, if temporary, cure for the apocalyptic blues. They sat around the kitchen table assuring these beautiful children that it was just a thunderstorm and helping them open to the beauty of it. They had been deeply moved to see the generation after them living through the same terror in which they had lived their own young lives.

These were strange times. Annihilation felt very real. The government seemed dangerously out of control. Three hundred thousand people marched down Market Street in San Francisco, completely filling it for as far as the eye could see. Buddhist monks were immolating themselves in Vietnam. A protester had incinerated himself with gasoline on the steps of the Department of Justice in San Francisco. Still the war went on.

It was hard to keep business-as-usual happening then, to grow up to be a welder, a doctor, a poet, a university professor. People gave way to crazy things, took desperate chances, followed the vanishing moment instead of the life-long plan.

At some point, Sheila and Ryan had packed their belongings into the Red Ant and headed for Canada. They had felt that it was not possible to lead a good life in the U.S. anymore; that if they stayed it would only be possible to sacrifice themselves, to live their lives in reaction to a war that seemed to be marching the U.S. into headlong destruction. As a conscientious objector, Ryan got an alternative service posting at a small Quaker school on Kootenay Lake. They had hoped that they could still make a life of their own in Canada.

Their dentist, Dr. Jack Rosenberg, who later wrote a book called Total Orgasm, and later yet founded a school of psychotherapy called Integrated Body Psychotherapy, warned them that they could not run away. He was a good and absolutely painless dentist who spent his spare time taking psych courses. He told them, rubber dams in their mouths, that they could not just go to another country and change their identity by changing their license plates. He told them that they had to stay and stick it out, bear the burden of their society.

They resented him for telling them this. They were twenty two and still childless. They found it hard to believe that they had a future. They went looking for one. They left.

In Argenta, they found themselves strangers in a strange land. All around them were back-to-the-landers, settling into gardening, goats, art, drugs and music; working naked in their gardens; playing guitars and singing to the moon from the front porches of their old houses; eating vegetarian meals pulled from the garden; skinny dipping in the lake. They had kaleidoscopically shifting relationships that made up in passion and angst for what they lacked in duration, relationships that were different from the stolidity and entrenched hostility that had characterised so many marriages of their parent's generation. Fritz Perls had laid down the relationship credo of the day: "I do my thing, you do yours. If we meet it's beautiful, if not it can't be helped."

Teaching was really only a small part of what Ryan did in Argenta. He also built stone walls, worked on the new student home, learned how to use a double bit axe to peel the slippery spring bark off fir poles, learned to use the same axe to cut flat surfaces on each side of the log so that one log could sit on another. He went on communal wood cutting trips with students and staff. They formed long human chains and tossed the cut and split rounds from hand to hand down the mountain and into the backs of trucks. At the school they formed another chain and tossed the wood from the trucks into the woodsheds. The stoves were like squat black gods that needed to be constantly propitiated by throwing wood into their hungry mouths. Thus fed they kept the icy forces of winter out of the classrooms. Sometimes on rainy days they would burn the chimneys—burn out the creosote before it could build up—to prevent the dreaded chimney fire. Standing by with hoses, they would pour kerosene down the chimney, light it, and then watch as small volcanoes of fire gouted from the chimneys and out over the roofs.

For Sheila, dissatisfaction began to grow at being left alone in the wilderness. Staying at home, pregnant and not quite a part of the school, she became a sympathetic ear to the students. They came up the trail through the orchard to visit her on their off hours. She poured out tea for them, and they poured out their dissatisfaction to her. She served muffins and jam, and listened to their complaints about the school and its rules, to their disillusionment about life, to their endless carping about the directors of the school. The wave of rebellion and psychedelia was crashing, even over this community that had placed itself in the wilderness, far from the corrupting forces of society.

Sheila felt impotent in the face of the student's angst which was too much like her own. She was frightened by the spirit of the community, its end-of-the-world self-sufficiency, its own freezer, its own walk-in cooler run with its own electricity generated by its own pelton wheel, its own Rube Goldberg crank phone system left over from another time, and most of all the scenarios of Armageddon that were on everybody's mind, the loose talk of "blowing the bridge" when the time came so that they wouldn't be overwhelmed by the hordes of desperate city folk who would come like locusts to eat whatever food the community had been able to store.

It was the ant and the grasshopper all over again, but in this version there were many more grasshoppers. They had been fiddling away in their luxury homes, watching TV, not paying attention to the coming winter. All the while their industrious country cousins had been piling away food for the karmic winter they knew was approaching. In this version the grasshoppers put down their fiddles and grabbed their guns. They climbed into their cars and took what they needed to stay alive.

The first encounter groups happened while Sheila and Ryan were in Argenta. Everyone was invited. They were led by a community member who had been to one out on the coast. The newer members of the community were trying to bring the older Quaker community into modern times, trying to heal the old issues that lay under the surface of their isolated community. They hoped that airing these old grievances would help all of them to become the loving, co-operative community that they assumed everyone wanted. Come together and love one another right now.

The invitation list included the old-timers, the children of those who had cleared the land and dug the irrigation system; the Quakers who arrived in the fifties with their ideas of Christian communalism, who built the cooler, the electrical system, the phone system; the Berkeley intellectuals who settled there for their own reasons; the latest wave of hippy drop outs. The old timers didn't come, the Quakers were pointedly invited and felt that they had to come, the Berkeley intellectuals hosted it, and the hippies came along for the ride. Far out, man.

Ryan understood little of what these all-night marathons were about, or what they were supposed to do, or even how to be honest. He did not dare to expose his inner world that was so full of pain, judgement, vainglorious dreams and shocking fantasies. He was convinced that all of this would only draw ridicule upon himself, hurt people and piss them off. As the poet said, "It would take a dump truck to unload my head."

Ryan faked his way through these painful evenings by doing a little of what it looked like the other people were doing. One night in the wee hours when people were shouting at each other and seemed to be getting nowhere, he crawled into a corner and went to sleep. He dreamed of a beautiful woman who came to him across a grassy field and invited him to shower with her. They took off their clothes and washed each other in an outdoor shower surrounded by men, women, children, parents and grandparents, who were eating picnics and singing to each other.

Sheila and Ryan went home in the morning, neither of them having talked about their dissatisfaction with the community, with each other, and with themselves. They were frightened by this process and drew more into their little world of coupledom, as uncomfortable as it was. They walked together down the early spring road, holding hands, tired from their sleeplessness and enjoying the morning sunlight. Their neighbour, Glen, one of the old timers, roared past them in his four-wheel drive truck that had pulled so many community members from ditches. He had not been at the marathon and was off to work, wearing his hard hat, the back of his truck full of tools. Always happy and pleasant, he smiled and waved at them.

Ryan would have liked to have been happy too. He began to dread going back to the Coleman Cabin at the end of the day. The walk itself was amazingly beautiful. Rather than the road, he took the old trail along the lake. It passed through an abandoned orchard whose bare branches, in the depth of winter, were covered with a tracery of crystalline snow. Snow fell silently in the dusk and the only signs of life, other than his own breath, were the tracks of the wild animals who had wandered through during the day. The dread came when he approached home and wondered what state Sheila was going to be in. Would he be hit by the waves of her dissatisfaction when he walked through the door? She had become the worm in his apple, always pointing out what was not working, rarely happy with what was.

They fought now, or spent their evenings in gloomy silence. He did not know what to do with her anger, the passionate intensity she aimed at him for taking the part of the school and not joining her in condemning its hypocrisy. He was cruel back.

Several months later Lara was born. As autumn began to close around them, in an attempt to pull their relationship together, they left Argenta.

And now, travelling wide-eyed along the back roads of B.C, they headed for their first Canadian city, Vancouver, hoping that they could build a life that satisfied them both; hoping to get settled before winter descended.

Tired, they continued their long journey through Keremeos (Keremeos Me Not on the Lone Prairie), along the Similkameen River, past the tunnelled rocks of Hedley, through Princeton, over the rainy mountains to Hope (there was always Hope); and then, as the sun tilted westward, glaring into their eyes, they drove along the long stretch of frenetic super-highway past Chilliwack, Mission and Langley; into the clustered towers and rainforest-modern of Vancouver.

17
Ryan And Sheila

It was not the smiling, benevolent Vancouver of summer, with long naked days at Spanish Banks; nor even the beautiful melancholy Vancouver of autumn where parting lovers walked through falling maple leaves on the little hill above Kits beach. All too soon it had become the austere slate grey Vancouver of winter.

It was Vancouver surrounded by forests so dark that the greens were almost black; forests smudged and softened at a distance by roving clouds of mist; forests in which the primal rituals of cougar, deer and bear still went on. Vancouver was a glistening city of light that had materialised like a fairy world only a century and a half before. It floated like a bubble on the primeval landscape, shining with radiance against the forests from whence it had come.

The wild animals saw it at night, shining through gaps in trees as they prowled their dark world. Cougars still wandered into town. They swam Indian Arm, shook themselves off as they climbed the stone ripraps of east Vancouver and walked past the grain elevators through the groaning harmonies of creaking trains. They sauntered into the city to see what it was about, feeling right at home, for, after all, it was an urban jungle.

Racoons screwed on the steps of city hall. On clear still nights, when the southeaster was asleep on its mother's lap, when the moon rose above Georgia Strait, you could hear the chanting and drums come floating down from the long houses in the north. Magic was still being made there. If there were words with the drumming, they would have said: "We were here first, we are here still, we will be here after."

That night, as Ryan and a young cougar explored this evanescent city of lights, a sifting of snow had begun to fall. Tomorrow, the mountains would rise like teeth above the dark forest, and the forest would be dusted white with snow. The air would reek with the fumes of oil furnaces and little black balls of soot would fall from the sky. At first the world would be pristine white; all the junk, all the candy wrappers, all the wine bottles and needles would be covered by this virginal bridal veil, but all too soon it would be churned into grey slush. In Vancouver, in winter, all colours sought grey.

As the storm closed, Ryan slowly climbed the steep slope that rose from False Creek into Kitsilano. His heavy Vibram soled logging boots—jaunty with their fringe of leather protruding from the bottom of each lacing—made lifting his feet hard work. As the lights of the city came on, the first snowflakes sifted down around him, staying for a moment on his woolen navy peacoat before melting into dark spots of water. He was dark, in his early twenties with shortish hair and a somewhat scraggly beard; here as a refugee from the Great-Country-To-The-South because he couldn't figure out how to deal with the death that that country was raining on the people of Vietnam.

This kind of winter was new to him. In California, where his great-grandparents had lived, autumn came as a quick swirl of falling leaves. With the first rains, the rolling hills lost their mane of dry grass and became brightly green. Creeks and rills appeared. Winter was simply a prolonged early spring. It was a time of rejoicing when the dry season ended and the enlivening water returned to earth. He remembered standing outside his and Sheila's old house in Oakland, face lifted, arms open to the sky, ecstatic at the first rain.

In Argenta, Ryan had gotten used to the freezes, the black ice, snow tires, studded snow tires, Stanfields, wood stoves, insulated snow boots and toques. Now in Vancouver torrents of water fell from the grey skies for days on end, sometimes driven by huge winds that buffeted the cliff-like high rises.

Ryan was an academic one step removed, which is to say, he was out in the world trying to live by the map of ideas that he had built during his 16 years in school. Rather than be elevated by the stored treasures in the repositories of western culture, Ryan had discovered a lot of very unpleasant things. Mostly he had discovered death. He had discovered that the democracy that his immigrant mother had called "pretty wonderful" was based on genocide, on the extermination of the native cultures, on the crushing of Latin America, on the subjugation of working people.

He was not alone in having stayed so long in school: many of his American contemporaries had also stayed past their individual ripeness for learning, stayed because dropping out—or flunking out—resulted in losing one's student deferment, which resulted in a free trip to Vietnam: "What the hell are we fighting for, I don't give a damn, next stop is Vietnam." So the song went.

Tonight, as the first snowflakes sifted down and the lights of the city came on around him, this was the baggage that Ryan carried as he walked up the steeply slanted blocks of Kitsilano. It was invisible, for how heavy is a thought? How heavy is the story that we carry around about ourselves? Even though his past trailed behind him like an invisible dinosaur tail, Ryan still looked distinguished in the neat slim lines of his peacoat and blue navy toque.

Also invisible was the bag of marijuana, called a "lid," signifying that it was more than a nickel bag, a matchbox, or a reefer. He had gone through the unnecessary trouble of opening the lining of his peacoat and sliding the plastic bag down inside the sleeve. This was the first marijuana he had bought in this country and also the first he had bought in a long time. He was quite afraid of being caught as he was a Landed Immigrant— Landed Ingrate he liked to call it—and could have been deported for any minor crime like the one he was committing. In Argenta they had deported someone for skinny dipping off the dock at Johnson's Landing, which had turned out to be a crime called "Moral Turpitude."

So Ryan did his best to look casual climbing into the Kitsilano sky, to look normal, whatever that was supposed to be. The year before, he had flushed his stash of Panama Red down the toilet to make peace with Sheila. He had watched it swirl around and disappear with that final little cough that toilets make. In high school he had started learning the art of looking normal on the outside while being very altered on the inside. If he got back to his apartment without being caught and tried for Moral Turpitude, he would face similar charges at home, for Sheila was death on drugs.

Also on this night, unbeknownst to Ryan, sixty five kilometers to the Northwest as the crow flies, as the owl flies, as the gull flies; on one of the last "primitive" islands in the Gulf of Georgia—no car ferry, no electricity, no phones, no paved roads, almost no people—Sarah and Nicole, sat in their small cabin. They were beautiful, in their early twenties. Long gold hair and long red hair flowed over each of their shoulders. Intelligence and laughter shone in their eyes. Gusts from the Southeaster bounced off cliffs above them and shook their cabin. Snowflakes had begun to swirl. By the dim light of their kerosene lamps Sarah played her guitar and Nicole wrote in her journal.

Their cabin was beneath the face of the local mountain in an orchard of unpruned apple trees; the grass of their clearing was kept clipped by the feral sheep left behind by the old-timers. Sarah and Nicole had walked the clearing and found the curlicued pieces of the wood stove and put it back together. It crackled and popped, throwing flashes of light through its seams onto the cabin walls. They had cleaned up the clearing, scavenging all the wood scraps, fragments from the endeavours of former lives. They were burning the past to heat themselves in the present.

Above this speck of light was the mountain, a solitary lump of basalt. It rose on sheer walls into a sky that was not yet whited out by the gathering snow. Its natural bonsais—twisted firs and pines—grew at impossible angles from clefts in the rock. Small but hundreds of years old, they set their branches at precise angles to the sun. The peak, the mountain's great stone knob, rose out of a fringe of old growth that had been beyond the reach of loggers. Below that was a ravaged plateau, a wreckage of stumps just beginning to come back in spindly first growth trees.

The mountain glimmered slightly in the light of a waxing (as they used to like to call it) moon. "Moons are born in the evening and die in the morning," Nicole wrote in her journal, "They emerge as a thin fingernail behind the setting sun and then, like a child hanging behind its mother, trail it further every night. Each night, on their way to oppositional fullness, they grow bigger. Then they begin their inevitable decline, falling behind, growing smaller and smaller, until one morning they fall in with their bright parent again. Then they travel as a dark disk in the womb of the sun. On the third day they are once again spit out as tiny bright slivers into the evening sky. And they do it every month. Every month!"

Nicole and Sarah knew this. They had watched it happen during the months that they had lived in this far away place. In summer they had spent whole nights up on the mountain. They brought no sleeping bags and remained ecstatically awake, as only youth can, hugging their knees for warmth and watching, in awe, the progression of the night, watching the many folds of forest beneath the stars, watching the open fields—abandoned homesteads—glowing in the moonlight like —as local poet Ned Varney had put it—"the luminous numbers on the dial of a clock."

Tonight, gusts of winds shook their cabin, rattling the plastic tacked over its empty window frames. Around them stretched nothing but the dark forest and a few far-away homes that were mostly lighted with lamps powered by gas generators that chugged away until late in the evening and then lapsed into silence, surrendering to the forest around them.

Everyone on Vasquez seemed to find a place that was as far away from anyone else as possible. For some it was because they wanted wilderness, primal solitude; for some it was because they couldn't get along with other people; for still others it was just because it was where they had found an abandoned house still standing. Houses built of logs take a long time to break down and decay.

If someone had been on the mountain this night, possibly the mythical crow, owl or gull that had flown from Vancouver, they would have seen the great storm blowing in from the Southeast, obliterating the sky, obliterating the distant lights of the city. The storm would have been closing fast, a giant white eraser washing away the stars, washing away the moon, washing away the luhm of the coastal cities, those clouds of light that billow up from beneath the earth's curve to compete with the light of heaven.

Down in the clearing, the gathering storm passed above and around Sarah and Nicole. It shook their little cabin, but they had become used to letting the great universe flow around them in all its unobstructed glory. To them the storm, along with sun, moon, stars, tides and the seasons was just another movement in the great symphony of their life.

Back in Vancouver, Ryan had approached the dealer's apartment anxiously, asking himself, "Is this going to be alright?" With trepidation he had rung the buzzer and asked for the dealer by name. "Is Randy there, Dave Classen sent me." He was buzzed in and went up to the fourth floor. It was a corner apartment with windows looking over False Creek to the east and Stanley Park to the north. He could see the towers of the bridge rising over the forests of the park. Behind the towers, West Vancouver rose, a mottle of houses and trees, transitioning like a water colour wash into the stern mountains behind.

The apartment smelled of dope and incense; Indian bedspreads were draped everywhere and Oriental carpets sparkled on the floor like signage from another world. Indian ornaments made of brass glittered on the mahogany tables. Bamboo chairs, cushions and hassocks were liberally strewn about the room. Framed Salvador Dali and Esher prints graced the walls, and also bizarre psychedelic paintings that looked like anatomical drawings dissolving into light. A large erotic canvas showed blue women with red lips, as sleek and jointless as seals. One was proffering her breasts like tropical fruit, while another held her labia open to show a universe— stars, moon, a galaxy—within. Her head was turned to one side with a look of invitation and amusement.

Sitar music emerged from large speakers—an evening raga Ryan thought; some kind of screen was oscillating in the corner of the room, strobing colours to the sound of the raga.

Even unstoned, Ryan felt that he was connected to a much larger universe, as though he was speeding through space on a magic carpet. Dusk began to fall. The city outside twinkled a bit as the earth hurtled along its orbit like a carnival ride. In the midst of all this, Randy sat between the corner windows, enthroned upon a high Balinese chair woven from rattan. Its tall peacock-tailed back surrounded him like an aura. His long red hair, looking very clean and washed, flowed over a white cotton robe which covered all but his face, hands, and silver embroidered Afghan slippers. With just a turn of his head he could look out the north window to see the mountains or to the east to look at False creek. Behind him, in the Southeast, Ryan noticed that a great roiling front of snow had already begun to obliterate the city. Some of the people in the room were occupied with art books, others sat looking abstractly at the ceiling which was painted the colour of twilight. It was covered with dangling gold stars that emitted little flashes of light as they twirled slowly on invisible threads. At the back of the room, sitting on a hassock, a couple kissed passionately. She wore a silk blouse that her nipples had lifted lightly off her chest.

In the midst of this Randy looked at home. A sleepy looking girl sat beside him on the floor, her chin resting on his leg. One of his hands was ever so lightly stroking her hair.

"Hi Man," he said to Ryan, "How's Dave doing?"

"Fine, he's moved into a new place over by Alma."

"Cool," said Randy.

Ryan felt out of his league, swept through a gateway into a psychedelia that he hadn't known existed. He had thought that buying dope would be a simple little one-on-one encounter, an exchange of money for a bag of marijuana. He didn't know that all these people would be here. He didn't want to make a fool of himself, to look un-cool (which he was pretty sure he was). He was weighing whether to say, "I've come to buy some dope." or, "Dave says you have some pretty good stuff."

As it turned out he was spared from having to reveal himself in language. Randy picked up a large brass hookah that sat on the floor beside the girl. He said, "Hey man, taste this stuff." He flicked a small lighter that looked like a miniature Aladdin's lamp and held it to the pipe. He sucked vigorously until billows of smoke began to emerge from the great red eye that glowed in its thickly packed bowl. Randy took a huge toke. He managed to contain it but not without a lot of gasping and sucking noises. He passed the pipe to Ryan, who took a more cautious toke, not wanting to embarrass himself with a bunch of racking coughs. Inhaling slowly and evenly, Ryan let in some cool air from around the corners of his mouth. He held his breath and started to returned the pipe to Randy who gestured for him to pass it on. He looked around and decided to hand it to one of the ceiling gazers who he hoped would not be too catatonic to take it, leaving him to choose someone else, certainly not the girl with the erect nipples.

To his relief the ceiling gazer, wearing the orange garb of a Sanyasin and a little Rajneesh mala around his neck, slowly moved his hand to take the pipe. Their eyes met for a moment and he gazed at Ryan from some very faraway place. Ryan noticed that he did not feel uncomfortable in the gaze and that the Sanyasin's pale blue eyes held a certain warmth.

As Ryan freed himself of the ornate pipe, Randy gestured him to a large cushion on the other side of his chair from the girl. Ryan sat down with only a momentary fear that Randy would start to stroke his hair as well. He was still holding his breath, letting the smoky resin permeate his lungs. As the drug entered his brain, Ryan remembered that one of the keys to the kingdom of psychedelia was just to be quiet and wait. Language, when necessary, was best left imprecise and open, so that everyone could understand it in their own way. Separate solitude's would not be jarred or challenged. He remembered that you could get by with just a few phrases: "Far out. Cool. Bummer. I've gotta split." It was like being in a foreign country. It really took only a few words to deal with the necessities of life. Ryan remembered that the Tao Te Ching said that it was better to let things unfold rather than to make things happen: "I'd rather play the guest than the host;" "It's better to retreat a mile than advance an inch." Way Wei Wu Wei.

Everything suddenly seemed so new. For Ryan it was like crossing a snow covered glacier, going very slowly, feeling for the crevasses, or like going into a jungle where no one had ever been. Clearly none of these people were travelling the timeworn, well marked roads of life anymore, the roads where there were signs to tell you what to do. Turn left here. Do not enter. They were making up the road, the trees, the wild figs, the pond where the women bathed, the python that was draped in the trees that they had just made up the moment before. When you were creating worlds, it was better to go slowly, for once placed, a tree could not be unplaced, once the river was there it must be crossed. Once the python had you in its coils...

Unable to hold his breath any longer, Ryan exhaled explosively. He realised that he had tripped out on a whole long train of thought about words, about psychedelia, about world creation. This is what he loved about drugs: his mind lighting up and thoughts racing through it. Other breaths blew out into the room as though from a pod of surfacing Orca, the great boom and spume of their out-breaths, the gasp of air before they dove back into deep waters as the pipe went around again.

Ryan sat in the room for a long time, aware that he should be going home, watching the light fade outside Randy's windows. The girl had laid her head sideways on Randy's leg and had fallen asleep there. She looked very sweet and innocent. Randy still stroked her hair. People came and went, tasted the dope, sat around, bought baggies and left. Randy sat on his throne, on top of it all, apparently unfazed by the constant inhalations that he was taking with each new customer. Ryan was shocked by the openness of it. He wondered if the marijuana had destroyed Randy's judgement, or if there was just a tremendous safety in this network of friends and friends of friends. He watched the transaction go down enough times to know how to do it and then bought his baggie and prepared to leave this floating world. He made a little bow at the door as he backed out, and Randy, sitting on his throne, the evening deepening behind him, returned it with the tiniest of nods, like an underworld king acknowledging a retainer.

Ryan closed the door. It seemed to him that this place was a concealed entryway, hidden in the midst of everyday Vancouver, to a world where the unconscious, the shadow, the psychic, the erotic, the metaphysical all emerged and came together.

Now, as he climbed the steep slope of Kitsilano, he was very stoned. That is exactly how he wanted to be. Everything seemed new and fresh, like after a rain. He moved through the external world while his internal world moved through him. He was enlivened by his heightened perception of both. The winter sky, not quite spring, was already going pearly grey, the colour it turned before dropping into final darkness. A few diminutive snowflakes swirled around him and caught for a moment in his hair and on his dark blue coat before transmogrifying into drops of water. It was good to be alive, to be a warm spark in this cold winter, to be bundled in his woolen coat and flannel work shirt. He came to Sheila's Kitsilano apartment and looked up at the warm lights. He put his key in the door and walked up the stairs out of the cold. In the living room Sheila was reading by lamplight in her favourite chair.

She was deeply immersed in her book and did not look up to greet him. Lara must be asleep, he thought, down for a nap. Darkness had fallen. Sheila looked peaceful and composed in the lamplight, enjoying one of the rare times when her attention was her own. He looked at her and his heart overflowed at her beauty, at her struggle to find meaning in life, at the rough journey that they had travelled together. He knelt beside her, took her hand and told her that he loved her. She tore her eyes away from the book, something on Hegelian dialogue, and saw that his eyes were glazed with marijuana. Maybe she smelled it on his clothes.

She was not happy to see him. He had been hanging around most of the day, sitting, reading, listening to the radio, making toast, commenting on everything from politics to the neighbours in the street, interrupting her precious silence when Lara slept.

This was not the way it was supposed to be. She was glad when he had gone out, but now he was back again, kneeling before her and telling her that he loved her. She could not rise to the occasion. Anger overwhelmed her. She said, "You're stoned. I was here caring for our daughter and you cut out and got stoned." She was implacable. He spoke of love, of a vision of happiness for them, of an open heart. She became angrier and angrier. He was crying beside her now. She rose coldly, went to the bedroom and shut the door.

18
Alone

As late summer came, the sea around Vasquez finally warmed up. The fields created by the old timers blew with long grass and sang with the voice of a thousand crickets. To Ryan, the long-dead old timers seemed like mythological titans from the time of creation. The apple trees they had planted were laden with fruit; the blackberry vines they had struggled to control were clustered with sweet ripe berries. All Ryan needed to do was reach up, like Pan, and stuff the ripe fruit it his mouth.

After Sheila and Lara had left, Ryan worked a little each morning to tend the garden and to bring in the firewood he would need for winter. He drove his much battered red Volvo to where it was permissible to cut wood on the road right-of-way and felled a fat white-barked alder. Filling the woods with noise and oily smoke, he lopped off its branches and sawed the larger branches into rounds. When the white trunk lay segmented like a butchered whale in its cradle of crushed undergrowth, he put away the chainsaw and took his sledge hammer and steel wedges out of the car. carefully placing them on the stump so as not to lose them in the chaos of broken underbrush.

As he split the rounds into pieces light enough to carry, the sound of his hammer ringing against the wedges made exclamation points in the forest's silence. Already the white flesh of the Alder was beginning to turn orange. He lugged the quarter rounds down to the car and filled its back with them. Back home he heaved them into the pile that was drying in the driveway.

He wore his plaid red and purple Chinese work shirt, his torn jeans, his deep sea diver logging boots, his gloves and ear plugs. He hadn't bought new clothes in a long time. Digging in the garden, kneeling, weeding, had compressed dirt into everything. Though he washed his clothes regularly, the dirt no longer came out completely. Cutting wood snagged and ripped things. Although he tried to remember which pockets had holes in them, at some point habits had taken over and the car keys had fallen through a holey pocket and disappeared forever into the underbrush. Now he started his car by twisting two wires together.

When he stopped to fill the saw, he loved taking out his earplugs: Suddenly, the silence of the forest was all around him, accented by bird song and gusts of wind in the trees. Sometimes he just sat, taking a break from sawing, and listened to the forest. It took him about two or three hours to bring home a load of wood. This was his day's work. He remembered an archaeologist in Nelson saying that the Kootenay Pit House People had worked about 15 hours a week. The archaeologist had waved his hand at the world around them and said, "And we call this progress?"

After bringing in the wood, Ryan changed into his Mexican peasant clothes: white shirt, white cotton pants (as white as they got), loosely woven straw hat to keep off the sun. Today he drove to a lonely beach that faced southwest. He took a long swim along the rocky coast, delighting in the rise and fall of the little swells that came up Georgia Straight. Huge arbutus trees leaned out over the cliffs to catch the sunlight. The ends of their branches were clustered with bright red berries. Their trunks twisted horizontally out over the cliffs, defying gravity. Their roots penetrated deeply into the rock to hold them up. Sunlight took precedence over uprightness. They were leaning out for love. They would lean that way forever.

When he was alone, he almost always thought of Ariel. In his inner eye, he saw her face in the sky, felt her to be part of the sinuous trees that leaned out for the sun, or the waves that lapped against the shore. With her he experienced the omnipresence that people usually reserve for God, Jesus, or other saints, believing that the beloved exists in everything. He swam like a dolphin, spending a long hour in the early autumn sea. When it had sucked out all of his mammalian warmth, he threw himself, shivering, onto the sunny beach to warm himself on its rounded pebbles.

He had only seen Ariel a few times since Sheila and Lara left. Now that he was a single man, she was wary of him. The easy visits on mail day had ceased. She was married and had two children. She had a sister on the island and also her sister's husband. Often when they met it was at a child's birthday party. In their small community of several hippy families and several old-timer families, you had to invite everyone to have enough people to have a party. When Ryan found himself in her presence, he made no overtures but was just happy to sit and talk, to listen, to be unobtrusively close to her. An observer—and everyone on the island was an observer—would never have guessed his feelings, or at least that's what he thought. He exchanged pleasantries that did not reflect the mystical depth of his feeling for her, and that she, he suspected, might have toward him. Or did she?

In summer most of these gatherings happened outdoors: there were potlucks under old fruit trees in abandoned orchards near the water's edge; stainless steel or plastic bowls of clams and fried chicken and potato salad. Sometimes they all sat together, saying little, watching the tide slowly flow into a lagoon. Eagles flew overhead, dropping their silver calls like coins from above. Ravens cawed from within the darkness of the forest. A rooster crowed on a far-away farm.

Usually there was a fire for roasting hot-dogs for the children. There was also wine, big half gallons of Calona Still Rosé which McElwaith called Still Rosy. If it was just newcomers, there was also reefer, which was not grown on Vasquez yet, but came from Mexico, Lebanon or some other faraway place. There was also conversation, endless conversation about gardens, wood stoves, chainsaws, fishing, boats, log salvaging; about working up the coast for fifty dollars a day, about chickens, about writing, about rock and roll; about bringing up children; about the world that they had all left behind, the world that seemed to be running further amok with every passing year. Conversation was their main form of entertainment.

They talked about how it got harder and harder to go back to the city, even to buy supplies or conduct business. Most people's idea of a job was to go away for a month or two and work at something that made them enough money to live simply all year, by eating out of the garden, by eating the feral sheep from the land and the fish and shellfish from sea.

Today, walking fully clothed to a beach below his house, Ryan thought about Ariel and wondered what she must be doing. As he approached the fork where one road diverged toward her house, he sent a wish that she come and meet him, called out to her in his thoughts. Sure enough, as he walked the forest floor she came the other way, alone, without children, without husband. He saw her far away through the tunnel of trees, walking with the light step of a hiker on holidays. She wore light green slacks and an off-white shirt with a colourful light shawl around her neck. She had cut her hair recently and it was almost a duck tail, swept back. They approached and met, exactly at the fork in the road, going in opposite directions. They stopped. She stood slightly above him, still on the road from her house. He had already passed the bifurcation and stood slightly below her on the road to the lagoon. Separated in this way they could stop and talk. It seemed safer this way, to show that he was moving along, that he didn't wish to detain her or walk with her. But he also knew that he must tell her of his feelings. There had been no time or place in the past months.

She smiled at him a bit warily. Her conversation strove for the normal. "Hi, how ya doin'?" she said brightly.

"I knew you would be here" he said, "We are always connected, even when we are apart, you must know this."

Her face became severe. "This is craziness," she said. She was talking to him earnestly, like she might have talked to one of her students who had stepped out of line, or who was thinking of dropping out. "Yes, I've felt this from you, every time we see each other, this intensity, but it's not real. I have my life, my family." And so she did. That he could not deny.

"Yes it is crazy, but real nonetheless. I don't know if anything can come of it, but something has happened and I feel connected to you in some deep way. I am always aware of your presence. You are in everything. I don't know what to say. I don't want to hurt or disturb you."

She was taken aback, rattled. She played with the ends of her scarf, twisting them around in her hands. She looked down for awhile and then back at him. They stood together, in this private moment on two different roads in the middle of a forest. They did not speak together in the patois of "far-out, groovy, wow." Something more formal had taken over their language: they spoke from a deeper part of themselves, something beyond the mask of the counter-culture.

They stood this way for a long time. There was really so little to say. Was it true he wondered, what she said about his feelings not being reciprocated? He thought of the laughter between them, the easy references and understanding of everything. He thought of her beauty. At some level he already suspected his love for her was some sort of worship of the feminine. It thrived on isolation, on non-consummation, on spiritual yearning. It could never come down to earth and be ordinary. It had nothing to do with companionship or raising children or helping each other through life. He did not think very much about the dimension in which she was also a woman, with a family, with financial worries, with security needs. She had become a goddess, present and omnipresent. His love for her was not about anything practical. Perhaps she was right that it was not real.

He thought that, for her part, while she understood the unreality of his point of view, she must have also understood that there was some truth to it: that there was a part of her that was beyond wife, mother, homemaker.

He relaxed in some deep way and just let go of all these questions, simply allowing himself to stand in the forest just a few feet away from her, to enjoy this rare moment of her presence. She stood too. They were just quiet together. He could not sort it out, the difference between her words and the feelings that he was experiencing. He did not know what was real anymore and had to reconcile himself to living with confusion and ambiguity.

She smiled, finally, and said "I gotta go." He reached out both hands to her on the road above him and they briefly squeezed hands as a farewell. She continued up the road and disappeared into the filtered green light, walking under a canopy of birdsong.

19
Alone

Sometimes Ryan would go to visit Sheila and Lara. Most of the time he tried not to think too much about them, but when he climbed the island's mountain and looked south toward Seattle, he would see the pregnant curve of the ocean arching its back up toward the sky and would ponder the great belly of troubles that had risen up between them. He would think with sorrow about Sheila and himself, and the blighted love that they had shared for so many years, and of Lara, her tiny fingers reaching out for his and her just forming use of language. The pain in his heart was too big in this lonely place and tears would fall down his face.

Then he would take the bus to Seattle and look at the night-time city lights through its tinted windows. They appeared green, a swirling maelstrom of electrical illumination. Who outside these windows could match his consciousness or he theirs? Surrounded by thousands of people, his loneliness was intense. He felt like he was from another planet. At least Sheila and he had some mutual understanding of who they each were, and of what being human meant.

When he stayed with Sheila and Lara, huge planes, their wings spread for landing, would float down over her house all day long, rattling the windows and emitting the sound of a thousand thunders. He could not get used to it. After several days, longing for solitude, he would climb on the green glassed bus again.

Back on the island it was a summer of bucketing around; it was a summer of home-brew and bottles of cheap wine; it was a summer of reefer, procured in Victoria and brought up the Island Highway. Between the cutting of wood and the growing of vegetables, it was an endless party thrown on the island's beaches and coves; it was a summer of oysters popping open beside campfires, of someone playing a guitar; of people in sleeping bags falling asleep beside the embers, of going home in the morning. It was a summer of freedom. There was no school, no job, no family, no obligations. It was a summer of hitchhiking and inviting the people who gave him rides to visit. He gathered clams for them from the beaches and served them dipped in garlic butter with fresh baked bread from the woodstove. The table was a huge cable spool set up under the spreading cherry tree that overhung his house. In spring, its blossoms floated down onto the table, into their food. In summer its dark canopy provided shade. Sometimes there were plates of steamed lamb's quarter or a salad of greens from the garden.

Marijuana was the lubricant of these fast flowing friendships. One toke and people would share their secret beliefs about what was happening. Everyone was a messenger. Meetings were not by chance. "What is it that this person brings to me? What do I have for them."

Often, the floor of Ryan's cabin was covered with the sleeping bags of these travellers in search of the grail. Those who he liked he encouraged to settle; took them around the island in his broken down car to see the houses that were still empty, or if they had money, to see land that he knew was for sale. There was nothing more important than to cook for these passerby, to make meals with what was around, to drink wine and smoke dope, hear the stories they had to tell, and to tell his own.

Several months after Sheila left, Julie, the striking Japanese-Canadian woman with whom she had shared the Pond House, moved to a smaller cabin—a fixed up feed shed—at the North end. The Pond House had become too big and lonely for her. She left Sheila's pots, pans, artwork, piano, and some of Lara's toys in the empty house. Ryan could not bring himself to go and claim them. When Julie moved, she told him that he'd better go and get whatever he wanted. She had said, "I don't think that stuff will stay around for long after I'm gone." It was only then he realised that she had been guarding it for him.

After awhile, people went through the unoccupied house. Each took a few things until it was empty again, its windows looking vacantly out on Main Road. When he visited friends, he found things that Sheila and he had once owned together. They were scattered all over the island: her long green mushroom batiks hung on a wall at the north end; the decorative brass bucket, a wedding present, held compost on a farm under the mountain; Her Swedish mushroom charts graced the walls of the north end commune; her piano sat in the dusty Pan-Abode (he always looked for cloven-hoof prints when he went there) beside Main Road. It was like she'd been torn to pieces and scattered all around. Mostly he just left these things where he found them. Sometimes, when he wanted something back, he simply walked across the room and took it. Nobody said anything.

Julie had long flowing black straight hair and classic Japanese eyes with dark disks for centers. From time to time she and Ryan had spoken a few words on the ferry, and he had given her and her parcels rides to the little house beside the pond while she still lived there. He never went in, though, even when Julie had invited him for tea, not wanting to confront what Sheila and Lara had left behind.

One night, after she had moved to the grain shed, he sat across a bonfire from her at a beach party. He looked across the circle of faces and sensed that she was attracted to him. The great cliffs that enfolded their little cove were illuminated with fire light. Sparks spiraled up into the sky. It seemed to him that when he looked across at her, their eyes caught. Moonlight glazed the water. Electric phosphorescence splashed as each little wave broke against the shore. When they swam that night, when they all had had enough wine and smoke and heat from the fire to take off their clothes, their splashings flew like sparks into the sky; their foreshortened bodies incandesced in the dark waters like creatures from the deep. He wondered what this magic was that let him know that she was attracted to him, this invisible, wordless, knowledge that opened a door to something beyond the limitations of the mind.

She had travelled a long trail. In her mind she was Canadian, adopted and raised by white Canadians. In her genes she was Japanese. During the war, the tomato farms, the green houses, the immaculately crafted homes of Japanese-Canadians had been confiscated and auctioned away, sold for a pittance to the envious whites who had always resented their success. Their neatly ordered, alien-looking gardens became the property of Caucasian neighbours who grazed cattle in them. Their green houses fell in showers of neglected glass. Their beautifully crafted double-ended fish boats were rafted-up in the mouth of the Fraser River, neglected and left to fill with water and sink.

The owners of all this were herded into stark camps in the interior. The marriage between Julie's parents unravelled in cultural disarray. Her mother, unable to cope, put her up for adoption. She was raised by well-meaning white people in Langley. Later, she travelled to California, lived in the ferment of Berkeley. Her exotic good looks opened doors for her. She had stayed with a U.C. professor who had tried to introduce her to the pleasures and pains of S&M. When the great exodus from Berkeley began, she was among those who left. People were seeking a life separate from that of being in perpetual reaction to the government. They were returning to the land. She found her way back to Canada, to the islands. She was a seeker, an adventurer on a voyage of discovery. She was Julie.

Ryan crossed to the other side of the fire and stood behind the log that she was sitting on. "Would you like a little shoulder rub?" he said. She looked back over her shoulder at him, a smile breaking on her Asian face. "How did you know?" she said. They both laughed at the assumption of clairvoyance, the understatement of what was happening.

This relationship that began by a fire was Ryan's first since Sheila left, and also the first since he had married Sheila. He was intoxicated by it and yet there was still his love for Ariel, and his love for Sheila and Lara. How could he reconcile these? He didn't know yet that the Greeks had as many different words for love as Inuit have for snow. Even the AM radio, his tinny little link to the outside world, crooned "If you can't be with the one you love, love the one you're with." It seemed worth a try. Where would it lead? To clarification? To letting go? To insurmountable confusion? Heaven only knew. He found it better not to think too much about this, and just to be in whatever moment he was in. Be Here Now—the motto of the time.

He approached love making with both ardency and trepidation. His whole being had been crying out for this meeting for years, but the absence of it in his previous life made him fear it. He wondered if he was flawed and that it would not work well. To his delight it worked beautifully. Julie and he found release in each other. For him it was a profound healing, and opened the door to relief and joy. She was also his spiritual teacher. One day he was helping her carry bags of food from his car to her grain shed.

One of the plastic bags had a small hole in it. As he carried it along, she noticed that grains of rice were falling out one by one, leaving a sparse trail across the gravel driveway, up the front porch, and across the weathered floor boards.

"Be careful," she snapped at him.

"But it's only a few grains" he said, his feelings hurt at this small step down from the near worship of first love.

"But each one is precious," she countered, bending to pick them up and put them in a small bowl. The idea that each grain of rice was precious was new to him. They talked. It was not just her limited budget speaking, but her understanding that the combined efforts of the plant and of the humans who had grown and harvested it had given value to every grain. Each must be honoured. Though Canadian, a part of Julie remained unacculturated and held the wisdom of another time and place.

Late autumn swirled around Julie and Ryan. They palled around together. Ryan wore his chammorrah; Julie wore her long flowing hand woven robes. Together they looked like ancient Mayans who had crawled up through a doorway in the earth onto the rural roads of twentieth century British Columbia. She liked kif and introduced him to its pleasures. There was a lot of hash and kif that was smuggled into Vancouver. Rumours had it that it was cast into hatch covers, suitcases and the like, and then fiberglassed. Later the fiberglass shell was cracked off and the kif was broken up into the tiny yellow grainy chunks that they bought. Everyone was a bit worried about inhaling the fiberglass resin, but they smoked it anyway.

Ryan and Julie borrowed Hirsh's latest car to drive to Victoria to score dope. Hirsh's cars were disreputable and just barely ran. They were cars that he picked up for $50 and drove until they died. He just walked away then, leaving them at the side of the road, and bought another $50 car. Hirsh had given Ryan elaborate instructions about how many times to pump the gas pedal and which wires to twist to get the car started. By following this procedure, Ryan finally, against all odds, got the car to cough into life.

He and Julie drove down the Island highway. Bright yellow maple leaves waved from the side of the road like banners advertising autumn:

"Now Playing." "See It Now." The day was glazed with pale sunlight that was pleasantly warm, warm enough to drive with the windows down, which was good, because one of them didn't close. Crickets sang at the side of the Island Highway. "Highway," they laughed. "We are travelling the high way."

The sunlight was made precious by winter hanging ominously in great cumulus towers over the mountains. The Cloud-Beings were stacking up and waiting to descend. It was definitely the time of the grasshoppers' last song and the human grasshoppers knew it too. Any day now the Cloud-Beings would come down and the deluge would begin, starting the long months of roiling cloud and streaming rain.

In Victoria, they stayed at the house of a man they didn't even know, not even a friend of a friend. His address had been written on a slip of paper handed to them by a hitchhiker they had picked up along the way. The man's name was Tom and he lived in a beautiful old Victorian house that developers had allowed it to fall into disrepair, renting it to hippies and Native Canadians until it could be torn down and replaced by an apartment building in which people would live stacked like cheeses, one atop another.

Tom welcomed them into his house without question. As they carried in their packs, Ryan noticed a grand piano gleaming amid the Salvation Army furniture; flowers shone out of a cracked jar on the scarred kitchen table. Tom turned out to be a young pianist whose talent far exceeded his years. Together they worked in the kitchen to make dinner. Ryan and Julie contributed brown rice, zucchini from the garden, and carrots with earth still on them. Tom had the tofu. As they cooked, they told stories about their lives and got to know each other. After dinner, Tom played for them. Later Julie and Ryan made a bed on the floor using couch cushions and their open sleeping bags. They made love, a simple surrendering to youth and beauty which was as natural as falling asleep or waking up. They drifted off to sleep in each other's arms, listening to Tom's improvisations coming through the wall from the other room.

The next day they drove to a dope-dealer's house out on Blenkinsop Road. It was a decaying white farmhouse, yard full of cars, people coming and going, rock and roll pouring out the open windows and wafting across

147

the autumn fields—summer's last hurrah. Ryan thought that the dealer might just as well have put up a flashing neon sign that said "Dope For Sale Within."

The following morning they slept in, listening to Tom's music filter into their dreams. When it was time to leave, Tom was still playing. They waved at him as they carried out their packs, and he smiled back at them. As they climbed into Hirsh's car, Tom's music sounded through the bones of the old house. They drove away.

It was late morning. Against all odds, the autumn sun had lasted for yet another day. They wound through the city streets toward the farms of Saanich, planning to cross Finlayson Arm on the Brentwood Bay ferry rather than, for the sake of the old car, make the long climb up the Malahat.

Several blocks into their journey a police car pulled out from a side street and began to follow them. Paranoia struck. They wondered if they had been followed from the dealer's house the day before. They turned right, out of the neighbourhood streets onto Douglas. The police car turned after them. They interrupted their route and took the long diagonal up Burnside. Still the police car traveled a short distance behind them. Panic was rising.

Julie reached in her bag and took out the small piece of kif they had bought. It was wrapped in tinfoil like the last square of an expensive chocolate bar. They passed under the highway and headed up into Saanich, the police car still behind them. She unwrapped the tinfoil and broke the piece of kif in half. They both knew what to do. They chewed and swallowed the grainy yellow substance, tasting the bitterness of it on their tongues. The perfume of cannabis pollen rose out of their mouths and into their noses. Ryan looked in the mirror, while trying to produce enough saliva to clean out his mouth. Julie rolled up the piece of tinfoil into a tiny ball and threw it out her window like a tiny shiny seed, one of her precious grains of rice. They looked at each other. They were clean. Ryan looked in the mirror. The police car had disappeared—off on its own mission.

They had been duped by the five coincidental turns, and now Ryan was anxious about what eating a chunk of kif would do to him. "What will happen now," he asked plaintively, "will we OD?" Julie just smiled at him. She didn't seem upset at all, so he relaxed and continued to drive.

There was a long wait at the ferry and they were incredibly high by the time the boat came skimming across the water on the thrum of its diesel engines. They waited in the inching line, inhaling the exhaust fumes from the cars in front of them. Their car was confining and claustrophobic. Once finally aboard, they left the car immediately and climbed a small ladder onto the ferry's upper deck. Finlayson Arm and the tall mountains around it were all shimmering in the late autumn sun. When the last car was loaded, the ferry moved out across the water. Ryan and Julie sat on the upper deck with their backs against the warm metal of the wheel house. Around them, the vibrations and overtones of the ferry's engines opened into a symphony of sound, and then, from high above, the sky split open and a choir of angels began to sing out god's thought forms, of which they, the ferry, the landscape, all seemed to be a part. Ryan looked at Julie. Her eyes looked like obsidian doorways into another realm. "Do you hear angels?" he asked. She simply nodded and smiled.

And so they sat on the deck of the Brentwood ferry, two tiny dots in an enormous landscape. They quietly held hands and allowed the choir of angels to exalt them above the diesel fumes; above the milling crowd of tourists who ate ice cream and looked at their watches. They had the upper deck to themselves. They sat back and allowed the comforting throb of the diesel engines to carry them into a world of motion and energy. Slowly, as they passed beneath the stern mountains of the Malahat, they began to merge with the greater creation around them. They were a part of it and a witness to it. They were holding hands and were all shot through with autumn light. When Ryan looked at Julie, her head was emitting the gold mosaic glow of a Byzantine saint.

20
Alone

With the cold weather, woodcutting started in earnest. The sound of chainsaws dominated the clear autumn sky. Summer had ended and with it the days of bucketing around in Ryan's now broken-down and haywired Volvo; the days of partying wildly at beaches, of drinking home-made wine, of roasting oysters over the open fire, of picking plums and blackberries. All this had come to an end.

Cutting wood was more enjoyable as a communal activity, so Ryan worked with his friend Reston. Reston had trouble folding his long slim body into the stooped confines of Ryan's Volvo, so they used Reston's army surplus combat vehicle which was much easier to fill and empty. They alternated taking loads to one house and then the other. At Reston's, his wife Mariel would come out to help them unload whenever the baby was asleep. They would leave the wood in a huge pile just inside the unpainted cedar picket fence that Reston had built for her. Mariel invited them in for strong tea and home baked cookies before they went out on the road right-of-way again.

Reston's hand-built house was in a small clearing in the middle of the forest. Old-timers, who prided themselves on living in proper houses, called it a "hippy shack." At the edge of the clearing, all around the house, stood huge first-growth Fir trees. Their gnarled tops, charred and broken by lightning, extended far above the surrounding second growth forest. Ravens used them as sentinel outposts. When Ryan and Reston heard flapping, they would look up and see black shadows flitting through the branches above them. Reston himself had fierce blue eyes and a sharply sculpted birdlike face. With his silky brown hair and trimmed beard, he reminded Ryan of a self-portrait of Gauguin that Ryan had once seen in the vaults of academe. Ryan sensed an affinity between Reston and these creatures of the air.

From the porch, these trees were extremely beautiful; their enormous trunks rose into the sky like the pillars of an elfin hall. One night when a raging westerly was combing out the forest's hair, Reston and Mariel looked through the skylight above their loft. They saw the trees tossing in the wind and felt their deep groans in the earth below them.

The next morning they walked outside and carefully examined each tree. One had a scar in it, a place where sometime in the past six hundred years its bark had been stripped away and the wood beneath damaged, perhaps by lightening. The scar was covered with moss and still dripping sap.

The skylight, meant to provide the peaceful pleasure of the stars, became a source of anxiety. Reston and Mariel would lay together on stormy nights and watch the tossing tree tops, wondering if one of them would come crashing down on their house, breaking it into matchsticks.

After tea and cookies, Reston and Ryan jounced down the road to find yet another old alder that looked like it might fall the right way. It took so many of these great trees to stay warm through the winter. After the tree came down, they would buck it up amid the roar and smoke of their chain saws. As they split the rounds, their axes swung like flashing pendula against the sky.

Sometimes they would just stop, short of breath, sweat dripping from their foreheads, and sit on the white alder rounds that lay in the crushed salal. At these times, when the saws and axes were quiet, they would take out their ear plugs and sit in the awesome silence. Sometimes they told each other stories from the past or talked about their present lives. They talked about their relationships, Ryan's that had just ended and Reston's which continued. Women were mixed in these conversations, two sided: purveyors of comfort and erotic pleasure, but also glowering controllers, demanding their will be done.

Autumn continued on in this way until winter began to make a few forays into the clear cool days. The Cloud-Beings came down, tentatively at first, just to try out their power. They would stay for a few days and then retreat back to their mountain fastnesses, as if they needed time to gather more strength. It was as though winter was refining its systems, adjusting its taps and spigots, finding out which ones were clogged, making sure they would all be open and ready to go when the time came, ensuring that there would be nothing to mar the opening chords of its devastating torrential downpour.

When the Cloud-Beings rolled in, there was a temporary end to the cold clear days of autumn, to the days of geese flying in long lines overhead, the days of being plunged into cutting firewood. There was a temporary end to splitting wood and stacking it in the woodshed where the white alder butts turned savage orange as they dried. There was a temporary end to pulling things out of the garden, to hanging tomato plants upside-down—all over the house—so the green fruit could ripen; to digging carrots and storing them in wooden boxes full of sand. There was a temporary end to stuffing fallen maple leaves into gunny sacks and covering the garden with them. On the days when winter flexed its muscle all this ended.

As for Ryan, the art of the homestead was almost complete. The square beds of his garden were almost covered by the rich burnt sienna of maple leaves. Piles of wood were stacked in the small shed where the suitcase of his illustrious ancestor was stored on a shelf. The suitcase, mouldering and splayed, was made of leather and was still covered with faded stickers from Europe's best hotels. Its seams had broken from all the tools, spare parts, bent nails, old chain saw files, that Ryan had stuffed into it. Access was by a small aisle between high stacks of wood. Wood was everywhere. It was stacked up to the roof of the shed and high up under the dripping eves of the house as well.

Sometimes when searching in the suitcase for a spare part, he thought of his family: his maternal great-grandfather, who came from Italy to work in the mines of California; his paternal great-grandfather, who had scraped soot from a roof near the San Francisco Mint and had panned it to get enough gold to make a ring for his wife. Things had gotten mixed up quickly as these two families came together in the marriage of his father and mother: many conflicting ideas, ways of being, beliefs about the universe were combined into a lumpy pudding, a geological aggregate, which Ryan tried to harmonise within himself.

To Ryan his illustrious great-uncle, owner of the suitcase, was just another family member rather than a celebrity. As a child, his father had told him the story of the mysterious injury over which so many critics had puzzled. He had also told him about his great-uncle's brothers and sisters, one also illustrious, one a suicide, one an alcoholic, one an invalid. Ryan knew firsthand about the dangerous blend of genius and self destructiveness that ran in his family. He had seen the darkness of it in his father and, more recently, in himself. His great uncle's suitcase sat surrounded by boxes of nails, old washing machine parts, salvaged axe heads—all the things on a homestead that are not thrown out because they might come in handy. Homesteaders tend to believe in reincarnation because they have seen flat tires become hinges; broken hinges hold a cracked chainsaw casing together; bedsteads become gates; spoons become waterwheels. There is a certain logic to it from a homesteader's point of view. Ryan also had his great-uncle's initialled gold pipe cleaning tool. He used it to clean his hash pipe. Things that are passed down in families get turned to other uses.

On days when the Cloud-Beings came down, there was only a small curl of smoke coming from Ryan's chimney. Not much fire was needed to heat his small house, so he had damped down the wood stove. Ryan sat inside and repaired things with spare parts from the broken suitcase, or he just sat by the fire and read. This was a picture of what winter would be like, a preview of things to come. Sometimes he donned rain gear and took long walks in the short pale days. He explored obscure little corners of the forested island and stood where it felt like no-one had ever stood before. Sometimes he visited his friends out across the island.

When he walked to Reston's, he often found him building something out in the tool shed, or working in the forest. He stayed outside in his raingear and helped Reston while they talked. On days when it was just too rainy, Reston and Ryan visited indoors. They sat in old overstuffed chairs by the wood heater and Mariel brought them something she'd baked. They drank strong coffee, shared a joint, and talked wild, entertaining talk full of speculation about the weirder side of life. Mariel listened and made the occasional comment, but always seemed too busy to sit down and join them; she was always doing a thousand things at once, bustling in her colourful hand knit sweaters and pastel scarves. Sometimes, at some particularly unfeasible part of their stories, she looked up at them with a grimace of utter disbelief upon her face. She shook her head and went back to her sewing. Her blond hair was tied at the back of her neck to keep it off her work. She looked through her glasses to see her fine stitches in the low light of the cabin. Sometimes she would come over and have just the tiniest toke before returning to her work.

Once Reston told Ryan a story about a friend who was in the U.S. Air Force. One morning at two AM his friend was awakened to drive in a secret convoy: sleepy soldiers moving out across the night, destination unknown. Rumour had it that they were driving trucks loaded with nuclear missiles. They drove through deserted, shut-down L.A. and soon, in the dead quiet of the 4 am city, arrived at huge service gates. As the gates opened, they realised that they were driving into Disneyland. They drove past the closed-down rides to another set of gates that descended into an underground world. They went through a long tunnel lighted by blaring fluorescent lights and ended up at yet another set of gates that let them into a huge underground military complex, a missile base hidden under Disneyland. How else could the government have built such a big installation without it having been spotted by satellite? The story seemed so typical of the US: all those children going on rides and enjoying their favourite Disney characters, while beneath them deadly nukes pointed skyward. Ryan wondered if the IBMs would launch out of the turrets of the Fantasy Land Castle. He remembered Khrushchev pounding his shoe on the table and demanding to be taken to Disneyland. Now he thought he knew why.

For Ryan's part of the conversation, he told Reston about a high school friend who had also joined the U.S. Air Force and had became a lieutenant in charge of a missile silo. The men whiled away their hours underground by figuring out how to circumvent the two key fail-safe launch system to initiate an unauthorised missile attack. The simplest system they came up with was to shoot the other person in the silo and then slip a fork over one of the keys, tie a long piece of string to it, run it across the silo to the other key, and viola! Armageddon. Ryan's friend was very proud of the 45 calibre pistol that as an officer he was entitled to wear on his belt

Such was their conversation on these days that were a prelude to winter. They were already enjoying the warmth of the wood that they had cut together, and for Ryan—the warmth of Reston's family—his wife and baby girl. Spending time with them filled some of the emptiness of his day. His talk with Reston reminded him of his first days of getting stoned, back along the Sausalito waterfront, of the surprising play of words, the unexpected double entendres, the hilarious imaginative creativity. He would say goodbye to Reston and Mariel and leave for home uplifted by coffee, by drugs, by family, sometimes by alcohol. As he walked out of the clearing, away from the giant firstgrowth firs that towered over Reston's house, he saw that all around him young trees were growing up out of the decayed stumps of the old forest. The forest was coming back. In his altered state it was not just a forest but a huge metaphor for life rising out of death, for rebirth coming from senseless slaughter. Or was that just what a forest was when one saw beyond the trees?

Ryan had a favourite tree: one of two huge firs that stood beside the artificial lake that had been dammed to gave water to False Bay. Somehow they had been spared the logger's saws. Neighboring trees, drowned by the lake's rising waters, stood dead and ghostly near the water's shallow edge. Ryan liked to stand next to one of the living firs. He would wade through the wet salal and put his back against the tree and close his eyes. He had heard that the huge upward osmotic energy in old trees pulled the kundalini up your spine. People said that this was a Native tradition—it was one of the myths that everybody seemed to know—but Ryan wondered how the West Coast natives had learned about kundalini. He didn't experience any kundalini but it felt good to be connected to this six hundred year old being that had persevered through so much time. He felt his awareness rise through it, as though through an antennae, and connect him to his far away daughter and wife.

When he arrived home he was wet, but his little house was still warm. He threw a couple of the logs on the embers and blew them into flame, and then changed into dry long johns and a sweater. He brewed himself some bancha twig tea, feeling sattvic after all his adventures in tamas land. He sat on the madras bed cover, comforted by the muffled popping of the fire

155

and by the sound of the rain drumming on the roof. He watched the rain drip from the cedar eaves. Outside his windows, the branches of the fir trees looked like stylised Salish fish tossing in the wind.

He knew that tomorrow the clouds might lift and he would be able to finish gathering leaves for the garden. With the bags filled and tied shut, he would stand in the forest for awhile, listening to its sounds and feeling winter come. There would still be stretches of fine weather, he knew, but they wouldn't last forever. He would be able to cut a bit more wood, would be able to climb the bluff behind his house at least one more time to see the whole world spread out below him in crystal clarity, all the way south to Mount Baker and the Cascades; all the way north to the fang-like mountain that projected out of the sea. But time was running out. Each time the sun came back, it came back for a shorter time; each stormy period cooled the air more and put more moisture in the ground, giving rise to more clouds. Each day was shorter than the one before. Clearly, the Cloud-Beings were winning. He was walking down a series of sunny steps into the unbroken darkness of a west coast winter.

21
Alone

And then one day it happened. The Cloud-Beings came down from the mountains, stalking on long legs of rain. They swept across Georgia Strait, each one perfectly cloud shaped with one great weeping eye in its exact centre. There were thousands of them and they came until they merged into one giant Cloud-Being with a thousand legs of rain and a thousand weeping eyes. They covered the sky, blotting out the sun, and wept upon the island, its inhabitants, its fields, its dried out pine-needle smelling forests, its dusty roads; they wept upon the stippled sea. They had all their spigots working now and their sorrow was immense. The ditches by the roads ran with water; dust turned to mud. The creeks became alive with froth and foamed their way back to the sea again. The remaining blackberries sprouted mould. The hummingbirds were gone.

The warm autumn days of long swims in the ocean and gathering blackberries for wine had long been over; so too the cool clear days of cutting wood while geese flew overhead in scintillating lines. The summer residents fled, scurrying to the ferry with their hastily filled boxes of belongings, leaving their respectable white vans parked for the winter at the Abandoned Church above the ferry.

The Abandoned Church. It had been abandoned by man but perhaps not yet by god. It had been built at a time when there were more people scratching out a living on Vasquez. Once a year a pastor was supposed to come by boat and hold a service for the remaining islanders, but it hadn't happened in a long time. The waves were too rough; Poseidon, ruler of the sea, conspired against the Christian god. Fishermen huddled home in fear as the southeaster beat against their roofs. The door of the church was always left unlocked. Sometimes it blew in the wind, as though spirits were coming and going.

The only service that Ryan could remember had happened once upon a Christmas Eve. It was put on by Brother William, an alcoholic, homosexual monk who had moved to the island in an unlikely attempt to see if rural life would quell his sorrows. Sometimes on the ferry, on early cold mornings, he would stand out on the back deck and say an Egyptian prayer as the sun rose like a fireball out of the south-eastern sea. He was already old compared to the rest of them. He wore his greying hair in a pony tail at the back of his neck. He looked at the sun through his old glasses and it illuminated the ridges and valleys of his skin which was already beginning to sag with age. He stood in his Salvation Army clothes and raised his arms to the sun: "O Atun, giver of life, thou art beautiful upon the horizon."

It had been a beautiful service. The church was lighted with candles that cast a warm light. Outside above the roof, the clouds wept, perhaps for the lost saviour, the elusive Mr. X—after whom Xmas was named—who was pitted, gutted, and spit out by the very people he had attempted to save.

The church was so cold that people kept on their rain gear, gum boots and woollen hats, but little bits of velvet Christmas finery shone out from under their collars. Marijuana rose like frankincense into the rafters. At the front, bottles of blackberry wine, the universal sacrament, and a splendid array of home-baked offerings graced the communion table. Brother William created an eclectic mass. As he spoke, children chased each other in the aisles while the clouds wept outside, drumming on the roof. Within, the community lifted it spirits on wine, on dope, on children's laughter, allowing itself to be led in a sacred celebration of the spirit of Christ by this defrocked monk, allowing itself to receive a blessing from him. The candles glistened with unusual brightness; as Christmas songs were sung, voices joined in a harmony that temporarily rose above the bickering and frustrations of rural life. After that night the church was truly sacred to Ryan. From time to time he came and sat in its quiet space, remembering the descent of spirit that had happened that night.

And Brother William? Years later, after a night of drinking and prayer, he disappeared when the island was asleep and there were no boats coming or going. People thought that he had walked off the end of the dock in his woollen Mackinaw and Salvation Army pants, but nobody was sure because his body was never found. Ryan thought he saw him once, many years later, sitting clean shaven in the Harold Street Caffé in Victoria, drinking wine with a man who looked like Adonis, but he couldn't be absolutely sure.

So perhaps it had been more of a getaway, as in D. H. Lawrence's *The Man Who Died*, where Christ, having survived the crucifixion, shacks up with a priestess of Isis somewhere on the coast of Lebanon. One night they hear the heavy boots of Roman soldiers tramping into the temple courtyard. With a final kiss, Christ simply slips away and rows silently— *Alone*—out across the Mediterranean. The night is clear and still and all the stars are reflected on the surface of the water. The sky and sea are one. There is no line between them. Having given it all once before, this time, when he hears the men with the cross and nails coming for him, he rows for the coast of Africa, his life to lead.

The Abandoned Church had a large grass parking lot that was meant for islanders, when there had been more of them, to park their trucks, jalopies, and tractors, when they came for services. The sheep kept the grass clipped. Now it served as a place for the summer people to leave their cars when they fled the weeping clouds and returned home to their electrically heated houses in Vancouver or Seattle.

Out on the island, the year-round residents had had their profligate summer of fishing, swimming and making love. Now the giant Cloud-Being gathered over them and wept for their sins. Grasshopperism was over. Gone were the clothes-less days and they scurried into clammy rubber rain gear and tried to get the last carrots dug up before the wire worms got them; tried to bring in the tomatoes to ripen on the window sill. Only the hardy kale and chard still raised their flags in gardens that looked like swimming pools. They tried to get the firewood that they had cut and split to heat their homes, to release the sun's stored energy in the rusty fireboxes of their patched together stoves.

The alder leaves fell. The maple leaves fell. The fruit trees were bare. Shining green was replaced by the tracery of bare limbs against the foreboding green of conifers and a sky of swirling grey. Water was everywhere, running, flooding, gurgling, dripping. Houses were filled with wet smoky clothes hanging on racks over smouldering stoves where wet alder, cut too late by these amateurish grasshoppers, hissed and sputtered instead of burned. Plumes of steamy smoke began to rise in the drenched clearings, like offerings to a god that lived beyond the Cloud-Beings, like pleas for intervention.

"Woe is me, woe is me, winter comes," cried the town crier in Everywoman's head, in Everyman's head, the town crier who wandered through the short grey days and long dark nights telling the hours, the slow passage of winter time.

In winter people's thoughts turned toward the reviled city, toward its bright lights, its electric heat, its shops, its movie theatres. The city was less despised now that the Cloud-Beings were weeping over the island, but the islander's beds had been made. There was no money to simply rent a little apartment in town and ride it out. There was small chance of a job with their long hair and the patchwork clothes that they wore out of need and principle. But there was the chance of a trip, a weekend away from the endless weepy-eyed clouds. For several days they could camp on a friend's floor and enjoy hot baths and warm rooms while their friends were at work paying for it.

Even trips to the town across the water, to buy necessities, became a welcome relief: Greasy breakfasts of toast and eggs after the nausea of the ferry trip; riding around in cars, some of which had heaters and defrosters; talking with normal people in stores; buying something new; bringing home chicken, pasta or lasagna noodles as a relief from oysters, chard and greasy island sheep; bringing home a bottle of wine, not the usual jug, but a green bottle from Spain or Portugal, something like Van Gogh might have painted, from somewhere sunny. Later in the cabin, by kerosene light, by the hissing fire, almost warm, they would drink it over the bones of a roast chicken or the remains of a lasagna casserole. Outside the Cloud-Beings would weep and weep as the winter night passed slowly on.

On one such night, after a ferry ride where the couches had slid and crashed from side to side, where soggy grocery bags had broken open and cabbages and oranges had rolled around the floor, where the passenger compartment had filled up with the smell of vomit, the debouched passengers staggered up the hill to the Abandoned Church to find their trucks and bring their sodden purchases home. It was only 6:30 but it had already been dark for two hours and it was pouring rain. Soaked, cloaked figures were waving flashlights around, trying not to lose their bags, their food, their chainsaw parts, their five gallon cans of kerosene. They piled into the backs of trucks and tried to cover things with plastic. They ducked down to protect themselves from the wind and rain, as the trucks, throwing a slurry of gravel and water, ground their way back up the hill.

Ryan sat huddled in the back of one such truck with Ariel, her children and her younger sister, Mel, who had come all the way from Edmonton. All night long on the ferry, before they had closed their eyes and become one with the waves to fight off nausea, Mel had been giving him the gears. She didn't like him. He was power-trippy and manipulative, she said. Perhaps she sensed his attraction to her sister and the threat it posed to her sister's family. Perhaps the sisters had talked. All her comments to him were laced with acid and sarcasm. But they had ended up in the same truck together, and gotten out at the same corner. Now they searched for their bags with flashlights while the clouds wept down on them and the wind combed out the branches of the Tree-Beings that stood above them in the darkness.

The truck rattled and banged off in the darkness, leaving them with their flashlights and their bundles. They walked down the road toward their homes, soaked and shivering. "Can we leave our stuff with you and come up and get it tomorrow?" Ariel asked.

"Sure, of course. Far out. Come in and I'll get a fire going and you can all warm up."

"Oh no," the sister said, "we just need to leave our packages." He could feel the daggers in her eyes trying to find him in the darkness. They walked in their gumboots across the gravel courtyard to the front of his house, wading through a wide shallow puddle. Ryan opened the door and walked in, finding with his flashlight the matches. They sat on the window sill in the head an old sledge hammer, rising out of its handle hole like a tiny bouquet of bright red and blue blossoms. They were called Eddy Strike Anywhere Matches, which sounded to Ryan like the slogan of a BC labour union. He took one out and scratched it against the side of the hammer head. It flashed into sulphurous flame. He lifted the chimney of his antique Aladdin Lamp, hoping that, like its namesake, it would grant him a wish tonight. He lit its circular wick and watched the flame crawl around it. He replaced the chimney. A smoky effluvium rose up until the draft caught and pulled the flame up into the mantle. Suddenly the room was filled with a white hot light. The storm beat outside.

Ryan had had the forethought to lay a fire in the curlicued wood heater. He dropped another match onto the soggy paper and watched blue flames crawl like worms up the pages of yesterday's news. Suddenly the paper caught and its flames rose into the cedar sticks that he had laboriously split—"making toothpicks" he called it—and all hell broke loose, cheery crackling, sparks spitting out, flashes of firelight lighting the room. He left the firebox door open to illuminate the house with its explosive cheer.

Ariel, Mel and the children had put their bags down just inside the door. Ryan looked in his bags for something to get them to stay. He offered the two soaked moppets hot chocolate and the adults wine. Mel begged off, saying that they must be going, but Jessie and Alia clamoured for the chocolate. Shivering, they had pulled the hoods off their wild blond hair and had already moved close to the stove, holding their hands toward the crackling fire. Ariel smiled and said "Yes, thank you. We'll warm up for a while before we head down the road." Mel looked disgusted but took off her coat and sat near the fire on one of the couches. They gathered around the crackling flames.

Ryan went to the cook stove at the other end of the room, clanged open the covers, crumpled paper into the fire box, broke cedar and soon there was a another fire. Tonight he used some of his precious pitchy fir to get things moving. It felt good to offer heat from the wood he had cut, split and dried. In the same way that a bee's honey tells the tale of the summer, the simple act of starting a fire felt like an expression of those bygone sunny months. He filled the aluminum kettle from the copper fixtures he'd soldered and clunked it down on the stove.

Wiley was gone. Ariel, Jessie, Alia and Mel were by themselves down at the house above the water. For him it was incredible to have Ariel as a guest in his house; all his longing went into being the host. He poured wine, the Portuguese kind, from its green bottle. He handed Jessie and Alia warming cups of hot chocolate. "Careful," he said, "it's hot."

He lit the five candles in the Mexican candelabra that had come from the deserts of Guanajuato. Its shape echoed the juniper tree that it lit outside the window. Even Mel began to loosen up in the crackling light of the house. They all took off their coats and hung them to dry on the racks over the cook stove.

After Sheila left, Ryan had dug up a huge sword fern and put it in an oak half-barrel between the kitchen and living areas of the house. The kerosene lamps cast leafy shadows against the walls. Ryan had also moved the madras covered single beds out into the centre of the room where they served as sofas. There were also thick couch cushions with velvety patterns of vines and leaves placed on a frayed imitation Persian carpet. One of the good things about the painful experience of breaking up was that finally, for better or worse, he got to be his own self rather than the compromise self of marriage.

In winter, cold air and drafts hung close to the ground, but other than that he found this arrangement sociable and wonderful. Some people felt uncomfortable with the unconventionality of the arrangement and didn't drop by much anymore. Others scarcely noticed as they drank tea, toked up, and ate curried lentils sitting Buddha-style on the floor: after all, this was not the 'other side' where, as Malvina Reynolds had sung, all the houses were made of ticky-tacky and everyone looked just the same. That was why they were here, wasn't it: to lose, with some help from drugs, that stifling sense of appropriateness and find out what was underneath.

Right now what was underneath was seduction, a pleasant playing with fire. The question was how to do this while surrounded by the children and a hostile sister. The rain continued to fall. Ryan offered dinner, refilled wine glasses. The house became warm and stuporous. Portuguese wine, pasta, a salad, the magic of lamp light, the sounds of the fires, the drumming of rain on the roof—the weeping of the clouds—the gusts of wind buffeting big fat drops against the windows, all conspired to create a trance of amiable inertia. He put on his rain slicker and slipped out to the woodshed where, flashlight in mouth, he pulled the cord that started the tiny Honda generator. He didn't use it much because, tiny as it was, it shattered the silence of the night. Once, on a full moon in February, when the roads, the hills, and the trees were sparkling with snow, he had gone for a walk, leaving his friends listening to music. Two miles down the road he could still hear the tiny generator fibrillating the crystalline night through the bare branches. Tonight it didn't matter. The storm drowned out all sounds from further away than a few feet.

He came back in and put on one of the reel-to-reel tapes that Sheila and he had made before coming to Canada. The women exclaimed and almost swooned as Bob Dylan came on in his new post-motor-cycle-accident voice singing, with Johnny Cash, "Lay lady lay, lay across my big brass bed awhile, Stay lady stay while the night is still ahead."

It was a married song, though, filled with love in the midst of struggle and working for a living. Ryan felt left out, but the music filled the room and held his guests for awhile more. As Ryan cleared away the wreckage of the dinner, they sat back and smoked cigarettes, their eyes staring off into the darkness of the fir ceiling. The girls were sleepy now, huddled on one of the beds. "Why don't you just lie down" Ariel said. Ryan brought them a blanket.

Mel, Ariel and Ryan sat on the couches listening to the music and smoking. After awhile Mel picked up a book and lay on other couch. She covered herself with a comforter and propped herself up on one elbow, holding her book so that light from the smoky lamp fell on its pages. After awhile she was asleep.

Ariel and Ryan talked softly, about Dylan, about whether his music after the accident was as good as the music before, about whether one could keep up the intensity out of which his early songs were born, or whether that great burning of energy had to come to an end.

They talked about marriage. He, having lost his, said, "But don't you think it's natural to come to the end of a person, of their influence, of what they have to show you? Don't you think it's natural to want to move on?"

She, still in one, said, "But don't you think that two people can keep exploring, go deeper all their life; that through one person you can know all people?"

It was as though a trance had settled in around them, a sleeping spell. They too were tired and lay down, in their city jeans and sweaters, on the remaining couch. The bed was narrow and after awhile Ariel and he were lying in each other's arms. For him, holding Ariel after all these months of longing was so intense that he could barely breathe. One by one the lamps and candles burned out, like the lights going down at the end of a play.

The music ended and there was the barely audible flap, flap, flap of the loose end of the tape going round and round. They held each other and drifted in the magic of the night. The little generator ran out of gas and coughed to a stop. The fires were damped down, just barely smouldering. The storm rolled outside, tossing the tree tops like masts. The forest around them creaked and groaned.

They lay in each other's arms, almost innocently, each in some way knowing that this was their moment, their only moment; that they could be lovers in spirit only. In this moment there was also a sign on the trail of love, "PRIVATE PROPERTY, DO NOT ENTER," a flaming sign left by an archangel to warn them that anything further would be of no avail, that it was all downhill from this moment where, passionately awake, entranced, they lay surrounded by her sleeping family.

22
Alone

In the morning Ryan tore himself away from Ariel before her children and sister awakened. Tip-toeing through the house, he quietly started the stove, filled the kettle and then went into the back bedroom and crawled under the covers to read. When he heard the sounds of their awakening he came out and made coffee with canned milk for the adults, hot chocolate from powdered milk for the kids. The sun had come out and the world outside the windows was glistening with rain drops. Ariel, busy organising the kids, was shy and friendly with him. It was almost like nothing had happened.

Ariel, Mel and the children organised their bundles and borrowed his wheelbarrow to take them down the road to their home. Once again Ryan stood on the porch and watched them go, as he and Sheila had done when they first met Ariel. Again, the children started laughing and talking loudly as they entered the forest, to dispel the imaginary creatures that lurked in the sword ferns, in the dark cedar groves, in the Labrador tea swamp.

The Labrador tea swamp. It lay just off the road on the way down to Ariel's. Ryan had discovered it while looking for thorn-apple trees from which to make the big wooden wedges he used to split buried cedars. The cedars, too big to haul out, had been left behind by the last generation of loggers. Forty years later they appeared as elongated mounds of humus covered with young plants—huckleberry, salal, salmon berry, Oregon grape. The roots of these plants ran along the fissures in the bark. As Ryan tore the plants out, great chunks of 40 year old humus flew off the log. The rest he scraped off with his double bit axe.

The logs were rotten two or three inches in, but sound and seasoned after that, perfect for fence posts. He started the split with steel wedges and, after that, used the two foot wooden ones he had made from thorn-apple branches to break them open the rest of the way. Work On What Has Been Spoiled.

Walking down the road, he had seen a few thorn-apples near its fork. Returning with axe and chainsaw, he struggled through the salal to get to them. He discovered that they were part of a great ring of thorn-apple trees that grew around a sunny clearing in the middle of the gloomy forest. Intrigued, he fought his way through the barrier of trees. The long thorns that grew from their looping branches caught his hair, causing him to stop and untangle himself several times. Scratched and punctured, he emerged into the large clearing, a swamp concealed in the middle of the forest.

He waded through the waist high Labrador tea bushes toward the center of the clearing, stopping to grab a handful of the leaves. They had long, almost chartreuse green tops and were covered underneath with orange fuzz. He crumpled them and held them under his nose, taking in their intoxicating, resinous smell. The ground was dry and the sun blazed down out of the sky. The whole clearing smelled of the leaves. It was silent except for the soft murmuring of ten thousand tiny solitary bees—the murmuring of innumerable bees. From the centre of the circular swamp he looked around the ring of tree tops. The sky above him was like a great open eye with the sun as its pupil.

Ryan found a dry place to sit, hidden among the bushes. He worried that he would be overcome by the scent of the leaves and drift off to sleep. He had a fantasy about his skeleton being found by another adventurer, someone coming to cut thorn-apple, in a distant future.

As much as he didn't want to fall asleep, he did. First he leaned on his elbows and then, a few minutes later, settled onto his back, hands beneath his head, knees up in the air—just for a few minutes he told himself. He had some thoughts that he was getting sleepy and should get up and start cutting wedges, but by then it was too late. The languor was delicious.

He dreamed of a faraway city sinking into the boggy plain on which it had been built. It was full of tilting stone churches and medieval statues that talked and pointed him toward a river. Angels with great flapping wings flew above the banks of the river and drove deformed beings into it. Among these were hybrid creatures with the heads of animals and the bodies of humans. There were men with pig's heads and women with elephant's feet. They were all tumbling into the water and being carried away by the great murky river.

In one of the ancient stone streets he met a hot young woman who had had a religious experience. Her genitals were in flame. She invited him up to her room where a fundamentalist preacher prepared to convert him. The preacher showed him a book that had pictures of his lineage in it, pictures of all the street preachers from the past. They were shown standing outside of bars, outside poolrooms and whorehouses. They were all waiting to lend anyone who had fallen a hard hand back. They were waiting for someone who was willing to be led out of hell.

When he awakened from the dream the sun was low on the horizon. He raised himself slowly onto his elbows and watched three deer browse on the other side of the quiet clearing. He replayed the images from the dream and wondered how his inner world could be so different from the world around him. He felt disoriented and wondered if he had been there for an hour, a few hours, a day, or several days. He half expected to see the handle of his axe eaten away by worms like in the old Chinese fairy tale; to find his chain saw inhabited by little solitary bees who climbed in and out of the muffler to get to their nest in its frozen cylinder.

The sun was no longer on the clearing and the bees had fallen silent. He imagined them sitting down in their burrows in tiny rocking chairs knitting black and yellow scarves. Suddenly he felt that a spell had been cast on him. He jumped to his feet and whirled around to locate the place in the trees where he had left his saw and axe. The deer scattered in leaping bounds and disappeared into the surrounding forest. He ran in panic through the snagging brush, and was relieved to find his tools intact, relieved to touch the modern manufactured goods, to feel the word "Homelite" stamped in the blue cover of his chainsaw, to start it and hear the roar of its engine.

Yes, he understood why the children shouted in the forest. Perhaps, he thought, a spell had been cast on him that day: his life was different now. He had no wife, no child. He was seeing a beautiful Japanese-Canadian woman. He was in love with his neighbour's wife. How did this all happen? When did it change? Was it that day in the swamp? Had the beings in the medieval stone city affected him in some way? Had the preacher set him a lesson?

Ryan's larder began to get low. He looked in the cabinets under the sink and found that the gallon can of safflower oil was almost empty, as were the bags of brown rice and whole wheat flour.

He opened the cupboard in the wall. Its door was of the same darkened fir as the rest of the house. Inside, it had shelves and screened holes that let in the cold air from the outside. In winter it served as a refrigerator. His block of cheese was reduced to a mouldy rind. There was no more peanut butter. Its can had already been fitted with a wire handle and had a jagged hole for a candle poked into its side to make it into a bug lamp. Held by its twisted wire handle with the open end forward, it became a little candle powered spotlight to light up the night. The five gallon kerosene can was also nearly empty, and he was almost out of dope. The local store carried only Cheesies and Aunt Jemima pancake mix. The rain fell outside. It was time for a trip to the city.

The night before the trip Ryan gathered his rain gear, a change of clothes, his sleeping bag, and put them in the his huge aluminum frame pack from REI. He would also use it to carry his food home. He put his gumboots by the door and in the morning left silently without taking the time to light a fire. He fired up the old red Volvo, which now had wires under the dashboard that he touched together to activate the starter. He drove it to False Bay, parking at the Abandoned Church.

It was a flat-calm day on the ferry. The sea was dull grey-green punctuated with bits of driftwood and seaweed. There was no bonhomie this morning, no conversation. People seemed withdrawn and in their own space. There was only the thrumming of the boat. Ariel was on board, as was Julie. This was a confusing situation. Ryan felt so close to Ariel but she was married and unavailable so he was sitting with Julie, with whom he was also close, talking softly. Ariel talked to McElwaith and began to laugh animatedly about something, beginning to build a hilarious atmosphere in the wet grey morning.

The ferry was full. Half the island seemed to be headed for the bright lights, escaping the dampness, the greyness, the darkness. They wore their gumboots, toques and raingear, proudly wearing the uniform of the back-to-the-lander, not bothering to change into "town clothes." Smelling of woodsmoke and sawdust, they liked to strut their poverty, their simplicity, their patched, free-store clothing. They were like monks visiting Babylon, all the while loving every moment of Babylon, its luxurious hot baths, its houses, its bright lights, its movies and restaurants.

Ryan's first trip to the city had come some months after Sheila had left. "I lived alone then," he had written in his journal, "with integrity. I was happy then, self sufficient, happy just to be with myself. I travelled to Vancouver, making the journey on foot, and brought back my pack weighed down with brown rice, with a shiny gallon can of oil, some figs, some cheese, some flour. I bought these things at Famous Foods. It felt good to be eating food that was famous. I was living very simply then, stripped of wife, of car, of job. I did yoga in the morning. I was truly celibate then. I lost this. I fell from that bright rim. I tumbled back into samsara, into the entanglements of desire and attraction again."

Now, sitting not far from two women with whom he was entangled in different ways, he felt an impending sense of moral doom, as if he had crossed a line and retribution was sure to follow. On the other hand, he thought, this might just be his conditioning, the things his narrow Christian culture had taught him to feel about love and sex and attachment. On one shoulder the preacher from the dream promised damnation, but on the other Crosby, Stills and Nash crooned "if you can't be with the one you love, love the one you're with." He relaxed a bit and sat back on the blanket-covered, vomit-scented couch and allowed himself to lean against Julie. She leaned back against him and they rode in mammalian comfort for awhile.

After a time, they went onto the back deck, the smoking deck as McElwaith called it. McElwaith was already there, cracking jokes. His curly blond locks hung out from under his toque and his eyes sparkled with a blue that was absent from the sky today. Ariel was there too, looking cold and shivery, hunched over a little. Julie and Ryan joined them. Together, standing on the tiny back deck, they looked like a renegade school teacher, a logger, and two refugees from South America. Their words, their laughter, were whipped out across the waters of Georgia Strait, as ephemeral and bright as rose petals on the Ganges. The inevitable joint came out. Elroy the cowboy appeared, his timing immaculate, making it five. They smoked and huddled out of the wind. The slick grey sea moved steadily past them.

After they had toked up, Elroy looked at Ryan and said, in his deep Texas drawl, "Man, where you headed?'

"Ahm outta awmost everything so Ahm headed for the big smoke." Ryan said in a fake Texas accent almost as thick as Elroy's. Elroy looked guarded for a moment, wondering if he was being mocked, but then saw the good nature in Ryan's eyes and laughed.

Ariel said, "Yea, me too. Goddamned cheques—the once a month shuffle. Like, I mean, why don't they just give you the money, send it out to you? It's like you earned it by paying into their system for years, right?" She told them that Mel was staying home to help Wylie with Jessie and Alia. "If we can get The Hotel running we can take it. I'm not going to drive it, though."

"Far out, what's happening with it?" Elroy was interested. He had a skill with cars that opened doors for him.

"Well, it might just need a jump, it might be okay. It might just need a push. It hasn't been used in a long time."

The Hotel. The Hotel was the ancient purple Plymouth that Wylie owned. It was shaped like a turtle, one long curve from windshield to back bumper, from eyebrows to ass. It was cavernous inside with plush grey seats. It was an antique, a car from the forties, but Wylie wasn't a collector. He had picked it up for $100 somewhere. It was unregistered and unlicensed. Most of the time, it just sat unlocked in the French Bay parking lot. It had come to be called The Hotel because it had become a refuge for people travelling up and down the coast. Since the most common form of transportation was hitchhiking in this travel-light, possessionless era, missed ferries were as common as missed heartbeats and missed periods. Having to rely on ferries cultivated an accepting Taoist perspective on life: "Well, if I make the 5:30 ferry I'll see you tonight, otherwise I'll be there in the morning."

People with cars drove like hell to catch the ferry. There were probably more wrecks on the Island Highway due to racing for ferries than any other cause. This was a consequence of driving fast with one eye on the rear-view mirror, looking for cops, instead of on the road ahead. When the frantic drivers pulled onto the dock at French Bay, just in time to watch the Vasquez ferry sail away without them, they cursed like hell. Sometimes they blew their horn, flashed their lights, or got out and waved their arms, trying to get the ferry to come back for them. The baleful Captain just laughed, a sneering laugh—one of his rare smiles.

The hitchhiker, on the other hand, was more philosophical: he thought, "maybe I'll catch it, and maybe I won't." In his stoned-out mind it was all the will of god, part of the path of surrendering ego. "Well, if I'm meant to get there tonight, I will. If I'm not it's because something else is meant to happen."

That "something else," for Ryan, was, more often than not, a night in The Hotel. That meant sitting in the comfortable back seat of the old Plymouth watching the light fade over the boat basin, watching people come and go in the harbour. It meant having dinner, pulling something out of his pack, like the remains of a loaf of heavy bread full of millet seeds that scattered and lodged in the upholstery, or a bit of cheese and some Polish sausage from Save-On-Meats in Vancouver. Then there was the ubiquitous Marijuana, so as night came, it meant having a toke and settling in to sort through memories, read a book or write a poem by flashlight in the womb-like darkness of the old car.

Sometimes a fellow traveller jumped into the car in the middle of the night. Ryan remembered one gnome-like creature that opened the door and entered like Rumpelstiltskin. He wore a little English felt hat over his long hair. "Hey man, cool. Wet out. Mind if I come in?" He called himself Phillip and had hitched all the way up from California to visit a commune on Denman. Everybody was on the move, looking for places to live. Somehow the word of this old car where you could sleep for free had travelled all the way down the coast. Phillip settled in. They shared a joint. There was a sense they were part of a great cosmic plan that was unfolding, a plan that was too large to see in its entirety, of which one could only get a glimmer. They talked about the spiritual unfolding that was happening, about Bodhisatvas which they believed that they all were, at least in some minor sort of way.

"Some of 'em are avatars like Christ, man," said Phillip, "like Quetzalquotal, realized beings, gods, who come down to enlighten humans. They take on the pain of birth, and often persecution, to show us the way and guide our evolution. Others, like Buddha, are humans, who through their own practice worked their way up."

"But where is this going, do they let go of their personality and merge with universal mind? Is there really only one being in many bodies?"

"I don't know, man, I don't know, but I don't think that would be so bad, do you? I mean, like, what are we letting go of, bad habits, hang-ups, individual tastes in food—like who cares if you don't like spinach—and then look at what we get in return, cosmic consciousness, I mean, like to merge with the mind of the universe. I mean, like fuck, that's why relationships are so crazy. It doesn't matter who you're with, it's like we're all the same anyway, what's all this about falling in love with one version, one set of looks, one history, one set of habits."

A wind had come up and the old Plymouth occasionally rocked with a particularly nasty gust. Rain blew against the windows and ran down them in long streaks. Out in the boat basin, rigging clanged against the masts.

"I don't know, man, it sounds kind of scary, like ants or bees or something." Ryan was still into individualism, invested in it. He carried his pain and history knotted in the layers of his body. He was almost bent over by his experience of being human, by stories from his parents broken marriage, by seeing farm land destroyed by suburbs, by years of rejection in school because his parents, out of principle, had refused to buy him the right kind of clothes. All this had to be worth something, right?

Ryan was shaped by it, warped by it like an old tree that had grown on stony soil and been shaped by high winds. Who would he be without this history, this tale of family, this tale of all the pain through which his young shoot had been forced to grow? A smiling hippy? Far out man? They were all so young to be thinking about such things, to be pondering evolution, spirit and the meaning of things. They were like street children who, without education, taught each other the ropes, the constructs that kept their shattered minds working and afloat.

Ryan looked like a hippy now. Anyone would have called him a hippy. There was the long frizzy hair that never quite stayed in pigtails, the Mexican dress, the endless smoking of dope and search for altered consciousness. It all said, "hippy." Then there was the patois, "groovy," "far-out," "man," but he was only hiding there—as were many others—in a simplicity of language that allowed them to meet and talk without the complexity of opinion or judgement. To him it was not quite real. He saw it as *epater la bourgeoisie*, as a variation on Baudelaire and absinthe, as a violent turning his back on the well kept houses and neighbourhoods that had kept him starved and empty for so many years.

The Hotel. Now, the ferry having landed, Ariel, Julie, Elroy and Ryan carried their packs to it. They had talked themselves into going to Vancouver, into bringing back cheap food, into eating Chinese, into seeing a movie, into staying at someone's house with a bathtub and central heating. There was no plan. It was spontaneous and last minute. Go with the flow. The Hotel had no keys, and you had to start it by twisting wires together and then turning the ignition with the screwdriver in the glove box. It seemed like a great adventure was about to begin. Amazingly, Elroy started the Plymouth with only a little coaxing. Ariel took some time to clean it, brushing crumbs and millet grains off the old plush seat and tossing out paper scraps. Ryan would drive because he still had a valid B.C. driver's license. Who would sit where, he wondered as he climbed behind the wheel. There it was again, hippy passivity: just leaving it up to the Tao, letting things unfold, having faith that whatever happened would be right; an unwillingness to intervene, lest the ego—the smaller self— bugger up some larger unfolding of the universe. They were all like egg whites being folded into a large batter, their individual bubbles breaking up to become the leavening for a greater loaf.

As it was, Julie climbed in next to Ryan and sat quietly at the other end of the long seat. There was a contained introspectiveness about her. Her hands were folded on her lap like she was letting life move by and around her. Elroy and Ariel climbed in back. Packs and bags were in the capacious trunk. Elroy's omnipresent guitar case with stickers of all the states he'd been through sat on the floor of the back seat.

They were off to Vancouver in this unregistered car, trusting in the Tao that they would somehow make it there in a society that frowned on both drug use and unregistered vehicles. Perhaps there was a magic mantle around them that made them look like they were in a nice 1972 Plymouth? Think Again. They looked like gypsies in their long hair, scarves, Stetsons, and proudly patched clothing. They looked like they had escaped from a

Furry Freak Brothers cartoon, peering out from the dark windows of their ancient car.

Perhaps, though, they would just slip through the cracks. How many cop cars were there in relation to all cars? What were the probabilities that a cop would pull in right behind you and notice the expired license plate? Later, when Ryan met Reina, she told him that her apache guru had said "There is really no room for us in society. We must live in its interstices." So off they went, hoping to surf the interstices all the way to Vancouver and back.

The ferry trip was uneventful. Ryan did yoga on one of the carpeted floors:

"Mommy what's that man doing."

"Let's just keep walking."

Elroy played his guitar, quietly, in an open place in front of the ship. He was clean shaven and somehow had managed to keep his jeans and western shirt with the pearl snap flaps over the pockets clean. His Stetson was spotless. Mothers didn't snatch their children away but sat quietly nearby listening to his songs. Children came and stared at him. One shy girl touched his guitar. Ariel bought a magazine. Julie sat contemplatively by a window watching the grey sea pass by outside. To the north they saw Vasquez, their world, reduced to a small grey hump sticking out of the winter water. It was hard to believe that so much Sturm und Drang was contained on such a small speck of land. The passion of an anthill.

The car lumbered out of the belly of the ferry, and amid trucks and buses, climbed the hills of West Vancouver. Keenly aware of their unregistered status, they tried to wedge themselves between large, slow moving trucks, front and back, to limit their chances of being seen by a passing cop. They passed the glass palaces of West Vancouver and threaded their way over the bridges to Kitsilano where they parked their car in a blackberry-lined lane behind Ryan's friend Rachel's house. They climbed the steps of the decaying Yew Street house and knocked on the door. Rachel was not home. She must have been working. Ryan left a note saying that they would be back tonight. They decided to leave the car in the lane behind her house to avoid being pulled over and ticketed in cop-thick Vancouver. They would run their errands, travelling on buses, filling their packs with staples until the packs became so heavy that they could barely lift them. Then they would meet back here at five, connect with Rachel, and see if it was all right to spend the night.

That night, instead of going out, they cooked together at Rachel's. Rachel was a Buddhist so they cooked a stir-fry with fresh tofu from the Sunrise Market, and served it over brown rice. They brought bottles of wine. For desert they had black bean cakes with red painted tops. They sliced them into thin fingers and passed them around on a blue willow plate.

Rachel was older than Ryan; her hair was growing grey. Ryan had met her when she and Sheila had been in some kind of Art and Spirit conference together. He had kept the connection. She worked in a ministry, the government kind, all day long, and was glad for a night of wild talk. She was amused by their tales of life on the island, by their talk about gardens and chickens. Ariel and Rachel found common ground about working in an office and dealing with the stupidity of supervisors. They shared stories and laughed about what it was like to be stoned at work.

Rachel had glaucoma and even now looked at them through thick tinted glasses. Marijuana helped relieve the pressure in her eyes and, living in a straight-laced world, she was grateful for the connections through which she could get it. Since he had started smoking dope again, Ryan always bought some extra to share with Rachel. Slowly, for medicinal reasons, she had become a hippy—very undercover. What she hadn't shared with them in the brightness of her conversation, was that blindness awaited her at the end. So she kept her job for the pension, enjoying each day of fading sight and saving for the time when she would live in darkness. She talked about impermanence, and about the puja she had attended the previous weekend. The islanders—marijuana Buddhists—knew the words; thought they knew all about it. They lived in the illusion that they were already enlightened or at least nearly so, "almost there." "The joke is," Ryan said, "that we are already enlightened and don't even know it, so we bring ourselves down by searching for enlightenment."

The wine was poured in Rachel's crystal glasses. The room filled with the scent of food and the perfume of hashish. By the end of dinner they were all in an altered state. Psychically Ryan was with Ariel. He

176

loved listening to the ease of her conversation as she got to know Rachel, listening to the effortless way she connected with everyone in the room. Now that they were here, away from the island, without their pasts, without their households, without their furniture, without their children, it almost felt like they were together. The only problem, as he periodically reminded himself, was that he was with Julie. She sat next to him, from time to time making soft asides.

Ryan felt Ariel's affection for him: her eyes darted toward him when she said something particularly funny. She seemed open and free tonight, but now he was the one with a partner. His relationship with Julie was not a formal one, they didn't live together, they didn't make plans together, but was there some expectation of their togetherness in this situation? Ryan wondered. He thought there was, but didn't really know. He couldn't tell.

They were thrown together in a strange effort to live a life where one's actions bore some resemblance to one's thoughts. Elroy was quiet, smiling, accepting. As he got more stoned his blue eyes got more crinkly. He spoke with them, smiled with them—beamed a shy acceptance to these older people who'd taken him in.

"Love the One You're With," the song said, but what if you were with both the one you loved and the one you were with? Ryan took one more toke in an attempt to rise to higher ground and see the situation more clearly, but only got more confused.

After dinner they donned jackets, coloured scarves, serapes, Stetsons and stepped out from under the still dripping eaves of Rachel's house into a night that had become star spangled and fiercely clear. The city was spread out around them like a glittering sequinned sari draped over the hills. It was full of neon brightness. A thousand electric moons burned along the streets and the three bridges were draped with pearls.

They took a Granville Street bus downtown and climbed out onto the wet, reflective sidewalks, strolling along with the mid-evening crowd of theatre and club goers, strolling past broken wino's and junkies who held their hands out for change.

It was inconceivable to them how people could wind up like this, stumbling, dirty, begging for change, sleeping in filthy rooms, stabbing each other for small possessions, their bodies winding up in dumpsters. The wino's and junkies seemed like living skeletons with just enough flesh to animate their wanderings through the arcade of life. Life was pleasant when you were full and stoned.

Ryan reached out and took both Julie's and Ariel's hands. Julie took Elroy's. They wandered up the street holding hands in a group, marijuana short-circuiting social rules and conditioning. It never occurred to them that their path away from their parent's sterile, well lighted homes could descend as far down as into the world of these slur-speeched creatures around them. It never occurred to them that some of these creatures had started out as they did, losing themselves in the revelry of their time, probably whisky and beer. It never occurred to them that in their time they too might have laughed at those who condemned themselves to the falsehoods of the classroom, the logging camp, the secretary's desk. Ryan could almost see the head of a dog, the head of a pig, the head of a jackal, as they wheedled and clutched around them, trying to get a dime or tell their blurry story.

The group had no plans. They had the idea that they wanted to take in a flic, but they hadn't looked in the paper to see what was playing or at what time. They rebelled against the clock: having to be someplace at a given hour vitiated the freedom of the moment. It was only the ferries that still exerted this tyranny over them. They simply wandered around this urban world, which transformed by drugs seemed like a fairy land. Its streets full of cars and people were so different from the silent forests that surrounded their island homes. They bought baklava in little paper trays at a Persian market that sold mostly pop and cigarettes. They continued their stroll, eating the baklava slowly, entering into a sugar reverie, the yoga of merging with food, the munchies.

Lighted movie marquee's were arrayed like oases along the night street. Each marquee was a tower of light, its pulsing reflections streaming onto the still wet pavement. Short lines of people clustered in front of the box offices as though they had come to get the latest news. The company of four wandered from marquee to marquee, looking at the posters, talking about actors and movies they'd seen. They were starved for movies. They were like Rip Van Winkle trying to get updated on the village after years of being away.

Ahead of them now, ahead of their sauntering non-attached, lingering, laughing foursome, a marquee arose with the word WOODSTOCK emblazoned in red capital letters across its fluorescent facade. The four of them were drawn to it as though by a magnet. Around them, people—some well-dressed, some in tie-dies and Afghani coats—paid their money and entered the doors of the theatre. Ariel, Julie, Elroy and Ryan looked at the posters. There were pictures of people sliding naked in the mud. There were pictures of a field full of people with great, loudspeaker-clustered towers looming over them like H.G. Well's monsters. In the sky, over the crowd's heads, were dubbed the faces of Jimmy Hendrix, Janis Joplin, Sly, and Joni Mitchell. They looked like the heads of Hindu deities in the process of materialisation. "But where are the fighter planes turning into butterflies?" Ariel asked.

They knew that this is what the universe had to offer them tonight. A ripple of electricity ran through them. They knew this was why they had been drawn downtown. They must see it.

"I almost made it, you know." said Ryan. "Like, some freaks came by the old farmhouse in Quebec where Sheila and I were living. They said, 'Hey, man we're going to this rock festival, do you want to come with us?' They had a yellow VW bus. We had met them while camping in New Brunswick. Man, I was so out of it, so in my own little world, like, I said 'Wow, like, what's a rock festival?' And they said, 'Man, it's like a lot of bands and a lot of people getting together.' Man, I had a baby. Sheila and I were just barely getting along and I said, 'Well, what if it rains?' Sheila and I talked it over and said 'no, like, it's too much.' Man, we didn't know what we were missing. It's like it wasn't even called Woodstock back then. Nobody had heard of Woodstock. It was just called a rock festival. I missed the event of my time, and someone had even driven right to the door to give me a ride. That's how out of it I was back then. I guess I learned that it's better to say yes than to say no."

Everyone laughed. Elroy, his blue eyes crinkling, said "Well man, here's your chance. At least you can catch it on film."

"Hey, it's, like, five bucks." Elroy pulled out a battered hand-tooled wallet that had only coins in it, not the loonies or twonies of today, but small coins—pennies, dimes, nickels and quarters—back from before Canada had become a third world country.

179

"Hey, well, like, what are they doing ripping us off like this, I mean, like they are making millions on this thing, right? And it's about our people isn't it?" It was Ariel speaking. She said this with just the right amount of lightness in her voice, just the right amount of laughing irony, to make it easily walk the line between joke and serious proposition. It was also an attempt to expand the possibilities of the moment, a veiled suggestion, presented with laughter, which could either be let go of or acted upon. If acted upon it became a kind of experiment. Would they actually be able to talk their way into the show? Ha, Ha, Ha. That was one of her gifts, to slip into madness and at the same time laugh at herself, at all of them, for being the madness of who they were. Ryan loved her for it.

Tonight they were stoned enough for this argument to make some sort of sense. A revolutionary zeal arose within them. They felt personally ripped off that the life they were trying to lead, a life of living on the land, of drugs and music and freedom, was being sold to the conformist masses—with jobs, apartments, central heating and running hot water—for vicarious pleasure. It just seemed terribly unfair.

Ryan felt some sort of power rise within him. Maybe it was too much dope and wine with dinner, but he felt unsinkable, like no one could attack him on the street, like no one could refuse him. He had expanded, for the moment, beyond the fears that lived inside him like cringing dogs, beyond the need to be polite, beyond the need to not make waves. He was giddy on it. He saw in this moment how the world was bound by the conventions and niceties of politeness, which functioned as a chastity belt against atavism. He also saw that anyone who stood outside them, even a little, even for a moment, could have whatever they wanted provided that the mob didn't destroy them first. In this state he rose to the possibility that Ariel had teasingly suggested: giving up hippy passivity, just for the moment, he decided to champion Ariel's words.

The manager of the theatre was an older man with a toothpick moustache and wavy white hair. He stood outside the door taking tickets. He wore a purple blazer with the logo of the theatre on it. Except for a slightly obsequious manner he looked more like a classical violinist than a theatre manager. Ryan approached him. His friends stood behind him.

"Hello!"

"Hello Young Man!"

"How are you?"

"Fine, fine,"

"We'd like to see Woodstock but we don't have the money. We think you should let us in because it is about our people and you are making lots of money on it. It's only fair to give some back."

Ryan was not aware that this was just the same old guilt trip between the haves and the have-nots that had caused him so many problems. (Otherwise known as "the Halves" and the "Halve-nots:" the former having enough that they could give away half of it, while the later had so little that they had to keep it all for themselves). It was also not exactly true that they didn't have money. It was true for Elroy, but only relatively true for the rest of them.

"Well if we did that with everybody…"

"Well we're not everybody. How many people have asked you this before?"

The manager kept tearing tickets in half as he talked with Ryan, taking time out to thank each of the people who were passing into his theatre. Ryan stood quietly, feeling that he was a force to be reckoned with. It was as though a powerful, manipulative, self-serving person—the very person that Mel has accused him of being—had been lurking inside his quiet, nice-guy homesteader persona, and now, Djinn like, it had escaped from its bottle and was offering the gratification of hitherto unsatisfied desires. Julie and Ariel stood beside him, both delectable in their own ways. Maybe he could have both of them. Why be limited to one girl friend, one wife. He could tell that they were enraptured, entertained by this little drama. For one who had never dared to push too much, it was an exciting game. Elroy stood a little back, somewhat shy, both amused and a little embarrassed by this grandiloquent show of language and concern for justice. The people in the line appeared to be listening closely.

"I'll tell you what, young feller," the theatre manager said "we'll compromise, you pay half and I'll take half price. Half price. Seems fair to me." The theatre manager was apparently a Halve.

Inside the dark world of the theatre, the cave against whose wall all things were projected, they heard the sound of a thousand thunders. The twang and snarl of guitars filled the darkness. Clouds passed quickly overhead as the cameras panned to the sky. The screen was filled with images of innocence and abandon, with images of the immensity of a gathered tribe, of safety and power in numbers. On the wall of the cave they watched the promise of change, the promise of thousands, nay millions, standing in peace, abandoning their worship of moloch, returning to the soil, living in love, singing in prayer. And they were part of all this. To them it told the very story of their lives.

They left, stunned and transformed, into a night where the stars had moved just a little; where the moon, old and crumbling, had canted only a little further west, perhaps to shine down on their island, out on the dark waters of Georgia Strait. The streets were almost empty at this late hour. The final shows had played. The lights were off in the tall buildings. They walked along through the darkened cliffs of brick and concrete on either side of them.

Together, they felt awed and peaceful. Perhaps the drugs and wine were wearing off, or perhaps the dark, yin energies of late evening had taken hold, but the expansiveness of earlier was gone. They were missing families and homes. There was the big family, the tribe, the Woodstock family, but there were also the smaller families of children, of husbands and wives, of islanders. The city spread around them with its miles of sleeping houses. Apartment buildings rose around them like storage units in which sleeping people were efficiently stacked, layer upon layer.

In the empty side streets, they walked past parked cars in which prostitutes were giving blow jobs. They walked over to Burrard and crossed the bridge. They walked under its ornate tower where Captain Vancouver stood in the prow of his boat. They stood on the bridge and looked up and down the inlet. Cars passed only infrequently now. The late night enfolded them in silence.

They came down off the bridge and walked past the brewery with its cloud of steam rising into the night sky; they climbed up into Kitsilano and up the creaking stairs of Rachel's house.

The porch smelled of rot and rain and piss. The old houses of Kitsilano had not been yuppied-up yet and were sinking back into the soil, turning into humus. Rachel had given Ryan the key, and he inserted it in the lock, turned it, and they tiptoed in, not turning on the lights. There was enough light from the surrounding city for their country eyes to see. Their bags and bedding were tucked away at the sides of the couch and behind chairs. They moved softly around the house, unpacking their things and spreading their bags on the tiny living room floor. They unzipped sleeping bags and spread them out in the middle of the room, chairs and couches surrounding on all sides. When they did speak it was only in whispers, partly not to wake Rachel, partly not to disturb the spell of the night. The distant sign of the brewery flashed on and off atop its tower. The room alternated between the soft red of neon and the dim white light of street lamps

"Shall we just put down one big bed, it that all right?

"Yea, we can get that blanket off the couch"

Ariel found throw cushions and arranged them as pillows. They tiptoed up and down the stairs for final trips to the bathroom and the brushing of teeth.

There was electricity between all of them, shared connection. The day's journey and visions of Woodstock danced in their heads. How was this all going to work, Ryan wondered: who was going to sleep next to whom? The chains of propriety were reasserting themselves. Could he just ask Ariel to sleep beside him? He remembered their night together in the rain so short a time ago. How would Julie feel about that, had she felt the undercurrents? How did Elroy fit into the picture? Elroy rummaged in his pack, quietly muttering to himself about something. Julie was in the kitchen brushing her teeth with the water running. Ariel was upstairs.

Ryan slipped off his clothes and quietly, invisibly, slipped into the mound of sleeping bags, Afghans, and coats that they had assembled into a bed. The heat was not on in the house and its bones creaked a little as it contracted in the cold night. Ryan lay not quite in the middle, leaving a little room on either side of him, leaving space to see how this played out. Hippy passivity had reasserted itself (if that's possible). Julie came from the kitchen and packed away her tooth brush in the beaded drawstring bag in which she carried her toiletries. She tucked it away into the huge woven shoulder bag that she had carried from the island. She slipped her shift over her head, folded it and placed it carefully on the couch behind them. Her body was illuminated with patches of colour—red from the sign, green and yellow from traffic signals, white from the street lights. She squatted down beside him and smoothed the pile of blankets, arranging it to her satisfaction before climbing in on his left, as she had so many times before on trips where they had slept on the parlour floor.

Ariel came down the stairs like a moonbeam in her white shift. Elroy, clutching the toothbrush that he had been searching for among capos, harmonicas, packages of Drum, Zigzag papers, spare strings, guitar picks, passed her on the staircase, wearing only his faded levies. They smiled at each other in passing. Ariel left her shift on and lay on the other side of Ryan, searching to find the right layer of the blankets. "Brrrr, it's cold," she said, and edged over toward him to press her arm ever so lightly against his. The three of them lay on their backs like mummies, no one moving. Elroy came down the stairs. From half way up he looked down at them and laughed. They laughed too. The tension was broken. He slipped off his jeans; his body was gaunt, white, very northern European. Body by Breugel. He slid into the last place beside Ariel. They all lay, boy, girl, boy, girl, watching the city lights flash and pulse on the walls of the living room. They were like children who had been put to bed too early, not yet ready to fall asleep. Ryan felt the intense, conflicted pleasure of lying between the two women with whom he felt deeply connected. Which way to turn?

There were no words to say in the intense hashish atmosphere of the room, in the sexual electric hotness that surrounded and enveloped them. They had made their bed, but could anyone really sleep in it?

For Ryan, his sexual energy had been in the background all night, like a power or uniting force. Now he felt its presence. He extended his hand to Julie, slipped it through the tunnel under her neck to the opposite shoulder. She turned toward him, putting a leg over his knees, tossing her long fine hair as she turned. She placed her lips quietly against his neck and they lay this way not really moving. The rise and fall of their breath was the only thing that moved them.

Ryan's hand rested lightly on Julie's spine. He traced the bumps and the valleys of her vertebrae with his middle finger. She made some little movements on his chest, slid a finger along the underside of his collar bone. He wondered how far they wanted to take this? What was OK, what was not? With them? With Ariel? With Elroy?

He could feel Ariel next to him, the warmth of her hip against him, the rise and fall of her breath. Their hands found each other and brushed lightly, just the microscopic ridges of their finger prints sliding in textural contact. All this seemed so momentous and yet was all so tiny and invisible.

Julie's leg slid up his and there was the tiniest suggestion of rocking in her hips, the hint of a push against the side of his pelvis. On the other side, Ariel's finger tips gently touched his, like a blessing, an understanding, a letting go. They lay long this way in the pulsing almost-darkness. Little by little Julie's leg slipped further and further over him. By invisible increments, as slow as the hour hand of a clock, she found her way on top of him. And little by little, almost involuntarily, as slowly as sunlight moving across a lawn, he moved under her, just a little away from Ariel, but his hand still gently rested against hers.

Julie's knee found its way into the space that had opened up between Ariel and Ryan. She closed over him like a forest, her long fine hair surrounding his face like a nomad tent. He felt Ariel's hand fade from touch, and felt her roll away from him in the darkness. He experienced a surge of loneliness and separation. A voice inside him cried, "No," but the ringing momentum of his and Julie's sexuality overtook him. The tent of Julie's hair closed him off from Ariel and from Elroy. He let go. They were like Bedouins in the desert, or Inuit lying together in the winter house. There was no stopping, no changing, no rest, no time to rethink things. The primal rocking began. The die was cast. He made love to the one he was with while the one he loved was somewhere in the dark beside him, as was the quiet cowboy who had so unassumingly entered their lives.

Ryan and Julie's coupling was short and fierce, carried out with the silence of refugees slipping past border guards. At the end she slid off him and they lay quietly on their backs, like mummies again. Did they sleep? Ryan didn't sleep. He lay very still not wanting to awaken those around him, if they were sleeping.

Ryan waited and wondered and worried. How was Ariel? Was this all right with her? It was not with him. It was as though the huge promise that had been building all night had just gotten dissipated, like clouds that passed without releasing their rain. Julie slept beside him, or he thought she did. Her breath sounded rhythmic and even. Next to him Ariel lay quietly on her back. He tentatively reached out to touch her hand, but there was no answer, no touch in return: a house with no-one home. He waited till almost dawn while the red sign flashed through the window and the traffic light continued to go through its cycles of green, yellow and red in the night.

In the early morning while it was still dark, Ariel stood quietly up. She smoothed her shift down over her body, and went silently upstairs. Ryan wanted to go after her and talk, but, before he could move, the bathroom door closed. He could hear water filling the Victorian bathtub that stood on its paint encrusted claws on the linoleum floor.

As morning dawned outside, Rachel, already dressed for work in a powder blue skirt, jacket with a ruffled white blouse, popped into the room and greeted them in her pleasant non-attached Buddhist way. She lived easily alone, without relationship and without obsessing about her lack thereof. Ryan had always wondered how she was so happy just by herself.

They got up, got dressed, folded their bedding, rearranged the living room and packed things away in their various bags. After Ariel came down they found their way one by one to the bathroom. There was little talk and little eye contact.

In the kitchen Rachel brightly asked, "So, what did you see last night? How did you sleep?"

She, making a pot of oatmeal for all of them, appearing far too normal. Breakfast was edgy, social.

"So how was Woodstock?"

"Far out. I liked Sly, dancing in his white jacket, playing a guitar that wasn't there, and Hendrix played this tortured version of the Star Spangled Banner, the Scar Strangled Bummer, Old Gory."

They could hardly meet each other's eyes, each spending an inordinate amount of time mixing the raisins into their oatmeal. They were not exactly like the Adam and Eve in Masaccio's Expulsion from Paradise, running out of the garden weeping and covering their genitals, but the mind-forged manacles had definitely made a reappearance since last night's hashish inspired reveries. Rachel rushed out to work. Each of them stood to receive a hug at the table. The door shut behind Rachel and they were left alone. Ariel was nervous, her eyes darted around and she looked at her watch. She was thinking about ferries, about home. Elroy spoke gently to Ariel, "Cahn Ahh take your plate?" He started cleaning up. They did the dishes and left them in the drainer for Rachel. They wiped the table; scraped the oatmeal pot. Ariel wrote a little thank you note with a flower on it. The flower had a face with a smile on it but there was something about the way the eyes came out that make it look wistful and sad.

They gathered their bags and loaded them into the 47 Plymouth that waited outside in the lane. The blackberries seemed to have reached several inches closer to the car in just one night, searching for another object to mound over. Julie scratched her leg on one of their long green tentacles as she climbed into the front seat. It had turned rainy again and water ran in long streaks down the ancient split front windshield and the little oval back window.

Elroy coaxed the motor into life, attaching the right wires, turning the screwdriver, and then he climbed into the back seat to make room for Ryan to drive. They settled in, amid their boxes of vegetable oil, bricks of cheese, bags of macaroni and brown rice. Ryan drove slowly out of the lane and began to find his way to the Burrard Bridge. Elroy procured a joint from the place in his bag where the capos, guitar picks, Drum tobacco, extra strings, harmonica and toothbrush lived. He lit it, took a deep drag and passed it around. "Where there's dope there's hope," he said, and they all chuckled, their first of the morning. They passed the joint around as they traveled slowly across the bridge toward the concrete canyons of downtown.

After toking up, Ryan became disoriented. He was driving slowly trying not to be conspicuous in a conspicuous car. As the dope expanded in his brain, there was a moment of feeling OK. The dope was much stronger than he was used to and the road broke up into four long directional planes. The windshield, the rear-view mirror, the side windows all become shafts of light vanishing off in different directions. They offered long perspectives that seemed to converge somewhere in the middle of his head. He watched through all of them, the world passing like a cubist painting. He turned left off Burrard, wanting to get to Georgia on the quiet, unpatrolled streets of English Bay, but it didn't work. Suddenly he found himself in a maze of one-way streets and was being funnelled off toward the noise and congestion of Denman Street. It was hard to drive. It was not just the optics of the situation but the fact that he was replaying last night, trying to reconcile lust and love, trying to re-gather the definition of himself that had spilled out from the cardboard box that he kept it in like the pieces of a jigsaw puzzle.

He was just telling himself that everything was all right, that it was just guilt and shame that he was experiencing, that life could go on, that there was room for experimentation and mistakes, even beginning to believe it and feel a little better, when a police car appeared in the rear-view mirror. Its siren gave a low moan to catch his attention and its red lights were flashing.

In his altered state Ryan's heart raced. Everyone had small amounts of dope in their bags. The car was un-registered with license plates that were at least ten years old. One of Ryan's inner cringing dogs wanted to stop and howl, but he knew that now was the time to keep cool, to act normal if he could. It would have to be an academy award winning performance.

There were no nearby parking places on the street, so he had to keep driving a little way, self consciously, moving his body like a machine, like a back hoe, this foot to the clutch, this hand to the shift, release foot, signal, signal. He had no idea if the turn signal really worked so he laboriously rolled down the window—partly to dispel the residual marijuana smoke—and crooked his arm outside. Inside his voice chanted "look normal, look normal." He wanted his mind-forged manacles back more than anything now. They would certainly be better than the steel ones on the officer's belt. He wanted to say the right thing, to appear pleasant and OK, as OK as possible for someone who had long bushy hair parted in the middle and puffing out to both sides of his head, who had dark soulful stoned eyes surrounded by red whites, who was wearing tribal Mexican clothes, who was in an unregistered car filled with boxes of cheese and cans of oil, whose companions were all carrying drugs and suffering from archetypal sexual guilt.

Ryan screwed his head around and caught the eyes of his friends. They were expressionless, like the eyes of Indigenous People before a firing squad. They were blank, like squid ink, designed to conceal, blank like the obsidian eyes of idols.

It was as though a report of their activities last night, of his arrogance with the theatre manager, of their sexual escapade, had reached the top level of heaven and an angel with a flaming sword, in the form of this cop, had been sent to punish them. Ryan saw himself in a cell in the basement of the Public Safety Building, otherwise known as the Cop Shop. The car rolled to a stop. He sat by the rolled down window with his hands plainly in view on the steering wheel. He knew enough to do that: not to get out, not to move fast.

"Wha the hell are you doin?"

The cop bent in and peered at everybody in the car. He had clipped grey hair, was overweight and had one of the strongest Scots accents Ryan had ever heard. "Oh, Jesus Christ, look a ya," he said when he looked inside the car.

"Did I do something wrong Constable?" Ryan asked. To his relief, his voice came out sounding normal, bright, and pleasant. A reassuring voice. He hoped that the shaking in his body didn't show. Adrenaline poured through the car. Their four externally imperturbable bodies looked more like mummies than ever before. Internally they wished they could tear their way out through the old steel of the car and run screaming down the street. Fight or Flight. Elroy started to laugh, but quickly controlled himself. No one else was laughing.

"DID YA DO SOMETHIN WRONG?" the cop shouted at him in his Scots accent. He sounded incredulous. He stood up and gestured with his large hands to the surrounding world, to the buildings, to the passing motorists. "DID HE DO SOMETHIN WRONG?" He repeated it several times, pointing at Ryan for the surrounding world to see. Then he bent into the window and shouted savagely at him. "NAY, YE'VE NOT DUN SUMTHIN WRONG, YE'VE DUN EVERYTHING WRONG, EVERYTHING."

His hands waved about as if searching for a reason to draw his gun. "I've been following ya since the bridge. Ye've done an illegal left off Burrard, ye've turned without signalling, ye've driven one block up a one way street the wrong way, one of your brake lights is out, ye have no stop lights, ye only signal half the time, you're driving so slow as to be a menace, there are no stickers on the plates, you're a mess, just look a' ya, look a' ya all wit your long hair and filthy clothes. YOU'RE DOING EVERYTHING WRONG! EVERYTHING." He shouted the word

EVERYTHING at him one more time. "Now, yer drivers licence and registration, please."

Water dripped from the brim of his hat. His face was florid with genuine anger but there was also an aura of fatherly remonstrance about him as well. Ryan saw that he was exasperated with them, that he saw them as unruly children that must be disciplined and taught the right way. Ryan shifted on to one bum cheek and pulled out his wallet, and out of it his driver's licence, a good B.C. driver's licence with his picture on it, taken just after he had immigrated, while he still had a wife and child, before he started participating in orgies, before he had fallen into moral turpitude. Ryan was relieved to see that in the picture he looked like a nice young man with a short beard and neatly groomed hair.

He handed it to the cop. The cop looked at it and looked at him, comparing the picture with the weirdo that sat in front of him. He shook his head in disgust. "Registration please," he said. Ryan began shuffling through the papers in the glove compartment for the registration that he already knew wasn't there. He looked among the candy wrappers and the little scraps of papers with names, addresses and phone numbers on them, under a tattered copy of David Lindsay's Voyage To Arcturus, under which was a can of oil leak treatment, and under that, receipts for various parts and pieces that had been used to keep the car running over the years. Ryan turned to Ariel and made a conspicuous show of asking her where the registration was.

"Isn't it there?" she answered with just the right degree of questioning and irritation."

"No I guess not." He pulled all the papers out on his lap and made a big show of going through them again, one by one.

"Oh shoot" she said, "I told Wylie to keep it in the car, but he thinks that someone will steal it and keeps taking it home. Maybe someone did steal it. I know he had just bought new stickers. I think he felt he had needed to get something to clean the oil off the plates before he put them on." She craned her head into the front seat. She looked out the window at the cop. "My husband has them," she said, "He's supposed to have left them here; I don't know WHY they are not here; he also was supposed to have put on the new stickers and I also don't know WHY he didn't do that." She looked at the cop with her eyes full of distress, unfeigned distress. Ryan noticed that even with her crinkled, worried eyes she was still very pretty.

"Look," Ryan said, "I know I was driving badly. I'm sorry about that. I live out of town in the country and am not used to the city. It's hard to see out of this old car. Usually we don't take it. We kept it parked in the alley all weekend and took buses. We wouldn't have taken it at all except that Julie had to have some medical tests." He turned sideways and gestured at Julie with his head.

Opportunely, Julie was starting to cry. Silent tears streamed from her Buddha eyes and slid down her cheek. Ryan couldn't tell whether they were tears of sadness or tears of rage at the lie he has just told about her, but whatever they were, they seemed to work. They had gained a little ground. The cop seemed a bit taken aback by their politeness, their respect of him, and Ryan's acknowledgement of the situation. Also, he didn't quite seem to know what to do with them. His lights continued to flash in the rear-view mirror. Rain continued to drip off his hat.

He slapped the ticket book several times against the palm of his hand. "Get outta town," he said with the utmost disgust in his voice, disgust that conveyed that they were beneath giving a ticket to, beneath arresting, beneath the dignity of the judicial system, beneath even his further attention, that they were like slugs that had entered the garden and he wanted them to slither and slime their way back to from wherever they had come. It was amazing what a few words and a tone can convey. Ryan could not believe their good fortune.

The cop brandished the ticket book in his face. "Jus get out of town. I would use up my whole ticket book jus to begin to write ye up. Now ye be out a here by sundown and I dunna wanna see ya back, ya hear? I NEVER wanna see this car again. You understand? NEVER."

There was a soft chorus of "Yes sirs" and "Thank you sirs" coming out of the car. It sounded like little birds chirping. The cop handed Ryan his licence and stalked back to his car, snorting with disgust.

So he was not going to ticket them, he was not going to search the car. Ryan twisted the two wires back together, Elroy whispering what to do, and turned the screwdriver. They were on their way again. Ryan watched in the rear view mirror for awhile. The cop followed them a ways, until they turned left on Georgia. Then he turned right and went on his way. All hell broke loose, animated discussion, everybody talking at once.

"What the hell was that all about? I thought we were fucked for sure." They were all still shaking.

Ariel spoke up, she was laughing again, amused by the situation. "I don't think he knew what to do with us. Just look at us! Just look at this car! It's like we didn't fit in! There was no place he could put us. He just wanted us back in our own time zone."

"Shit, Ahh was praying," said Elroy, "Shipped back to the States for sure is what I was thinking, next stop Vietnam." He took off his Stetson, put it on his lap, and raised his hands in prayer in front of his chest. His eyes rolled upward to heaven like those of a Renaissance saint. "Thank you lord," he said. They all laughed, but he was serious.

Julie said, in her small matter of fact voice, "I think he has kids of his own, like us, I mean like we all have parents, right, his age. He pulled us over because he wondered what his son and daughter were up to, right? He hadn't talked to them in awhile because he's so pissed off at them. I think we confirmed his worse fears, but also maybe he saw that we were people too. Like he wouldn't have wanted to see his own kids in jail, right? So he decided not to search and arrest us. That's what I think."

Elroy sang softly in his cowboy voice:

Senators and congressmen please take a stand
Don't criticize what you can't understand.
Your sons and your daughters are beyond your command,
Ooooh the tiiiiiiimes they are a chaaaaanging.

They all joined in despite themselves and sang riotously, chapter and verse, as the old car climbed the big hill to the upper levels, past the mall where Moloch (Mall-och) lived among his fancy refrigerators, expensive clothes, sports jackets and other fashion statements. They were relieved to be headed back to their land.

Once again the ferry opened its mouth for them. It bellowed as it left the dock, its great pipe organ horn resounding off the surrounding mountains like a Bach fugue. They stood like refugees on the after deck for awhile. Ryan put his arms around Julie and Ariel. Ariel slipped her arm over Elroy's shoulder. For a moment they stood together this way, accepting fate. Then they went separately for coffee and magazines.

192

Ryan just sat in one of the chairs with the chrome arms by a window. He slouched back and stretched out his legs in their deep-sea diver logging boots. The vibrations of the ferry lulled him to sleep. He dozed for awhile and then reawakened. He looked out the window and saw Ariel leaning on the railing, her back to him. She was looking out over the Strait of Georgia. Their island was now in view. Composed of a lot of little dark humps, it looked like a pancake rising unevenly on the griddle of the grey sea. The rain had stopped coming down but the decks were still wet. Ryan went out, buttoning his coat and leaned on the rail beside Ariel. It was the first time they had been alone since last night.

She turned on him with vehemence, her eyes narrowed, her voice full of pain, grief, and anger. "I feel horrible you know. I can't tell Wylie about this. Now I have to keep it all to myself." She turned away from him and cried bitter tears. He wanted to comfort her, almost extended a hand to her but he could feel the ripples of anger emanating from her shoulders and knew that his hand would be shrugged off. He felt that he was to blame for all this confusion.

It had been a long elaborate seduction gone wrong. Ryan had set the table: they had travelled together, he had suggested a place where they could stay, kept the energy flowing with drinks, with dope, with movies, with little street theatre acts as they strolled along. It had been a magic night. But when the feast was served, when the silver lid was lifted, the wrong dish was on the plate. But the energy had been created, and had to run its course. In the end, social conventions prevailed and their love had come to this. He stepped away from Ariel and went back inside the ferry.

They all sat separately in their favorite places on the ferry, paced the deck, or read magazines. When its great horn sounded again, they walked down the long staircases, climbed back into their old car and drove up island through the dull flat day to the Vasquez ferry—home again.

"Look, there's an article about the Commune in Maclean's," said Ariel in an excited voice. She thrust the magazine she had been reading into the front seat between Ryan and Julie. Looking down from the road in little glances, Ryan could see a picture of the Commune's guru, Bob, standing on the wharf at False Bay. Ariel read part of the article out loud. It made the Commune sound like a place of dreams and magic rather than a camp of programmed zombies. "What a bunch of bullshit," Ryan said.

They arrived at French Bay with only minutes to spare and scrambled to carry each other's boxes down the wharf. Ryan parked the Hotel in the gravel parking lot where it would peacefully sleep until its next adventure. He sprinted across the parking lot and ran down the gang plank and jumped on the ferry at the very last minute. The deckhand pulled the hawser off and jumped on right after him. The ferry reversed and then snorted in forward out of the harbour.

They all talked animatedly with other friends as the ferry made its crossing. At least it was flat calm today. At False Bay Wylie was already there. He had borrowed McElwaith's old blue truck and carried Ariel's boxes up to it. He had to leave it running, probably because it wouldn't start except by rolling down a hill. Elroy met a friend and decided to stay with him awhile. He gathered his boxes and guitar and said goodbye to all of them with his shy smile. Ryan got his car, the much battered but still running Red Ant, and brought it down the hill. Julie and he loaded their belongings. They drove past his house to her home and up her driveway. He helped her carry her boxes in, being extra careful with the bags of rice. She asked him if he wanted to have some tea. He said no, that he wanted to go home and put his food away. They hugged for a long time and then he went out to the car.

His world was a mirror that had broken into slivered pieces. At home, he tried to put them back together as he found places for the things he'd brought back. Some went in the screened cooler, some went in the mouse proof bucket under the counter, some went in the water-tight bucket that was submerged in the well. As the fire crackled into life, he tried to make sense of what had happened, of his fractured relationships, of the loneliness he felt. He brought the galvanised wash tub in from the shed and filled it with water that he had heated on the stove top. He hoisted himself into it and had a bath before going to bed. His arms and legs hung out except when he sat cross legged in it like a yogi.

Climbing into bed, he blew out the lamp. In the darkness, the woodstove made little pinging noises as it contracted into coldness. Everything was much as it was the night before his trip, when he lay alone in the cabin thinking about the next day, but he knew that in some way everything was different now.

23
The Commune

After their ill-fated trip to the city, Julie and Ryan started seeing less of each other, eventually becoming "just friends." One day, just before Ariel went to the Commune, before Elroy and Miriam had gone, Ryan went to the grain shed where Julie had moved to bring her some of the tofu that he had learned how to make. He found her home immaculately scrubbed and empty. She was gone.

She had left a few things, wrapped with origami precision in newspaper and labelled with the names of various people on the island. Ryan found a package on the table with his name on it. He opened it and found one of her two porcelain rice bowls, blue and white with willows and bridges. He put it in his pack and carefully put the crumpled newspaper and twine in the tin heater, leaving the cabin as neat as he had found it, like a shrine.

Panicked, he made the rounds and found out from Alexis and Sammy that she had packed up her two or three bundles and hitched a ride to the great stone house of the Commune. Alexis and Sammy said they had given her a ride part way in their old truck. Alexis was raging as he paced up and down his living room telling Ryan about leaving her off at the Commune road. "It's mind control, you know, it's fucking mind control. They have some kind of Power. It's probably some kind of CIA experiment." Sammy made a face. Ryan thought she saw his distress and was trying to paint a kinder picture. "You know, she actually seemed to be all right. She was just curious, you know, she just wanted to go up there for awhile to see what was going on. She's a strong person; I think she'll be all right."

To Ryan it was a more personal failure. What if he had taken their relationship more seriously? What if he had invited her to live with him? What was there to have kept her in the world? Living alone? The silence of her little cabin? Their attenuated friendship?

Julie had been the first of Ryan's friends to go, followed in all too short a time by Ariel and family, by Elroy, by Miriam. Since then, he had seen Julie only once, from the back of a pickup in which he had gotten a ride. A crew of Commune members had been at the side of the road filling the Commune's truck with alder rounds. Ryan had never seen just one of them. They were always in a group, like ants. They had formed a long line and were passing alder rounds from person to person. There was no playing around, no tossing the rounds to each other like he and his students used to do in Argenta. They were collected and serious.

Always looking for her, he scanned the group. At the last moment he spotted her. Gone were her exotic peasant clothes. Gone was her luxuriant long hair. She wore drab work clothes and an army green wool cap. She was surrounded by other similarly garbed people. Ryan shouted her name and flung his arm up in a greeting. She looked up for a moment and gave him the most cursory of nods. The others simply kept attending to their work. The truck rattled around the corner and she disappeared from sight but not from mind.

Before it took Julie, the Commune had not seemed dangerous. Sometimes he would see groups of commune members, glistening in their hooded rubber rain parkas, cutting alder on the road right-of-way. Sometimes they would stop work and watch him pass, looking at him with big empty eyes, like those of the pulque stoned tribal people he had seen by the side of the road in Mexico, or like children, staring in open wonder.

During the winter, the flow of visitors to the Commune had dropped off to nearly nothing. The short days, the rain, the darkness, the Great Wave landscape on Georgia strait, had made it difficult for people to come and check it out. To keep themselves going, Ryan and his friends threw winter parties. Warmed by fire and wine, they would sit around at night and freak each other out with ghost stories about rain gear clad zombies moving toward them through the dark forests and dripping ferns. They recalled the Manson Family killings and talked about the dead and unspontaneous look that Commune members had. Ryan wondered if it would have been different had they worn saffron robes instead of hooded rain gear. He didn't think so: There was none of the sparkle or play that he had seen in the eyes of Tibetan monks. There was something dark about them.

When spring came again, the article in Maclean's renewed the flow of pilgrims to the Commune. The previous summer, people had stopped at Ryan's house and ask him how to get there; sometimes they spent the night before continuing on their way. Now, not wanting to participate in anyone's induction, Ryan had built a gate, a primitive affair with split cedar pickets and tire tread hinges. People passed his house and moved on.

Ryan and his friends read the Maclean's article with interest, trying to find out what was going on. When the leader had been asked what they were doing, he said "The truth is evanescent, like dream material, if you try to grasp it, it is gone." The article made it sound like a great and enlightened place. To Ryan and his friends it felt more like a cancer growing in their midst.

After Julie, Elroy and Ariel also went to the Commune. Ryan felt responsible. Certainly his longing for Ariel and his lack of commitment to Julie hadn't helped. He felt that he had become an agent of the Disintegration, the great wave of experimentation, confusion, wildness, and ecstasy that was tearing everyone apart; that his allegiance had switched from Apollo to Dionysus. As the weeks turned into months, and nobody but Miriam had come out, Ryan began to feel that he needed to take some action to try and pull his friends out while their homes were still empty. To make amends.

He decided that the best way would be to express an interest in joining the Commune. This seemed credible since so many of his friends were already there. Then he could live there for awhile, using his time to talk to the people he loved and persuade them to leave. The more he thought about it, the more plausible it seemed.

24
The Commune

The road to the Commune was long. Ryan started early, hitching and walking, turning on to smaller and yet smaller roads as the morning wore on. After passing below the Commune's expansive orchard, empty and silent, he finally came to stand at the great gate. The entire area in front of the Stone House had been fenced off, not with a ramshackle hippy fence but with a massive fence of peeled and verathaned new wood. The gate was on a bank high above the road. The bell that everyone was talking about—a large polished brass bell—hung next to it. Steep stairs with varnished rails of peeled poles ascended to the gate. As with the ancient pyramids, Ryan thought, one must ascend to meet the high priest.

Rumour, the great god of small communities, had it that the Commune was no longer letting everyone in; that visitors must stand at the gate, ring the bell and state their purpose. Then they were then let in—or not—according to some unknown criterion. A man, a little older than Ryan had come all the way from Winnipeg to join the Commune. He had been told that he couldn't come in. Thinking that it was some sort of Zen test, he had decided to camp by the gate until they reconsidered. Finally, losing patience with him, they threw him, tent, backpack and all, down the stairs. Broken and dejected in spirit, he spent the night on Ryan's floor on his way off the island.

Ryan climbed the stairs to the gate. He saw that in the middle of its heavy plank door was a small wrought-iron spyhole that appeared to open from the inside. The roof and upper portions of the Stone House loomed above the top of the fence. Its stone walls and heavy beams made it feel like a great and brooding presence. The morning was remarkably silent. There were no sounds of work, no voices. Ravens called from out of the forest and a hummingbird whirred around a honeysuckle planted near the gate.

Ryan just stood a while. Ringing the bell seemed like such an act of assertion. He knew that whatever happened after that, he would have brought upon himself. He wondered how to announce himself: A timid little tap? A great clanging alarm? He imagined that those within would notice the exact ring. Ultimately he decided on something orderly and controlled: three moderate, evenly spaced clangs of the bell. He let each tone fade into the forest before he sounded the next. No one came. He stood at the top of the stairs, feeling the morning sun on his face, listening to the sounds of the forest. He was sure that the sound of the bell had been heard, so he just waited. Finally, with a click, the spy port opened and a pair of pale blue eyes looked out at him.

"Yes,"

"I live on the island. Some of my friends have come to live here and I've been thinking of joining them. I'd like to talk to Bob about it, if I can." Ryan was polite and supplicant, as he had learned to be in university when asking a professor if he could turn in a paper late. Who says that a university education has no practical value?

"What is your name?"

"Ryan." He resisted the temptation to ask in return, "And what is yours?"

"Your last name?"

Ryan told him and he said, "Wait here, please."

The spy port snapped shut and he was left alone in the quiet morning again. After a while, the gate opened and two men were there. Their faces were carefully expressionless.

"He will see you, please come with us."

Ryan walked through the gate. The man who had spoken led the way and the second man fell in behind Ryan. They walked the short path to the house. It was surfaced with fine beach pebbles and edged with smoothed beach stones. The grounds were manicured. Even the dead lower branches of the trees had been cut off to give a clean park-like feeling to the landscape. The twigs that normally littered the forest floor had also been removed. The fine pebbles they walked on, gathered from the shores of the island, had been recently raked, leaving a wave-like pattern in them.

Ryan's un-named leader opened a side door to the mansion. They entered and walked down a hallway paved with stone into a great church-like room. Stone walls and massive roof timbers framed a large meeting hall with ordered rows of benches. On a slightly raised dais at the front of the hall, Bob sat in a chair next to another empty chair. He was dressed in a pastel plaid sport shirt and what looked like a pair of stay-pressed pants. He had penny loafers on his feet. His thick glasses, gave him a myopic slightly owlish look. His shortish red hair was parted and combed to the side. Behind Bob was a window. Through it Ryan could see people coming and going on their business, carrying shovels, axes, saws, pieces of wood. One of his escorts motioned him to the bench in front of Bob and said, "Have a seat."

Ryan sat down and his escorts sat on either side of him, not crowding him, just sitting there.

Bob simply said, "Yes?"

His tone was neutral, not friendly, not unfriendly.

"My name is Ryan. Some of my friends have come to live here, and I want to see if I can live here too. I want to see what it's like here."

His resolve and bravado were vanishing by the second. Despite his nerdy clothes, there was something so intimidating and powerful about Bob's presence. Ryan wondered how he could possibly have thought that he could have come up against him and lead his friends back out.

"Well, what are *you* looking for?"

Ryan was at a loss. He made some stuff up, some clichés of the time, right out of *Be Here Now*. "I want peace; I want to be in the present. I want to be connected with nature."

Bob mercifully cut him off with a horizontal slice of his hand.

"It sounds like you really don't know what you want. It's hard to make good choices when you don't know what you're looking for."

Ryan felt like he had been weighed and found wanting. Any idea that he had of challenging this man, was now gone. He was just a humble, polite supplicant sitting before this guide of some eighty people, the ruler of this small empire, the leader of....what?

There was a long silence. Bob said, kindly, "Well, it's OK not to know. Actually, it's better not to know than to think that you have it all figured out. At least not knowing is a start. At least then you can begin to find out what you do want, when your head's not all full of ideas and theories."

200

Ryan floundered around, trying to ask some questions. His questions were general and trivial: "What are you doing? What is your purpose?" His mind, usually so active and speculative, seemed to have gone blank. Bob mostly answered his questions with questions of his own: "More importantly, what are you doing?" "What difference does our purpose make if you don't know yours?" The challenge of "You don't know what you want," had put Ryan on guard and he was afraid to ask real questions for fear of being laughed or snickered at. He felt like he was the only one here who didn't know some great secret.

Finally, Bob took pity on him and gave him a few clues: "We work to become empty. To empty out all the crap we have accumulated, all the chattering, all the planning, all the conniving, all the posturing. We are nobody here. We are nothing special. We don't have special clothes, we don't have rich or poor, we don't have popular or unpopular. When we are empty enough then we can be filled in a different way. We might just See something."

"But what is it that you do all this for? What is it that you want to see?"

"I don't even want to talk about it because then your mind will take it and make some fantasy of it, some make-believe version that you can pretend is real. Your mind will say, 'Oh yea, I know that.' Then you just have one more fantasy to live, and the fantasy world isn't over for you yet. The story of you goes on."

A woman had come in and sat in the chair next to Bob. Unlike the other people he had seen walk by, she was not wearing drab work clothes, but a simple dress of deep green velvet, cut long and falling nicely along her supple figure. Her long dark hair was tied back in some kind of silver comb. She carried a plate of biscuits which she held out toward Bob, silently offering him one. He took one but didn't eat it. She sat down in the chair next to him. He held the biscuit in his hand and continued talking to Ryan, speaking rhythmically in a warm sympathetic voice. To Ryan's horror he found himself beginning to warm up to the man, beginning to like him and wanting to be liked in return.

"One reason people stay stuck is that they want guarantees, they are afraid to take a step without knowing how everything will work out in advance. We are all about faith here, about not knowing everything in advance. We are about jumping in and living rather than letting life be an endless rehearsal. We are about letting go of the need to know. This is what we call *the gateway*. We say that you have already looked in your mind, you have explored every corner of it, you have explored religion and physics, astronomy, micro-biology, sex, celibacy, spirituality and drugs. You are still lost and confused. It's like when you lose your keys and find yourself wandering around the house looking for them, feeling in your pockets over and over again, and, of course, each time you feel they still aren't there. Why do you keep looking in your pockets? Why don't you just realise, after the first time that they are not there?"

The part about the lost keys struck a particularly sensitive note with Ryan.

Bob continued: "This is what I'm saying: You've looked everywhere and are still lost and confused. Now the question is, are you ready to try something different, to just let go of all that? Are you ready to just live quietly and see what happens? Are you finally ready to See?"

Ryan took exception. Now he was angered by the presumption of this man who scarcely knew him calling him lost and confused—even though, inwardly, he knew he was lost and confused. He stood up for himself. "I'm not lost and confused. I'm just curious. I just want to know what is going on here."

"A person who is satisfied doesn't keep on eating. If you really knew who you were, you wouldn't waste a precious day of your life coming down here to see me. You wouldn't need to. If you want to pretend, ok, then go on pretending. You can go back to your farm and pretend for a while longer, have more pretend occupations, more pretend relationships, more pretend ideologies to pass the time. Don't you see, the beginning is just to honestly admit that you don't know, that you are lost. Then you can commit to what is real. You can begin to See."

Through all this, the woman next to Bob sat in her chair impassively munching biscuits. She just looked at Ryan and chewed, only breaking her gaze to look down and brush off some crumbs that had fallen on her lap. It was like she had heard this dialogue a thousand times before and had just come to hear it play out.

Ryan began to feel like an insect wriggling on a pin. He felt that the façade he maintained—that he was OK, competent and resourceful—was

202

being pried apart, board by board, by the crowbar of this man's words. His edifice was crumbling. He looked around the room and saw that a few people from the Commune had wandered in and had quietly taken seats in the pews at the back. They gave Ryan friendly little nods that seemed to say, "It's all right, man, we've all been there." He noticed that they all had little knowing smiles on their faces, like they had come to hear the truth and sweetness of the Master's words, or perhaps they had just come for entertainment, to watch the surgical ease with which the Master stripped away Ryan's defences, the falsehoods of his ego, the encrustations of his life.

Bob looked through his owlish horn rimmed glasses at the biscuit in his hand. He turned it around and around, like he was looking for a message on it. Then he looked back at Ryan, who felt like crying for all the pain and confusion in his life, for the loves he had lost, for his far away wife and child. He wanted to start blubbering at the Master's feet; to admit that his life had come to naught, but the small part of his pride that he had managed to salvage forbade him to do that.

"I wonder if I could just see my friends," he asked, surprised at how very small his voice had become, "just to ask them what it's like here?"

Bob shook his head and smiled sadly. "I don't think they want to see you right now, Ryan. They have a new life and don't want to be drawn back into all the problems they had before." He looked meaningfully at Ryan. His eyes looked huge behind their thick lenses. Then the woman reached out and touched Bob gently on the arm. Their eyes met for just a second, and then Bob looked back at Ryan.

There was another silence in which Bob looked at his biscuit again. Then he looked up and began talking. This time gently.

"You know, it really is all right. It is only by living that we come to this place. It is only through defeat that victory can be born. There is nothing as lucky as bad luck because it brings us to our knees. We surrender. If we have a house, if we have a car that runs, a wife, children, a job, then we can go on thinking that we are OK all of our lives. We will never even know that we have missed the main course. We will be content with the appetisers. Defeat is a kind of Victory. There is no success like failure."

Ryan shivered. How did Bob know all about his life, his missing keys, his broken down car, his distant wife and child, his lack of purpose? If defeat was victory, he thought, then I must be royally victorious. He wondered how he could possibly have screwed up his life any more than he already had. He wondered how he could possibly have believed that he could come here, like Orpheus, and lead his friends back out into what he considered to be the world of the living. Confronted with his own brokenness, the uselessness of his own life, with how little he really had to offer anyone, he was inwardly struggling to just get his own ass out of there and not succumb to a life of planting trees in docile silence.

Bob continued gently talking. "We live, we work, we eat well. We don't take drugs. After awhile, without drugs, the confusion dies down and you will be happy to simply live again. That is how we were meant to be. Rise with the sun, sleep with the night, peacefully do our work by day. We've lost all that and then we get it back again. It's our second chance. We believe in being healthy here, in taking good care of our bodies. Everyone who comes here becomes strong. We eat good food. Work strengthens us; we become whole beings again. People gain weight, not flab, but muscle. There's not a flabby soul among us. In silence, the mind becomes quiet and the senses become sharp again, and we learn to See."

The gentle words, the compassionate naming and acceptance of his confusion, the promise of a way out, had moved Ryan almost to tears. They were rising in his chest, as was the need to be comforted, to be forgiven and to be shown the way. He had the absurd idea that he would fall at Bob's knees and that Bob would put the biscuit in his mouth and bless him. He was even liking the idea of having a strong pioneer body, hardened by work and sleep and food, but just at the very moment that Bob had said "There's not a flabby soul among us," an enormously fat man, carrying some sort of bag, jiggled and rolled past the window behind him. Suddenly Ryan's mind, which had been lulled to sleep by metaphor and rhythmic speech, was on red alert again. What he had been hearing, the rhythmic words, the shifting of meanings, the confusion of opposites, "weakness is strength, strength is weakness (and that is all ye need to know), came tumbling down in the knowledge that what he was being told was not what he was seeing. Now he was ready to run and flee instead of surrender. Perhaps, in just the short time he had been here, he was already beginning to See.

He was instantly, for better or worse, his truculent old paranoid self again. He was too frightened by this powerful man to make a grand gesture, to stand up and knock over a pew, to denounce him in front of his acolytes. It was all he could do just to slink out.

It required every bit of his will to simply stand up and force his legs into action, to say, "Thank you, you've given me lots to think about."

Bob looked down at his biscuit, the wasted sacrament, and then back at Ryan. He shook his head ruefully as if to say that Ryan had missed the whole point of it. Then he raised the biscuit to his mouth and began chewing. Ryan was backing away from him now, toward the door. His escorts had also stood up and were walking with him, relaxed, and faintly smiling. They exchanged a glance with Bob.

"Yes," said Bob, "Go back to your farm for awhile, go back and live out several more cycles of life, go through all the motions. You are free to do that. You are also free to come back, this door will be open to you when you realise there is nothing more for you out there. And your old friends will be here to welcome you."

Ryan was almost to the door when Bob said one more thing. Ryan turned to look at him. "When you cut off a chicken's head, it flaps and runs around the barnyard for awhile, like it's still alive, but it's really not. You might find that your life no longer holds the same satisfaction it used to."

Bob stood and the woman in the green dress stood with him, brushing more crumbs off her dress. She had finished the entire plate of biscuits. The escorts fell-in line with Ryan, one in front and the other behind him. Bob and the woman watched him go down the hallway and into the world of groomed trees. He tried to walk jauntily like he was full of confidence and had not a care in the world, but it was hard to do. He tried to catch a glimpse of the plastic village that he had heard so much about, hoping to see his friends, but the village must have been down somewhere among the trees, out of sight, and his escorts seemed determined to keep him on the trail. They took him to the main gate and nodded goodbye to him. They were no longer expressionless. There was a bit of a smirk on their faces now.

Ryan walked back along the road, below the orchard where thirty or so people were now working silently with shovels and mattocks, clearing the land of salal, salmon berry and sword fern. Each one briefly looked up at him as he passed, just a glance, and then went back to work. The late morning air was full of the sounds of their shovels, mattocks and axes scraping away at the soil, cutting out roots.

Ryan felt very glad to be out of the oppressive stone house and back in the open air again. He felt that it had been a close call. He had almost taken the proffered sacrament, almost traded his life in on the one that was going on in the orchard. He was grateful for that fat man who had walked by the window, who had pulled him out of the singsong of words and similes. Yes, his life was broken, and that part hurt, but he'd rather fix it himself, thank you very much. He entered the alders that grew where the road dropped down beneath the orchard. Their smooth white trunks rising into the leafy canopy comforted him. Alders are humble trees, he thought, the dispensable foot soldiers of the forest. They grow just to provide shade and ground cover so that the long-living climax types, firs and cedars, can get started. Then their mossy bodies fall and rot quickly to provide food for the emerging conifers. Each generation rises to shelter the one coming after it and then falls to make room for it. Suddenly, he felt like crying. What was life without understanding? What were the stars without the mind-prints of the constellations to give them a story? He drank from the stream at the bottom of the hill, and felt the water flow into him, nourishing him as it nourished all creatures along its way. He felt a great refreshing coolness run into him, into the forest of his cells and rock bluffs of his bones.

What had happened was that he now had a bit of hope. It was not inevitable that he and all his friends would be sucked into the realm of stone and silence. He had visited and emerged, without his friends, true, he was no Orpheus, but at least he had gotten himself out. He worried about Bob's prediction that he would be back, but he really didn't think so. He had learned that his life, even such as it was, was worth living. He looked forward to his home, even to his loneliness. Today he would soak soybeans for tomorrow's tofu. Each day was the seed of the next day, a series of successive plantings as they said in the seed catalogues, and who knew which of today's fragile dreams would sprout in the future. It was this little rivulet of optimism that kept him walking down the road. Precious substance? Wellspring of delusion? He was not quite sure.

25
The Commune

There was still a lot left to the day when Ryan got back from the Commune. His legs were tired, but he rejoiced in starting the spring chores that in his funk he had neglected. It seemed of the utmost importance to put his life in order.

Even shovelling out the old outhouse didn't seem so bad. He wheeled its contents, reduced to clean and earthy loam by their year in the ground, down to the composter. When darkness began to fall, he called it a day and went to lock in the chickens, already roosting in their coop. As he returned to the house, two figures with backpacks came down the road in the falling gloom. They saw him by the chicken coop and called out to him across the fence. He went over to talk. They were two teenage girls from Prince Rupert, Anne and Daphne, both blond and cute. They had dropped out of school and were tripping down the coast to explore the counterculture. The sky was fading and a few fat drops of rain were beginning to splatter the road. Eventually Anne asked, "Do you know anywhere we can crash for the night?"

"You can stay here for a few days if you want." It was not just hospitality that motivated Ryan, but also wanting to provide people with an alternative to staying at the Commune. Anne and Daphne reminded him of his students in Argenta: open, spirited, and searching for something more meaningful than the life that awaited them in Prince Rupert. Perhaps he did have something to offer, a roof at the least.

They accepted his invitation, and they all walked, on opposite sides of the fence, back to the creaky picket gate. He opened it for them and they came into the yard. In the house they took off their heavy packs and outer layers of clothes.

Ryan built a fire and cooked for them. It was hard to find things to talk about. The conversational burden fell mostly on him. They said "wow," or "far out" to most of the things he told them but didn't have very much to say back. After dinner they did the dishes. He showed them the couch/beds on which they could sleep, where the lamps and matches were, where the outhouse was. As they began to unload their packs, he retreated, lamp in hand, to the back bedroom to read.

A few days turned into a few weeks. Mostly they hung around and listened to the conversations that went on in the house. They met his friends, and, during the day, traveled around the island and began to make a few connections of their own. Ron dropped by one mail day and was delighted to find two girls his own age. He invited them down to see his tiny float house. Other of the island's young bachelors began to find reasons to drop by and visit.

Many of the conversations in the house were about the Commune. People talked about the friends they had lost to it. They speculated about who would go next, and talked about how they had taken to dropping by friend's houses to make sure that no one was slipping—or gone. They talked endlessly about Elroy, about Ariel and Wylie, about Miriam, about Julie, trying to make some sense of their defection. At first the two girls didn't understand. "Well what's happened to them," Anne asked after listening quietly for awhile, "did they all die or something?"

Alexis, Isaac, McElwaith, Sherry and Ryan were all sitting around the table. They were taken aback. "No, they just joined the Commune."

"Oh well, then what's the big deal about?" ventured Anne.

They all laughed. Anne's exclamation shocked them back into a sense of perspective. From the mouth of a babe came wisdom: afterall, their friends were not dead. Things lightened up a little after that. They got back to their gardens, their fences, their psychic explorations. For Ryan, it brought up the Greek question again. Perhaps it was better to let your children live and be taken captive by the Turks. At least there was a small hope that they could someday escape and find their way to freedom.

Several weeks later, much to everyone's surprise, Miriam came out of the Commune. Back at the farm, she was importuned with questions. "What are they doing there?" Everybody found their way to the south end to find out about the mysterious power that drew people to the Commune, and why she had been immune to it.

"Nothing" she said, "They just quietly go through their lives. They don't talk except when necessary, they try to spend some time alone on the bluffs each day. They sit with Bob in the big house. It's like a congregation. They believe he sends his consciousness to them; that he can hear their prayers and send them visions. For me nothing happened. After awhile I got bored. I wanted conversation, my own house, my own garden, tasty food. I got tired of being around seventy other silent people all the time." She laughed her New York laugh.

She was reclining on the old couch in the living room, looking like a princess in a Pre-Raphaelite painting. On the improvised coffee table in front of her, made from old boards and weathered crates, Isaac placed plates of plums and slices of Miriam's home-baked French bread. He was bringing yet more delicacies from the kitchen. She took a sip of apple wine from their one good glass, the flaring crystal one that Isaac had found in the barn.

Isaac and Miriam had made up a story about this delicate treasure, so out of place—with its fragile stem and frieze of flowers—among the old harnesses and yokes in the barn. In their story it had been set down long ago by a couple sneaking away from a party to a tryst in the hayloft. In the aftermath of arranging clothes and getting hay out of each other's hair, they had forgotten the glass. The couple had walked back through the dark trees of the orchard to the lamp lit house. Colourful Japanese lanterns, lit with candles, were strung across the porch. A slightly past-full moon, looking like it was made of crumbling rock, hung over the bluffs to the east.

Sounds of laughter and drunkenness came through the darkness. A fiddle and guitar were blending their soft tune with the song of the crickets. As the couple walked, they could see other couples weaving past the windows to a waltz. Perhaps the party had been a housewarming, thrown to celebrate the completion of this house when its lumber and shakes still had the gleam of new wood. As the couple approached the dark porch, voices greeted them. Some men were sitting and drinking on straight wooden chairs in the shadow of the porch. "Nice night for a walk," one of them said. She wondered if there was a bit of a snicker in his voice.

"Yep, sure is." her companion said, covering for them in a voice that put everything into a normal conversational pattern.

They stood on the porch and talked with the men about a Model T that was stuck down Rouse Bay Road. It had lost its brakes and gone into the creek at a crazy angle. "They are going to have to get Thompson's cat to winch it back out."

Standing in the dark, away from the light inside, she was glad for this chance to compose herself. The men offered them drinks from the bottle. She declined and he realised that they had forgotten the glass that they had been sharing in the barn. He couldn't go back now, so he went inside to find a new one, finding only a used cup. He rinsed it under the single tap in the sink and came back out. He smiled at her as he stepped through the curtain of light onto the darkness of the porch. One of the men filled his cup and he offered her the first sip. She accepted and felt the heat of the whisky go down her throat. They shared the cup with each other, passing it back and forth, in the soft summer night.

To Miriam and Isaac this glass was precious because of the story that they had made up. They were surrounded by ghosts on this old farm, by artifacts of other people's bygone lives, things that were not taken when the farm was abandoned. Having no money, they used these things and, like archaeologists beginning to live the life of the people whom they were studying, making clothes of fur and chipping tools from flint, they began to understand the people who had been on the farm before them. Slowly they became like them.

Isaac was unbelievably delighted that Miriam had come back. To him she was Persephone returned from the underworld, bringing springtime back into his life. He knew that their relationship was unstable and, like all the ones in his past, probably wouldn't last. He didn't even hold out hope for that anymore. "Live Happily Everafter," had gone through a progression of downward expectations. At some point he thought maybe his parents had the right idea, to stay together and "Live Unhappily Everafter." But even that modest goal didn't seem to work. He tried giving up on "happy" or "unhappy" to see what "Live Everafter" was like, but the Everafter part didn't work. So now he was simply down to "Live."

He and Miriam were like children from a fairy tale. They had escaped the crumbling city. Against her parents' wishes they had travelled the long road through the Adirondacks, then west through the industrial states, then through Iowa, Nebraska, Wyoming, Montana and north into Canada. He was disappearing from the evil emperor's army, from being forced to fight hopeless battles against relentless Asians with whom he had no quarrel. He and Miriam had hitched this distance together, freezing in snow storms, sleeping in green fields of wheat. She was a princess in rebellion against her wealth. Though it was not her wish, there was still a place for her to fall, to return to. Her family had built up wealth and fled in poverty and built it up again many times in its long European history. She wished to build another kind of wealth, a wealth built on the love of nature, on the sensual appreciation of life, on community. Her parents, disapproving of this uncouth painter, had chosen to starve her out by cutting off her funds, confident that she would be coming back to the comforts of the castle. They would not make it hard for her; they would be welcoming, pretending that it had just been a lark, a giggle.

Isaac had nowhere to fall, no place to go back to. He had wild hair and a long beard, looked like a mountain man, someone from another time. This flight with a bundle on his back was a thing his people had done before. At some level he was not unfamiliar with it. There was little money between Isaac and Miriam. Sometimes, in the cities, he did street art, painted portraits on the sidewalk in pastels, puts his cap out on the ground and rapped madly with the passerby who looked at his gallery. Because of the dearth of money between them, they treasured the ten or so dollars he got for an afternoon of talking and drawing.

Isaac and Miriam had some clothes, their sleeping bags, a tent, a little stove for cooking, a couple of tiny camping pots whose lids served as dishes. Isaac had a small bag of paints. Before he left New York he had cut a long narrow strip from one of the great canvases he used to work on. Big had been where it was at in the New York art world then. He rolled the canvas around dowels to make a scroll and carried it in his bag along with the paints.

Sometimes they camped in the mountains for several days to wash their clothes and bathe in the lake. When the weather was warm enough for paint to dry, he did small sketches of where they were. They were pale and faded since he mixed the paint with turpentine and put it on like water colour so that it would have time to dry in the sun. He painted himself and

Miriam into each scene of this evolving scroll, tiny figures in a huge landscape. In each scene he was sitting somewhere, maybe under a tree, painting, and she was dancing or combing her long thick hair. Even in these miniature drawings, really just expanded lines of paint, her luxurious femininity was abundantly expressed. Were they in love? Probably not. But they were excited by this adventure and by the intimacy they felt with each other as they made this long journey together. Isaac knew that this too would end, that someday his alcoholism, his ignorance of feminism, his lack of interest in it, would get to her. But in this moment, on their farm, on this island, sharing delicacies with visitors, she had brought back the summer and he brought to her the fruit of the fields.

Ryan was delighted that anyone at all had come back from the Commune. It gave him hope. Miriam reclined on the couch holding court. She had the hottest story on the island. "Life in the Commune: Get a first hand report!" Isaac adoringly served her as she regaled the stream of visitors with what it was like, and how their friends were faring. She was used to luxury and used to being served. Isaac was from a long line of serfs. He was used to being of service.

There was something about their relationship that was built around his willingness to serve and her willingness to receive: during the day he painted and worked around the farm. She grew flowers and read novels and cooked marvellous things out of the simple food that they could afford and gather. At night they ate together, pretending that they had made the greatest feast from the oysters and herbs that they had gathered and served with brown rice from the city. His day was through, his jobs were done, and now he granted her every whim. He was hers on these long passionate evenings. And this she hadn't experienced. Men had used her plenty but never had a man given himself so readily to what she wanted. A part of her stood aside, was critical of his goodwill clothes, his lower Bronx chatter, his constant drinking, his cultivated disregard of all the social graces. But the little surprises, the adventures, his way of taking each ordinary day and turning it into a dramatic triumph or defeat, kept her enthralled. He made life up as he went along. He invented each day for her like a magician pulling a coin out from behind her ear.

Mostly, the novelty of their life delighted them: living on an abandoned farm off the coast of British Columbia, living with almost no money, growing their own vegetables, heating their house with wood they had cut themselves, gathering food from the sea, eating chunks of sheep and deer that the neighbours dropped off, picking apples and pears and storing them in the cellar for winter, borrowing the neighbour's cider press and making apple wine from the apples in the orchard, finding morels under the same trees in spring, gathering the eggs from the three chickens that the same neighbours had given them, carrying water from the well in buckets, bathing in a galvanised wash tub heated on top of the wood stove. All this seemed strange and marvellous, especially that they, of all people, should be doing it—and surviving. They had been here several years now and their relationship had weathered her going to the Commune and coming back. Mostly in her life, when she had gone to do something else for awhile, whoever she was with would have gotten angry and moved on. So this was also new, to be with a man who let her go and then was still there when she came back: not angry with her, not punishing, but glad to see her.

On a small island everything affects you. There is nowhere for events to go. In a city, things happen and then spread out in ripples, like seismic waves, disappearing into the countryside. Here things hit the shores and bounced back. It was as though news, gossip, events, couldn't travel over water. They bounced back, were replayed, talked about and considered from every angle. Sheila's and Ryan's break-up had shaken Miriam and Isaac. They had been their best friends, their artistic and intellectual compatriots, fellow refugees from the war and from Usa, the industrial Moloch to the south. Sheila and Miriam were also Jews. When Ryan and Sheila broke up, Isaac and Miriam questioned their own relationship. When their friends abandoned their lives and went on down to the Commune, left their homes empty, their doors ajar (When is a jar not a jar? When it is adored.), their things scattered on the floor, Miriam wondered what was going on. Was there a secret that she wasn't in on?

Miriam took things seriously. She went to see. Now she was back. There was something in her coming back that helped Ryan to let go of his lost friends and lovers. It was their own life, he realised, and regardless of how it seemed to him, they had a right to do with it what they wanted. They would come back, or not, in their own time. For him it was time to move on and find new friends; to affirm his own life, the life of a single man living on a small farm, the life of a man with an ex-wife and daughter living in faraway Seattle.

26

Delicious Disorientation

Time hung vacant on Ryan's hands. Ariel and Julie had dissapeared into the Commune. His house was empty. His sodden garden lay covered in its blanket of umber maple leaves. The shed was filled with wood. His car sat permanently at the edge of the road. Rain fell relentlessly.

Every day in the early afternoon, while there were still a couple hours of light left, Ryan had a toke, donned his raingear and walked to get out of the cabin. All of the ditches and creeks were full and running. Water was everywhere, playing a great symphony to gravity as it ran down the roads, gurgled through the dark forest bottom, rushed down the sides of rock bluffs, cascaded in rivulets and creeks off the island. As he walked along the waterways, Ryan listened to its sound and reflected on the downhill nature of everything, on the co-identity of gravity and time. There were also voices in the water, distant angelic choirs singing of creation. Often the sun broke through, like a favour from god, a gesture of mercy based on the compassionate understanding that it would be too cruel to take it away for an entire day. Darkness came at four.

Aside from his teenage initiation into peyote, Ryan's adventures in altered states had been limited to marijuana. As altered as that world was, it finally became humdrum and ordinary. For years he had resisted the world of psychedelics out of the fear of REALLY losing his mind: in Marin County, the sidewalks had been littered with people who had "blown their minds," never quite come back from acid trips. His friend Peter had told him of his first experience with acid, of eyes and teeth springing out of the lawn that he had been lying on. Ryan was afraid that under the force of such apparitions, his sanity—fragile at best—might crumble like a foundation whose concrete had been mixed with too much sand.

For him it was an ambivalence: wanting to lose the mind-forged manacles and fearing the loss of them. It was finally Jake, a small time drug dealer and redneck ex-truck driver, who gave Ryan his first dose of acid. Moon-faced country boy Jake was huge, looked like a farm boy used to hard work, told bad, coarse jokes, pulled stunts like coming to a party wearing Groucho Marx glasses with a penis for a nose. He had simply dropped by Ryan's one day in his four-wheel drive invasion vehicle—the same one later owned by Reston—grinding to a halt outside the door, saying that he had some very pure acid that he'd just smuggled back from the States.

Acid had strange names then, like Purple Microdot, Heavenly Blue and Clear Light. He took out a Ronson lighter that had had its guts removed to make it into a smuggling case. He removed some cotton batting and spilled some tiny pills out into the palm of his hand. He was very proud of his lighter. He had soldered an upper compartment into its body that still held lighter fluid. He could flip it open and light a cigarette while talking to the customs agent who was searching his car. With surprising dexterity he picked up one of the tiny pills with his large fingers and gave it to Ryan. He put the rest back into his lighter, stuffing the cotton wad back in after them. Opening the top of the lighter, he flicked the wheel with his thumb and let the flame burn briefly. Ryan and he both laughed at the trick. The acid was a gift. Jake simply assumed, with the force of his powerful personality, that Ryan would want it.

While not exactly Aldous Huxley nor Stanislav Grof, Jake nonetheless came with simple authority, like a messenger from the gods. To Ryan, who now lived fully in the realm of omens and portents, he might as well have been wearing a silver helmet with wings on it. Jake left again, not even taking the time to sit down, grinning as he ground off down the road in his huge redneck, military-surplus, four-wheel drive, bullet-proof combat vehicle to distribute free chemical enlightenment to the rest of the citizens of this west coast Islandia.

As the great grinding of gears disappeared into the silence of the winter morning, Ryan sat down and put the pill in the palm of his hand to examined it. It looked like Krishna in tablet form; was tiny and blue with a small red dot that looked like a bindi on it. Did he dare to take it?

He decided that his time had come. After all, it had been brought unbidden to his door by Jake this morning, in a multi-geared truck that resembled Ezekiel's wheels within wheels more than anything else on the island. And the truck, he reflected, had been laboured on as surely as the pyramids, by the struggling souls in the mines, by sweating workers in the foundries, by more workers somewhere in Detroit; had been created just to bring him this particular speck of chemical matter. Synchronicity and wonders! In years to come he would introduce Jake as his acid guru: "I'd like you to meet Jake, my acid guru," he would say, and they both would laugh.

The quiet of the morning was unbroken by passers-by or cars. To Ryan it seemed that a space had opened up to have this experience, a quiet eye in life's storm. He took the pill with a tulip shaped wine glass of clear well water. He held the glass up to the window and watched the morning light filter through the water. He saw the inverted image of the cherry tree in the glass, the world turned upside-down. He put the tiny pill on his tongue, the miniature blue body of Krishna, and swallowed the sacrament with cool clear clean well water.

He cleaned his house a little, much as Sheila and he had cleaned their house while waiting for Lara's birth. He washed the dishes and swept the grass matting. He changed his clothes, taking off his work shirt and putting on clean—as clean as they got—Mexican whites. Knowing that this was an occasion worthy of respect, he wondered what happened when ordinary people like himself, people who hadn't been burned clean by fasting in the desert, experienced biblical visions.

Then, in the quiet of the cabin, he waited, listening to the ravens in the forest and reviewing the twists and turns of his life that had brought him to this moment.

27
Delicious Disorientation

At nineteen, Ryan had been in his second year at SF State, living at home in Marin County, helping his mother and sisters cope with the death of their father. He had a part time job driving a Cushman truckster between the various clinics of Kaiser Hospital. As a university student, he had no experience with the world of black working people and felt totally incompetent in it. He could barely read the doctor's illegible handwriting to sort out the lab slips each day, while the agrammatical people around him were able to do it with ease and aplomb. Not knowing the rap and patter of the everyday world, he was awkward, uneasy, and felt out of place. Besides sorting lab slips, his job involved driving x-rays, charts, lab samples, and the occasional body part (usually eyeballs), in the Cushman Truckster between Kaiser's various clinics on Geary Street. All day he drove 'round and 'round like the wealthy farmer that Han Shan compares to a bug circling the bottom of a pot.

Work, school and his girlfriend Diana took most of his time, but occasionally he hung out with his old high school gang. Living at home, he sorely missed the heady freedom of his San Francisco apartment and radical roommates of his previous year.

One of these old gang members was Larry, fat, moon faced, and intolerant. Larry had dark stringy hair that he wore parted on one side, Hitleresquely oiled down against his scalp. When it fell on his forehead, he pulled out his comb and put it back into place. Larry always wore light blue cords and a light blue plaid Pendleton shirt: many identical sets of these hung in his closet at home. He was what today would be called a science nerd and had an imperious, peevish, fussiness about him that would have befit the vizier of an Age of Reason king. Enormously intelligent, he used it only in service to the dark side. Beneath his bland, controlling exterior was a darkness that none of the rest of Ryan's old gang could even approximate. He kept his place in the group by fascinating them with glimpses of the dangerous double life he led: showing up at parties with a gun, or heroin; smirking at their cautions to him, at their refusal to participate.

Years later Larry became Laurie. Ryan never saw him after the gender change, but could only imagine an overweight, malicious, and terribly unattractive woman. The only foreshadowing that Ryan remembered had been so insignificant as to have meant nothing at the time: he had phoned Juanita's asking for Larry, who had a part time job doing dishes there. Juanita herself, foul-mouthed, answered the phone. As a joke, Ryan had asked for Laurie Jones instead of Larry Jones. He heard Juanita bellow for Laurie Jones. When Larry finally came to the phone, to stop her bellowing, he was angry and chagrined and said that he would break Ryan's arm if he ever called him that again.

Juanita's was an all night diner on a derelict ferry boat, the Charles Van Damme, that sat at a crazy tilt in the mud of San Francisco Bay. Juanita, rumour had it, was an ex-madam. Hugely overweight and wearing gigantic brightly coloured tent-like mu-mus, she sometimes emerged from the galley to unrestrainedly and foulmouthed yell at staff and customers alike. As a teenager, it was always scary to be there, not really wanting to be noticed by the bikers, the hustlers on the make, the drug dealers, the old beatniks, and mostly by Juanita herself. The dark nooks and crannies of the ferry made it safer for Ryan and his friends to be there, as they could usually find a table in the shadows where they could watch the action without too much fear of the spotlight being turned on them.

As a senior in high school, the gates of freedom had finally blown open for Ryan. He belonged to a small group of outcasts who ate their lunches together on a hidden lawn behind the school. They had read Huxley's Doorways to Perception, Visions of Heaven and Hell; had heard Ginsberg read Howl on tape, the enchanting hypnotic rhythms of his vision of America as Moloch eating its own babies.

Ryan's friend Harry had a horrifying old Triumph motorcycle with bald patches all over its tires. He took Ryan, terrified and clinging to his back, thundering through the scented summer nights to Sausalito, suburbia's own little piece of post-beatnik culture. The mystery of how

Harry was allowed to do this lay in his father's statement that "I would rather have him run it out now than in his thirties, when I did."

Sausalito promised everything that the bland suburbs denied. Ryan and his friends sat in coffee houses sipping espresso and listening to folk music in their dark glasses—which they called shades. The beatniks were over and there weren't hippies yet, just drug addicts, blacks—called spades—bikers and artists. Gradually a group of young people began to emerge and connect at Juanita's. Refugees from high school, from suburbia, from affluence, they all hovered at the entrance to this dark world, poised for descent.

At Ryan's school, the drop out was despised. Disaster, poverty and destruction were believed to be on the other side of dropping out. The door into the world of drugs, sinners and renegades, into the world of the shadow, was a dangerous door, but it also seemed that it was an entry way into the world of creativity and psychic exploration; that those who lived on the other side—though their lives were often marred by poverty, addiction, and broken relationships—had some kind of knowledge, some *Je ne sais quoi*, that was utterly lacking in soulless white Marin County.

Suicides, those who were so drugged-out, stoned-out, lost, that they couldn't stay in the world anymore, took on a special spiritual significance. Even when he was in high school, contemporaries on their way to suicide were walking the streets, gone beyond the pleasantries and petty concerns of society, wired into the despair of hard addiction, their unborn dreams going down with them, living the tragedy of the noble derelict, the tragedy of what they could have been; living in contact with death, the grim reaper; travelling an alternate road ever deeper into the dark paths of the underworld; voiceless Orpheuses with no-one to sing to.

The ex-girlfriend of one of these high school derelicts, James, told Ryan about the time James had showed up at her door. She had ended her relationship with him because it had been too painful to watch him self-destruct. It was a hot, dry, late summer day, and when she had opened the door, there he stood. He looked like shit and asked her for a glass of water. She had been so manipulated, so fucked around by him, that she just said no. She asked him to leave. He went, walking through the crackling leaves in his long sad winter coat, walking with a stooped and yet aristocratic bearing. The next day she heard he was dead, overdosed, leaving her to

221

wish that she had given him the glass of water. Had it really been too much to ask?

This was shockingly real: life punctuated by death, given significance by a dark reality that Ryan and his circle of friends could not comprehend. It made their plans and dreams, their little rooms with coloured glass decorations from Cost Plus, their little forays into drugs, sex and art seem somehow trivial and insignificant.

Later, in a cultural context, there was the Counsel in Malcolm Lowry's Under the Volcano. There was Janis Joplin and Jimi Hendrix and much later Kurt Cobain. All dark heroes travelling the road down to death, travelling the road that nobody wanted to travel, travelling the road that everybody was trying to avoid, winding down that dark path that always stands next to us. A few songs, a few lines maybe, drifting up from the chasm, a small record of the dissolution of the body, and maybe, just maybe, a spangled glimpse of what lay beyond.

The Charles Van Damme, captained by its opulently sweaty Charon, became a boat of the damned for some. Many of the young faces who gathered there, eager for experience, betrayed their promise in addiction, in overdose, in psychosis or in suicide: "I have seen the best minds of my generation destroyed…" Some still live to this day in trailers at the edges of towns, sorting and re-sorting the vestiges of their dreams.

Ryan had not been so quick to succumb. He had had the example of his father who fell apart completely after dropping out just short of his PhD, surrounded by accolades and requests for "more" from his professors. His thesis had been on the psychology of tattooing. As part of his research he had wandered the lower waterfront streets. Something about this experience, or about his war experience, something he never talked about, germinated the seed of destruction inside him. He remembered standing by his father's sickbed, having one of their stilted and truncated attempts at conversation. He told him that he was studying psychology and his father, in his haunted broken voice, his tongue oozing yellow pus from radiation treatments, replied: "Don't go into psychology—go into one of the sciences—in psychology the more you know, the less you know."

Terrified by his father's decline into alcohol, cancer and pain killers, he remained a weekend drop out, keeping one foot in high school, and following it with the other in university. He was terrified to leave the paths of structure and sanction completely. He feared that somewhere inside he too had this place of disintegration that would not hold without the Salvador Dali crutches of conventional reality: that the center would not hold. At SF State he vowed to himself that he would never drop out: no matter what, he would keep putting one academic foot in front of the other; that he would become a professor of something or other, even if it meant having to write a thesis on fart taxonomy.

Larry was terribly overbearing. One weekend, Larry, Ryan, and a friend named Tom Kousamano took a drive-away car to Reed College, a Mecca of post-beatnik culture. From beginning to end this was a Larry adventure. He was always up on things that the rest of them didn't even know about, like drive-away cars and the drug culture at Reed College. They suspected that his nerdy suitcase contained more than blue corduroys and Pendleton shirts.

Larry took control of the entire trip. The car, which they got to drive for free in return for transporting it back to the rental agency, was in Larry's name and he felt that gave him the right to say when they would stop, where they would eat, and when the bathroom breaks would be. In Portland they turned the car in and spent some days at Reed. The Students there had set up an enormous board game of world domination. Some of them were flunking out because of it. The game kept evolving, getting bigger and more complex; drawing more and more students into it. Students were afraid to go to class, to sleep, or to study, for fear there would be an urgent crisis and their country would be invaded while they were away. A system of runners had been set up. They entered classrooms, a math class with complicated formulae on the board, an art history lecture where a many-armed bronze Shiva danced on the lectern, a literature class where ancient Greeks chased each other around a vase in priapic ecstasy. The runners slid through the aisles, whispering to students who hastily left and ran down the corridors to the war room in the basement.

In the war room was a huge hand-painted map of the world spread out on a giant board made by pushing together four Ping-Pong tables. All the countries of the world were represented, their resources and military capacities. The map was littered with charms and symbols. Related information was scrawled on the blackboards that circled the room. Students crowded around the table as the dice were rolled and the fates of hapless nations unfolded.

Hitching home, Tom and Ryan grew tired of Larry's domination. They ditched him at a convenience store, running into the night while he was inside making them wait yet another time. They plunged through the lighted streets of Portland, out of breath, until they came to the darkness of the railway yard. They inquired of a switchman the whereabouts of a southbound train. They walked across the darkened train yard, counting tracks to find the train to San Francisco. They lay on a flat car, freezing, as it moved slowly out across the moonlit Oregon landscape; freezing as ghostly, silver-clad fields moved slowly by them; freezing as the train stopped and waited on sidings every half hour. On one of these waits, they saw a boxcar with an open door far ahead on the curve of the train. They ran for it, afraid the train would start without them, and hoisted themselves into its dark space. They found it occupied by men who were lying on the floor and had covered themselves with torn paper grain sacks. Boxcars, boxcars, boxcars.

It was at Larry's small house in the Fairfax hills that Ryan had first taken peyote. His little group of friends had heard about peyote rituals. They knew about the Native American Church, and now they sat around while Larry ground up peyote buttons in a blender and showed them how to fill gelatine horse capsules with chunks and powder from the sacred plant.

Larry's real talent, if he had one, was for connecting with the underbelly of society. As they stuffed capsules he told them about taking peyote with his biker friends one night. They had driven faster and faster, screaming, on the twisting roads of Mt. Tamalpais, certain that monsters were rolling up the highway like a carpet behind them, trying to capture their car in it. After having swallowed the capsules, Ryan realized that he didn't want to be in an altered state in this house. Larry was just too scary and Ryan was sure that he would power trip him—scare him or mess with his mind—as soon as he was stoned and helpless. It was not Demonic Disorientation that Ryan was looking for.

Ryan asked how much time it would take for the drug to come on and figured that he had time to get to his girlfriend's house in SF. He knew it was uncool to accept drugs and then walk out, but he did it anyway. As he left, Larry was already beginning to look a little strange. Ryan wondered if his incisors were really beginning to hang out from under his upper lip, or was he just hallucinating?

Out in the Marin county twilight, the wooded hills were alive with the sound of crickets and sprinklers. House lights shone through the trees. Ryan got in his car and started the drive to Diana's out across the bay. The drug was just coming on as he hit the Golden Gate Bridge. The lights of the city became twinkling gemlights. The distant street lamps looked like strings of pearls draped across the hills. The span of the bridge was catching the last fractions of sunset and looked like a giant harp left behind by a Celtic god. The wind thrummed through its strings. San Francisco floated on its pale cerulean waters like the celestial city come to Earth.

Most of the night he was frightened. He felt nauseated and his body ached. Diana gave him her bed and slept with her mother. From time to time she came back in to check on him, gently rubbing his back and assuring him of his earthly existence. Infinity kept yawing open around him in a most unsettling way. Every time he closed his eyes, he dropped through the sheets into a great void and floated in emptiness. Toward the end of the evening, after he had vomited several times, the trip turned mild and he experienced himself as a coloured flower, swaying slightly on its stalk, blowing in an infinite field of other coloured flowers. Their colors were luminous, pure and from another dimension; like nothing he'd ever seen before.

He rushed off to work the next morning, sleepless. Back at his job, driving the truckster full of x-rays and lab specimens around Geary Street, he was a changed person. Last night's visions of endless dimensions beyond his little world of sex, work, and learning had captured him. He would never be able to settle into being that smug and comfortable professor anymore, living in the exalted halls of past knowledge. All morning, going around Geary Street, like Han Shan's bug, he remembered himself as a flower, one of many, glowing in infinity's field.

Somehow, roundabout, the selective process of his life, of choosing this and not that, had taken him from this early initiation out to an island that was far from everything to which he had once aspired. It was a world of sky, rock and trees; a world where talking ravens sent messages out across the dark forest in their stentorian voices. Often as he walked, he heard them call, passing news across the hills and valleys of the island. They spoke in an elaborate series of coded caws, whistles and clicks; sequences of twos and threes, single clicks and double clicks; a soft tonal hoot that he had yet to decipher. He wondered how long it took their news to get from one end of the island to the other. Not very long, he thought, as he heard their messages repeated at ever greater distance.

He wondered about the essential barrenness of American culture: that nothing satisfied, that everything seemed so boring. Locked in the hall of mirrors, the fun-house of empty entertainment, he sought Delicious Disorientation, a concept that he had come upon when he was seventeen and lost in the slums of Mexico City. Unwittingly he had crossed a line and entered so deeply into the land of the have-nots that people didn't even think to ask him for things. He walked with relief in this poor area where there were no beggars to say no to, no vendors at whom to shake his finger. He was being followed by a pack of playful children who wanted nothing of him but contact. The children were just excited to see a young foreigner wandering in their world, a thing that maybe they had never seen before. They wanted to engage him, to play with him and find out who he was—this stranger who might as well have dropped from the sky.

Far from the landmarks of the tourist world, lost in the hugeness of the city, he walked for miles through nondescript streets of stone and concrete buildings. He thought he was walking back toward downtown, back to the world where he belonged, when suddenly, in an opening between buildings, he caught a distant glimpse of the Monument of the Revolution—in the opposite direction from where he expected it to be. The place where he was trying to go was glimmering far behind him in the afternoon sunlight of this ancient inland seabed. Space, the model of it that he carried in his head, shattered and the world literally spun around him as he reoriented himself. He reeled with it, dizzy and stumbling in the streets. Delicious Disorientation.

In long retrospect, it was not just an escape from reality that he was seeking, but a return to reality. The barren culture he had grown up in was devoid of gods and angels, ghosts and demons; devoid of magic. These had all been debunked, banished by western rationalism, yet he still sought them, sought the magical realism of Latin writers, the old deep magic carried like a treasure in the rotting carcass of Catholicism. He had not yet realised that these things, even if they didn't exist, must be made up to provide a world rich enough to nourish the folds and convolutions of the human psyche; that the psyche cannot thrive, will actually seek death, in a world of gas station realism and clean-restroom empiricism. Despite the influence that Galileo still exerted from his grave in Santa Croce, he was returning to a world where each person was the centre of their own universe, the eye from which the universe peered out all around at itself.

There was little left for him since the university had taught him not to believe in anything that could not be measured. In their little study group in Argenta, he had fought Chardin, tooth and nail, could not separate the Christian trappings, the graveyard smell of the inquisition, from the root of Chardin's ideas. On a hillside somewhere is a graveyard, stacked deep with the tiny bones of all the babies that have been thrown out with the bath water.

Marijuana, then, became a way of slipping off the mind-forged manacles and providing Delicious Disorientation more or less on demand. In Sausalito, he and his stoned friends had laughed gratefully at the complexity and nuance in everyday speech, the richness of double-entendres and multiple meanings that they hadn't heard before; at the richness in music of which they had been previously unaware. One of the first times that he smoked alone, he took his camera and walked through the Marin County hills, gazing through the viewfinder at trees, seeing them in a way he had never seen them before. He found himself transported to a world different from the one in which he thought he lived: a world where the ordinary was extraordinary.

He loved this world but eventually gave it up to keep peace with Sheila. She was afraid of drugs, afraid for him, also afraid for the sanctity of her own mind and the integrity of her personality. In Vancouver, he flushed his stash of rare Lebanese marijuana down the toilet. He watched it, reddish brown in colour, swirl and disappear down the drain with that final cough that toilets make, leaving not even a stain in the clean white bowl of western rationalism. In this sinking moment he even missed the washroom of PEMEX station number 44, just outside of Nogales, with its filthy toilet, its unclean floors, its missing seat, its rusted empty toilet paper rack. At least there were signs of life there, signs that someone had passed.

He lived the next few years straight and unhappy, feeling banished from the garden. He listened for hours to Sketches of Spain, and watched coloured spots behind his eye-lids, trying to recapture a pale imitation of peyote visions. His sister, visiting, found him this way one day and asked him what he was doing. "Watching spots," he said, which she found terribly funny.

After Sheila left, he took up smoking again, with an intensity to make up for lost time. At first it was wonderful. One day he smoked so much that the trees seemed to go into the landscape rather than stand out from it. A new dimension was born, a world of recesses. The hollow tree trunks were indents in the canvas around him, the roads were incredibly detailed oriental scrolls intaglioed with fir needles and willow leaves. This was the Delicious Distortion he'd been craving, but it lasted only a few seconds. Quickly it became jaded. Rather than amuse him, the multiplicity of meanings in language left him confused and paranoid. He wondered what people were really talking about. More often than not he got caught up in the world of thought rather than the light of the senses. Still he persisted at living in a heightened reality. His body began to ache and his lungs to feel scorched. He coughed endlessly. He moved to a water pipe, but by now it was of little use. His energy sank. He slept and ate a lot. The farm sank into semi neglect. His lungs felt so burned that he began to wonder if he had cancer. Still he smoked. He felled trees and cut firewood in an altered state, learning how to do the most complex things while stoned. Everybody on Vasquez seemed to be doing the same thing. Even a visit involved coffee and a joint. Doing things stoned forced a certain kind of awareness on him. He needed to watch and organise things that would otherwise have been automatic.

As a teenager Ryan had read Ray Bradbury's *Fahrenheit 451*, in which the protagonist escapes a repressive futuristic society. He follows the San Gabriel River out of Los Angeles, up into the mountains where he discovers, living by campfires, a world of literate hobos, the world's remaining free spirits. Books have long been banned, seen as the carriers of subversive ideas, but each hobo has memorised one or more books and they tell each other these stories around the campfire at night. At the end they see the flashes of yet another nuclear war lighting up the night sky over Los Angeles, seeing in this tragic ending a new beginning for humanity.

Now, out on Vasquez, Ryan found himself living a version of Bradbury's fictional reality. Life had imitated art. He and his island friends passed old paperbacks, held together with rubber bands, from hand to hand. Sometime the stories they told about them, the plot synopses, were more entertaining than the book itself. Some of their books had been left behind in the city or had just disintegrated. So, on rainy evenings sitting by their wood stoves, they retold the stories from these lost books, mustering all the detail they could remember. The written tradition had begun to slip back into the oral.

Ryan was amazed at how much his formative reading of *Fahrenheit 451*, had influenced his life. Another formative book was Norman Mailer's *The Naked and the Dead*: as a young boy when he had been reading guts and glory war novels, his haunted, dying father had tossed it on his bed. "Here, read this," he had said. Ryan read Mailer and knew beyond doubt that this was how war really was; the scales had been pulled from his eyes and he understood that a person of his fears and sensitivity had little chance of surviving combat. The Naked and the Dead had started him on his journey toward conscientious objection.

One of the tales that the islanders shared was a story by H.P. Lovecraft, in which a man takes vast amounts of hashish and leaves his body. He flys across space and enters a palace where a Sultan with a cruel and infantile face is sitting on his throne, watching some poor soul being flayed alive, his skin being removed inch by inch. Suddenly the Sultan looks directly up to where the hero hovers and says to his guards: "There is a spirit in the room." The man watches helplessly, transfixed by the sultan's eyes, as the palace guards, huge muscular eunuchs, start spooning

229

handfuls of hashish from a huge jar into their mouths. He is unable to move as the guards rise out of their bodies, take his ethereal arms and fly him out across the Mountains of Madness, where they drop him screaming into the void beyond.

Ryan and his island friends also read Paul Bowles' stories in which kifers wandered across the desert in piss stained robes. They laughed at these stories and embraced their heroes as cultural ideals unattainable by anyone as middle class as themselves. This, and home-made music, was what took the place of TV on rainy winter nights.

Later, Ryan tried to grow his own marijuana. At first, thinking wishfully, he wandered the island country side with a tobacco can—one of the big round ones—full of pot seeds. He scattered them at the edge of swamps, in places where there was water and where it looked like the open range cows might not go. He naively fancied himself a later day Johnny Apple Seed—Johnny Pot Seed—and envisioned himself strolling at the end of summer through luxuriant groves of sacred weed, pipe in hand. Retracing his steps in early autumn, he found not a single plant. The feral sheep and free-range cows had scoured every bit of open land. Nothing escaped them. They were like bio-vacuum cleaners, lawn mowers that constantly trimmed the green carpet that covered the island. Other than some strange moos in the woods on summer nights, nothing had been gained.

Ryan had learned that Cannabis is a plant of civilisation; created by long centuries of attention and cultivation, as much a product of the human imagination as human imagination was a product of it. To grow well, it needed the adulation that he would later learn to give it. He had never grown the plant before, and only knew what it looked like from pictures. There was a popular book at the time called "*The Secret Life of Plants*," that claimed all sorts of sentient attributes for plants. Ryan read it and wondered if plants were aware of the secret life of humans.

The next summer, he wandered into Wylie's vegetable garden. Wylie was busy carrying buckets of water to his plants, gently pouring it around their roots. Ryan walked around with him, chattering amiably while Wylie responded with terse and faintly interrogative responses of "Oh yea?" Suddenly, there in the parched taupe sand of Wylie's garden, was an amazing plant. It looked as though it was carved out of jade. The leaves were draped and green like bamboo. It was as graceful as a kimono and radiated psychic energy.

"Wow, what the hell is THAT?" he asked Wylie.

"A pot plant'" Wylie replied dreamily.

So this was the living being whose flesh he had been smoking all these years, the plant that had given him a sense of relief from gas station realism. Now he had met it in person. It was like nothing he had seen in a garden before. It stopped him in his tracks.

They both just stood in silence, gazing at it, looking like the man on the Seven of Pentacles tarot card who is watching his garden grow. Wylie poured a little water around the plant's base. Ryan gently lifted its leaves; bent down in the sandy soil to smell its perfume.

Ryan said, "It's beautiful."

Wylie said, "Oh yeah?

28
Delicious Disorientation

And then it happened. The sound of a car on Main Road brought Ryan back into the moment of sitting on the bed waiting for the acid to come on. He thought that maybe he could feel something in his body and, eager to notice the first signs of what was to come, paid attention.

It was as though someone was slowly turning up the dial on his sensations. More and more he became aware of the tight achyness that he carried around with him at all times. It was the invisible background to his life, something that he had learned to tune out in the interest of functioning. Next he noticed a creeping of his skin and the sense of a huge, electric energy beginning to stir within him. It felt as though, coincident to his physical body, there was a body of energy that was beginning to awaken. He could not tell whether one housed the other or if they simply coexisted. The cabin began to breathe eerily, to expand and contract a little; the grain of its fir boards, blackened by the wood-smoke of many winters, began to flow and swirl as it once did in living trees. He looked at his arms and saw that a small arc of a great wheel was passing through them. The wheel was as big as the solar system, very baroque and intaglioed, full of curlicues and flourishes. The fraction of it in his arm, moved minutely, slowly, just under the skin. He looked up and saw that it moved through everything, through the fir boards, through the window glass, through the trees outside, a great invisible rose window. The sun and moon were part of it, painted on the sky, as were night-time's constellations and planets. It was the wheel of life and death slowly passing through everything. Ryan watched the skin on his arm and saw the wheel's slow procession through his very being.

The ghost of electricity begin to howl in the bones of his face. He thought "to reach the realms of energy I must first undergo physical dissolution." It was as though the molecular bonds holding his all too solid flesh together were beginning to break down. He felt like a cicada shedding its skin, as though a tender green winged creature was about to burst forth from the underground potato bug in which it had been living for so long.

At the corner of his vision was a great yellow light that shone into the dark little world of the cabin. It disappeared when he tried to turn his head and look at it. What was this light he wondered? Could it be what the Quakers called the inner light, or Buddhists the clear light? At that moment, two little girls from the house at the edge of the forest dropped in for a visit. He heard their chatter, their footsteps on the porch, their knock at the door and said "come in." They opened the door but didn't come in. With one hand on the door knob, they held back and shielded their eyes against him as though against a bright light. Then they abruptly said goodbye and left. He heard their laughter and chatter fade up the road and wondered what they had seen with their innocent unconditioned eyes.

Alone again, he understood that this was different than anything he had experienced with peyote or marijuana. His body felt heavy, squat and muscular. He smelled of sweat and sex. He felt black like the devil and had to go look in the backroom mirror to see if he had sprouted leathern wings. He locked the door and took off his clothes to look at himself, as if for the first time, at his dark Italian body, its skin, its muscles, its penis, its long brown ringlets of hair all flowing and pulsing with the miracle of life.

The urge to express all this became overwhelming. He put his ordinary work clothes on and pried open a can of paint from the store room. He found a brush and began painting on the plywood panel that screened the hot water heater from the front room. He moved and the paint continued his movement. He watched it run and flow and become alive. The whole world was flowing and swirling around him now, the paint, the grain in the wood, the walls. The grass on the knoll outside the window moved slowly, like an echinoderm, engulfing the rock bluff outside. Even the forest moved, sent out small trees to engulf and close the clearing, a rent in its continuity.

In the midst of all this there was another knock at the door. Reston and McElwaith, on their way to Alexis', had stopped to say hello. Ryan stood wild-eyed at the door, paint brush in hand, the very personification of a mad artist. His eyes gleamed with electric fire like twin flashlights.

"What's happnin', man." They looked at him with a mixture of amusement and concern.

"I just dropped some acid that Jake left off. Wow"

Reston and McElwaith, in their ordinary reality, looked small and innocent, like boys going fishing. Their clothes, their belts, their shirts, the pack that Reston was carrying, all looked like clothes that their mothers had dressed them in for making a journey. Ryan ushered them inside and showed them the flowing paint. He had painted an eight foot tall creature with a hexagonal head. It towered over their small human forms, like a Hopi Kachina just arrived from the other world. Ryan was so excited to see the paint still flowing and moving long after he had put it on. It was like time had spread out and let many moments flow into one moment, like seeing the world through time-lapse photography. Everything was unfolding around him, being born, maturing and dying, in a second or in a lifetime.

Somehow this had gotten into the painting. Below its hexagonal head there was a series of radiating, spider web circles joined by a wavy spring-like spine that held them all together. Ryan gesticulated madly toward the plywood panel. "Do you see how the paint flows and moves? It circles in the circles and runs down the line, then it flows straight back up to the top of the spine." Reston and McEleaith exchanged glances, then McElwaith laughed, "Slow down, slow down, Ryan, you're stoned on acid and we're not, we can't see it. We'll come back sometime when we're stoned on acid."

Ah, the old problem. When Diana and he had first started experimenting with cannabis, Ryan had been amazed at the realms of word play that it opened up for him and had wanted to write a stoned book. He envisioned it as having a little pouch inside the back cover, like a cartridge belt, that would hold enough neatly rolled joints for the reader to stay stoned for the entire book. State-specific consciousness: if someone at the pub promises to help you build a fence, you have to get them equally drunk again to redeem the promise. Someone once asked Salvador Dali if he took drugs. He replied "I am drugs!" McElwaith and Reston went on their way, letting Ryan know they were going down to Alexis' to spend the afternoon and invited him to drop by if he felt like it.

Later, when flowing walls and the dark heaviness of his body had become too much for him, Ryan put on his coat and boots and walked down the road to the house where Alexis had moved. Now it was his turn to feel like a boy whose mother had dressed him. The alteration of his consciousness had gone on too long and he didn't know if he could take it anymore. It felt like his energy was drawing on some inner source that was coming to its end; like he was going to collapse in on himself, become a tiny two foot tall wizened old man. As painful as they were, he craved the comfort of his very own personal set of mind-forged manacles again. Like a prisoner who has been released, he was looking for the crime that would get him back to the comfort of prison. He knew McElwaith had chlorpromazine, an emergency drug that would bring him down. He sought help and company. The world of energy and light was too lonely, too non-human. He walked through the windy day to his neighbour's house, the wind seeming to blow through him as well as around him.

The dark forest stood on either side of the narrow dirt corridor on which he walked. He remembered that the corridor was called a road. Civilisation, the work of man, was just this narrow strip cut into the primal landscape. The forest hovered at its edges, just waiting to close in and reclaim it. Within the road's margin of young second growth trees stood the great black stumps of the former forest which had been cut down and carried away. The stumps were sometimes eight or ten feet high. Ryan felt a huge sadness permeate his body and wept by the side the road to see the remnants of these broken giants. They brought him into the realm of brokenness, the subset of brokenness, the warehouse of brokenness, the category of brokenness, the platonic ideal of brokenness, the place inside that held all spoiled and broken things. His mind was placed in brokenness, and there he found his father, dispirited, broken, blasted with cancer. He felt his love for this remote man the way he felt his love for these elder stumps. One must love to feel sadness.

Then, standing still, he saw that each stump was a garden: that moss, ferns, salal, red currants grew out of their tops and cascaded down their sides. Out of these gardens young trees were rising, protected by the height of the stump from the sheep and deer who would otherwise have eaten their tender buds. Life arising out of death; life and death so inexorably entwined that Ryan could not clearly separate them.

He started to walk again and all around him saw life rising out of death in its various forms: the old forest dying down, becoming mulch and soil while the young forest rose out of it, not even waiting for it to be decently buried; young roots attaching to the punky wood of dead trees not yet turned to soil. He felt within himself cells dying and new cells being born; he felt his spirit's growth and his body's decline into the grave.

The trees around him hummed and sang in the great wind that was sweeping across the island. He was a tiny being walking in the midst of this great melody that carried within it the smell of cresting whitecaps and spices from distant lands. It flowed by like a slow dragon, endless in its undulating coils. The trees were bending in the wind like the masts of a ship. The island sailed through time and space like a floating Atlantis driven before an approaching storm. The wind tossed the branches of the trees and every branch had coloured lights burning at the end of every twig. The whole forest was alive with light and music, flowing, popping and flashing around him. He began to dissolve in this sea of energy; to merge into everything.

Overwhelmed and feeling that he must be dying, he staggered to the side of the road and stumbled a few feet into the forest to hide himself from passing trucks. He sat cross legged in the ferns, tears running down his face. He closed his eyes and a huge space opened up inside him. It was a heaven, orange and yellow, swimming with tiny dragons. Ahead of him burned a huge sun, throwing out giant solar flares. Only vaguely aware that his body was still sitting in the damp ferns, he was being pulled by the sun into its blazing yellow core. In the midst of it, an orange triangle opened up in his third eye. He passed through it, gaining speed, travelling in light years per second, passing through triangle after triangle, each one bigger than the one before, in a tunnel opening to infinity. Not prepared for the immensity of this dissolution, he thought about his daughter, about his lost loves, and wanted to come back. He needed to return. He followed a sprout of himself, a rootlet, back down into his own body. Finding it, he straightened his legs, feeling like a new born calf trying to stand. He forced his eyes open and by that act retracted himself from the leagues of space into which he had travelled. He stood in the blazing forest. It was all light and colour and felt as though it could be sucked, at any second, like a silk scarf, through the triangle gateways, leaving nothing but a great emptiness in its place.

He made his feet move. Returning to the road, he walked along it to seek succour from his friends. He knew that they had adventured here before and, if he could only get there, would know what to do. He looked down on himself from above, a man, stooped over as against a wind, wearing ordinary work clothes, walking down a country road. But somehow he was all of this too, almost crushed by it, just barely moving along.

He traveled down a long dip in the road and stood at its bottom where a deep creek ran through a culvert. Listening to the creek's song for awhile, he let it sooth him. The creek flowed and gurgled among the roots of great old firs that had secretly survived the logging. They were a comfort to Ryan, their roots holding the creation together; the water that flowed by them cooling down the explosive energy of all this fire and air that seemed about to disperse at any second. The clay at the side of the road was wet and Ryan connected with it, feeling its moisture and solidity. He was standing on the ground, a part of and surrounded by Earth, Air, Fire, and Water. He was experiencing an ancient view of the world, something that had been hidden in writings and graven upon stellae to be passed along, and now, today, it had found him. He was in a great Shinto shrine praying to the elements, the gods of the trees and earth, to send him succour, to tie him to them with their tendrils. He knew that ancient man had walked in this realm, had seen nature and themselves this way. He knew that he had been living in the top drawer of an ancient cabinet, in one room of a huge mansion, not knowing that the rest was even there. He laughed and cried at this rude awakening, grateful that he had found it; angry that his culture had hidden it from him; frightened at its hugeness; knowing that he was just peeking through the key hole.

He walked on, up out of the hollow. At the top of the hill Alexis' house hove into view, smoke curling out its chimney; a human outpost in the flashing non-human world through which Ryan walked. Ryan walked up their pathway, and arriving at the door, knocked. Sammie let him in. She looked deeply in his eyes and called out to the others in the room, "Ryan's here." They were sitting in the living room, glasses of home brew before them and a slight smell of hashish in the air. They all looked up at

237

him, saw the wildness in his eyes and gently laughed. McElwaith laughed out loud, finding mirth in this situation as he did in most situations. Reston nodded his head in a slow affirmative way, showing understanding. Ryan realised that these people had all been here, had walked in this dimension, had already been blown away. They lived with this knowledge. They had made lives in this world of flux and fusion. Panta Rei.

"I'm scared," Ryan said in a voice that surprised him with its smallness and meekness. They looked at each other and back at him and laughed gently again. It was a laugh full of kindness and understanding. As hypersensitive to criticism as Ryan was, he did not feel ridiculed, only understood.

"I'm scared, I want the Chlorpromazine."

"We can get that for you," said McElwaith, "I can go home and get it, but why not just sit down and have a bit of wine. Chlorpromazine is a drug too and can have its own unpleasantness, so it's better just to sit down and sip some wine and see if you can come down by yourself. It's better. If you can't we'll get the chlorpromazine, OK?"

McElwaith's blond curls and short blond beard framed his bright and shifty blue eyes. He chose not to look like a hippy; he could have been an ordinary everyday fisherman or logger. Ryan sat and tasted a bit of the blackberry wine that Sammie brought him. It was from last summer. It tasted like autumn fields with bees and wasps. Looking around the room at his friends, he wondered, was anybody ordinary? He thought of his wife and daughter, so far away, and was sad. It was hard to be this open, this vulnerable with people—this helpless. He cried like a child. It was hard to rely on their good will.

In the shelter of the house they talked him down. He sat and listened to conversation and music until the magic began to fade and the world started to become familiar again. They fed him soup and bread, and he slowly moved from the world of energy back into the world of the body. Alexis played a basic blues run that Smiley had been teaching him over and over again. Ryan had never heard anything so sweet.

Reston sat back in his chair by the fire, smoking a hash pipe. He had straight brown hair just over his ears and a short groomed beard that framed his long face, with its hawk like features and troubled blue eyes. His eyes could also light with laughter. Puffing on the hash pipe to get it going, he looked very ancient, like someone out of the Arabian Nights, a time traveller swept on to this desolate island by the hand of fate.

Ryan listened to their stories, slowly taking food into his mouth, taking the earth inside of him, entering into the amazingness of taste. Reston told him about a time in Portland when he had taken 40,000 micrograms of acid just to see what would happen. "We were just too stoned and went to the emergency room to get a shot to come down. As we sat there, the gold flecks on the linoleum floor kept swarming up our pant legs, like aphids, and we kept trying to brush them off. Then a nurse, all dressed in white with a white cap, came in carrying what seemed to be the world's biggest hypodermic needle. It was so frightening that we just ran screaming out of the room and into the street. She was running behind us, still holding the needle. I ran to a friend's, and just sat at a table for three days. There was nothing going on. People came and went. They had their meals around me, went to work, came back, went to bed and got up again. Outside the window, I saw the sun pass across the sky three times. Every now and then someone would put food in my mouth."

Ryan had only taken 400 micrograms. He couldn't even begin to imagine what 40,000 would do. His friends clearly knew the world of altered realities better than he did and he felt a deep kinship with them. Outside, rain began to lash the windows and blow puffs of smoke back through the vent of the tin heater.

He thought about the influence that these people had on him. In his previous world he would never have met them. One by one and two by two, like the animals on the ark, they had arrived on this island, refugees from a civilization that appeared to be racing toward Armageddon. In the small confines of this pre-apocalyptic world, they were like classmates in a new school in which he was enrolled; they touched him deeply.

Returning home, he was well fed and coming down, but still in a world where all living things had an electric aura. His friends had comforted him like mothers, gently helping him back into the human world of bodies and food. The forest around him was no longer threatening, just alive and magic. As he entered his house, the painting no longer flowed, but there was definitely a suggestion of movement, a ghost of electricity. He hoped that on future trips it would flow and move again.

239

He went out into the yard. The wind had shifted to the northwest and the last of the high clouds were still lighted by fractions of the sunset. In the dim twilight, he looked around and saw the old junk with which he was surrounded: the remains of the old house behind the one in which he lived, bits and pieces of lumber and hardware that he had saved because they might someday be useful: his very own pre-apocalyptic junk pile. He was overwhelmed by the amount of old stuff around him, the accumulations of the past.

He went back inside and got some newspaper and kindling. He used the news from several weeks ago to start a huge bonfire. Here, tonight, before the magic wore off, he tried to connect with what was new and fresh in his life, tried to make a new start by burning everything that was old and decayed. As night seeped into the clearing, the fire burned brighter and ever brighter, lighting Ryan's small shake house and the trees that towered over it.

He circled wider and wider, gathering more and more bits and pieces. Somewhere in all these broken boards was his own growth tip, just waiting to have the debris lifted so that he could grow freely toward the sun. He kept throwing things into the fire until it was just too dark to collect anymore. At some point he realised that he could not accomplish this task all in one night; that getting rid of the rotting past would be a long term project.

He dragged out a chair and sat and watched the fire burn down to embers. It burned long into the night as he watched the past disappear, watched the colours that appeared in the flames. When it was almost gone he scried the glowing embers for images of what would come. All around him, in a night that had turned northeaster clear, distant stars were burning. He had started out the day with Krishna the Preserver, his blue body and red bindi in capsule form, and ended it with the fires of Shiva the Destroyer. Totally exhausted he entered his quiet cabin and climbed into bed. Little images still trickled past his eyes. He watched them as he slipped into darkness. He dreamed that his spirit was being carried out over the world on a great wind that passed high overhead.

29
The Commune

After the novelty of hippiedom had worn off and days of being stoned had brought too much lassitude for his active nature, Wilf, the strong local boy who drummed at the Legion, began to wonder what the Commune had to offer. When he presented himself at its gate, Bob simply told him that if he stayed around for awhile he would see a few things that were far beyond what he had already seen in his young life.

This was of interest to Wilf. He was so strong and rooted in his body and this world, that the drugs of the hippies had barely made an impression on him. Hallucinations seemed silly, like cartoons, and the endless hippy philosophising about spirituality seemed like elevated bar talk, the same old bullshit that was passed back and forth over pitchers of beer at the Rod and Gun--locally known as the God and Run or the Rotten Cunt—a pub in the town across the water,. There was a seriousness about Wilf. If there was something other than this reality, he wanted to know about it. Bob talked to him about silence. He said that it was through being quiet that one learned to see.

Silence sounded good to Wilf and he decided he would give it a try. They started him out working on the fence, but it soon became apparent that he was skilled in everything he did. Next they asked him to take over the butchering of the Commune's cattle. With his knowledge of how to live in the country, he soon became indispensable. He began to work with Tim, Bob's right hand man, on the Commune's large construction projects. Tim went over the plans with him and Wilf organised the work. He had never had sixty people at his command before and was amazed at how much he could get done in a day. He began to extend his vision into the projects, sharing his ideas with Tim, who took them to Bob. Wilf's ideas began to be incorporated into the projects. While the other members silently worked, awaiting their visions, they saw Wilf with the Commune

241

leaders, pointing at the emerging buildings and fences, talking softly so as not to disturb their silence. He was even invited to eat up at the house occasionally, but felt uncomfortable and usually stayed down in the village of plastic shacks. Nonetheless, he became one of the inner circle.

Even in the midst of all this heady stuff, he did not forget his purpose. After a year he arranged to talk with Bob. He was persistent. When they finally met, he said "I've been here for over a year now and haven't seen anything beyond the ordinary things we do every day."

Bob said, "First you must learn patience." He sat on his chair in the great stone house and asked Wilf. "What if you were building a house like this and someone came to you after a month, one of the workers, and complained that you had promised him a house and all that he could see was torn up land and foundations going in? What would you say if he asked 'where is the house you promised me?'"

Wilf laughed his good natured laugh. "I'd say it'll be here a hell of a lot sooner if you get back to work and quit your fuckin' belly achin'." Bob and Wilf looked at each other and laughed together. Wilf got back to work.

He came to Bob on the anniversary of his second year and asked again. "You said if I stuck around I would see a few things, and I ain't seen nothin' yet."

Bob said, "You're a good man Wilf. You really keep this place going, perhaps too much so. It takes a lot of thought to do what you do. Maybe you should cut back. Spend a couple hours on the bluff before sunset each day and see what happens."

It went against Wilf's active nature to do nothing, but each day after dinner he went up on the bluff and watched the island tilt into darkness, watched the sea turn blue and then black, watched the stars come out and the clouds sweep by overhead. He tried just to listen and see, not to follow the thoughts of tomorrow's projects that crowded into this head. Sometimes he remembered something essential that had to be done next day, like sharpen the chain saws before they went out into the woods, or talk to Tim about ordering more concrete in on the next ferry. Keeping the now over 100 people occupied required a lot of thought and organisation. He took to bringing a small notebook so that he could write these essentials down and not have to think about them. He envied the people who were just told what to do each day, who dreamily peeled poles or carried them up to where the fence was going in, the people who didn't have to keep track of things. Sometimes he felt like a sheep dog in a flock of passively grazing sheep, always alert, always sniffing the wind.

Everyone around him looked so beatific, which made him wonder what they had seen and if perhaps he was the last one who hadn't seen anything. There was no way he could find out, as conversation that was not about a direct need was frowned upon. He felt he could only contribute by working harder for everybody; that that was what he had to give.

One day, up on the bluffs as evening came, Wilf opened his eyes to write down some nagging detail and found that Bob was standing quietly next to him. Bob smiled at him with the warmth of a father. It seemed to Wilf a special blessing that Bob had sought him out and had come to see him here on the bluff. Before sitting on the rock besides Wilf, Bob touched him on the top of his head, just held his fingers there ever so lightly. "Just allow yourself to relax Wilf, just breathe." was all that he said. "Try not to work so hard. You are so good at that, but what you're looking for comes through not trying harder." Then Bob sat down next to him on the sun-warmed rocks. They sat together as the day died down around them. Wilf forgot his book and let go of the next day's duties. At first he was afraid that with Bob sitting right next to him, he would dissolve or find himself somewhere else, but then he calmed down. So what! That was what he was here for, wasn't it? So he just sat and closed his eyes and listened to the wind sweep over the bluff. He didn't see anything, didn't have a great vision, but he loved the deep silence of the evening. He realised that this is what he had been missing with all his thinking and wondering and planning: he hadn't even enjoyed his time up here in the evening. He had been trying too hard for something to happen. It was so different to just sit and breathe...just breathe. Later he started to nod off and then jerked awake to find that darkness had descended and Bob was gone. The hippies had told him stories about Indian gurus who had appeared to someone who later discovered that the guru had actually been a thousand miles away. In the darkness Wilf wondered if Bob had really been there or whether he had simply appeared to him.

Wilf picked his way down the bluff and through the groomed grounds. He had been having the work crew lop off the scraggly lower limbs of the trees to give the grounds an open park-like appearance. He walked through the streets of the plastic tent city, past the cook house that served the communal meals, past the rows of tables under their plastic roof. There was still a Coleman lamp on in the cookhouse. Wilf knew the routine. The dish crew was silently drying and putting away the last of the evening meal's plates. They would also soak the beans for tomorrow's meal so that the morning crew could set them to boil.

Other than the cook house, most of the other houses were already dark. People had worked hard and were tired by the end of the day. Since reading, music, and talking were frowned upon, they retired early and slept so that their bodies could become strong and healthy; they rose and retired with the sun so that they would once again fall into the natural rhythm that would give birth to the consciousness that they were meant to have. Wilf went to his own plastic house in the sleeping tent city. It was a little better built than the rest of them. He bent back the plastic door flap and stepped inside. Lighting a candle, he looked around at the carefully peeled and joined poles that formed the framework, at the ladder he had made that went up to his loft. His was the only house that had a loft. He had built it above the one room with its table, its chair, its tin heater, its place to hang clothes. He took off his clothes and climbed the ladder into the loft. Blowing out the candle and opening the plastic hatch that he had made above his bed, he lay listening to the night and to the occasional sounds made by the hundred sleeping people around him.

30
The Commune

As his third anniversary in the Commune approached, Wilf began to doubt his ability to experience the other dimension in which those around him seemed to blissfully live. He considered giving up his responsibilities and asking to be just a worker so that he could enter deeper into the silence, but the thought of mutely doing simple, unchallenging tasks every day felt like a living death to him.

Three winters had passed, long wet winters of working in the woods, of wearing clammy rain gear, of clothes never being completely dry. He envied the people who had come with families. Perhaps they had whispered conversations at night while they lay in their winter beds and the rain drummed on their plastic roofs. He was always directing groups of people at work, often using just gestures. He used words only as backup when the sign language didn't work. Even then he spoke softly, in a whisper, just to keep his large assertive voice in check.

In his loneliness, he took to directing a number of the small, one person projects that needed doing. He would pick a person, and then help them carry the necessary tools and materials to the site. Once there he worked with them for awhile to show them how to do it. At first it was mostly silent. He applied the wood preservative to the fence and then passed the brush to the other person who did the same. He watched to see if they had the knack of it, enjoying these simple acts of one-on-one companionship.

Later, alone in the woods, doing something like showing someone how to scrape away vegetation from the bottom of a fence post, he began to indulge in some idle chatter just to hear the sound of voices. He would say something simple like "How did you like those potatoes last night?" or "What do you think of the new cook house?" Because he was seen as part of the inner circle, this seemed all right to the people with him. To his surprise most of the people he talked with seemed to delight in this opportunity for chit chat. Sometimes they would just sit idly on the hillside and chat for awhile about what they used to do, where they had come from, what was it about their past life—as it was called—that hadn't worked for them.

He was curious about what other people were experiencing during their quiet concentrated work. This curiosity began to guide the conversation. "So what's it like for you; what have you been seeing?" To his surprise most of the other men—it was unthinkable to go off alone into the bush with a woman—had not "seen" any more than he had. He got answers like, "I'm still quieting my mind." "I know that someday it will be revealed to me." "It takes so long to undo the years of conditioning." Some, however had experienced visions or insights, or heard voices up on the bluffs. Others believed that Bob was god. But mostly, Wilf was surprised to discover, the silence he had taken for enlightenment was only the same mute wondering and dissatisfaction that he had.

He also came to realise that many people really didn't care about the spiritual vision of the Commune: they just liked the simplicity, the peaceful daily routine, the simple rules to live by; the lack of room for ambition or failure. They had simply come to annihilate the complicated messed up lives that they had created for themselves. Then he remembered having read in one of the books that hippies had lent him, that the meaning of nirvana was "annihilation." He realized that some of the people were here simply because their lives had stopped working.

He also learned that his fellow Commune dwellers were not all losers: there were ex-doctors, lawyers, business men, realtors, professors in the group. Wilf found out that they had sold their homes and liquefied their assets; that they had donated everything to the Commune; that there had been no satisfaction in their seemingly elegant lives. The Disintegration had rendered their relationships, their homes, their sports cars, their degree of fame or fortune meaningless. "Everybody comes to the Commune with nothing," Bob had said, "everybody signs over what is left from the past. Only the Commune—all of us—owns anything."

There were people here who had had nothing, and people who had had it all. Now they were more or less on equal footing, except for the people with special skills, like himself, who had taken on some specific task for the good of the Commune: to treat its sick people, to cook for it, to deal with its legal problems, to design its buildings. This was not seen as a special status, but as a sacrifice: to be willing to spend some time away from blessed simplicity in order to serve the greater good.

"We must get beyond this idea of individual survival," Bob had said, "It just intensifies the illusion of a separate self and filters everything we see. It hides the great vision of who we are. This path is not for the faint hearted, not for those who would hold something back, some secret bank account. If there were the possibility of retreat, you would take it rather than reach the goal. We are all together here in our commitment to the journey. Like mountain climbers, we make our ascent tied together."

There were things that Wilf found out that no-one should have known: while they were all supposed to be in the eternal present and to have died to what they had before, in reality, many of them found this eternal present boring. They had thought that it would lead to cosmic consciousness, or at least some understanding of the divinity that Bob kept saying was in everyone. But for most of them, as far as Wilf's clandestine little survey had shown, it was simply mute boredom, lacking the fun of conversation, the die tosses of success and failure, the spark of flirtation.

Even the marriages were picked by Bob. People who he saw would further each other spiritually were married in a group wedding each autumn when the sheep were mating and the inflamed bellows of the free range cattle echoed in the woods. The brides and grooms stood together in the great meeting room, two by two, wearing their marriage clothes: the simple cotton dresses made by the sewing team for the women; peasant white shirts and pants for the men. After the ceremony there was a special meal with desert. Each couple was given several days to merge their households and bond with each other. They could be seen walking hand in hand, still in their marriage clothes, under the groomed trees of the Commune grounds.

Occasionally, word was given that the whole Commune would meet as a group to hear Bob speak. Some of them knew that in other traditions this was called Satang or Darshan, but here, simple and unpretentious, it was just called a Talk, or Conversation. There was excitement when this happened: all day long people smiled at each other. There was even some whispering about it. After the day's work, after dinner, after showering in the communal bath houses, one for the men, another for the women, they changed into clean clothes and walked up the groomed trails to the great house where Tim and Mariel waited at the door holding candles, silently greeting each person as they filed in and found a place to sit on the varnished wooden benches.

"Tonight," said Bob—he sat in his great chair on the low stage in front of the group—"I want to talk about obsession. Almost everybody out there in the so called 'real world'"—people laughed—"lives for an obsession. Some of these are easy to see. The person who is obsessed with sex, or with alcohol, or with their weight, or with a specific breed of dog"—everyone laughed again—"yes, some people's purpose in life is to breed those little wrinkled up Shar-Pei dogs." They laughed together. Bob threw back his head and his horn rimmed glasses twinkled in the electric light provided by the generator. He wore his usual stay-pressed slacks and pastel plaid sports shirt with a corduroy jacket. He looked more like an advertising executive or accountant than the magnetic leader of a rural Commune. They all enjoyed this moment of lightness. It was beautiful to hear Bob speak.

"But most obsessions have come to seem normal. They don't even seem like obsessions anymore. Some are even seen as desirable and are rewarded. Think about gaining wealth or power or fame. Think about the obsessions with being beautiful, with security, with worrying all the time, with wondering if you are going to have enough money for your old age." The older people in the group had a harder time laughing at the last one than the younger people. "Then there is the obsession of raising the perfect family, of implanting your children the right obsessions, the ones that will get them ahead in the world. All of our time goes into these obsessions. Like dogs worrying our fleas (we seem to be into dogs tonight), our whole life is usually spent trying to satisfy some dumb obsession, so that we never really wake up, we really never find the one thing that we were born to discover. We have sold our birthright. It's like the story of the beggar who saved the king's life and was offered anything he wanted. Because he was a beggar and was obsessed with getting enough food, all he could think of to ask for was a sandwich." There was more laughter.

"It is like the hung-over Irishman who is walking home along the beach, in the blazing sun of morning. He finds an old barnacle encrusted bottle and pries it open with his pocket knife, hoping it's full of booze. He pries off the old lead stopper and an enormous Genie rises like smoke into the sky above him. 'You have freed me after countless kalpas of imprisonment. For that I give you three wishes.' The first thing that comes to the Irishman's mind is booze, so he asks for a cold beer. The Djinn hands him an open bottle of ale, pulled out of thin air, exquisitely chilled with little drops of condensation running down its green sides. The Irishman tosses it back, and to his astonishment, as he turns it upright again, it refills itself. He tosses it back again and again and each time is amazed that it refills itself. Meanwhile, the Genie, anxious to be off to wrack vengeance on the descendants of those who imprisoned him, impatiently says 'you have two more wishes.' The Irishman, without an iota of doubt, says 'could I have two more of these, please.'"

They all laughed together again. Then there was a silence broken by faint after-chuckles and the distant susurration of the generator.

"So this is our castle." Bob gestured around him. "It's not my castle, it's not your castle, it's our castle. There is no me and no you here. We are all together. What unites us is that we are not satisfied to live in obsessional reality. So we take our chances. We live a life that will deliberately undermine our obsessions. You are all very brave. It is hard to let obsessions die. At every step of the way there is the desire to run. Some of you have probably even wanted to go get a job at the dry-cleaning businesses in the town across the water or even at the Chevron Station." There was nervous laughter at this one. "Anything but stay here for another day. You all know the feeling. You all know how hard it can be just to be here, to live authentically, to live simply, just to be forever in the present. It goes against everything for which you were groomed. But when the sky opens, as it will for each of you—that is my promise—you will weep with joy that you have stayed the course to receive the gifts that await you. We will Converse. Conversation Time is to inspire each other. This is the true purpose of Conversation. It means 'to keep company.' We all carry our own weight on this path, nobody can walk it for us, but we can keep each other company as we walk along."

This was the time for questions and answers. They all knew that it had come. Hands were raised. There were some testimonials. People stood up and talked about their realisations. There were some mystical experiences, lights approaching them on the bluff, inner voices giving direction. All heads pivoted around toward whoever was speaking. People nodded in recognition at some of the stories. Only one poor woman raised her hand and asked Bob for help. Nothing like this had ever happened to her. She was depressed, day after day, just like she had been before. She said that at least before there had been some escapes, like going to a movie or having lunch with a friend. She started crying. The group was silent.

"You are very brave," said Bob, very softly projecting his voice directly to her, across the room. "You are living with your suffering. You are embracing it and experiencing it directly. It is through merging with our depression, our ennui, that we move through it to the other side. Sometimes what you are experiencing is called the 'corridor of madness,' or 'the dark night of the soul.' Know that it is the great darkness that precedes the dawn." He raised his voice to the larger group. "Honour and protect her, surround her with your love. She is your leader. Follow her into the darkness so that she will be able to lead you into the light." The people next to the crying women extended their arms to her and held her. "Let's just sit for awhile," said Bob. "Let's just be with this."

After a while Bob simply nodded at Tim and Mariel. They took two candles and walked down the aisles at either side of the room. People began to file out after them. The crying woman was no longer crying but left looking very wilted, supported between the two people who were holding her. Despite the crying woman, there was a happy buzz as they filed out.

It troubled Wilf, as he lay in his loft, that what people said to him in private was so different than what they said at the meeting. More and more, anger began to rise within him, and his great muscular body tossed and turned on its little bed. The slim poles of the plastic house creaked and groaned with his movement. He got up and lit a candle. He went down the ladder and paced around for awhile in his small space, and then, feeling too confined, dressed and went out into the dark night.

31
The Commune

Wilf slipped out the commune gate onto the darkened road. He walked past the great clearing of the orchard, now silent and claimed by the night. A small moon hung over the trees and an owl called. He followed its voice down into the forest and travelled the road's twists and turns until he came out on Main Road. He walked through the night until he came to the cabin he had built on his parent's land. He found the key under the stone where he had hidden it three years ago, and unlocked the padlock. Once inside he lit a lamp.

Everything was more or less the same as he had left it, except that it was dustier and the stuffing of the old easy-chair, where he used to sit and read, had been chewed and pulled out on the floor by mice. Noticing the black conga drum that he used to play at the Legion, he gave it a thump. It sounded dead from three years without a fire. The cabin smelled musty, so he left the door opened to let the fresh night air into the lamp lit room.

He could, he thought, just stay here and not go back. He could pick up the threads of his life where he had left it three years ago. He could write off his experience at the commune, call it an experiment that failed. But he was angry at the bullshit, the promises, the waste of his time—he was also afraid.

Many times Wilf had accompanied Bob to the gate when people were leaving. He had heard their parting conversations, ranging from angry, shouted recriminations to pathetic, tearful excuses. When Bob got wind that people were leaving, he walked them to the gate in an effort to dissuade them. Wilf had often been asked to be there, because of his strength, in case the people became violent toward Bob. If the shouting and gesturing became too big, Wilf, the victor of many a barroom brawl, simply walked in and stood between Bob and the angry departees.

There were several tacks that Bob took with departing people: one was "You are making the worse mistake of your life. Yes, of course, this gate is open; you are free to leave any time. You think you can go back to your old life, but you cannot, you have already changed too much. You can go through the motions of your old life or pick up a new one, but you will always feel like a ghost living in a world that is unreal to you. You have already seen too much to be satisfied by that" –he gestured out at the world in general—"any more."

For others he said: "You've almost formed your eternal soul, an adamantine consciousness that can live forever in the present; that can live through death, catastrophe, the end of the world. Why throw your work away now, when just a little more perseverance will get you what you came for? Perseverance furthers. Then you can leave, do whatever you want, once the job is done. Without finishing, nothing else matters. No matter what you do out there, no matter what success you have, when the time comes, you will simply die like a dog. There will be nothing left. You will perish. Your body will go back to the elements. It is only by finishing the crystallisation of your eternal body that you can pick up this thread: go through the space between lives and be born into this work again to complete your evolution."

Sometimes the disaffected people were persuaded and walked back with Bob and Wilf. They went back to their plastic house and unpacked their bundles of belongings. Sometimes they left. When they left, Bob watched them walk down the road and shook his head. "It's too bad," he would say, "their obsessions were too strong. It will be many lifetimes before they get this chance again, if ever. To die like a dog is to have done nothing here, to leave nothing, to have lost eternity."

On the way back from one of these tête-à-têtes at the gate, Wilf had asked Bob about crystallising the soul. Bob told him: "It would not further you to talk about that right now, Wilf. One must have seen, at least a little, had a glimpse, before we can talk about that. Just keep doing your work 'til the first opening comes. Then we can talk about what is next. Thank you for being at the gate with me today."

Standing in his lamp lit cabin with the door open to the night, Wilf didn't know about any of this. He did worry, though, that if he left he might be sacrificing the unique opportunity of his life. He did worry, as he

252

looked around his musty cabin, that perhaps his old life would no longer have any flavour. He just wanted a vision, some talisman of the different reality that Bob had promised.

So far, he had seen the people who left as being weak and not able to stick it out. He had worked at so many shit jobs in his young life that he could stick out almost anything. Now, he admitted to himself that he was definitely thinking of leaving. Voices arose within him: "Wimp. Pussy. Quitter." He also knew that he could just go back and that no-one would be the wiser about his little walk tonight.

The night-hours passed in his cabin. He built a fire in the wood heater and closed the door. He didn't feel he could just quit. That would be saying that it was his fault, that he was deficient in some way. He knew that to leave in this way would leave him feeling defeated and scared for the rest of his life. Somewhere he knew that to be true. He had gone to the commune; he had worked hard. He had given three years to the experiment. How much was enough? It was like fishing, he thought. How much patience was enough? Was it foolish to just keep fishing in the same spot when there were no bites? Or, if you left, were you giving up just before the big one struck? At what point did you decide that there were no fish there and try another spot?

No, he realised, it was not all his fault. He had waited; he had done what he was told; he had worked hard and contributed; he had sat on the bluffs. Still nothing. Bob had not delivered. Somehow this was all an elaborate masquerade to keep all these people enslaved and in a stupor. Bob held the purse strings, kept them in line with promises of paradise and threats of the loss of their soul. In short, he had been sold a bill of goods. Was it safe to admit that now?

He remembered the time when he had spoken up on a thinning job above the Alberni Pass. He had confronted the management about the food, about the hours they were working, about their deferred wages. At first everyone had been afraid to back him up, afraid of being canned and losing the time they had already put in. He remembered how he had risen from his seat and shouted the bosses down. They were afraid to touch him, afraid of the strength and violence that lived in his young bull-necked body. He had just stood there and kept shouting them down when they repeated their bullshit stories. At first the men around him were filled with embarrassment for him, he could feel it, but he had just kept shouting and exhorting them, "What are you, a bunch of pussies? Are you going to let these assholes treat you this way? Are you going to let them feed you shit, work your asses off and then not pay you til the contract is over? What if they don't pay you at all when the contract is over? What if it's just a sweet fuck-you? Fuck that! We want our money every two weeks and you owe us for four now!"

Eventually the men had stood up with him and added their voices. Someone had even thrown a few chairs around. The bosses were taken aback and left. They had climbed into their truck, and said that they would check it out with head office. "God-dammed right you'll check it out," Wilf shouted after them. The next morning no one went to work. They sat in camp, and practiced throwing axes into the sides of fir trees. At noon the truck arrived with a new cook and everybody's pay check.

Wilf shut down the wood heater, blew out the lamp, and padlocked the door behind him. He put the key back under its stone. On the long way back, he walked off his anger and adrenaline. The next day he went about his chores, directing his crew, but there was a sarcastic edge to his voice. It was loud now, not the enlightened whisper any more. He shouted to people who were fucking up. "Hey, you better stack that straight or the guys up in the house aren't going to like it. They might take your soul away." His voice was full of anger, but also had a snicker in it. People didn't know how to take it. There were a few comments like "bad night?", or "Hey, take it easy we're not here to kill ourselves." Wilf ignored these, or simply snorted.

32
The Commune

Wilf waited his time until the next "talk" up at the house. When it came, he filed in with everybody else. The focus turned out to be on respect and Wilf felt the talk was aimed at him. Bob's theme was about how those who organise the work for the commune are not bosses but are there to serve the other members. He also addressed unnecessary talking as a distraction from what they were trying to accomplish. "Conversation, like we have here, is sharing the journey together. Talking is just more mind chatter."

When Conversation Time came, Wilf was the first on his feet but Bob called on a woman who stood up in the front row. She talked about the sense of relief she had at not having to *be* anything, not having to *do* anything special. All her life, she said, she had jumped through hoops for people and now she was just here. She talked about how connected she felt to everyone even though they didn't talk. "Just a sympathetic glance, just a smile of recognition gives me more of a sense of connection to all of you"—she looked around the room—"than all the intense late night conversations I used to have before."

Wilf was on his feet again, ready to speak, but Bob held up a hand and stopped him. With his other hand he pointed to a man standing at the back of the room. Smiling at Wilf, he said, "Let's let Bill speak first, he hasn't spoken before."

Wilf sat. It seemed to him that he was deliberately being gagged and shunted to the side. He waited until Bill had finished talking about feeling healthy for the first time in his life; about how he loved the physical work, the early nights, the rising early in the morning. "It's so simple," he said, "really it's all a miracle, just getting up in the morning is a miracle." There were ahs in the group and Bob beamed benevolently at Bill.

Wilf was on his feet again, standing large in the middle of the room. Bob gave him a look of query. "You seem to have something that won't keep tonight," he said mildly.

"Dammed right I do," said Wilf. The anger and snarl in his own voice surprised him. It traveled like a shock wave through the group and disappeared into a deep silence. People craned around to see who was speaking and then turned hastily away. After a moment Wilf realised that no-one was looking at him. *So it is going to be like it was on the Alberni Pass*, he thought to himself. Only Bob was looking at him, with a look of sympathy on his face, his brow drawn into wrinkles, like a great concerned panda bear.

"People have noticed you seem a bit angry lately," Bob said with a pleasant paternal smile. "It's good to talk about it, get it off your chest, rather than to let it seep out everywhere. Especially to let it leak out on people who are just trying to do their jobs."

"Yea, you're damned right I'm pissed off," said Wilf. "I'm pissed off at all the bullshit that goes on around here. I came here three years ago and you told me that if I stuck around, I would see a few things. Well, I've been sticking around and I've seen exactly sweet fuck-all, I mean like diddley-squat. I thought it was just me, but I've been checking it out. There're lots of people that haven't seen a fucking thing." He turned around the room, gesturing with his hand. "I know damned well that most of you haven't seen anything either."

"You're pretty scary when you're mad Wilf. I wonder if people just tell you what they think you want to hear because they don't want you to feel bad or are afraid to anger you." Bob said it as a gentle question.

"I don't think so," said Wilf, "I think everyone goes along with it because they don't want to feel foolish. It's like The Emperor's fuckin' New Clothes. There's not really a lot happening here, just a lot of control, a lot of stupid rules, a lot of bullshit, like all the 'this is all of ours' bullshit." He waved at the room around him. "We live in plastic huts at the bottom of the hill and live on oatmeal and lemonade. You live up here in the castle. The meat we eat doesn't even belong to us. I know we don't own the fucking cows we kill. So do you. A lot of people put in a lot of money to be here, what's happening with all of that?"

256

The fear in the room was palpable now. People had turned around to look at him. Some people were leaving, running out of the room. A group of women held each other at the back and cried.

Bob seemed un-rattled. "This is just not useful, Wilf. We gather here to inspire each other. Conversation Time is about sharing our light and leading each other on. You are welcome to come and talk to me about all of this, I'm happy to work with your confusion. You deserve it. You've given us all so much. It happens to everyone along the way. The ego rebels at having its props pulled out from under it and lashes out at everything around. I'll bet everyone here, at one time or another has felt the way you are feeling now. How many people have felt like Wilf is feeling now?" He looked around the group with the slightly myopic look that his thick lenses gave him. A smattering of hands went up. "See, you're not alone. The important thing, though, is not to lose it, not to act it out and give it power over you. You must remain free and in command of yourself. You are acting it out, Wilf, you are beginning to lose it. In so doing you are bringing yourself down and all of us down. You are one of us. Please come back." He opened his arms in a gesture of invitation.

Part of Wilf felt like crying, like surrendering. But another part was too mad for that. "Bullshit, you have to have an up to have a down. We just have this controlled stupor that we walk through each day in. It's not our fault; it's not that our ego is rebelling or whatever you call it. It's that you really have nothing to offer. You've promised more than you can deliver!"

"That's all, Wilf," Bob said. He stood up in a no nonsense sort of way. "Go get yourself together and we'll talk about this later. You're scaring everybody. We can't talk about it when you're like this." He turned and headed for one of the little doors at the side of the stage.

"Bullshit," roared Wilf, "We'll fuckin' talk about it now." He emphatically stabbed his finger toward the ground beneath his feet, as if "now" was the ground that he stood on and his own personal possession. "I know god-damned well I'm not the only one, and I'd like to hear from some of the rest you." He stood in the middle of the polished benches and gestured to the silent commune members around him. He turned slowly around the room, taking them all in. He muttered a few names as he turned. Most of them looked horrified to see someone who they had regarded as part of the inner circle fighting with Bob. Some clung to each other. "Yeah, now is the time to speak out. I'd like to hear from some of you who've told me what it's like for you. How 'bout you Ben? Arly? Tom?" They each shook their heads no and turned desperately away.

Bob was turning from the door and gesturing to Tim and several other of the people who lived in the House with him. "I said, that's enough Wilf, I meant it. I'm responsible for the safety of these people. I can't allow you to terrorise them like this."

"I'm not terrorising them. I'm just giving people a chance to speak how they really feel. It's about time, don't you think?" He cast his gaze around the room trying to catch someone's eye, but they were all looking down at the floor.

Tim pushed his way down the aisle to where Wilf was standing. People stepped out of his way, stepping over benches to make way for him "Come on Wilf, we'll go for a walk and talk about it." He tried to take Wilf's arm, but Wilf easily shrugged his grasp away. "No fucking way," he said, "I've waited three years. We're going to deal with this now and were going to deal with it here in front of everybody."

Several other members of the inner circle were now working their way through the pews toward Wilf. These were the people who had come to Vasquez with Bob, the group around which all the other members had coalesced. Theodore, one of these original members, worked his way toward Wilf from the aisle on the other side. "Come on Wilf, he said, let's not get ugly about this." Bob was talking to other people at the front, mobilising them. He talked to the commune doctor who hastily left the building.

Samson, another member of Bob's household, so called because of his huge bulk, was rapidly stepping over the benches, moving directly towards Wilf from the front of the room. He was moving fast, like a linebacker diving through a scrimmage, and people were springing aside to get out of his way. Tim tried to grab Wilf's arm again and this time Wilf pushed him. Tim stumbled backward along the aisle until several people caught and steadied him. "Isn't anyone going to speak up with me?" Wilf shouted. Theodore came up behind Wilf from the other side of the aisle and tried to pin his arms by encircling his body, but Wilf easily broke his grip by simply flinging his powerful arms upward. He was just starting to turn to face Theodore when Samson came like a freight train from the front and with a tremendous shove sent Wilf flying backwards over the bench behind him. Wilf's knees buckled against the bench and he went down, crashing onto the floor between rows. On the way down, his hit his head on the bench behind him and lay dazed for a moment, a moment in which Samson leapt over the bench and sat on top of him, pinning his arms to the floor. Tim and Theodore each grabbed one of Wilf's legs that were still draped over the bench, holding on to them for dear life. Wilf struggled for a moment but the combination of Samson sitting on him, Tim and Theodore holding his legs, and the position he had fallen in had immobilised him. He gave up and lay still. "That's it'" said Samson, "just calm down and relax Wilf, breathe, you're going to be all right."

The room was in chaos. There were screams and shouts. People stood in knots not knowing what to do. They all looked to Bob who was still standing in the front of the room dispatching people on errands. Several more men came and sat on the floor next to Samson, taking hold of Wilf's arms.

One of the men next to Bob shouted loudly to get the groups attention and once there was silence Bob spoke softly. "This is unfortunate tonight. It is unfortunate that Wilf got violent and we had to subdue him. We will take care of him now and help him regain his balance." He walked over to Wilf and looked down at him. "We're sorry Wilf, but this place is for people who have the necessary stability and maturity to live peaceably together. We'll see what we can do for you." He turned back to the assembled group. "It would be good for everyone to go home now. Michael is on his way to get his medical supplies and he will help Wilf. We'll see that he is safe and alright." People began to leave, casting backwards glances over their shoulder at the knot of people holding Wilf down.

Michael was the commune doctor, tall, thin and withdrawn. It was hard for him to meet people's eyes. He came with his black medical bag, sidling past the people who were filing out through the door, inching down the aisle behind Wilf's head and setting his bag down on one of the now empty pews. He took out a syringe, removed it from its plastic wrapper, twisted on a needle, and filled it from a vial. "This is just to help you relax Wilf. Don't worry we aren't going to hurt you. We just want to see that you don't harm yourself or anyone else. We want to see that you don't do something you regret. We can talk about it all in the morning."

Wilf strained at the arms that held him, almost getting his right arm free before another person jumped in to help restrain him. The pew that Tim and Theodore were sitting on rocked with his effort to free himself, but the grips of those around him held. "This is bullshit," Wilf said, "this is illegal; you guys are going to pay for doing this to me."

"Just relax," said Michael, "things will look a lot different in the morning." He tore open an alcohol swab and cleansed a spot on Wilf's arm. He flicked the syringe with his middle finger to tap out the air bubbles and injected the clear fluid into Wilf's arm. Wilf craned his neck forward to watch the injection, muttering imprecations under his breath, and then, as it took effect, slowly slumped backward.

When Wilf was in a groggy stupor they carried him like a tranquillised cougar into a small room near the entrance to the Stone House. It was known as the Guest Room because the reporter from Maclean's had been housed in it and visitors who came to see if they wanted to join, or parents who wanted to see their children stayed there. The commune gave them three days of hospitality, in accordance with some ancient tradition, and then they had to decide whether to stay or to leave. Wilf was laid on the guest bed and his arms and legs were expertly bound with soft rope cut from a cotton clothesline. They carefully checked the ropes to see that they were not cutting him. Six people kept watch over him, silently sitting in straight back chairs, making an effort to stay awake. In the small hours of the morning the doctor came and gave Wilf another shot.

Down below, people whispered about the events of the evening. Up through the trees they could see the lights of the Stone House burning late into the night. No one could sleep. They lay in their beds and listened to the muffled sound of the generator running at the bottom of its enclosed pit.

In the morning, half an hour after dawn they heard the great roar of a float plane landing in the long finger of the bay. Theodore, Tim, Samson and several others from the house carried Wilf, sedated and tied to a stretcher down to the small floating dock that the commune had constructed at the edge of the bay. The sea plane taxied to the float on the high tide of the placid bay. Two paramedics climbed out and put Wilf into a restraint system and belted him securely into the back of the plane. The doctor climbed aboard and the plane taxied back down the bay. At the end of the bay its engines roared as it took off into the Northwest wind. Wilf and the doctor were gone. The commune members began their walk through the day.

33
The Commune

Wilf was flown to Riverview Hospital where Michael used his authority as a physician to commit him for observation. After filling out the forms, Michael flew back to the island. In the Stone House that night they had a talk about the importance of emotional maturity and a small ceremony wishing Wilf well.

In Riverview, Wilf asked to have the restraints removed. He said that he was not violent, not crazy; that he had gotten himself there for standing up to a fanatical cult out on a remote island that nobody in the hospital had heard of. Unfortunately, Michael had committed him as a delusional paranoid and these protestations were exactly what everyone expected him to say. They were in no hurry to remove the restraints. Wilf quickly realised that he must be a model patient if he was to be listened to and ultimately freed. He became quickly aware of the seriousness of his situation and the things that they could do to him there. He had read *One Flew Over the Cuckoo's Nest,* and visions from it sent cold chills down his spine. He became quiet and polite—he had been raised well and knew how to do that. Containing the great rage that was burning inside him, he calmly asked to call his parents to let them know where he was.

After half a day, they began to believe that he was not violent. They lowered the dose of tranquillisers they had him on and gave it a try without restraints. They kept him in an isolation cell with a window in the door. Someone sat outside on a stool all day and night and watched Wilf through the window. He was aware of the shift changes and always waved at the new person as they came on the job. Though angry, he managed to be meek and rational. When they asked him about what had happened to him, he told his story in a logical and contained sort of way. The staff discussed his case. They noticed that he seemed to be clearly in possession of himself. After a week they took him out of his padded cell and tried him on a closed ward. He was restless and paced around looking out of the screened windows. They noticed that he was willing to engage the staff and other patients. He even played checkers with some of the patients. One of the nurses noticed that he seemed to be teaching the elements of the game to some of the more deranged patients. After a week of boredom, he set up a poker game. They used the little packets of sugar that came with the meals for currency. These became valuable items on the unit. The staff noticed that Wilf enjoyed talking and that there were wild entertaining conversations during the poker game.

After several more days, they cut back more on his tranquilizers. At his psychiatric appointments Wilf told a strange story about being subdued by a commune out on Vasquez Island. His parents came to visit him. They were old homesteaders who knew about chainsaws and fishing and how to prune trees. In their interview they confirmed Wilf's story, that the commune was nutso, a bunch of zombies, and that they were relieved that their son had finally gotten himself out of it. Wilf told his psychiatrist that there was an article on the commune in an old McClean's, but that it only told half the story.

Dr. Peters, to whom Wilf had been assigned, knew something about Brother Twelve and some of the other cults that had sprung up like mushrooms on the rainy BC coast. He knew about deprogramming, a controversial psychological process that was used to bring young people who had been recruited into these cults back to their senses. He had treated kids who had blown their minds with too much LSD. He had treated kids who believed that beings from the Pleides were communicating with them; kids who felt that the apocalypse was coming; kids who felt the west coast was about to fall into the Pacific; kids who thought that the icecaps were melting and that the world's cities were about to be drowned; kids who believed that the RCMP was preparing concentration camps in the interior, like the ones they had put the Japanese in, to put all the hippies in; kids who believed in the second coming of Jesus; kids who believed that they *were* the second coming of Jesus; kids who believed they had been abducted by flying saucers and experimented on. It was a hell of a time to grow up, Dr. Peters conceded. On his desk was a picture of his two golden girls, one a freshman at UBC, the other an honour student in grade 11. He was god-damned lucky he realised. He was also interested in Wilf's story.

263

In the end, Wilf was subjected to a battery of psychological tests and the staff agreed that he was as normal as any of them. They released him and wrote a report saying that the commune doctor, a G.P, had apparently misdiagnosed Wilf, judging a situational outburst of anger as a psychiatric disorder.

Wilf's parents came to take him home. On the way home, they stopped in Nanaimo and took a hotel room. Wilf reported the whole thing to the local detachment of the RCMP. He told them about the cattle rustling, gave dates and locations. He told them he could lead them to where the bones of the cattle were buried.

34
The Commune

There was a flurry of activity on Vasquez as the police interviewed various residents about the situation with the cattle. The cattle owners, some of them absentee landowners, were contacted and there was a roundup and head count. The island's old corrals were fixed up and filled with cattle for several weeks. Wilf, dressed in his cowboy clothes and riding his brother's horse, led the roundup. He took the RCMP, armed with a warrant, onto the commune land. Bob and Tim didn't make an appearance during the visit. The man at the gate simply took the warrant up to the house and returned after a while and opened the gate for them. Wilf showed them the plank-covered pit where the bones of the cattle lay in their dark underground chamber. He took them to the various sites where cows had been slaughtered.

Charges were laid and it all played out in the headlines of the local papers. CULT CHARGED WITH CATTLE RUSTLING. Reporters traveled out to the island, relishing their day on the water, relishing being driven around by Deana in her old VW van. Islanders were only too willing to tell their theories about the commune, which were even stranger than its reality. They talked about voodoo, zombies, CIA mind control experiments, alien domination, and devil worship. There were stories about secret passages in the house, strange meetings in the woods, loudspeakers on the bluffs. All this filtered into the Vancouver Island papers and even into the august Vancouver Sun. It was one of the strangest and hottest stories to hit the press in weeks.

While the trial was ostensibly about cattle rustling, the prosecutor used every opportunity he got to ask about the strange goings on at the commune. For Wilf it was great to see Bob and Tim, indicted as the defendants, sitting at the defence table, dressed in their suits, looking stiff and uncomfortable. The defence tried to block questions about life at the

Commune as irrelevant but the prosecution persisted, pleading that it was important to establish the deviant nature of the leader's thinking and the gullibility of his followers in order to prove how easy it was to slip into cattle rustling. "Once we have deviated from the common morality, once we have dismissed that as irrelevant, then it is easy to rationalise all sorts of things that are not really acceptable." Every time the prosecution described the commune as "a cult," the defence objected. Finally it was simply called "the commune."

The defendants, Bob and Tim, pleaded ignorance about the ownership of the cattle. They tried to turn it back onto Wilf by claiming that he had assured them he was taking care to slaughter only the commune cattle. The claim was laughable. The prosecution pointed out that the commune owned twelve cattle and according to local cattle owners over forty were missing. Did they think that cattle bred that fast? There was even some laughter in the courtroom.

But the main problem for the prosecution was its inability to show that Bob approved, directed or even knew about the slaughter. The judge ruled that even though Bob was the leader of the commune, he could only be convicted for crimes that were committed with his knowledge. He also ruled that it could not be proven that Tim knew about the ownership of the cattle; it could not be proven that the remains belonged to the missing cattle as there were no ear tags or other identifying marks to be found. There was also a reasonable doubt that some of the missing cattle might have been killed, eaten and disposed of by other island residents. In the end, in accordance with mild Canadian justice, the charges against Bob and Tim were dismissed, but the reputation of the commune was badly tarnished and its cover blown.

The membrane that had kept the world from peering too closely at the commune's affairs had been breached and the commune was exposed to the scrutiny and opinion of the obsessional world that it had so long spurned. It did not stand up well to having the light of adverse publicity shone upon it. Some members had already left after Wilf was flown off. After the verdict they were followed by others who quickly packed and and took the next ferry off the island. Those who stayed did not read papers or listen to the radio. Bob simply told them at the evening talks what was going on. He told them that the world did not appreciate people who tried to transcend its mediocre values, and, in accordance with this, they were being persecuted for a minor infraction based on Wilf's wilful deception as to the ownership of the cattle. The world had found them, he said, and now they would have to find a more remote place to continue their work.

In the following months, they sold the great Stone House to an American from Seattle, who also bought their orchard and the waterfront land. A great barge was towed up the narrow bay below the house. In one long night of lights, of the green wasp-like truck buzzing back and forth, of an ant-like procession of commune members carrying flashlights and bundles, it was loaded with all the commune's possessions. Just before dawn, the commune's machinery was winched aboard followed by the truck. The remaining members climbed on and the whole crew disappeared. By daybreak the house, the orchard, the manicured grounds were all silent and empty.

As the tug and barge became a speck on the Sabine channel, it was as though a dream had ended.

35
Alone

After the commune sailed away, there was only the emptiness of Ryan's cabin, the rain, the brokenness of his car. To escape, he hitched to California, staying in Marin County with Dave.

In the years since Dave's visit to Vasquez with Celia, he had reinvented himself as a hippie contractor, specializing in the restoration of elegant turn of the century houses. He salvaged redwood boards from other houses that were being torn down, carefully pulling out the nails, and running them through a planer to make the seasoned lumber gleam like new. The redwood forests had been cut down to make this lumber. Dave thought that it was precious and saved it from winding up on a bulldozer-splintered rubble heap. All around, there was a sense that anything that could be pulled from the swirling rampage of change was sacred and worth saving. Dave drove an almost new truck with a stereo in it and lived in an elegant home.

Dave and Celia, had long since broken up. Celia had moved to the mountains to live among the followers of her guru. The guru had told her that to attain enlightenment she needed to give up her family, so her son Thompson now lived with Dave. Though well cared for, he seemed sad and missed his mother. The glitzy young women who passed through Dave's house, his lovers, gave Thompson attention and were kind to him. They played at being mothers. After awhile, Dave tired of each of these women and moved them on. He had already tired of Diane, a warm curly-haired beauty with a light nymph-like body. One night, knowing that Ryan was single and lonely, Dave simply asked, in a voice full of despair, if Ryan liked her. He suggested that, if so, he might court her. It was harder for Dave to get out of relationships than into them.

Everything was just as fractured in Marin County as it was in the Canadian bush. It was glitzier, the cars were better; people were taking expensive spiritual workshops. They lived communally to afford beautiful homes. Everyone had a roommate. Everyone was broken up. Every marriage had ended. Everyone was one, two, three relationships past the one in which they had started out. Children climbed on planes to visit far away fucked-up fathers and missing mystical mothers. Dave's friend Brian owned a beautiful house in San Anselmo. He was occasional lovers with his two roommates (and tenants), Eileen and Cher, but they were all free to pursue other relationships.

With difficulty, Ryan arranged to meet Celia in Grass Valley. His experience with the commune on Vasquez had left him full of apprehension about what shape Celia would be in. Nevertheless, he hitched across the Great Valley and up into the the thin air, sparse pine forests, and scooped-out mountains of the Sierra Nevada, whose towns were full of stone buildings from a time when men sluiced for gold and lived in a savage way. As Ryan stood by the side of the road, winter's silver sun filtered into everything.

He met Celia at a church that she had told him about. They walked arm in arm through the pioneer graveyard, among the trees and tombstones. She seemed fiercely determined to transcend the human condition, referring to herself as "this machine" rather than as "myself." When Ryan asked her about Thompson, she said, "Yes, sometimes this machine feels sad when it thinks about him, but I know I am not this machine."

It broke Ryan's heart to see her this way. Dave had told him that Celia made money for the commune by doing portraits for people in city parks. He said that part of the idea of the commune was to learn to live by one's wits. According to Dave, the leader had used the money earned by the wits of his followers to buy great art in Europe, saying that enlightenment was transmitted through the paintings. His followers got to be enlightened by the art while serving in their master's household. Digging the Rembrandt while dishing the soup.

Ryan wanted to do something to shake Celia from her ideological fastness, but their friendship seemed too tenuous for any kind of confrontation. She burned with a belief that this path would release her from life's suffering. Besides, what did Ryan have to offer? A falling down farm? A life of broken relationships? A child lost in the concrete jungle of Seattle? Drugs as an escape from all this? He wondered if his precious individuality was any more wholesome than Celia's devotion to her master. He even wondered if he did have any individuality, or was he just as much a slave to the zeitgeist, to the religion of sex, drugs, and rural survival, as she was to her master's beliefs? Were they both just leaves being swirled along in separate currents of one great river, each believing their own leafness? There was a song that went, "We are dust in the wind."

Ryan gave Celia a little book on Gurdjieff. On the book's green cover was Gurdjieff's circus strong-man's face with its one droopy eye and great walrus mustache. The school Celia belonged to claimed to have its roots in Gurdjieff, though Ryan didn't think that it really had much to do with him. While he didn't dare tell Celia this, he hoped she might see for herself from this little book that she had fallen into a hapless cult. He hoped that it might be an antidote. He had somehow managed to ignore the fact that the author of this book was reported to have married twelve of his disciples. According to his followers, it had been a beautiful wedding. On top of the cake, there had been one groom surrounded by twelve brides—one Ken and twelve Barbies. The guru's followers, the sangha, laughed about this. They thought it was so cool, the ultimate in *epater les bourgeoisie*. They were so sophisticated that just about anything went.

Many years later, when Celia was a social worker, reunited with her children and devoted to her grandchild, she told Ryan that she had showed the book to her teacher who dismissed it as the inauthentic "wiseacreing" of a fraud, of a power tripping control freak. "You have to be careful about what you read," he had said, and she decided not to read it.

The late afternoon sunlight fell through the trees onto tombstones of mountain granite. All around Ryan and Celia were the names of pioneers who had lived their lives in these mountains, much as Ryan and Celia were living theirs now.

After Dave had left, before she became a follower of her guru, Celia had moved with Thompson to Berkeley. There, in that steaming cauldron of revolution and change, she had bonded deeply with a therapist who helped her in ways that were not easy to put in words. He lived his life in a wheel chair, from which he helped others, less visibly wounded than himself, to find peace, joy and meaning in their lives. Then one day he drove himself to the desert in Death Valley.

He parked his car at the side of the road, unfolded his wheel chair, and wheeled himself out into the desert, his chair leaving tracks in the blazing sand. There he sat and cooked himself to death in the fiery loneliness. While this was happening, he appeared in apparition to Celia in her Berkeley home, sweat pouring off his face, his expression both humorous and imploring. She immediately tried to call him but his phone rang emptily. Days afterward, she learned what had happened and wondered if his apparition had been begging her forgiveness. Shaken, feeling her own grip on life to be tenuous, she thought that Thompson would be better off with his father for awhile. She left him there and sought her teacher in the mountains.

It was a time of psychic leakage, of visions and telepathy, of the boundaries between separate people breaking down. It probably had something to do with the drugs that everybody was taking. People who just a few years earlier had been solid individuals—Vira, Chuck and Dave— were totally unprepared for the paradigm shift that assaulted them from their little recreational forays; for the disintegration of the consensus reality by which they, their parents and grandparents before them had all lived.

Tripping on "recreational drugs" was like buying a roller coaster ticket for fifty cents and getting the thrill of your life when the whole damned roller coaster fell down; it was like buying a ticket for a carnival ride and being catapulted into an alternative universe where everybody was green and had two heads. People simply pulled themselves up out of the rubble and tried to live their lives again, with all their friends broken up, or in communes, or just strung out.

"There must be some way out of here," said the poet: like believing in Jesus, or Krishna, or Buddha. The veil had been ripped away, the veneer of civilisation shattered, and who had been prepared for this while just trying to have a little innocent fun? The wounded must go somewhere.

271

Returning to Dave's, Ryan called Cybele, an old high school friend that he and Sheila had known. Cybele lived across the bridge in San Francisco. Her house was out in The Avenues, otherwise known as the Sunset District, that great decline of nondescript houses that falls block after block, through the wind and fog, down to the sea. Ryan thought of it as a buffer zone between the sea and the sunny Hispanic heart of San Francisco, placed there by providence to protect the Mission district from fog and sea: the sea would first have to crumble down all these respectable houses before devouring the old Mission, the taco stands, the downtown bars, the decaying Victorian houses.

Ryan knew that this was a very long term and somewhat racist view of the function of the Sunset District—that all these respectable white people had been put on The Avenues to simply keep the sea from eroding away the Hispanic heart of San Francisco—but long term views were *au currant* then. Everyone had read Velacovsky's theory that change didn't come in long geological millennia, but overnight, with cataclysm, with meteors striking the earth. They all knew, years before it had become a mainline idea, that the ice caps were melting. They anxiously walked the beaches to see if the waters were rising.

Time lapse photography in combination with too much drugs ("drugs" as a singular noun) had allowed people to see things erode away right before their eyes. Things that looked stable were really moving and decomposing, dying and being reborn. The old forest fell and died; new seeds sprouted from its rotting trunks. Anything that wasn't busy being born was busy dying. They had geological eyes.

And then there was the bomb. Sirens in the night had taken on new meaning. Everybody let go of plans and began to trust the impulse of the moment; relationships were for now rather than later; consequences seemed a thing of the past; all the frantic coupling seemed to come from the fact that no one could find a credible version of a future; the erotic chemistry of the moment seemed much more compelling than some plan about a life together; immediacy was put above coherence. Bonds broke down. Molecules flew about. The centre would not hold. There were no real families to turn to. Whatever you needed you'd better grab it fast. Even the carpet was moving under you. Comfort came as it might, in chance—or synchronous—meetings in the dance of life. There must be some way out of here.

When Ryan entered Cybele's house, he was surprised to find Reina there. She was a friend of Sheila's who had come with her to Vasquez on one of her occasional visits. While the children had slept and Sheila had read, Reina and Ryan sat with their backs against the fir boards of the cabin, drinking tea out of small Japanese tea cups. They talked about the Upanishads. Later she sent him a copy.

Since then, he had seen her once when he was visiting Sheila and Lara in Seattle. She had been working at her sewing machine, meticulously stitching rich scraps of salvaged fabric into thick medieval looking drapes to block out the sound of the freeway, the endless river of cars and trucks that flowed beneath her window. Ryan had sat and talked with her while she had sewed.

Like everybody else, her relationship was gone. She traveled with her five year old son Francois in another old red Volvo, a coupe, not a station wagon. For awhile she and Francois had lived in Hawaii with her teacher, a guru of apache descent, and his followers. Most of the time they lived off pineapples and mangos plucked surreptitiously from the edges of unguarded fields.

That had ended for Reina one night when the young women who were the guru's followers decided to surprise him with a fancy meal. At the Laundromat, the girls had found a tattered Ladies Home Journal. In it was a recipe for a sweet potato casserole with a melted marshmallow topping. They meticulously prepared it for him, set the table with a cloth, dressed up, bought wine. When they served it—with great fanfare—he got an unbelieving expression on his face: "What is this shit?" he thundered and threw the whole casserole, pan and all, dripping down the wall. The dressed up girls trembled in terror, thinking that this must be a profound spiritual teaching, something they didn't understand about combining sweet potatoes and marshmallows.

There had been too many scenes like that. Shocked by her teacher's abusiveness, Reina retreated back into her own life. It was very confusing. The first time she had met her guru, he had given her a hug and worlds had opened for her, a vision of endless space and an immensity of peace. Now

273

she wondered how could the same person who transmitted this to her also be so petty and volatile?

Reina was staying alone at the house out on The Avenues. Francois was with his father and his father's new girlfriend, younger than any of the previous ones. Ryan greeted Reina and they sat around Cybele's huge oval table drinking tea with the other people in the house. Cybele had two small children, black and beautiful like their father, a sculptor who had died of cancer. Around the house, his marble cats sat in the eternal meditative poses of cats, as if turned to stone by a magician. They were so realistic that no one would have been surprised had one of them suddenly leapt up and rubbed against their leg. It felt like they would soon come to life.

The talk was ordinary around the table, but they all knew they were looking for a spell that would take away the pall that lay upon the land and make it green again. Reina sat back a little, listening and laughing with the conversation. From time to time she got up to replenish the tea pot or bring more Chinese pastries to the table. The light from the window highlighted her light brown hair that was tied in a pony tail behind her neck. Ryan noticed that the bones of her face, her cheeks, her jaw, were precise and delicate. Her long flowing skirt was in contrast to the jeans that other women were wearing. Occasionally she smiled at Ryan across the table, a hint of gentle laughter in her green eyes at the forebodingness of the talk.

Also at the table was a young French woman—a housemate of Cybele—who was a student at San Francisco State. She was upbeat, cheery, seemingly immune to everyone's portentousness, bringing a particularly French lightness to this otherwise depressed company. The talk around the table was about Canada, about the draft, about the underground railway, about LA falling into the sea in "The Big One."

After awhile, Reina asked Ryan if he would like to see the rest of the house. The grand tour ended up in her attic room at the top of the house. They stood at the flaking paned windows and looked out at the grey swirling world outside. A chorus of foghorns with different tones and frequencies hooted and moaned in the solemnity of the late San Francisco afternoon. They looked at each other and knew their moment had come. He took her in his arms and they walked backward, she standing on his feet, until they fell effortlessly on the lace bedspread that she had salvaged somewhere from the disappearing past. The sky faded around them. Downstairs, far away, they heard the phone ring. It was for Reina and they heard the French girl say "I am sorry, I sink she is in zee bed." Reina whispered to him "we've all been trying to get her to say 'in bed' rather than 'in zee bed.' In her French accent it just sounds too suggestive."

The house on The Avenues was frequented by all sorts—to use Emily Carr's words—a constant stream of dealers, artists, musicians, and students. No-one seemed alone anymore. Gone forever was the type of private apartment that Sheila and Ryan had once shared with each other. It was pretty much like living in a circus. People brought groceries and cooked dinners, served wine, smoked dope, brought guitars, played music, stayed the night. All this was unplanned and uninvited. It just happened. There was a network of homes through which people flowed back and forth.

Melissa, who came to the house often, had four husbands. She and her husbands lived together nearby. She only came with one at a time, but Ryan got to know them all, during his stay. One night at a party that had organically grown out of the swirl of people, everybody was in the living room talking and sipping wine. A fire blazed in the fireplace as a shield against the foggy skies.

Melissa, sat on the floor, leaning back on her straightened arms, her legs wide open to the fire, soaking in its warmth. She wore a see-through silk blouse and green silk harem pants that clung to her body. Not a great beauty by cultural standards, her face was somewhat plain, her body compact and muscular. One of the cats—one of the ones that had not been turned to stone—came up to her and started rubbing against her open legs. Purring, it began kneading her delta through the silk of her pants. She threw her head back and moaned with pleasure. Conversation stopped for just a beat and then went on as though nothing were happening. Ryan wondered about their arrangements at home, what it was like sexually, but he never asked her or any of her husbands. It would have been much too uncool to satisfy this basic curiosity. The mode of the day centered more on acceptance than understanding. It was easy to have an arousing fantasy about her.

How do relationships become relationships? The days grew longer. It became time for Ryan to hitchhike back to his far away farm and turn the soil of his garden. He said goodbye to Reina. Their time together had been long, sequestered and passionate, full of walks in the park and browsing in San Francisco's bookstores. The Haight Ashbury was past its prime, a shabby and touristy remnant of what he remembered from a few years earlier when, as a young academic, he had only dared peek from the corner of his eye into that world of abandon.

He went to Marin for a day to say goodbye to Dave, and the next day he put on his pack, leaving with almost as little as he had come. Dave gave him a ride to 101, the Redwood Highway. After a goodbye hug, Dave drove off in his truck full of tools and lumber. Ryan watched him go and then put his thumb out into the stream of traffic, wondering who fortune would throw him with today. After awhile he simply sat by the side of the road and played a small mandolin that he had been given. When he got tired of that he wrote in his journal. Later he juggled by the side of the road, working on a new trick that he had been learning. The moment was everything, getting there was nothing. The bigger new trick was to enjoy the day, the sun's position in the sky, the quality of light, the *fin de siècle* streaming of the endless traffic on the highway.

There were enough of his kind so that he knew he would eventually get a ride. Hitching was really a school to him, a shuffling of the deck to let synchronicity connect him with whomever he needed to hear from: princes in rags drove old cars along the roads and picked up hitchhiker-philosophers. They shared experiences and told each other the cosmic news as they rattled along. The day edged onward as the sun travelled on its arc. Ryan got rides from kindly bewildered parents who helped him because they had children wandering the country; from a cowgirl drinking beer to assuage the pain of her broken marriage; from a man in a Star Trek uniform with Elizabethan puffs on its shoulders who told him about Reich and Orgone. They stopped at his house for lunch, and before travelling on, toked up and sat facing each other in the time traveller's orgone box. After awhile, in the dark chamber, Ryan could see the other man's outline—Elizabethan puffs and all—as a dim green field of energy.

Ryan traveled along the winding Eel River through giant redwoods into storms from the north. He stood in the rain in Garberville for awhile, looking up at the bare hills that rose above the mist spattered redwoods. Now he did have his thumb out. He posited a hitchhiking law: *The Longer the Wait, The Better the Ride.* When he finally did get picked up, soaking wet, it was by a van full of Vietnam vets who had been discharged because of their wounds and had joined the anti-war movement. They were all missing parts of themselves. The van was filled with a formidable collection of wheelchairs, crutches and prosthetics.They turned the heater up high so that Ryan could warm up and dry out. Listening to the Moody Blues and toking up, they wound through the redwood forests toward Eureka and Arcata. The longer the wait, the better the ride.

Pulling into Eureka, they stopped to see the opening of an anti-war show that some friends had put up. They trundled out their wheelchairs and aluminum crutches, strapped on legs, and limped and wheeled their way to the gallery. Inside, wearing their military jackets, headbands, long hair, and coloured beads, they wheeled around, looking at photos of small naked children running in terror as bombs exploded behind them; at a huge American flag where the red stripes turned into blood and ran down the wall, where helicopters flew among the fifty stars, where tanks and foot soldiers ran in procession along the white stripes. There were photos of peace marches in the cities of America; there was Marijuana art and Make Love Not War art. In one painting, a couple passionately embraced on an American flag. The man held himself up above the woman. He wore only an open army shirt and had glass beads and dog tags dangling from his neck.

Wine was abundant and they were all a bit tipsy when they headed back to the van, a bit inspired by the sensual, sexual, non-violent uprising of which they felt themselves to be a part. They cranked up the stereo and wound through the rain around the great shallow windswept bay to Arcata. There, they left Ryan in front of a hotel, telling him that it was a way station, a cheap place where good people stayed. He stood with his pack and watched the van disappear into Arcata's rainy streets, its rock and roll fading, its tail lights making red streaks, like the stripes of the American flag, on the wet pavement.

After it was gone, he walked a few steps through the rain to the grand entrance of the old hotel. It had seen better times but was still respectable; had not yet fallen into the hands of drunks and junkies. He walked across the polished stone floor to the counter where a small hunched woman with grey hair tied at her neck rented him a room. She welcomed him as though into her own home, giving him the key, and taking his seventeen dollars. His room was on the third floor, up a carpeted grand stairway from another time. As he walked to his room, he noticed that many of the doors were left open. The hotel felt like a large house. People looked up as he passed and gave him a nod of greeting. His room was clean and well made up. Its high ceilings and deeply recessed bay window gave it a palatial feeling. The steam radiator poured out heat. Outside the bay window, Northern California rain fell in sheets. Ryan showered and changed into a cotton kimono he had picked up in SF's Japan town. He draped his wet clothes over the radiator and sat on the bed, luxuriating in the dry warmth of the room.

After awhile Ryan opened his door. Sitting clean and dry on one of the room's two chairs, he softly played his mandolin. After awhile a woman came by, holding her little daughter by the hand. She was tall with soft pale skin and dark eyes. There was an aura of sadness about her.

She said hello and stood in the doorway listening for awhile with her daughter twirling at the end of her arm. Ryan stopped playing and they talked. In his kimono with his hair tied up, he looked like a samurai resting between battles. They talked about the roads they had travelled, the cities they had known, the places they had lived. She said that she and her daughter lived in the hotel. Estrella was her name; her daughter was Star. "Our names both means star," said Star before twirling shyly out of sight behind her mother.

Ryan was hungry but did not want to put on his wet clothes to go into the rain. Estrella told him that the hotel restaurant, having made concessions to its hippy clientele, had some vegetarian dishes including some good imitations of Mexican food. They ordered dinner to be sent up to his room. Estrella went and got a cloth from her room and spread it on the bed. They pulled up the room's two chairs and used the bed as a dining table. Star sat on Estrella's lap. The food came on plates with metal covers over them: great oozy vegetarian enchiladas bubbling with cheese and red chilli sauce, red mounds of rice sopa, tortilla's, refried beans on the side, perfect food for such a cold and rainy night. There were even a couple bottles of Sol.

The equation of dairy with evil hadn't been made yet. Most vegetarians still ate eggs, cheese, yoghurt, and milk. They knew that technically they were lacto-ovo-vegetarians. Everybody seemed up on these things.

After room service cleared away the dishes, Star, blond, lovely and very tired, fell asleep on the bed. Estrella went to get her sewing. Returning with it, she sat in one of the chairs and stitched while Ryan sat and practiced his mandolin in the other chair. From time to time they talked.

How do relationships become relationships? While Estrella and he sat and whiled away the evening, Ryan thought of Reina and the time they had spent together in San Francisco. He could feel the place in Estrella that wanted a father for her child. So many women were travelling alone with their children, looking for a man with whom to make a family. So many men were off on some quest or other, exploring psychedelic shamanism, hitching the roads, making protest in the cities. It was as though everybody had been drafted, whether or not they were in the army.

The rain continued to fall outside; great luminous clouds passed slowly over head as the sky clock ticked westward; the moon cast its occluded light on the world. The restless cars pulled over and stopped moving; their drivers climbed out and went into their homes. House lights winked out leaving only doorbell lights glowing like pilot lights in the darkened streets. A spell of silence fell on the city.

Estrella finished her project, a skirt for Star. She held it up to look at and then packed it in her sewing bag. She picked up Star, speaking softly to her and quietly left. Ryan opened the door for her and watched her carry Star along the hotel's dimly lighted hallway, passing door after door, now all closed, winding through the labyrinth of her time, trying to see and understand. As she disappeared around the corner, he closed his door with a tiny click. He turned out the light and climbed into bed, listening to the rain fall outside. As he drifted off to sleep, he thought of Reina and savoured the connection they had forged in San Francisco, wondering if it was mutual or whether she had already forgotten him in the swirl of life. It was a time of no guarantees.

36
Endstorm

The millennium has turned. The last day of the nineties ended with a moody sunset over the Strait of Juan de Fuca. The sun sank through bands of clouds with great shafts of light falling onto the sea. A lone photographer stood on Beacon Hill in Victoria and recorded this with a single snap of her shutter. She then climbed on her rusty bicycle and rode home in the darkening light. None of the bad things happened that were predicted to happen. Life simply went on, business as usual. Ryan had scoffed at the Y2K doom seers. He had simply lived through too many alignments of the planets, too many California-falling-into-the-sea earthquake scenarios, to still believe any of that.

Back in the old days, he had been on top of the mountain on Vasquez when the Amchitka nuclear blast went off. A group of his friends and he had climbed the mountain, guitars and flutes in hand, to watch for the tidal wave that was supposed to cleanse the west coast of the parasitic civilisation that was sucking and chewing on it—might as well have a front row seat. The tidal wave never came but a good time was had by all on the mountain top. The Ghost Dance again.

Now it is summer, July, and the weather has finally turned hot. It is a fine day, and Ryan is driving up the island highway in a red Jetta that is only eight years old—his newest and best car since the days of the Red Ant. He had discovered that downward mobility was easy, but that it was harder to go the other way. He is dressed in shorts and a T-shirt. The sunroof is open and he is enjoying the warmth of sunlight on his bare legs. He is clean shaven. His white hair—what's left of it—is short and balding at the back. The CBC is on, whispering like a serpent in the garden of his driving. He hasn't been to Vasquez for almost thirty years; hasn't wanted to face the memories of his failures there; hasn't wanted to see the old friends who know too much about him. Now there is a retreat—one of his colleagues has a summer home there—and for the first time he feels he can go.

Just before Nanaimo the highway changes into a huge California type affair. It soars through nondescript evergreens and is marked by enormous overpasses with illuminated overhead exit signs. Somewhere down below are the little towns through which he used to drive, places of congested traffic, ice cream, pubs, hardware stores and fishing shops. Nanaimo is only an exit, marked by stylised ship's masts that rise beside the overpass. A sign proclaims it as The Harbour City. Who needs a computer to experience virtual reality?

It is only after Ryan has driven ten more miles, that he realises that he has missed Nanaimo completely, its nucleus of winding streets and stone buildings—B.C.'s answer to Guanajuato—its cytoplasm consisting of miles of car lots and logging equipment depots. Where has it gone? He comes out of his driving trance with a start. "Where am I? Have I fallen asleep and awakened on the other side of it?" He feels like Rip Van Winkle driving through a land that has profoundly changed during an afternoon's inattention. He looks around. Yea, the mountains of Vancouver Island have become stacked with tract homes where before there was nothing but second growth forest and logging roads.

He has trouble figuring out which exit to take to get to the familiar boat basin where he plans to catch the ferry to Vasquez. One thing remains the same: racing for the ferry. He realises that he needs to choose exits wisely: there is no time to miss an exit and drive twelve miles to the next one and then back again. He's not sure to what the exit signs refer, but manages to take one that drops him down to the little town where he used to shop when he lived on Vasquez. The town itself has changed completely. In the elapsed thirty years only a few of the old buildings—which were new in his time—remain. The rest of the town is filled with malls and fast food concessions, a perfect example of the Californication of B.C. Well, he was one of the ones that brought that here.

Everything is so different that he is anxious that he has missed the boat basin or that the route to it has been changed. Finally he sees it, the old green sign that says Vasquez Ferry, a small Department of Highways sign that hasn't changed—it's just that everything around it has. As he

281

turns right, it feels like he is back in his own time again. He is relieved that things still look more or less as he remembers them: the clutter of boats and masts, the parking lot full of rusted trucks and opulent cars. Some of the rusted trucks look like they have been here since his time. What is more eternal than a rusted truck?

The parking lot, though, has been re-organised: it has been paved and the parking places marked with different coloured lines to indicate different types of parking. There is boat parking, resident permit parking, and transient parking. He realises that he must fall into the transient category and finds a white slot at the back of the lot. He gets out and grabs his pack from the trunk—he left with only a sleeping bag, a pillow, a swim suit and a change of clothes. A woman walks by and he asks her if he needs to buy a ticket. She says yes and tells him to buy it over at the warfinger's office. She points. He looks at his watch. Ten minutes to go. He leaves the trunk open and runs at full tilt to the warfinger's office to buy the ticket. He runs back, slaps it on the dash, grabs the pack, locks the car and runs for the ferry.

The gangplank down to the floating wharf is now a slip-proof metal grate instead of the old wooden one that had wooden cross pieces nailed to one side and long smooth planks on the other. The smooth side was used to slide heavy boxes down to a catcher at the bottom. The ferry is the fourth generation replacement of the rusted logging crummy, each one growing longer to accommodate more people and freight. As yet there is no car ferry. As in the days of old, scruffy people laze around talking to each other while others carry heavy objects onto the deck of the ferry — today's feature is a table saw.

Near the time of departure everybody shuffles on board. The ferry is packed today, most of the people choosing to sit outside on the aluminum luggage racks rather than on the plastic seats in the stuffy cabin. The racks themselves are heaped with every type of pack, box, and package: there are groceries, hardware, laundry bags, classy shopping bags from The Bay; the latest fad seems to be large plastic totes with locking lids.

Right away, he recognises Florence, the woman who came to Vasquez with Dave when he had left Marin County. After Dave had broken up with her, Florence had lived for awhile as a joyous single woman, earning money by using her dental hygienist skills to clean the teeth of fellow islanders. Ryan remembers lying on his back in a field full of small daisies outside her house, resting his head in her lap while she used sharp steel instruments to scrape away the plaque on his teeth. She had a large crystal goblet of home-made blackberry wine from which she asked him to swish and swallow from time to time. She laughed and told him stories as she cleaned his teeth on that summer day. Such was been the state of dentistry on Vasquez in the old days.

Now she is talking animatedly to another older woman. Ryan looks out at them from inside his own old body, and realises that they have come to look like the old homesteader women, the "old timers" who were already on the island when he had first come as a young man. Their bodies are marked by hard work. They are a bit heavy-set, a bit wrinkled, a bit grey, going through what he thinks must be the difficult passage of losing their youth: becoming rounder and heavier as their estrogenic fertility fades away. He has seen his own wife struggle against it, rub "natural" hormones into her skin at night, work out harder and more often to keep the weight off, deny herself even the small delicacies that until now she had allowed.

With an electric start, he realises that the other woman is Ariel, as animated as ever, her face going from concern, to gaiety, to excitement, to disgust several times a minute, just like the alternating clouds and sunlight passing over the Strait. He decides that he will find a time to talk to her on this voyage. How can two people share such intensity and then just become old people who greet each other sedately across time?

Mid-channel, lulled by the rocking, he catches her eye and she comes over with animation and pleasure. They sit next to each other on the baggage shelves, feet propped out in the aisle against the roll of the boat. As in so many meetings across time, they do not talk too much about themselves at first. He finds out that she works in Vancouver teaching music to schoolchildren, going from classroom to classroom with her box of rhythm sticks, bells, triangles, and little cymbals—coaxing voice and rhythm from her young charges and then moving on. She also works with words—apparently a long journal. Are they both trying to make some sense of the lives they have led, he wonders. After awhile they reveal a bit more about themselves; what their children are doing; what their ex-partners are doing. It turns out that Wiley was killed in a logging accident and one of her daughters was lost at sea while sailing back from Hawaii with her boy friend. Their boat never arrived, disappeared without a trace. They talk a bit about the pain of that. They talk a bit about other things in the past but do not go right to the heart of it: what was there between them in that time so long ago? Ryan still wonders. Was it all one sided, all his projection, or was there some faint echo returned by the married woman who he loved back then? It becomes all too serious and they climb back out of the graveyard of the past, relieved to stop chewing on the bones of the dead. Ryan can see that she is glad to get back to Florence and talk about what is real and what is now.

As the ferry pulls alongside the long slope of the island, before it makes its turn into False Bay, Ryan sees that there are a few expensive summer homes built along the little bays and points of what used to be a wild coastline. Two kayaks paddle tranquilly along this stretch of coast. As he watches, he talks with a colleague who is also coming to the retreat. They talk about the formation of a new professional association and about an acquaintance who's application was denied for providing false information, but another part of his mind is living in its memories. He remembers fighting tooth and nail against the subdivision of which these houses are now a part; how the realtors came on a huge sail boat called the Dragoon and tied up to the dock in False Bay, opening a floating real estate office. The whole community worked together to fight the parcelling up of this land; to fight the suburbanisation of their wild island; to stop the wave of conventional people that would follow as soon as there were tiny lots to buy. Their efforts were like castles made of sand: washed away by the advancing tide. They fought and lost.

Ironically, Ryan wishes that he had had the foresight to buy one of these lots: now he would like to have one of the tranquil summer homes that he sees basking in the mild July sunlight, inhaling the scent of low tide and lit by the reflections that flash off the water. He would like to be responsible for a small lot with a few of the best trees carefully preserved, with no fields to keep free from alders, no chickens or goats to feed twice daily, nothing to keep him tied down. No fence posts to replace as one by one they rotted away.

On the dock he meets Thomas and Dorrie, people from his time, older, wrinkled but essentially the same. They recognise each other instantly, across thirty years, and greet each other as if time has not intervened, as if Thomas is still the elegant young man in ragged British woollens who looked like he had just stepped out of Sherwood Forest. Dorrie, stands beside him. Laughing with people, she radiates warmth. She is no longer the sylph of earlier times. She's weathered child birth several times, cried tears for those around her, and nourished her little community in the woods. The girl is gone and the older woman, not quite crone, has emerged. With a twinkle in his eye, Thomas refers to himself as a land developer. He is still slim and elfin. His hair, no longer red, still flows down his back in a grey pony tail. He still has his loving, easy smile, with new laugh crinkles around his eyes. As Ryan talks with them, he realises that he and they have all gained more wisdom, yet are also still the same. He wonders what the stubborn essence is that keeps a person who they are, the laugh, the voice, the basic temperament that is there for a lifetime, like it or not.

In his twenties Thomas had come out from England to claim the bit of earth that his father had left him, his father who had died in a boating accident—the same dangerous speed boat that Rosa and Karl had come on. The land that his father left him turned out to be several quarter sections of undeveloped forest and coastline, worth millions. Instead of cashing it in and living a life of ease, he had decided to live on it. For many years they had no real roof on their house. Their living room, their bedrooms, and their kitchen were all covered by a huge translucent white tarp stretched over a wooden framework. It had the advantage of letting its white diffused light into every nook and cranny of the house. It was like having your roof be a window, or like having an open grey sky over your head

Thomas formed a land co-op so other islanders could build houses and gardens in return for paying a share of the taxes. Deep in the woods, he started a button factory. Powered by a polished Datsun engine neatly mounted on two concrete pillars, it was a place where the co-op members could earn the money they needed to live.

Ryan thinks that Thomas's life embodies the ideals of the arts and crafts movement: each person surrounded by things of beauty and having a livelihood that is dignified and contributes to the good of all. Land rich and cash poor, what money Thomas and Dorrie have came from gathering ancient juniper twigs out on windswept islands and polishing them into agate grained buttons in the depth of the woods. Once a year they put on their best clothes and went off to the button shows in Los Angeles or New York where they schmoozed to find buyers for their product. Ryan imagines that, smelling of juniper and wood smoke, they bring a sweet naïveté to the glitzy world of gift shows.

The next morning, while his colleagues go to the café to drink coffee and share life stories, Ryan walks up the hill to visit Emile, the stepson that he helped to raise in the days after the commune. Emile is now thirty and building an amazing house.

The road to Emile's runs steeply uphill and is cut through the salal; in many ways is more of a path than a road. Barely wide enough to get a truck up, it preserves much of the forest floor rather than being lined with crushed rock. Ryan notices that the road is marked with oyster shells placed every twenty feet or so, pearly side up, in the moss at he side of the road or at the base of a tree or stump: it's an old squatter's trick, to mark the trails with oyster shells so that you can see them glowing white when you are staggering home full of homebrew on a dark night. Ryan mentions the shells to Emile who says, "Yeah, Susanna and I aren't so big on flashlights."

Emile's house is meticulously framed with lumber that he has milled himself. He has traded work—milling, carpentry, wiring, growing a small crop of marijuana, to gain the money needed to build his unfinished mansion. Atop the house, rising two full stories higher than the rest of it, is a half finished Florentine tower. Emile's Italian genes seem to have taken control of the house design. Ryan and Emile climb the flexing aluminum ladder to stand on the still swaying platform at the top. On the way up, Emile explains that the diagonal sheathing will add rigidity.

The top of the tower catches just a glimpse of Georgia Strait and Mount Arrowsmith. Ryan and Emile stand together above the treetops, looking out over the island. Ryan notices a cell phone, folded like a clam, on one of the fir sills. Emile explains that the tower is the only place that he can get reception in the island's crazy quilt of rock bluffs and cedar swamps. While climbing back down to the unfinished kitchen-living room, they laugh about it being his communication tower. In the main part of the house, the windows are still sheeted with plastic. Everything is on crude temporary shelves or counters of green fir. Paintings and tools hang on the exposed studs of the wall. Except for the fine framing and precise joints— a big except—the room, in its unfinished utilitarianism, looks a little like an old hippy shack. The difference is that it will grow up to become a house.

They eat bread that Emile has made from organic flour milled with a high tech mill that he has bought for $200 from a couple in Washington State who had a Mercedes in their driveway. Emile tells Ryan that the mill usually costs $450. They make toast in an antique toaster, of the type where the coils glow red and you have to open the side doors to flip the piece of bread. It's powered by a bank of batteries under the house. A pelton wheel, somewhere far away, is charging the batteries. The blades of the pelton wheel are made from soldered silver spoons. Deep in their casing, the antique spoons turn and turn, making electricity for the house. Ryan and Emile dip their toast in a bowl of extra virgin olive oil with a bit of balsamic vinegar in the bottom—the Italian genes again. The bread is delicious and sweet in a way that store-bought bread is not.

Emile remembers his childhood on Vasquez as a golden age. He questions his use of electricity; he fights the changes on the island; he is furious about the paving of the first 100 yards of the road that comes up from the dock, the same road where people's tires used to spit gravel on everyone as their trucks lurched up the hill. From the sea, the island now looks more or less like every other gulf island, its ribbon of paved road disappearing from the ferry slip into the forest. When Ryan had walked from the ferry, he noticed the place where the pavement abruptly ended and the old gravel road began. He thought it should be marked by a small sign: "Civilisation Ends Here."

The coast of Vasquez seems to be going the way of the other islands: expensive summer homes for the upper crust. The interior, though, is still dedicated to the old ways: homesteads and unusual handmade houses. Emile's house is built on the land co-op that Thomas created. Several other second generation island children also live on the land co-op. There is an enclave of them. Another of Emile's old friends, Reilly, has managed to buy back the homestead that his parents sold when they moved to the city. The money came from pot gardens hidden in tangled, inaccessible corners of the land. The Vancouver Sun has proclaimed Marijuana the biggest industry in B.C., out stripping timber, mining, and agriculture—seven billion dollars annually.

In the afternoon Emile and Ryan walk down to the small art gallery that has been built on the banks of Mud Bay, next to the post office. On the way they stop at a house that is being built by Theresa, another second generation Vasquezian, born from Ryan's generation of homesteaders. One of her paintings hangs within the framework of her partially finished home. It is a self portrait in which she shows several aspects of herself. In it she is standing with her spirit hovering over her. Her animus is to her left; her inner child sitting on the ground in front of her.

Samuel, another child of the island, also lives in this cluster of houses. Their houses are all slightly out of sight of each other, a conclave of school friends who are now moving into homeownership. Ryan remembers Emile and the other children building elaborate villages along the banks of the road ditch; building tiny houses of twigs, complete with roofs and porches; building piers on which to tie their tiny twig boats. He didn't realise that they were building a model, loosely based on what they saw around them, of the world that they would create when they grew up.

At the Gallery there is an opening of an island arts and crafts show. Local musicians play jazz on the grassy lawn outside the Gallery. Home-made wines in funky bottles with tattered original labels still stuck to them are being served in plastic cups for a dollar a glass. While the adults talk and listen to music, children splash in the warm waters of the bay. The tide is in and the water has been warmed by having inched along the mud flats.

Ryan thinks that the art is incredible: beautiful paintings, baskets woven from local cedar bark, carved wooden bowls. After touring the gallery, he sits outside on the grass and listens to the music. It is a good day on which to have come. He talks with many of the people who he knew so long ago. They are all old and wrinkled like himself but still seem to be celebrating the lives they have been given. Everything, Ryan knows, has come harder here. They have not only made the art, but have had to build the gallery. They have also probably had to cut down the trees and mill the lumber. Without exception they give Ryan a hug, across thirty years of time; welcoming him like a prodigal son returned home. It is as though he never really left at all; as though his experience here has made him a part of this tribe forever. A beautiful old women—who he recognises as Sammie—comes up and hugs him. She is wearing sparkles on her face and has tied her grey-black hair in bright silk plaits.

The next day, when he and his colleagues leave, the ferry is not running. It seems that its two employees have joined a union and are now striking for higher pay. The local fish boats have capitalised on the situation by offering to take people on and off the island, for an exorbitant $12.50 each way.

Ryan and his urban colleagues climb aboard a fish boat named Silver, a green tub with a skull and cross bones engraved in rust on its flying bridge. A large German shepherd stands on its hind legs looking out of the upper part of the wheelhouse's Dutch door. It gives the impression that the boat is from a children's book—that the skipper is a dog, that the deckhand a sheep, and so on. In reality, the skipper wears a black beret and looks a lot like Bug Rogers, the beatnik spider from the Gordo comic strips of Ryan's childhood. Several large marijuana plants are growing in full sight, in plastic buckets, on the flying bridge.

The skipper already has a full load of returning city folks and decides to leave early. Why wait until the appointed departure time if you are already full? He unties the boat and leaps aboard. He climbs into the wheelhouse, pushes the dog aside, revs the engine and shoves the boat into reverse. He guns the engine and they make a long backward arc out into the bay, turning so that they are facing out to sea. Just as he shoves the Silver into forward, Sherry—McElwaith's ex wife—comes racing down the dock in her truck. She jumps out of the cab waving a package and shouting, really pissed off. Her long kinky golden hair is flowing like Rapunzel's down over her shoulders as she screams at the skipper.

"You've left early. Sarah is waiting for this package on the other side. Now she's not going to get it."

The skipper is not about to be deterred, not about to return to the dock to pick it up. It is not about courtesy or service but simply about who has the right to tell whom what to do. The skipper says nothing but sets his jaw and determinedly shoves the throttle full speed ahead. The boat goes snorting out of the bay, leaving Sherry screaming invectives on the dock.

Out on the water, the day is flat calm. Ryan stands on the deck talking with his colleagues about the island. He chuckles to himself about how little things have really changed; about how, through it all, the island has managed to preserve its primitiveness. There is still no car ferry and no Hydro. Perhaps, he thinks, there is some sort of geomagnetic field that causes machinery, families and real estate schemes to breakdown and fall into chaos and acrimony. He does not know.

37
The Commune

Back in the old days, in the spring when Ryan had returned from hitching to California, he asked after Ariel, Wylie, Julie, and Elroy. What had become of them?

People said that they had not gone with the commune: Except for Elroy, they had all moved to towns up and down Vancouver Island; had applied for welfare and started looking for work. They were trying to rebuild their lives.

The commune barge had sailed north to a huge piece of land that Bob had bought on an island half way between the north tip of Vancouver Island and the south end of Haida Gwaii. There was 400 inches of rain up there instead of the 45 or so that fell on Vasquez; there were great soggy forests full of salal, and swamps full of reeds, lily pads, and skunk cabbage; there were mosquitoes and black flies. The commune, now reduced to about forty members began to rebuild its empire. First they cut poles to build a corduroy road across the swampy terrain. Then they bought a cat and built plastic shacks in the dark forest to utilize the shelter of the trees.

It was different living in a cold climate full of relentless rain. One by one the commune's members left to try their luck in civilisation again. Soon there were not enough left to build a new life. In the end, Bob took the remaining members back to Vancouver Island. He left them standing with their bundles on the dock at Alert Bay, refugees from spiritual experimentation. The great tract of land was sold and Bob left with his inner circle, the same people with whom he had come, the same people with whom he had lived in the great stone house. For many years no one knew where they had gone. They had just packed up and disappeared.

Several months after his return Ryan saw Elroy again. He was on his way back to The States, and had come to Vasquez to get his guitar and the few belongings that he had stored at Isaac and Miriam's house. On his last night, on his way to the ferry, he stayed at Ryan's. Broken in spirit, he told Ryan that he didn't know how he could find a new life that had any meaning. Ryan tried to comfort him, saying things like, "Well, spirit belongs to everybody, it's not like something that people can give us or take away from us," and, "If that's your path, you will find it again." Elroy was not cheered. Looking at the floor and speaking in his soft Texas drawl, he said, "You don't understand, Bob was different. Bob was like god."

Years later Ryan heard that Bob had gotten out of the commune business entirely. He and his small original group had moved to the South Seas were they lived a life of decadent ease. Ryan thought about the Berlin Wall, the Soviet Union, about all the great tyrannies that have such a short life span. He thought about Shelley's Ozymandias, a great broken monolith out in the desert: tumbled arms and legs of stone, a cruel commanding face buried like a football in the sand. The pedestal on which this heap of rubble had once stood was engraved with words nearly erased by wind and sand: "My name is Ozymandias, king of kings: Look on my works, ye mighty, and despair!"

Isaac moved to the South Seas as well. A few years after the disintegration of the commune, he too stopped by Ryan's house on his way to the ferry. Carrying only the pack he had come with, he said he was leaving on a pilgrimage to find a place where the climate was better, the living easier and the women more submissive. Years later Miriam told Ryan that she had received a postcard from an island in Indonesia that wasn't on any map. In the postcard Isaac told her that an old friend in New York had connected him with a seashell wholesaler, who paid good money for him to collect shells and ship them back to New York.

Ryan chuckled to himself: he could see Isaac walking down the beach, wrapped in his Sarong, skin the colour of bronze; he could see him, stooping to pick up a brightly coloured shell, and then put it in the woven bag he wore across his shoulder. Or, maybe on other days, he went out in a great canoe with the men to bring back fish. Ryan imagined him living in a small thatched house with a devoted local wife who cooked exquisite meals for him from the fish he brought home. She cooked for this Big American because he himself was such a catch. It was not just the envelopes of cash that came in the mail every few months, but also his broadmindedness and his kindness to her, far greater than that of the local men. She waited on him hand and foot. Well, who wouldn't?

Ryan saw him carving the door posts and lintel of his house; painting magic symbols on the sides of canoes. He saw him fathering a belated child or two with his young bride, and pointing up at the sky when a great plane passed overhead, telling them what it had been like to ride in one. At night he sat in the lodge and joked with the elders, speaking a version of their language that was totally gibbled by his strong Bronx accent. They laughed and were delighted at the way he talked. He sipped from the gourd of Kava that they passed around. He spat out beetle nut juice and laughed with them through his broken purple teeth.

38
The Commune

The painting is twelve by seven inches, a little lopsided because of the home-made stretcher bars. It is crudely framed with salvaged cedar. The wood of the frame—sun darkened from years of having lain in a field with sheep passing over and around it—marks it as having come from Vasquez.

It is a strange picture, painted Van Gogh style in fat oils. A bright orange August sun with concentric yellow lines radiating out from it beats down on a dry grass landscape. Ryan remembers the heat of that day and the sound of crickets. As an old man, he can't hear crickets anymore—too much chain sawing back on Vasquez has taken away the high range of his hearing. The summer tinkling of crickets: a small but immeasurable gift from god—forever lost. What is left is to remember crickets, to write about them and all the other lost things, like the passionate and confused sexuality of his youth. Sometimes he thinks that in working so hard to tame sexuality, we lose it: that the very confusion we seek to eliminate— that bowing down to a god that is beyond our control—is part and parcel of sexuality itself. He keeps the painting in his bedroom, away from the public parts of the house.

In the painting there are also some rickety fences, sun blackened, like the wood of the frame. A grid of sagging page-wire hangs between the fence posts. Some small fruit trees—maybe prune plums—look dry like bones in the August sun. There is a gate. Beyond it are the tree tops of silent firs, thrusting up into a yellow sky. It is late afternoon, and their deep blue shadows are beginning to lengthen, to bring coolness to all this blazing sunlight.

Leaning up against the gate is a huge carrot wearing a Stetson. On the cross-piece of the gate, above the carrot's head, above the shadowed underside of the crosspiece, sits a wiry black cat. At the bottom of the painting, painted in large scrawling letters it says, Ryan as a Carrot on the Farm Last Summer."

The painting is one of Isaac's. It looks like a fantasy of midday at the cross roads, the cat sitting in the sun above the hat, but it is just what Isaac saw when Ryan visited one day. Ryan remembers leaning against the gate in his old Stetson, the one that he had painted a face on. He remembers the cat sitting above him. He doesn't remember being a carrot. Perhaps it was the drugs they had taken, the drugs that Isaac's friend from New York had brought. Perhaps Isaac had just seen that Ryan was slowly becoming a vegetable.

Isaac often did small studies: A mushroom on the window sill—the shadows under its gills, the purples fading to black—contained the whole story of the evening being born, and of every evening that ever was, and of mushrooms and fields and old houses. Infinity in the palm of your hand. His talent far surpassed the time he actually spent painting, far surpassed his belief in himself.

Isaac's paintings often had a certain prophetic edge to them. Once, even before Miriam's stint in the commune, he had been working with the Minotaur theme: a large, for him, canvas that he had been painting on for days in the few good minutes when he was not cutting wire worms out of carrots, or drying the fruit that ripened around him, or serving delicacies to Miriam, or brewing antique crocks full of fruit wine. Yes, it was autumn.

In the painting, the dead bull lies on its back on the altar. The priest holds a curved knife aloft, ready to make the first cut. Around him are the participants in the ritual, classical Mediterranean men and women, wearing togas and flowing robes. They are sexy in their almost undress, their eyes play toward each other across the dead bull's body. A woman with a red mouth drinks wine from a golden chalice. Everybody seems to be pleasurably anticipating the cut that the priest is about to make. Is he cutting out the bull's heart? Is he cutting off its huge balls that loll like cantaloupes behind its upturned legs?

While Isaac painted in the house, the commune truck, like an evil green wasp that buzzed around paradise, pulled up in his dusty driveway. Isaac was too engrossed in his painting to even notice. He was too surrounded by the cool interior of the summer farm house with all its windows open, too immersed in the deep inner world of imagination, in watching it magically emerge onto the canvas, to take any action or go out and greet people. He was almost paralysed; had surrendered to the inner world of inaction and imagery: his gift was that when he was in this inner world, he could still move his fingers and eyes to make representation of what he saw there.

It was Miriam who went out to see what they wanted. They had been driving around looking for their herd of cattle. The cows, ranging freely, had wandered through the broken down fences into Isaac and Miriam's field where they were vacuuming up the sparse dry grass. Now that the commune members had found their cattle, they wanted to use the farm to slaughter one for food. They wanted to use the picnic table to butcher it on. They would bury the guts and wash the table afterwards. They would leave Isaac and Miriam some meat.

Miriam came in from the late afternoon sun. Why do these deeds so often happen as the day edges toward night, as the sea of darkness sweeps through the trees and the alternate world of stars and night birds begins to replace the world of the sun? She was flustered and spoke to Isaac in the dark living room, her harsh New York accent spreading out into the Canadian countryside. "Isaac, it's Tim and Wilf. They want to kill one of their cows here and butcher it. They will leave us some meat. Is that OK?"

Isaac was too far gone into his painting, into the ancient world of the Minotaur, to give much of an answer. The world of the painting seemed more real to him than Miriam. It was her distant voice that was flat and two dimensional. In his periphery he saw her form and heard her voice coming toward him. She sounded anxious and in need of his help. She never knew what to do in situations like this. He knew he must answer, come out for a moment, if he was not to be completely pulled away from the ancient world he was painting. So he managed just a nod, a small nod, and she, used to his ways, left and went back outdoors.

Later there was a shot. Its sound entered into the mythological world of the canvas through which Isaac's brush moved. Isaac was also vaguely aware of voices entering from far away. They were the modern authoritative voices of men organising something, giving instructions.

Later, the blue he painted shadows with ran out. He came back into the ground floor of the house and squeezed the tube, but no more paint came out. He set crumpled tube next to the sheet of old window glass that he used as a palette. As he stretched he realized that that was it for the day; he would need someone to pick up a tube of blue for him from the other side. After appraising his painting and the progress he had made, he went over to the mantle and shook out his jar of coins, putting enough money in his pocket for a tube of paint. Taking his brushes, some rags, a jar of turpentine out into the porch, he painted out his brushes on the porous boards of the front steps and the hot afternoon became infused with the smell of turpentine. As he finished each brush, he laid it on the top step of the porch. A neat row of clean brushes.

He walked back around the house and pulled up a bucket from the deep well, removing a homebrew from the ones that he had managed to save, and then lowering the bucket back down. He opened the long necked beer bottle with his mountain-man belt knife and took a deep cool swig before walking across the hot field to the knot of people in the shade of the apple trees where they had killed the bull.

They had shot him in the shade where he had been grazing, and had brought Isaac's sturdy picnic table—the one he had built from old fence posts and salvaged planks—over to where the bull lay dead. They had brought enough people to lift the bull onto the table so that they could butcher him. Now the group stood around the table and watched. Wilf had already made the long incision from the animal's throat down to and carefully around its penis, scrotum and anus. The huge balls of the dead animal lolled out behind it on the weathered boards of the table. Someone made a joke that Isaac couldn't hear and a little laugh went up. Miriam was at the edge of the circle, watching. She also laughed, and then took a sip from her canning jar full of apple cider.

For Isaac it was a moment of supreme disorientation. He was back in the painting again or the painting had landed on his farm. He looked around the circle and saw the very people he had painted, that he had imagined. They were in jeans and T-shirts instead of the garb of classical Greeks, except for Miriam who was wearing a light flowered blouse, but their faces, the likenesses, were the same. Their positions around the table were exactly the same. Miriam was even wearing red lipstick.

During the trial, the painting had to be hidden. The likeness to commune members would have made it compelling evidence, even though

Sammie and Alexis—the painting's owners—knew that it had been painted before the deed that it depicted, but no one would have believed that story, so they took it off the wall and slid it down behind the couch for the course of the trial.

39
Ryan and Sheila

He had heard about her long before met her. His friends, a small group of aliens like himself, talked about her; quoted wise things that she had said. Her name came up—Sheila—a rebel, an intellectual, a bright light, with cream coloured skin tending to freckles and silky long black hair. They met when they were entering high school, and for a long time remained just friends, amiable wandering intellects who enjoyed each other's company. They were each with other partners who didn't share their bent for bitter alienation, partners who had the temerity just to try to enjoy life in an easy sort of way.

Later, when they were at San Francisco State , after having broken up with their partners and living alone in pain, they reconnected. It was a time of revolution and change. They walked together through the foggy streets and talked about the bitter lessons they had learned in relationship, their pain and loneliness pulling them together. There was not much sexual energy between them, but one night they decided to sleep together anyway. She wore a long, tent-like, vertically striped, red and white night gown and turned off the light before getting into bed. That was how they started. They became a couple.

They were of like mind, connected through art and philosophy, but lacking an easy affinity of body. Slowly, over many months, frustration and anger become their lot. They thought it was where they lived and moved every six months, hoping that if they found the right spot their lives would fall into place: the geographical cure. Thus began a nomadic odyssey that left them perennially rootless and more unsettled than ever. San Francisco; Oakland; Marfil; Acopilco; Marin County; Argenta; Bellingham; Vancouver; Victoria; North Hatley; the squatters cabin on the North arm of the Fraser; Kitsilano; and then Vasquez Island, last stop, everybody out.

Each place had its charms, its dreams, but it didn't take long before the ill-omened birds of dissatisfaction settled around them again; it became time to pull up stakes and make another desperate attempt to move to where the birds couldn't find them.

As Ryan writes this memoir about Sheila, he sits inside a wide arch on the island of Kythera, the birth place of Aphrodite. It is Sunday. The arch is on the lower floor of the large house where Ryan is staying and holds up the rooms above it. It looks out over the blue sea toward Crete, looks out past the great rock of Ithra that looms off shore. It is painted a faded crackling blue inside, like a sky with shepherd's clouds.

As he prepares to write the next paragraph, Ryan pauses to gaze over the Aegean—a time honoured source of inspiration. Now an old man, he looks at the pink and red oleanders below and hears the cicadas rhythmically chanting. Ahhhh, the pleasures of the present. If only he'd known them then, been introduced, he wouldn't have rushed into things so much, or so quickly...

There is a story about Brahma who incarnates as a pig and has a sow and many little piglets. He lives in mud, loves his piggy family deeply and forgets that he is a god. The other deities are distressed that he has left his throne. Heaven and earth are in chaos. So in love is Brahma with his sow and with his piglets, so in love with rolling in the cool mud and eating delicious slop, that the gods cannot awaken him to his true nature. In desperation the gods kill his piglets one by one in front of him, each squealing and screaming its lifeblood away, and then finally, ditto, his sow. Brahma is beside himself, rolling in the mud, squealing and screaming in rage and pain. And finally, as they hold him down, everything he loves gone, he awakens to his true nature and welcomes the knife that will release him from his earthly form.

In the Greek plays, the chorus chants. Wearing antique masks and robes, they sway like ancient figures awakened from the dead, like bodies made of seaweed swaying at the bottom of the sea. They chant, over and over again, as the drama plays itself out: "Man must suffer to be wise."

300

Ryan stops after writing this note. He wonders if the reader has ever heard a pig scream its life blood out.

It is the night before a Mexican wedding. It is in a small Mexican town where Sheila and he lived for awhile. The pig, still snuffling in its stone pen, will be served the next day as succulent carnitas to the guests of the wedding.

The groom, an American writing student named Ray Whearty, is marrying a Mexican woman. He performs the ritual. It happens in the small hours before dawn; before the heat of the sun; before the flies. It happens early so there will be time for the skinning and butchering and cooking of the pig before the celebration. Ray and his friend Steve sit on the pig to hold it down. Ryan watches while Ray slits its throat. It screams and screams, mournfully, in the pre-dawn Guanajuato night while its life blood runs out. By the end Ryan swears that the pig is crying, just for a few final sobs. After it is over, Ray puts his Stetson back on his head. It has been knocked off by the pig's struggles. His friend, Steve Gaskin, then a writing instructor and not yet the guru he was to become, says, "Looks like you got some blood on your sombrero, pardner." It is Ray's wedding sombrero. He takes it off and examines the spot of blood on it.

In the predawn before the wedding they have taken a life. It is as though a life must be taken and eaten to provide nourishment and make room for the new lives that will spill from the marriage. This is the ancient ritual, the ancient understanding. No namby-pamby veganism here. All this happens back when they are all still young, an accidental meeting, in Marfil, a small village outside of austere Guanajuato, who's shuttered stone eyes look forever inward at its colonial past.

For Ryan, the old man out where where Aphrodite was born, it is difficult to write about his time with Sheila. He avoids it by pausing to gaze out at the rock of Ithra on its blue waters.

The Greek version of Aphrodite's birth is not as pretty as the Botticelli painting would lead us to believe: Zeus castrates Cronos whose penis falls into the Aegean, becoming the rock of Ithra. Ryan looks out from the arch and imagines that, at certain times of day, in certain times of shadow, he can see the face of Cronos out on the towering rock, monumental and stern, still peering into the deep blue waters, searching for his lost penis. Out of the blood and foam of this deed Aphrodite is born. Primitive male sexuality is laid waste so that feminine sensuality and love can appear on the scene. After this horrendous birth—and aren't we all born of blood and foam and does not the sacrifice of the pig happen, in some way, for everyone—she swims the distance to Kythera, half way up the coast to a sheltered bay where she comes ashore.

Kythera is on a great swath of blue sea where huge white waves crest and roll with the wind. This is where three seas come together, the Ionian, the Cretan and the Aegean. The water is turbulent, treacherous and portentous. One can almost see the goddess, swimming naked and bodysurfing the great waves, the rock of Ithra towering above her, a fecund moon high in the daytime sky, dolphins arcing beside her, escorting her to safety as she swims up the arid coast. When she reaches the ledge still called Lotous Aphrodite, she climbs out onto the land for the first time. She leaves the dolphins behind and trades them for the sunlight, the buzzing cicadas, and the warmth of the land. Beautiful in her nakedness, she climbs up to the ledge, a place of safety, and warms herself, rests, in the afternoon sun. Everything changes for everybody.

That night, in the tomb-like stupefaction of a room closed up against mosquitoes, in the white noise of the air conditioner, Ryan dreams he is in an ancient city.

There are street people living in the ruins of a Roman amphitheatre surrounded by high-rises. Man must suffer to be wise. Are there any shortages of berths on the voyage that gives the opportunity for wisdom? Are there any shortages of actors to play the parts?

In the dream, one of the street people gives him a folded wad of newspaper with something inside. He opens it and discovers that it contains a well developed foetus, looking like a butcher shop chicken, but definitely human. He is appalled, "I will take it to the police," he says in the dream. He is the only respectable one who the police would not arrest, whose story the police would believe, who would not be a suspect. But he cannot find the police. He carries it around the city. He does not know how to use the phones in this country. He takes busses, trolleys, trains. A man comes after him and pushes him off the train, crushingly, onto his back.

At last he arrives at his friend Pat's, a university professor on sabbatical in this city, hoping that she will help him. The package is now falling apart, the worse for his flight across the city, and has become grease soaked. He knocks on the door. Pat answers and he cuts off her effusive surprise at seeing him. She has guests. Through the doorway he can see elegant people sipping cocktails and talking to each other. He signals her not to introduce him and goes straight upstairs to use the phone. He opens the package and finds that it now contains cooked chicken and fries. He forgets its origin and, hungry from his flight across the city, reaches in and pulls off a moist chunk of soft cooked flesh and pops it in his mouth. He licks his fingers; then he is appalled. Now he will make his phone call. He will turn himself in for eating chicken.

He awakens the next day, Monday, and opens the curtains to let in the breeze from the sea. Ithra looms in the cerulean light outside his window. He will take this day as a day of rest. The small amount of writing that he has been able to do has frayed his nerves. He will use this day to figure out how to use the curtains and the electric vaporisers to keep mosquitoes out so that he is not sealed in a tomb at night. He will walk to the cave of Aggia Sophia, through the cicada buzzing groves, over a ridge on ancient stone paths and down through cypress, olive and palm to the great arch of the cave. A German tourist has written a small Xeroxed guidebook to out of the way places and marked their difficult trails by painting small dots of red paint, like spatterings from stigmata, on the sun-baked rocks.

The cave was once the home of a hermit and has a small chapel in its dark mouth. Though not Orthodox, Ryan decides he will light some candles. They are left haphazardly on a small blue wooden table, with a box for coin and a BIC lighter for fire. He will light candles for his dead mother, for his sick wife and for himself. It is a day of atonement. He looks like an ordinary tourist, though, and wonders how many of the other tourists he sees are carrying similar packages into the caves of hermits—people who have lived outside the web of relationship—to seek absolution.

40
Ryan and Sheila

It is eleven o'clock at night. Ryan's hundred year old house sleeps in its quiet neighbourhood above the sea. In this light it is a large dark cube with a huge Irish yew growing in front of it, a yew that has escaped from its trimmed columnar shape to resume its wildness in the genteel streets of Victoria. A small westering moon hangs in the haze above the Strait of Juan de Fuca. In this sedate district only the occasional car whooshes by on its way home.

When the phone rings, Ryan is already asleep, his grey head on the pillow. He sleeps with the curtains open to be in contact with stars, moon and the passing night. The phone rings in two places: downstairs in the kitchen and across the hall in his office. Its double ring sifts softly through the bones of the old house and into the world of his dreams. "Is that the phone?" he says as he struggles to waken. Disoriented, he jumps out of bed, cursing softly. He's learned that phones at night do not bring good news. Naked he walks across the hall, not turning on the light, into the little room where he writes. In the darkness—a darkness he can see in—he picks up the phone and in a voice that surprises him in its sleepiness and blurriness says "Hello?"

It is Lara on the other end: "Hello dad, I'm in the hospital in Olympia, mom has had a cerebral hemorrhage; she is not expected to live through the night." He is too sleepy to do what he knows how to do. He asks a few questions: Andrew is with her. They were in Seattle recording. Sheila's exchange students found her in the morning when she did not come up for breakfast. She will call him in the morning. Ryan is so sleepy that he forgets to get her number. He forgets to tell her to call him anytime in the night if she needs help. He forgets to tell her what he knows about dying. He forgets to comfort her. He realises all this after he has hung up. He goes back to bed and talks with his wife Cora for a short while, soft voices in the quiet dark house, and then they drift back to sleep.

In the morning he finds the hospital number and calls. A small group is gathered in Sheila's room. Lara comes to the phone. They are deciding whether to take Sheila off life support.

He checks the airlines and finds he can get a flight, gathers a few cloths, a copy of the Tibetan Book of the Dead and races out the door, driving hard for the Airport. Cora arranges to have a rental car waiting at Sea-Tac. From the plane, the Strait of Juan de Fuca is a burnished mirror below clouds. As Ryan makes the short flight across the waters to the good ol' USA, shafts of light come down through the broken sky and land on the sea's polished surface.

Carry-on in hand, he goes through the familiar drill: customs, the subway train to the car barn, a great concrete building full of nothing but rental cars, and finally the freeway. Its green signs direct him down the long straight road full of rumbling trucks to Olympia.

He finds the hospital easily, directed by omens and portents. He knows Lara and Andrew are there, Peter, Sheila's lover for awhile after him, is there, Susan her friend is there. Michael Thomas one of their students from Argenta days is driving up from Portland to say goodbye. They have been waiting to disconnect life support until her living will is found and everybody who wants to see her has arrived. Just before Olympia Ryan sees the big H that denotes a hospital. It is on Peter Way so he decides it is worth a try: it might be the place even though the exit is well before Olympia proper. He asks at a gas station. "Where is Saint Michael's Hospital?" and finds out that it's only blocks away. He buys a bottled green tea drink to fortify himself and drives on for two blocks, turning right at the light, like the man said.

The hospital is unusual, a concrete monolith to be sure, but rising abruptly out of the surrounding forest. Its parking lots have not been cleared of trees. Rather, parking bays have been scooped into the forest leaving plenty of trees, moss covered stumps and under growth. The parking is free and there is even volunteer valet parking for those who want it, a far cry from the Canadian health care system. After much driving around under the trees, he finds a space and, as he gets out of the car, sees Andrew who has come out to check on their dog. He feels well met, that in this huge uncharted space he has arrived to a friendly face, a hug, and the story of what is happening.

They walk the long polished corridors of this temple of suffering to the room where Sheila lies among her friends and ex-lovers. She lies like an Egyptian queen in the process of mummification. There are tubes in her arms and tubes going down her throat, breathing tubes and suction tubes. One of her eyes is open and glittering a little, like the eye of the ancient mariner with a tale to tell. He merely nods at the others and goes to her, takes her hand and tells her that he is here with her. When he starts to speak to her in a low voice, Peter asks if he would like some time alone. Ryan nods and Peter and the others file out of the room. Lara is somewhere getting a bit of sleep, they tell him, in some little room with a couch that the hospital has reserved as a place for exhausted family members when they are no longer able to sit at the bedsides of their beloveds; where they can slip into their own realm of inner darkness and sweet peace for a few blessed hours of oblivion.

In the empty room with Sheila, Ryan is surrounded by machines that hiss and breathe. He looks out the window and feels supported by the forest that comes up to the walls of the building. It hides the cars, the streets, the Seven-Elevens, the very ordinariness of what goes on below; it makes the hospital seem like a Mayan temple that stands alone above the forest canopy, a place that catches the solstices and equinoxes and sees the stars; a place to get a glimpse of eternity.

Ryan pulls up a chair and bends close to Sheila's open eye and looks deeply into it as he speaks. He speaks of their life together; he asks her forgiveness for the ways in which he had not been a good husband. He forgives her for all the things he had resented during and after their marriage. Knowing how hard it must be to leave a child alone in the world, even an adult child, he swears to look after Lara. As he says these important things, he can see Sheila's single eye, semi open, the lid, swollen, almost veiling it, scanning, scanning. At the times when he says the really important things, she jerks, sending a jolt through her arms. This seems to him her way of acknowledging—the only way she has left.

He assumes that she can hear him, that she is aware, if not with her body, with some spiritual sense that pervades the room around her. He assumes that her consciousness, embodied or disembodied, is still present. It is just that its link to her body is very attenuated. He tells her that she has had a stroke, that she is dying, that her friends have gathered around; He tells her that as she lets go of this body, this lifetime, these friends, that what will be left is the pure endless consciousness that underlies all this; that this is her true self; that it has never been born and never can die; that it will always be there; and that since this is who all of us really are, those close to her will still be travelling with her. Then, all this said, he sits quietly among the wires and tubes and holds her hand, waiting for the others to return. The warm afternoon sun shines in on them through the western windows. When her friend Susan comes in, he sees the jerk of recognition as she comes up to the bed. It again affirms for him that some sentience remains even though there is little she can do to express it. She is buried in a body that doesn't work anymore. It seems so important to keep her company; to provide comfort.

Susan brings a bag of cookies to sustain them. She lost her husband less than a year ago, the husband she married young and had lived with all her life. Toward the end, he had been released from this very hospital, where he and Susan had spent so much time, to return home to die. He and she had slept together during these final days, enjoying a few more precious nights of holding each other. On the night that he died, he turned to her in the darkness and gave her a little back rub as she drifted off to sleep. In the morning he was gone.

The present situation brings back for Susan all the hours in the hospital with her dying husband. Now Sheila, the dear friend who supported her through all that, is also dying. Besides bringing home-baked cookies, she had also thought to arrange a place for Peter and Ryan to sleep, in a small residence that the hospital runs out among the trees.

When darkness falls, Peter, who has been here since the night before, goes to their room to get some sleep. Susan goes back home. Lara sleeps on the couch in the little room with Andrew on the floor beside her. Ryan sits alone with Sheila. They have not yet cut off Sheila's life support. The living will arrives tomorrow. Then they will see.

Ryan arranges chairs, one to lean back in, one to rest his feet on, and lowers the light. He realises that he cannot sleep this way and soon will have to leave. He needs to get some sleep tonight. For now, he sits with Sheila. They are together once again in this hospital room.

He remembers the long journey of their time together: SF State while living in Oakland and San Francisco; marriage in the Sierra Nevada; their house in the woods in Fairfax; Mexican adventures in Acopilco and Marfil; difficult times in Argenta and Bellingham; Victoria and the magical birth of Lara; the East Coast escapade and the farmhouse in North Hatley; the squatter's cabin on the Fraser for him and the Kitsilano apartment for her; and, finally, their last days together on Vasquez Island.

In the midst of these reminiscences, Kay, a young Japanese exchange student who used to rent from Sheila, comes to take over the vigil. Sheila had adopted her; had spent long hours on the phone helping her with her life when she had moved away to the Dakotas. She sits with Sheila in tearstained grief while Ryan goes to the little room he shares with Peter.

At six in the morning—not too hard as he is an early riser—he walks to the hospital, to take his place beside Sheila again. On his way he enjoys the beauty of the early dawn light filtering through the branches of the forest. He starts with coffee in the cafeteria. This is the hospital routine that he got to know when he had sat for ten days with his dying Aunt Lenora, only a short eight months before. Little breaks. Coffee. A cookie. Last night he had gone out to bring back Chinese food for everybody, delighting in his few minutes of driving around in the world of the living.

Lenora, his mother's sister, had been childless. Her husband had died six months before her. Ryan's sister, Elena, and he had taken turns sitting by her bedside. Cousins who he hadn't seen since childhood came and sat across the bed from him, sharing stories in soft voices during the long evenings while Lenora slept.

When he had sat with Lenora, he would leave at eleven at night to sleep on the couch at his uncle's—her brother's—house. He would return at five-thirty in the morning, driving through the December darkness, coming and going through the dark to enter the fluorescent world of the hospital, a world where stricken parents wheeled terminally ill children in and out of elevators. He treasured his two-hour lunchbreak when his eighty year old uncle would come and take his place. He would buy an excellent hamburger from the little diner across the street and then drive his rental car into the light of the California hills. Finding a little enclave of nature in the suburbs, some grassy hill with oaks on it, he would climb up into it to eat his lunch. Then he would spread out his leather jacket, a gift from Cora, and sleep for an hour in the pale but still warm winter sun.

Sometimes on his lunch, he went to find classical music tapes that Lenora could listen to to drown out the hospital noise, or books that he could read to her. It was just before Christmas; carols of joy were playing mechanically everywhere. The city of Walnut Creek seemed like a huge shopping mall with people coming out of shops and dumping piles of bright presents into the trunks of their shiny cars. It all seemed unreal to Ryan. He had one foot in the land of the dead, living all day in a place of suffering, sitting beside an aunt whose breath constricted more with each day, who was living bravely in terror of the end, of what her final suffocation would be like. She was surrounded by denial, by social workers who made plans for her to go home, by a loving brother who counted on her to get better. He read to her from Isabel Allende's *Daughter of Fortune*, read for hours. During one of the sexual scenes, Lenora chuckled through her respirator at how inappropriate it was for her nephew, who she had know since a boy, to be reading these lurid scenes to his old Auntie. They continued the readings but never did finish the book.

After Lenora died, it took Ryan weeks to get back into the land of the living; to enjoy the simple things we all do. When he came home, Cora gently nursed him back, with meals, with walks, with simple tasks around the house. "Would you mind fixing that cabinet for me?" He left Lenora, thinking he would come back after Christmas—his own denial—and spend more time with her. She was gone in two days, dying in the arms of Elena, who had taken over after Ryan left. Elena called Ryan in tears at eleven at night to let him know that Lenora had just died. He asked her to say the Invocation to the Clear Light to Lenora and dictated it to her over the phone. It was awkward. Elena said, "why don't you just read it to her and I'll hold the phone to her ear." He read it twice. "You are the clear light of consciousness...you have never been born, never died... never real... never unreal...not the void of nothingness but the endless endlessness of the absolute." Elena, a nurse by profession, came back on the phone and said that even though Lenora was clinically dead, her eyes seemed to move behind their lids as he read.

After Ryan hung up, Elena left and started the long drive home to Sonoma County where her husband lay sleeping in their little house by the Russian River. She turned on the radio and Vaughn Williams *Ascending of the Lark* came on. She listened to it on the dark streaming highway, and later sent Ryan a CD of it.

Why did Ryan, who had no memory of having undergone death and rebirth, offer Lenora these readings? As a boy of nine, on a camping trip, when all he wanted to do was catch fish and swim in the lake with his sisters, he dreamed, as he lay in his sleeping bag one night, that his family had pulled into a dusty, old-fashioned gas station. In the dream, as his father was gassing up and tightening the ropes that held the boat on the car, the kids, as was their wont, went looking around for curios or gum machines. It all seemed very ordinary, very real. He was looking in the window, at the coca cola posters, at the sun glasses, at the cards of coloured plastic bug deflectors, when suddenly he saw a sun-faded poster entitled "The Eight Ways Of Dying." It showed eight different photographs of an emaciated looking Asian man lying on a bamboo mat in different positions. He looked at these and suddenly realised that it was really weird to be seeing this in a gas station. His scream awakened him from the dream, and the whole campground from its sleep. It was twenty years before he discovered that these positions existed and were used for dying.

During his stay with Lenora in the hospital, Ryan had made up visualisations of going into the clear light to help her get to sleep at night; he hoped that facilitating the little letting go of sleep might help her later with the bigger one of dying.

Lenora was open to all this. Though a Catholic born in the hills of Reppia, as were Ryan's mother and all his aunts and uncles, she had gone beyond, in her later years, attending yoga classes and other spiritual workshops. The year before she died, Lenora had gone with Elena to a Thich Nhat Hanh workshop. At lunch she said, "I have to see who this man is." She wandered down the aisles of the huge theatre, a tall old Italian lady with curly grey hair, a school teacher all her life. She wandered by herself backstage and looked around, opening doors and looking for Thich Nhat Hanh. She opened one door after another and suddenly there he was, surrounded by those close to him, eating lunch with chopsticks. She excused herself and started to back out, but he said, "Please join us." Someone pulled up a chair and she sat down and was given some chopsticks and a bowl of take-out Chinese food. She had lunch with Thich Nhat Hanh.

In the morning, Sheila's parents find her living-will and fax it up from Mendocino. It is beautifully crafted, a testimony to the clarity of Sheila's mind. Reading it is like having her present with them for a moment. In the will Sheila is very clear that she does not want to be kept alive on life support if two doctors concur that she will not recover. "Concur" –such a sickly word.

Ryan feels grateful that Sheila has left this will; that the decision to unplug her has not been left up to Lara; that it is not something that Lara will have to bear onto herself. The second doctor explains, graphically, that Sheila is not really alive according to the brain scans. He tells them the brain is very delicate, about the texture of grape jelly, and that a haemorrhage of this magnitude is like turning a fire hose on it; that Sheila's brain has been scattered and rearranged within her skull, lost and forever broken. He shows them the scans of what has happened inside her head.

Later in the morning when all have arrived, from their homes and the couches, rooms, chairs, and floors on which they have been sleeping, they stand around as the tubes and suction devices are removed. Immediately Sheila's breath takes on a deep rasping sound. All the monitors, the computerised graphs, are also disconnected and turned off, and they can no longer distract themselves with these visual representations, no longer take their eyes away and stare at the screens above her. There is now only Sheila, her face swollen, both of her eyes shut, her breath coming in laboured gasps full of bubbling fluid.

Susan arrives and leads them in the songs that she and Sheila used to sing on road trips. Michael Row the Boat Ashore, Swing Low Sweet Chariot, Kumbaya. During the day they sing softly to Sheila from time to time. Her eye now stays closed. She has gone inside to cope with the business of dying. They sing quiet songs as her oxygen saturation levels drop, as her breath slows to a laboured rasp.

Exhausted, Lara climbs on the bed and sleeps beside her mother, holding her, in the late afternoon light that filters in over the tree tops. The forest is reminiscent of all forests, reminiscent of the redwoods in Comptche where Lara and Sheila lived when Lara was a child; the light is reminiscent of all light, of the inner light, which Ryan hopes is dawning for Sheila as the outer one fades.

Sheila's parents, old, grief stricken, live in their little house in Mendocino. They want to come but the long day's drive to the airport in San Francisco is daunting, and Ray, at 82 is not well enough to be left alone. So they stay in their house, a house filled with the paintings and sculptures of departed friends, and, as the hands of the clock move slowly, listen to the steady sigh of the whistle buoy and the booming of waves on the headlands. Miriam calls the hospital often. "How is she?" Her voice is full of tears. She is endlessly weeping over her comatose daughter. Ryan can only imagine what it must be like to have a child die before you. In his mind it is he who dies, saying goodbye to his children who are in the fullness of their lives. This seems so wrong: to witness, in your old age, a child struck down in the middle of her life. Miriam says, "and things were getting so much better for her."

That night people find their way home. Susan asks to be called if Sheila passes. Lara, Andrew, Peter, and Ryan are left. They stand at Sheila's bedside. The kind nurses have given them a portable CD player, but the only disks they have are donated disks of rain falling, surf crashing, jungle noises, and thunderstorms. On one of his breaks, Ryan goes to K-Mart and finds among the numerous pop CDs a disk called Baby's First Classical Music. It is from a series of disks—remaindered—to play for your baby to make it smarter. In this case, he grimly reflects to himself, it will be Baby's Last Classical Music. As the sun sets behind the firs, he plays Bach, Mozart, Beethoven, Pachelbel from the magical silver disk. He hopes Sheila can hear the beautiful music. It lends a splendour and solemnity to these last moments in the light as the red streaked sky fades outside the tinted hospital windows.

As darkness settles around them the nurses bring in a folding bed so that Lara can sleep beside her mother. Ryan asks the nurses to check

Sheila's oxygen saturation levels. They are dropping into the low sixties. It feels like the final vigil has begun, but Sheila's hold on life is tenacious. She hangs on to her bubbling and painful breath. They continually wipe away the yellow sputum that begins collecting on her lips. The nurses talk about people not leaving while their loved ones are around and they begin to wonder if their very presence is keeping Sheila suspended in this painful state. The nurses give Sheila morphine to ease her breathing. They suggest that everyone take little breaks, walk the corridors for awhile to give her a space in which to let go, but no-one wants to be too far away. Ryan goes down to the chapel to pray and do Bardo readings for her spirit, but at this hour the chapel is locked. He returns to the room and leans over Sheila's bed and says the Invocation to the Clear Light softly to her in a variety of different ways, hoping it is all right with the others present and doesn't clash with their beliefs.

He knows that Sheila has never been particularly religious or spiritual, so he says "as you float above this hospital you see a beautiful clear light moving across the sky toward you. You see within the wonderful clear light all the artists, the poets and philosophers who have guided you. They reach out to you, welcome you, and as you enter the clear light you realise that you are not separate from it or from them. That you are the clear light itself; that this is your true nature. That you have never been born, never died. That you are the endless endlessness from which all things arise."

Each breath comes harder now. They all stand by the bed, continuing to wipe her mouth and stroke her hair. Lara, exhausted, distraught, says "You've got to let go Mom, I can't do this much longer." The breaths become rougher, the spaces between them longer, and finally, after many almost-last-breaths, there is an emptiness, a no return. Several tears stream down Sheila's cheeks in these last moments. A sentient being is in there, expressing her sorrow at leaving life, at leaving her daughter, at leaving her family and friends.

At the moment of death, the room becomes psychedelic to Ryan. The colors swim a little, the colour of Sheila's face settles quickly into a marble white and her features take on a look of deep nobility. Lara laughs out loud. After her long ordeal she says "You mean this is it, this is what we've been afraid of?" Peter says he felt a gateway to another world open

313

for a moment. All of them feel that they are not afraid of death after this experience. Dying is another story.

Ryan says over and over again the invocation to the clear light. Then they disperse to different phones in the hospital and call those who want to be told. Ryan tells Ray and Miriam about Sheila's last hours.

Kay and Susan return. It is just after ten in the evening and the hospital ward is hushed. They sit together for a little while and talk softly in a small corner lounge outside Sheila's room. The ordeal is over. They take turns sitting with Sheila's body, now so cloaked in mystery and a peace beyond suffering. They tidy the room where they have spent so much time, packing up personal things, throwing out food boxes and old Kleenex.

Exhausted, they make plans to meet for breakfast tomorrow and then leave for the night. Each says final goodbye to Sheila before they disappear down the long corridor. After they are gone, Ryan sits a long while with Sheila, to give her spirit some time to leave her body before it is moved or wheeled away. He recites the prayers for the dead several more times and after an hour leaves. He asks the nurses if they can leave Sheila's body undisturbed for as long as hospital routine allows. They look puzzled but are glad to comply. They say no-one is coming in tonight and they can leave her in state 'til the wee hours of the morning when they will call the morgue to come and get her. Ryan leaves them the classical music he bought so that it will be on the ward.

He walks down the long reflecting linoleum corridors and out into a night alive with the scent of fir trees. Behind him the hospital rises over the forest, looking more than ever, in the star lit night, like a candle lit Mayan ceremonial centre. No cars disturb the night. Sheila's body is alone in this tall building which houses so much suffering and compassion. The stars glimmer overhead and there is sacredness all around.

He walks through the forested parking lot to the room he shares with Peter, entering quietly so as not to wake him. He lays in his small single bed, his body silent, his head replaying the day's events. After awhile he goes to sleep, falling into the depths of his own blesséd emptiness.

314

41
Endstorm

Ryan sits in a small guest cabin on Lara's property in Comptche. Across the way he hears her family getting up, the clanging of their wood stove burners. He looks out the window at their small low house and the great redwoods that rise above it. The grass in the clearing between the two houses is autumn brown. Inside the picket fence, the garden looks dry and at the end of its season. He sees the smoke from their morning fire begin to rise out of the chimney. In a few minutes he will walk over for coffee. In the meantime, he returns to a chapter he has been working on:

We stand like sentinels at the gates of the past, a poisonous past that we have tried to ingest, to eat, to get rid of. Poison eaters.

What have we done for our children? Have we broken the mold, the shadow of the bland fifties in which we grew up, beneath which a thousand desire demons surged? Have we eaten or been eaten by these demons? Experiments it was called.

But in some way, we hope, we have made it unnecessary for our children to follow: these little ones saw us and knew this lifestyle was not for them. We were the generation of chaos, rebelling against the generation of fakeness. Our children are neither fake nor chaotic. They have reinvented families where children sleep cuddled up with their parents under the passing moon; they have rediscovered Love rather than living out all the forms of love.

We would like to think, beloveds, that we slew the dragons and let the dragons slay us, so that you could find a life that was real, so that you could bring sanity into the world; that we were the alders that came before the firs.

But why does the past, which is supposedly behind us, need a gate? So that its bad things cannot flow forward into our children's lives? So that the dead stay buried? So that it will be over and done with? So that a new generation can live without the haunting dreams of Auschwitz? So that cannibalism will not happen? So that the bomb will be a distant memory of horror, something that is not really relevant anymore, like the iron maiden or the sieges of the Black Death?

There used to be keepers of the past. Are we them? Standing like sentinels at the gates of the past so that it may sleep; so that its billions of mouldering corpses may remain stacked like tombstones; so that our children may enjoy the archaeological present, the growing surface full of flowers; so that they may create a new world without the weight of the old.

Who says that those who don't study history are condemned to re-live it? Perhaps it is the other way around: that those who study it get caught in its snare and repeat the intricacy of its spiderweb patterns.

Blessed be the forgetful for they shall sleep in the arms of the present.

June 1, 2003, Comtche

316

42
Endstorm

As an old man, Ryan has come to believe that his purpose in life, after all the other things he's done, the professions he developed, the children he helped to raise, was to tell this story.

It feels to him that he was placed on Vasquez—even if he didn't know it at the time—just to observe and to tell this tale. He wrote down nothing, just lived his life there and then went away. He was like that wrestler who went to Japan to learn Sumo wrestling. The wrestler put on two hundred pounds by eating three chickens and five loaves of bread a day. When he had gained the necessary weight, he competed and acquitted himself well. Then he lost all the weight and went back to America to take up his ordinary life again, probably with a few stretch marks.

Ryan went there, took the drugs, entered the altered reality, then stopped and went back to the ordinary world again. Now the memories have come back to him, confused and blended. What of this tale is memory? What of it is imagination? Whatever it is made of, it is like cheese or wine that has aged. Through entering this time again, he has hopefully caught some essence of the story that he lived.

While writing, many voices tell him to stop. To cease and desist. To have done with it. What a waste of time. Don't you have anything better to do? How could one rather unexceptional life be of interest to anyone? At best, perhaps, some distant relative might be interested, see strands of themselves coming from 'ol great grandfather who scribbled in his deluded later years. He thinks that if he types it, maybe someone will even read it, unlike the poems his father wrote that still lay unread in a shoe box because of the impenetrability of his handwriting.

He fights back, trying to reassure himself. He says: "At the very best there is the example of Frieda Kahlo who created a body of work simply by painting herself." Then, as the tale begins to work deeply in his unconscious—like antibiotics, inoculations or Chinese herbs—an answer comes that each life is a jewel. Bright jewels full of love, bloody jewels full of pain and suffering (Frieda painted blood), dark jewels full of cruelty and hatred; that any life enunciated is a story of god unfolding one of his/her many robes and trying on one of the vast array of beings s/he has created, and then in death, in submission, folding and repacking it, putting it away again: "And if this vainglorious idea be not true," he thinks, "well then, anyway, this is my material, me, my life, even in the thousand disguises of imagination in which I have cloaked it."

"Furthermore, having gone through an evolution, having come to some kind of understanding through the living of my time, often by floundering around and cavorting like a lamb with the spike of a maguey stuck in its throat, I wish to share this understanding, the small wisdoms and cautions, with others on the path. Like a collection of signs that say 'go here' or 'don't go there.'"

But maybe this is just an elaborate rationalisation, he thinks: Maybe I just want to tell my story so that it doesn't sink into darkness; maybe I want to remember and extract some of the sweetness from it, to have it count for something at least, so that it will not have been for naught, the tale of an old idiot; maybe I just wish to attach enough beads and feathers to it so that someone might pick it up and have a look at it, or even hang it on a wall. To die without having told this tale would be almost to not have lived.

He tries to shape meaning and make sense of so many things that at the time just seemed to happen. Introverts write books because so much is happening in their inner world that there is never time to communicate it. They surrender to the hopelessness of expressing the ten thousand reflections passing through their overheated psyches. Their silence, often mistaken for shyness, becomes books. Books are the footnotes to what actually happened. The footnotes become longer than the text they comment on. "There is one God and that is Allah. There is one scripture and that is nature."

Now, re-reading the preceding paragraphs, he wonders, like a drunk trying to deal with the morning after a particularly magnificent bender, how to pick up the thread again. This book is finished, this tale is told. He sits in his office, the little corner room that used to be a closet, looking out at the bright morning sun lighting up the trees and roof tops of Fairfield. The filing cabinet is open, that great beige beast that has held his papers for so long, a gift to his wife from a supervisor at the Provincial Mental Health Centre where she once worked—"Just take it," he had said, "no one will really miss it." The blue plastic recycle bag bulges with the papers he has thrown out, whole file folders he has emptied.

He remembers cleaning out his mother's house after she died, heaving into the back of the truck his father's old clothes that still hung in her closet. His father had been dead for twenty years. He remembers sorting through boxes and boxes of papers, old bank statements from 1950, everything had been kept, nothing had been thrown away. He remembers having at least a quick look at everything and deciding what should be saved, and what should be thrown out. He remembers throwing out his father's old PhD thesis, the one he never finished. His father was researching anti-Semitism, whether people could really identify Jews by their looks. There were all the mug-shots that he asked people to classify as either Jewish or Gentile. Ryan's uncle's photo was in there, a smiling swarthy young man, Dino. Most people pegged him as Jewish and, as children, they all laughed because he was their uncle and they knew he was Italian. There was his father's elaborate statistical analysis of this; everything he abandoned, sad, intricate, brilliant. Ryan looked at it for one last time, appreciated it, his father's work, his mind, before consigning it to oblivion.

Why did his father not finish? Why did he not make his statement in life? Ryan's mother said it was because he got cancer, but Ryan thinks he stopped writing long before that. He thinks of an old girlfriend of his, Selene, telling her mother "You'd better finish it soon (her great history of the West) because I'll be damned if I am going to find a publisher for it after you are gone."

He went through boxes of old family linen, most of which had been eaten by moths. He divided up the remnants of the family silver, most of which had been stolen and pawned by his mother's tenants, wild students to whom she rented rooms in her declining years, as much for their company as for the money. She lived in her house surrounded by the drugs, intellectual ferment, rebellion, stormy love affairs of these young

319

people. Hadn't she had enough with Ryan and his sisters? She was a mother to them, an old Italian lady who would say a few wise things and give them a glass of wine and some food when their troubles overwhelmed them. In need of company and companionship, needing to be useful, she turned a blind eye to their pilfering and debauchery.

Ryan vowed then that he would not leave a bunch of junk for his children to sort out. It would be such a sad task, to sort through all his loose ends and unfinished projects, pages and pages of disjointed writing. The time has come. He does his own sorting. He throws out all the old posters, old lesson plans, catalogues of articles on healing, note books full of I-Ching tosses and dreams. It all goes. It's amazing, he thinks, how little from a life is worth saving, how much of it was just for the moment; how the laboured-over lectures and lesson plans, the ads, the business flyers really have little meaning in the end. He sets aside a folder of letters he wrote to Sheila in the years after their separation, some of them vituperative and poisonous, taking her to task for the way she separated him from Lara, some of which—thankfully—he never mailed. Does he want Lara to find these and know how he felt, or does he simply want to leave her the untroubled memories of her mother? He will think about it.

This book is his testament (or maunderings); it is what he has completed. It is what he will leave, all tidily wrapped up, about that time in his life and that time in history. Everybody in his family seems to leave something. It is also his guide, for if there is a Bardo, a space between lives and a coming back, a sleeping and an awakening, then perhaps he might find this book, a new him in a new time, man or woman, might find this book and read it.

And just how would he find this book if he comes back? And how would he know that it was written for him by himself? Well, he knows he will be a reader—he always has been. Maybe his samskara's, his karmic tendencies, his DNA, will bring him this way again, like all those kids in Nelson who are doing the whole hippy back-to-the-land thing all over again. Recurrence, our worse fear: that there is no evolution, personal or otherwise, that we just do the same thing over and over again, like Bill Murray in Groundhog Day.

In this lifetime he read Mailer, Bradbury, Lowry, Keroac, Ginsberg, Snyder. Maybe, just starting out again, just 19, he will find this book in a used book store, or left on a shelf, and recognise the spirit of the writer as his own, and, maybe, or maybe not, not need to repeat this same journey twice.

He might read it out on a porch in the late summer evening, looking up from time to time to watch the great freight balloons ride the trade winds east against a summer sky that is filling with stars. Or he might read it when there is death and destruction all around, when humans are showing their worst face and it doesn't seem like things can go on much longer. Maybe it will remind him to go to Florence and look at that Benozzo mural in the Medici tomb that shows Lorenzo riding out with his entourage on a fine spring morning. Lorenzo looks sideways from his horse, directly into the eyes of a viewer, who in some future age will be standing there. Living in a time of war and treachery, he was, just for that moment, looking into the future, betting that someone would be there to meet his gaze.

The future. Maybe it will remind him that there is a future; that life moves on through black times, through holocausts, through wars, through plagues, through global warming. Maybe it will remind him, that even though we are always riding through the valley of the shadow of death—even as Lorenzo, on that deceptively beautiful morning—birds in the trees, spring all around him, beautiful men and women clad in silk on fine horses—was riding through this very valley; maybe it will remind him to live his life well, do something creative, not wallow too much in sexuality, to create relationships with integrity, serve the life force, raise his children, work for the good. Maybe it will remind him.

"Now I am done," he thinks, "I will carry this huge blue bag down to the recycle box. I am glad I left this guide for myself. Now, perhaps I can tie up the tomatoes."

43
Endstorm

On this late winter afternoon—almost evening, almost dark—a great storm races up the Gulf of Georgia. It blows in from the Southeast, a giant white eraser washing away the stars, washing away the moon, washing away the luhm of the coastal cities. All up and down the Gulf of Georgia, the rain turns to snow.

In Vancouver, as the front hits, a light sifting of snow begins to fall. Tomorrow the mountains will rise like teeth above the dark forests, and the dark forests will be dusted white. The air will reek with the fumes of oil furnaces and little black balls of soot will fall from the sky. At first the world will be pristine white. All the junk, all the candy wrappers, all the wine bottles, all the needles, will be covered by this lovely bridal veil. Soon it will be churned into grey slush. In Vancouver, in winter, all colours seek grey.

Andy sits at his writing desk in his Shaugnessy manor. An Arts and Crafts lamp casts a puddle of yellow light around him. The rest of the room is dark, panelled in shadowy oak that has been stained the dark brown of another time. Outside it is barely light. The great storm has just hit, shaking the windows and spattering them with hail. The house shudders with a gust and then seems to bear itself up. Still holding his pen, Andy walks to the window. He is still in the running pants and sweat shirt from his after-work run. Standing against the window, he is bent almost into a S, his hips pushed forward, his chest back, his head forward. The light of the lamp reflects off his bald head.

He looks out at the shrubs, the elegantly landscaped borders of his garden and watches the wind bend the ornamental trees low. A gush of water and leaves runs down the window from an overflowing gutter. He walks back to his desk to make a few more notes, flipping through the pages of his scrawled yellow legal pad, adding a bit here, crossing out a bit there. He finds just the right place to put his ideas. He is working on the closing argument in a case where the wealthy client stands accused of scalding his two small children to death in the bathtub. He is even more stooped and bent than he was when he was on Vasquez, though one could also say "coiled." On the courtroom floor, dressed in one of his fine suits, he emanates a formidable reptilian power. "They are entitled to a defence," he once told Dorrie when she had challenged him about the clients he chose to defend, "that's the way the system works." He looks up as the storm beats against the windows and then back down at his speech. "This should do it," he says to himself as he reads aloud his eloquent and impassioned words.

In the West End, high up in a glass penthouse, Thornton Fatherson III talks on his cell phone. He is gathering backers for a new company that he is floating on the Vancouver Stock Exchange. His patois is jocular, full of irreverence, inside jokes, and subtle little innuendoes. He flatters his listener into feeling that he is in the know, in on a grand scheme, an opportunity that is not for everyone, that is only for the discerning few. He walks to the window and watches the storm close, listening to something, maybe a list of considerations from the person on the other end: "Uh-huh, Uh-huh, yes, Uh-huh, No, No, Oh Hell No. I don't think so, Bullshit, that's really bullshit. It comes down to whether he has the balls. Yea, what a pussy, eh? Yeah, maybe a testosterone patch would help! Nope. Bullshit, Yes, Yes, Uh-huh. Yes. If you ask me, we have them by the short and curlies. Right, Uh-huh, yes, yes…"

He talks more or less automatically as the storm sweeps toward him across the city's roof tops. As he talks he is becoming isolated by the haze, the rain, the snow, the hail of the storm. The city begins to fade into the swirling white, to disappear around him. His cell phone begins to crackle but the connection holds. Hail thunders on the roof. The patio outside becomes a slushy lake. He is standing, warm and comfortable, in the middle of a lake in the sky, connected by his cell phone to the rest of the world, finding just the right words to reel this sucker in. In the beginning was the word. That has not changed much.

In the bowels of a TV studio, completely buffered from the storm, Alexis sits at an editing machine. He doesn't even know about the storm outside. He cuts and splices, making seamless reality out of hours of scattered footage. It hurts him to cut some of these scenes. He remembers the fun and high-jinx of shooting them. Now they will never see the light of day. A voice comes from the other end of the room.

"What are you doing, Al."

"Killing my babies," he says.

It hurts, but he knows that anything that doesn't contribute must go. It is a small simplified world that he is creating, with its own laws and creatures. Of the ten thousand things, he has assembled maybe ten or twelve, to bump up and play against each other. As he looks as the screen, somewhere above him a branch falls on a wire and the screen goes into darkness. "Shit," he screams. The room falls into darkness. The voice comes again from the other end of the room.

"Did you save it?"

"No, Shit, I lost it."

He doesn't know what happened to make the lights go out.

Across the Burrard inlet, up against the foot of the mountains, Elroy hears the first fat rain drops splatter against his window. On this side of the water, for some unaccountable reason, the storm comes as rain rather than snow. He gets up, holding his papers in his hand and looks out at the Vancouver sky line, the dark green mound of Stanley Park, white monoliths rising all around it. As he watches, it is being obscured by a great swirling cloud that breaks and rolls over the skyline.

Long ago Elroy gave up his music to become a preacher, Ellerton Thompson, D.D. Sometimes he still plays the guitar to lead his congregation in song. Only a few people still call him Elroy. He is pacing back and forth, reading tomorrow's sermon to his wife, his best critic and adviser. Sometimes he gets mad at her when she finds a flaw in his thinking, but usually, after he thinks it over, he comes to realise that she is right. Whatever that glimpse that he got from Bob was, he never got over it. He returned to Texas and started in at bible school, in a stab at fundamentalism, but what the bible school offered, regardless of its other merits, did not even speak of what he had experienced out on Vasquez.

Travelling eastward, going through seminaries like playing cards, he wound up a Unitarian, an assistant pastor in Boston who still spoke with a gentle southern twang. When a church came up in Vancouver he jumped at the chance, free-trade enabled, to go back to the Raincoast of his youth.

Tomorrow he would present his congregation with an idea, from Avaita Vedanta, that god is ubiquitous; that god is the great sea of consciousness that gives rise to everything; God is in everything and everything is in God. He has decided to make it practical by talking about how one can, just by withdrawing some attention from the messy chattering of the brain, find silence; how by going into it, one can know and become one with this great wordless awareness that is the mother and underpinning of everything.

His Yankee wife, spunky and charismatic, sits in a chair listening to his sermon, her grey hair in a jaunty pony tail. She had to finish the dishes and fold some clothes before she could come and listen to his talk about transcending the messy details of life. Outside the storm knocks something over, maybe the garbage can, and Ellerton goes out into the night to investigate. When he comes back, raindrops are dripping from his thin but still red hair. He continues the sermon, his wife attentive. "It's interesting," she says, "In this version, god is not a person, is really nothing like a person. It's just this great sea of awareness and love that gives rise to and sustains everything. But you never said what you believe. Do you believe in this vision that you are writing about?"

"My job," he says, for a moment speaking in his mellow preacher's voice, the voice of a singer, "is to promote inquiry, not belief. What does it behoove me if I tell them where I stand. It's a losing proposition. Either way, half will embrace me, and half will dismiss me. It's better to let it niggle at them, let them figure out where they stand for themselves. You have to be careful with words."

Outside the window the southeast storm continues to rush over Vancouver and continue up Georgia Strait, lashing the waves into blowing foam, dappling the sea with rain and hail. In the dark blue-grey world of the evening, the sea fades into blackness as the storm blows over Vasquez, over its old homesteads and boarded up summer homes. Some of the homesteads are empty again, awaiting another batch of inhabitants; some are still lived in by the new old-timers, those who had settled in the seventies; some are lived in by a few of their children who have chosen to stay.

Outside the window the southeast storm continues to rush over Vancouver and continue up Georgia Strait, lashing the waves into blowing foam, dappling the sea with rain and hail. In the dark blue-grey world of the evening, the sea fades into blackness as the storm blows over Vasquez, over its old homesteads and boarded up summer homes. Some of the homesteads are empty again, awaiting another batch of inhabitants; some are still lived in by the new old-timers, those who had settled in the seventies; some are lived in by a few of their children who have chosen to stay.

Deep in the forest, Dorrie sits in her kitchen braiding strings of garlic. As she does this, Thomas reads to her from a book on quantum physics and healing. Their children are long gone, left for the city their lives to lead. The doors of their empty rooms are closed to save heat. It is already dark and the battery operated electric lights are on, each shining like a little star on a specific area of their life. Above them the wind combs out the branches of trees. Dead branches, rain, fir cones and needles, swirl around the house as Thomas reads to Dorrie about the dance between matter and energy. He stops reading and looks up, as though he can see through the roof. After all these years they finally have a real roof over their heads. He hears the windmill damp itself down and turn itself out of the wind, so that the storm won't blow it down. "Maybe we should have a fire tonight," he says, and Dorrie answers, "Yes, that would be nice, it's gotten cold." Thomas opens the woodbox in the wall and carries an armload of cedar, some old newspaper, yesterday's stories, over to the wood heater and opens its creaking iron door.

At the foot of the mountain rain blows through the pane-less windows of a small weathered cabin. A few tatters of plastic still flap from the cedar battens that used to hold it in place. Behind the cabin are the remains of a garden. Its fence posts have been knocked down by the cattle and lay tangled in the rusty page wire that they used to hold up. The forest around the clearing is decimated, rutted by skidders, a valley of stumps and unburned slash piles, rotting and full of weeds. Suddenly there is a clap of wind and two birds startle from the bare branches of the ancient apple trees behind the cabin. The birds spiral upward In the fading light, soaring effortlessly through the first snowflakes, making minute adjustments of their pinions to each gusts wind. They rise higher and higher, finally disappearing into the darkness of the mountain, like guardian spirits merging with creation.

Higher on the mountain the rain has already turned to snow, covering the island's dump, the excavated hillside of rusting tin cans, torn black garbage bags, useless appliances, broken sheets of gyprock. To one side of the dump are the remains of an old broken Volvo. Its hood is missing, revealing the empty space where its engine used to be. Snow begins to form a cap on its roof. It drifts in through the broken windows and collects on the tattered plastic seats. Soon it will be all white, like a snow drift. In the fading light, black sockets stare out from where its headlights used to be. Long ago it carried Sheila, Ryan, Lara and all their things to Canada; it drove to parties, carried wood, carried seaweed, gave people rides; it came and went on many errands, to and from its island homestead.

Earlier in the day, in Victoria, at the foot of Vancouver Island, the storm has already been blowing for several hours. Julie holds open the back door of her Lexus and opens a large red umbrella to cover her passengers as they slide out across the seat. She is showing an elegant waterfront home along Beach Drive. She wears a dark blue suit accented with a single string of pearls. She wears her Asian hair straight back, secured by a carved ivory clasp at the back of her neck. The group, huddles together under the umbrella as it makes its way to the door. This is not good, Julie realizes: the view of Juan de Fuca and the Olympics—the house's major selling point—will not be visible today. She can only hope that the proximity of the storm, the waves breaking on the rocks below the living room will be exciting to them; that they will come back on a clear day to get another look. They arrive under the portico and she furls the umbrella and leans it against the wall. Her key turns in the lock and with a tiny click the door swings open. She steps aside, gesturing for them to enter.

Ryan sits in his closet typing just a few last words, an epilogue called End Storm that he just couldn't resist adding to his already complete book. He writes: "Each small place has its mythology, its creation tale, which makes it different from every other small place, which makes Vasquez different from Saltspring, from Denman, from Galiano, from Valdes, from Lasqueti, from Saturna." He thinks for awhile, then he writes, "The world is saved not by ideas or political action but by the transformation of human nature."

There is a little thrill of satisfaction as he sees the final words rolling off his finger tips. Rain drops mixed with snow pelt the sides of his old Edwardian house, sticking to its sage-green paint. There is an arctic howl as wind whips in through a window that he has never been able to get to close properly. As he writes these final words, he thinks: "The world is easily hypnotised by words." He leans back and looks at them on the screen. "This should do it," he says out loud. "It is as though we really existed, that I existed; that there was an Ariel, a Julie, a Reston, an Isaac, a Miriam, a Sheila, an Elroy; and that this is what it was like. "

Outside the storm picks up in ferocity. All up and down the Gulf of Georgia the rain turns to snow. In Vancouver, out on the islands, in Vancouver Island's little cities, in Victoria, flakes begin to fall, whiting out the lights, whiting out the moon, whiting out the stars. A great white eraser moves over the islands, up Georgia Strait, over Vasquez, obliterating everything that was visible only yesterday.

Acknowledgements

I would like to extend thanks to: early readers Susan and Laurie Geddes, Doug MacDonald, Lhasa Hetherington and Peggy Hansen; to Laura Anderson for both early rading and encouragement prior to publication. Special thanks to Doug for his thoughtful suggestions. Thanks to Ann Eriksson for her comments about the original manuscript being too large for publication. They led me to splitting it surgically into two books, *In a Time of Magic* and *Back to the Garden*. As sometimes happens with the separation of Siamese twins, some parts were needed by both books so they share certain elements.

Thanks to Susan Breiddal for her skilled and heroic editing; to Peggy Hansen, Jim Drake and Donna Hansen for copy editing and helpful suggestions. All remaining errors are obstinately mine alone.

Thanks To Doug Hamilton for his chapter on the Sideras Commune, *The Asking,* in *Accidental Eden* by Douglas L. Hamilton and Darlene Olesko.

Thanks to Brian Pitt and Lawrence Fisher for their encouragement after reading the proofs of Back to the Garden; and their advice regarding the fictionality of my characters. Gratitude to Madeline Walker for her encouragement in the days leading up to publication, and for her profound support in helping me to see the value of my own work.

Thanks to the fabulous painter Alan Abrams for the cover illustration and to Doug MacDonald for the digital rendering of it. Thanks to Lhasa Hetherington for the cover design and help navigating the digital world; to Peggy Hansen and Madeline Walker for the back cover description.

Thanks to Nicola Furlong for her excellent course on online publishing and to Fran Aitkens for help with designing the print version.

Thanks to Gabriella Onderwyzer, Manfred Wolfe, and Ray Rice for recognising my writing ability and, each in their own way, encouraging me to continue. Thanks to all the people who shared this time and place of history with me for all the lessons—both expansive and humbling—that I learned from you.

Most importantly, thanks to my wife Peggy Hansen for her support during the years of writing this.

About the Author

In his youth, Arnold W. Porter lived as a back to the lander on one of the Gulf Islands in British Columbia. In writing *Back to the Garden* he has drawn on this experience, as well as his degree in literature from San Francisco State University, his interest in Taoism and Eastern religions, his master's degree in counselling from the University of Victoria, and an understanding of human nature gained through 35 years as a counsellor. He currently lives with his wife in Victoria, BC where he writes, plays music, practices tai chi, and works as a hospice counsellor.

www.ingramcontent.com/pod-product-compliance
Lightning Source LLC
Chambersburg PA
CBHW061927170626
46813CB00006B/2327